Kate Tho— —as born in Belfast. She came to Dublin — —nly French and English and had a successful career as an actress and voice-over artist before ditching the day job to write full time. Her four previous novels, *It Means Mischief, More Mischief, Going Down* and *The Blue Hour* have been widely translated. Kate divides her time between Dublin and the West of Ireland, is happily married and has one daughter.

STRIKING
POSES

Kate Thompson

BANTAM BOOKS
LONDON · NEW YORK · TORONTO · SYDNEY · AUCKLAND

STRIKING POSES
A BANTAM BOOK : 0 553 81431 1

First publication in Great Britain

PRINTING HISTORY
Bantam edition published 2003

1 3 5 7 9 10 8 6 4 2

Copyright © Kate Thompson 2003

The right of Kate Thompson to be identified as the author of this work has
been asserted in accordance with sections 77 and 78 of the Copyright
Designs and Patents Act 1988.

Set in 11/13pt Baskerville by
Phoenix Typesetting, Burley-in-Wharfedale, West Yorkshire.

Bantam Books are published by Transworld Publishers,
61– 63 Uxbridge Road, London W5 5SA,
a division of The Random House Group Ltd,
in Australia by Random House, Australia (Pty) Ltd,
20 Alfred Street, Milsons Point, Sydney, NSW 2061, Australia,
in New Zealand by Random House New Zealand Ltd,
18 Poland Road, Glenfield, Auckland 10, New Zealand
and in South Africa by Random House (Pty) Ltd,
Endulini, 5a Jubilee Road, Parktown 2193, South Africa.

Printed and bound in Great Britain by
Cox & Wyman Ltd, Reading, Berkshire.

For Malcolm – not before time

Acknowledgements

Thanks are due to the following: Marc O'Neill for allowing me to snoop around his studio, and Emma Elliot for scrutinizing an early draft. Conor Horgan, for kindly letting me sit in on one of his fashion shoots. Willy Siddall and Vincent Lavelle for the diving advice. Eileen Colquhoun for helping me map out Troy's psychological journey. Monica Frawley for her non-pareil design savvy and Marian Smyth, style suprema. My friends and family for putting my books face out on the shelves (apologies to all booksellers affected by this!). Sarah Lutyens and Susannah Godman for everything they've done for me. Cathy Kelly and Marian Keyes for being the kind of friends you dream of having. Sadie Mayne (for being unflappable), Beth Humphries (for being eagle-eyed) and all at Transworld, especially Francesca Liversidge, my fantastic editor: a buddy who surfs the same wavelength. Finally, my daughter Clara and my husband Malcolm: the best things that ever happened to me, and without whom I would be utterly lost.

Chapter One

'We are suffering. Dear God, how we suffer!' A meaningful pause. The English subtitles streeled across the bottom of the screen while the actors droned on in French above them. 'We are suffering from that mutual solipsism that only lovers suffer.'

'I don't want to hear this.' The leading lady glared at her male counterpart with smouldering, kohl-smudged eyes. Why did French actresses always have smouldering, kohl-smudged eyes? 'Your voice gives me a pain. Here.' She seized her skull with both hands. 'It thuds in my head like a pile-driver.'

Tell me about it, thought Aphrodite Delaney. She'd sat through an hour and a half of dialogue so ludicrously ponderous that she wasn't sure whether she wanted to laugh or cry. It didn't help that the English translation was inept. She'd tried hard to concentrate on just listening to the French, but her leaving cert French wasn't good enough to make sense of this drivel without the help of the godawful stilted subtitles. Hell's teeth! This film had got rave reviews! What was wrong with her that she hated it so much?

On screen the actress threw back the white sheet that covered her and crossed the room to stand pensively by the window. Her mass of tousled black hair snaked down her naked back. 'Oh God! Your buttocks!' moaned her lean and gorgeous lover, gazing at her as he lounged against a bank of snowy linen pillows. His eyes were all half closed and slanty. He was an undeniably sexy piece of work, but you sensed that he knew it, and that – for Aphrodite – was his fatal flaw. 'Your buttocks move me so intensely, Minette.'

Aphrodite couldn't help herself. The laughter that had been building up inside her for the best part of half an hour finally burst out. She heard the person sitting behind her give a little 'tch' of annoyance, and she regained control with an effort.

At the window the sultry actress was twisting a strand of her hair, and saying in an irritating singsongy voice: 'Snow. Immaculate white snow. How pure it is. How easy to defile.'

The camera panned in on her lover's face. He narrowed his eyes even more.

'Snow looks ravishing when it has fallen on a roof of terracotta tiles,' murmured the actress. She smiled to herself as she gazed out the window, and then she stretched luxuriously. Another close-up of her lover's face. 'It takes on the texture of an eiderdown. But when it begins to melt a little, it enters into all the cracks so that the roof looks scarred, defaced. The virginal white is most attractive. But unfortunately,' here, a sigh 'ephermeral.' She turned and scowled at the bloke on the bed, and then inserted a suggestive thumb between her bee-stung lips (How come all French actresses have bee-stung lips? wondered Aphrodite. Botox or its oral equivalent, probably), and sucked on it. 'J'ai envie de te baiser encore une fois,' the actress was saying, and Aphrodite was suddenly reminded of that in-your-face sexy ad for Gucci's Envy. They were all at it, these gorgeous broads, going round sticking their thumbs in their mouths as a prelude to sex. Maybe she should try it next time she met someone she fancied? She just couldn't help it. Another snort of laughter escaped her.

'Sh!' from the person behind. Aphrodite rooted in her bag for a tissue and held it against her mouth.

The actress continued to rub her lower lip with her thumb as the camera moved in on her eyes, and Aphrodite found herself wondering what trick she had played to get her pupils so dilated. 'Shall we make love again?' drooled the subtitle.

Oh *no*! thought Aphrodite. Not *again*! She was fed up with seeing the camera rove lingeringly over the actress's physique. It was so perfect it looked as if she didn't even have to hold her tummy in. Aphrodite would need to be permanently attached to a Slendertone machine if she wanted a tummy like that.

The actor on the bed glowered meaningfully. 'Perhaps,' he said. 'Of course, when one makes love, one is engaged in a peculiar kind of dialectic – one that prevents us from achieving true happiness, according to Spinoza. Or was it Schopenhauer? It's not important. What is important is that – we suffer.' A single piano note rang out. 'Do we not suffer?' The screen went black. The titles began to roll in silence. Aphrodite wasn't interested in who'd done what. She

11

stood up before the first title hit the top of the screen and slung her bag over her shoulder, noticing in the half-light that all the other members of the audience in the small art-house cinema were gazing at the unfolding credits with rapt reverence. They'd sit on through key grip, best boy and catering credits, she knew, then turn and nod sagely at each other when the lights came up.

As she strode down the passage between the rows of seats a man in an aisle seat uncrossed long legs and got to his feet unhurriedly. 'Load of crap, wasn't it?' he said under his breath as she passed him. She paused, turned and smiled.

'A *very* peculiar kind of dialectic,' she said. The man laughed, and someone in the audience went 'tch' again.

'Well. We philistines are obviously in the minority,' he said, throwing a jacket across his shoulder and joining her in the aisle. They walked out of the auditorium side by side. Outside the door they paused and looked at each other. 'Fancy a drink?' he asked.

Aphrodite bit her lip, looked away, considered for a second, and then looked back at him. His eyes were heavy-lidded and lazy-looking, with a barely perceptible, very sexy cast, and with lashes that drooped over the outside edges so that the whites were almost obscured. They were the most come-to-bed eyes she'd ever seen. He raised a vaguely quizzical eyebrow. 'Well?'

She nodded. 'Sure,' she said, immediately wishing she'd demurred just a fraction. She'd always been crap at game-playing. She also wished she'd washed her hair, made a bit more of an effort with her make-up, and wasn't wearing the T-shirt her friend Lola had given her for a joke that had: 'Beam Me Up, Scotty' emblazoned on it. She had done a massive double-load laundry that day, and it was the only clean item of clothing she had apart from another joke T-shirt (again courtesy of Lola) with a lewd invitation on it. At least she wasn't wearing *that*. Still, she made a mental note to keep her jacket on.

They made their way through the lobby to the bar, and the man indicated a corner table. 'Sit down,' he said. 'I'll get them. What'll you have?'

'A glass of Guinness, please.' Aphrodite sat down, and busied herself with a little bag-rummaging. She took out a tissue and blew her nose, she located her mobile and switched it on, and finally she submitted to the irresistible impulse that was urging her to take another look at her new friend.

There was something a little intimidating about him physically, but he was no thug. He was tall, heavily built and rather shambling in the sartorial department. He was wearing baggy moleskin trousers and a loose shirt in dark blue brushed cotton. The suede jacket he had slung over his shoulder had been expensive when he'd bought it, but had obviously been battered about a lot since then. He hadn't bothered shaving this morning and he was overdue a haircut. He looked lived-in. The girl behind the bar was looking animated.

He glanced over his shoulder at Aphrodite and she returned her attention to her phone like a shot, hoping he hadn't caught her watching him. The display told her there were two messages for her.

One was from an advertising agency asking if she'd be interested in doing some set-dressing on a television commercial, the other was from the artistic director of an impoverished theatre company asking her to get back to him a.s.a.p. if she was interested in designing a production of *A Midsummer Night's Dream*. Shit. It was the story of her life. Of course she was interested in designing a production of *A Midsummer Night's Dream*! It was one of her favourite Shakespeares. But there was no way the theatre company's budget would stretch to the kind of lavish production values she'd aspire to, and the money would be crap. If she was lucky, she might just earn enough to cover her expenses. She'd have to go for the set-dressing option. It was the kind of job she'd never, ever have envisaged herself doing while she was training to be a theatre designer, but there was silly money to be made in advertising, and she'd got a heavy letter from her bank this morning. She knew that another, even heavier letter would be clunking onto her doormat within the week if she didn't do something about her overdraft very soon.

She rummaged in her bag again, this time for her notebook so that she could jot down the phone numbers that had been left on her voice mail. No notebook materialized – she'd left it by the phone at home, she remembered. What *did* materialize was a photograph that had been taken several months ago, when she'd been on holiday in France with her then boyfriend, Bradley the Bollocks Boyd. It must have fallen out of an obscure section of her wallet. Why on earth had she kept it? she wondered. She studied his beautiful face and wished she had a sharp object handy to scribble over it. Then she studied her own smiling face and wished she hadn't been such a walkover. Bradley had treated her so appallingly that she left the 'r' out of his name now any time she referred to him. Scrutinizing both of them together, she felt a slight pang of regret. She looked much better then than she did now – slimmer, tanned, and with gamine hair. She must have put on half a stone since the summer, and her gamine hair was at that horrible grown-out stage now. It was all Badley's fault. She'd gone into a complete decline when he'd decided he was bisexual and had left her for an actor fresh out of drama school, and her self esteem was still brittle after the battering it had received. She tore the photograph into the smallest pieces she could manage, then sprinkled them into the ashtray.

'Your Guinness.' The man who wasn't a thug set the glass in front of her and sat down in the seat opposite. She noticed that he had to slide it back a distance in order to accommodate his legs under the table. 'Sláinte.' He raised his glass.

'Cheers.' Aphrodite mirrored the gesture, and took a sip of her stout. All at once she was at a complete loss for anything to say.

'I wasn't aware that that film was meant to be a comedy,' he remarked, wiping a trace of Guinness foam from his mouth with the back of his hand. 'I wish I'd been sitting beside you. We could have laughed our asses off together.'

She smiled. 'We wouldn't have been very popular with the rest of the audience.'

'The rest of the audience was comprised, to my mind, of fatuous farts. That was one of the most pretentious pieces of cinematic shit I have ever had the misfortune to sit through.'

'Why didn't you leave?'

'Why didn't you?' he countered.

'I wanted to see if it got any worse.'

He smiled. 'It suffered from that brilliant paradoxical thing, didn't it? The worse it got, the funnier it got.'

'Yeah. It *snowballed.*' He gave a gratifying laugh at her little joke. The name of the film had been *Chose de Neige*, which translated badly as 'Thing of Snow' – presumably to underline the 'ephemeral nature of life' as waffled on by the black-eyed, black-haired, botoxed actress.

'It also suffered bigtime from *Emperor's New Clothes* Syndrome.'

She gave him an enquiring look.

'"Everybody's raving about it, so it *has* to be good."' He adopted the kind of monotone a talking sheep might use.

The place was filling up now. The main screen was disgorging its audience, and those doughty intellectuals who'd stayed on for the French film credits were trickling up to the bar. Aphrodite recognized the director of an avant-garde theatre company talking earnestly to one of his satellites, who was nodding equally earnestly in agreement. Discussing the artistic dialectic of that poxy film, probably.

Her phone rang, and she hit the 'off' button. She didn't want to talk to anyone about work right now. She didn't want to talk to anyone about anything. The man sitting opposite her was an exception.

He gave her a smile of approval. 'I'm glad to see you've got good manners,' he said.

'I hate this thing. But I'd be lost without it.' The lives of most media people depended on their mobile phones. Aphrodite loved watching the way they indulged in ostentatious mobile one-upmanship. Every time the newest, gimmickiest, must-have Nokia came on the market, they all went into competition orbit to be the first to get their hands on one.

He was giving her an assessing look, as if checking her out. 'D'you know what's worse than the person you're with taking a call?'

'The person you're with *making* a call?'

'Nearly. But not quite. It's when someone you're talking to on the phone says: 'Oh – just let me access "call waiting" –'

'And then gets back to you and says: "Sorry – I have to go – talk to you later" –'

'Neatly implying that the person on "call waiting" is *much* more important than you.'

Aphrodite laughed. 'I got rid of "call waiting" for that very reason.'

'I got rid of my mobile phone. I'd love to get rid of my land line.'

A moment of silence descended. Aphrodite took another sip of Guinness, and then realized something. 'Hey – you still haven't answered my question.

Why didn't *you* get up and leave that film if you despised it so much?'

'I wanted to meet you.'

Oh! For the second time since meeting him she hadn't a clue what to say. 'Why?' was all she could manage.

'Because I suspected we'd have a rapport. It's not every day you come across someone with such a healthy disrespect for the Emperor and his new clothes.'

The way he was leaning back in his chair studying her with undisguised interest was starting to faze her. She fumbled further for conversation. 'It got some extraordinary reviews. The *Independent* loved it.'

'I never read reviews. I hate critics. Sam Beckett was right when he proclaimed that the term "critic" was the worst insult he could level at anyone.'

'Vladimir in *Waiting for Godot.*'

He raised an impressed eyebrow. 'You know your theatre.'

'It's my profession.'

'You're an actress?'

'No. I'm a designer.'

He took a swig of his Guinness, observing her over the rim of his pint glass. 'I wonder if I've seen any of your stuff?' he said, as he put the pint back down on the table. 'What's your name?'

This was the bit she dreaded most when she met someone new. She took a deep breath. 'Aphrodite Delaney,' she said.

'Beautiful name.'

She shook her head and made a face. 'I hate it. I've

often thought about doing the deed poll thing, and I've *never* forgiven my mother for landing me with it.'

'It's unusual, that's for sure. Very theatrical.'

'So's she.'

'Your mother?'

'Yes – she's an actress, so at least she could have assumed a stage name if she'd hated her real one as much as I hate mine. Hell – I couldn't even manage a decent nickname.'

'Why not?'

'Try it. Most nicknames are diminutives, right? Deborah, Deb. Patricia, Pat. Juliet, Jules. What could I call myself? Aph? Aphro? Dite? They all sound crap.'

'You're right,' he conceded. 'Aphrodite it had to be.'

'And you're . . . ?'

'Jack Costello.'

'Nice to meet you, Jack.' They shook hands across the table. His hands were big and hard, like workmen's hands. She wondered what he did for a living, but felt embarrassed to ask. It was usually the third banal question asked by people who actually didn't give a shit what you did, the first one being: 'What's your name?' and the second: 'Awful/wonderful weather we're having, isn't it?'

He took another swig of his pint, then glanced at his watch. 'Do you fancy going for something to eat? I haven't had anything since breakfast.'

'I can't,' she said. *Rats!* she thought. What a missed opportunity! 'I arranged to meet someone here at half past seven.' And suddenly, to her horror, she heard herself saying: 'We could do it another time, though?'

'We could. But not for a while. I'm going to the States tomorrow.'

Oh! 'Oh? Business or pleasure?'

'A bit of both.'

'How long are you going for?' She tried to make the question sound conversational.

'I'm not sure. A couple of months. Give me your phone number. I'll call you when I get back.' He slid his jacket off the back of the chair and trawled through the pockets. The detritus that emerged included a roll of film, a slim, very well thumbed volume of Catullus, a pack of French cigarettes, a fountain pen and a condom sachet. Aphrodite hoped he hadn't clocked her clocking the condom. He handed her a book of matches before stuffing the rest of the junk back in his pocket. 'Here,' he said. 'Write it on this.'

The matchbook bore the logo of the Merrion – one of Dublin's most upmarket hotels. Posh, thought Aphrodite, unzipping the pocket of her backpack where she kept her stylograph. She'd taken her mother to the Merrion for afternoon tea on her last birthday, and had almost passed out at how much it had set her back. Her hand when it emerged from her backpack was black with ink. The bastard pen had leaked again.

'Hell,' she said, ineffectually rubbing her palm with an old tissue. 'It's always doing that. It's about time I got a new one.'

'Use mine,' he said, delving in his pocket again and handing her his fountain pen. It was a Mont Blanc – very elegant, very understated.

'Sexy pen,' she remarked, examining it.

'It was a present.'

From a girlfriend, probably. Only lovers gave each other presents like Mont Blanc fountain pens. Did he have a current girlfriend? she wondered. Was he the type of man who could blithely ask a girl to go and have something to eat with him while his partner was engaged elsewhere? She remembered the condom in his pocket. Maybe it was just as well he was going away tomorrow. This man could be dangerous. Still . . . She scribbled her phone number down on the matchbook and handed it back to him. Their fingers touched, and she knew that he was as aware as she was of the physical contact. As their eyes met she resisted a sudden urge to slide her thumb into her mouth.

'Aphrodite!'

She looked up. Lola was heading in her direction. Lola had been a year ahead of her at Central St Martins in London, and was – like Aphrodite – back in Dublin trying hard to interest the major Irish theatres in her work. 'How's it going? I'm early for once!' She pulled out a chair, sat down between them, unwound a length of bronze organza from around her neck, and then cocked her head flirtatiously at Jack Costello. 'Hi! I'm Lola MacBride,' she said.

'Jack Costello.'

'Jack Costello? The photographer Jack Costello?'

He inclined his head in the affirmative. Ow! thought Aphrodite. How stupid of her not to have made the connection.

'I loved your spread in last month's *Individual*,' gushed Lola. 'It has to be the most imaginative fashion shoot I've seen in years.'

'Thank you. It was bloody hard work, that shoot. It's gratifying to know it paid off.' He stretched, then got to his feet and shot another look at his watch. 'I don't mean to be rude, but I need to get something to eat before I pass out. It was good to meet you, Aphrodite. I enjoyed our "peculiar dialectic". I'll be in touch when I get back.'

'Good to meet you, too,' she said, hoping she sounded casual. 'Thanks for the drink. And enjoy the States.'

'I will.' He gave her one last smile with those extra-ordinary eyes, and then he was gone, manoeuvring his way through the crowded bar.

'Well, hell!' said Lola, looking intrigued. 'What were *you* doing with Jack Costello?'

'He took me for a drink after the film.'

Lola looked even more gobsmacked. 'He picked you up?'

'*No!* I mean, no, not really.' It hadn't *felt* as if she'd been picked up.

'How did it happen then?' Lola was lit up with curiosity.

'I'm not quite sure. We both found the film unin-tentionally hilarious, and we just got talking.'

'He picked you up.' It wasn't a question this time. Lola gave her a shrewd look. 'Watch it, Aphrodite.

He has a desperate reputation, you know. Although I suppose that can't be helped when women throw themselves at him all the time, like suttee widows onto funeral pyres.'

'I did *not* throw myself at him!' Aphrodite was indignant.

'I'm not saying you did. But I know loads of women who would if they got the opportunity. He's brutishly sexy.'

'He's not at all good looking, really,' said Aphrodite, in a pathetic attempt to deny to herself the truth of Lola's words.

'Good looks have nothing to do with it. He's still brutishly sexy. *And* he's got a dead sexy job. Did you see that spread in *Individual*?'

'No. What was it like?'

'Sexy. Hey – finish that drink and let's go get something to eat. It's too crowded in here, and there's that spooky Finbar thingy ogling me.' Finbar de Rossa was an actor who liked to think he had a mesmeric effect on women. 'Where'll we go?'

Aphrodite started to do mental arithmetic. She couldn't afford anywhere too pricey right now. 'Giraffe and Grasshopper?' she suggested.

'No. The staff there are so fucking superior. You'd think the place was the bloody Criterion and not just a tarted-up burger joint, the way they behave. Let's go to the Troc.'

'OK – but I'm only having a starter. I'm under serious budgetary constraints at the moment.'

'I'll treat you. My budgetary constraints have disappeared into the ether, and I'm celebrating. I landed that gig in the Chamber, Aphrodite.'

'*Oedipus*? No shit! Well done! The champagne's on you, sister. When do you start?'

'Not for ages. But I've got some great ideas.'

'Tell.'

'Well, I'm going to do something totally audacious and dress Oedipus as a transvestite.'

Aphrodite looked so staggered by this that Lola couldn't continue. 'Joke!' she chortled, delighted by her little wheeze. 'Come on. Let's go and get drunk.'

* * *

Many glasses of wine later, they were comfortably indulging in gossip in a booth in the Trocadero. The Troc was a theatre people's restaurant. Punters often came just to luvvie-spot, hoping some of the theatrical glamour might rub off on them. The fact that the glamour had a vaguely tarnished edge just added to the allure of the joint. It was filling up now with a post-show crowd. People were queuing by the door, and waiters were turning tables round as fast as possible. Aphrodite knew that she and Lola were sitting too long over their coffee, but having consumed the best part of a bottle and a half of wine, neither of them was feeling too much guilt.

'Have you heard the latest about that gobshite Damien Whelan?' Lola sloshed the last of the red into their glasses.

Damien Whelan was a designer who worked non-stop. He was also such a vicious queen that he made Snow White's stepmother look like Mother Teresa.

'Let me have it.'

'David Lawless is directing a production of *The Seagull* at the Phoenix and guess who's designing?'

'Damien Gobshite Whelan?'

'Right first time.'

'Oh, no, no, no, no, *no*!' Aphrodite slumped forward with her head in her hands. 'I've always wanted to design that show! Oh, Lola! Why is life so *unfair*?' She looked up again at her friend. 'D'you know what I've got to look forward to next week? I've to dress a suburban kitchen set for a teabag commercial. Do you know what that means?'

'Placing product strategically around the place?'

'Yeah. And tweaking tablecloths and blinds, and trying to decide which is the least tacky-looking mug for the housewife to pretend to drink her tea out of.'

Lola made a sympathetic face. 'At least there's a few bob in it.'

Aphrodite shrugged. 'Yeah. I know I shouldn't complain. And I really could do with the money right now. But *The Seagull*! And Damien Whelan! It makes me want to throw up.' She took a great swig of wine, and then leaned forward with her elbows on the table. 'D'you know how *I'd* do it, Lola? I'd set it in the West of Ireland in one of those gorgeous dilapidated Georgian mansions. I'd do big Connemara skies overhead – you know those incredible mackerel skies that look as if they've been brushed by a giant white wing? And all the costumes would have ornithological touches.'

'Ornithol– You mean birds?'

'Mm-hm. Nina would wear all white of course, to

begin with – sprigged muslin with a feather-trimmed cape for her first entrance. And in the last act her costume would be spattered with mud from where she's been wailing and wandering round the fields, so she'd be a bit like one of those poor seagulls that's been through an oil slick. Arkadina would be a peacock, obviously; Konstantin a raven –'

'Trigorin?'

'A vulture. I'd give him a topcoat with an astrakhan collar, and I'd make the actor playing him shave his head. Oh God – I have so many ideas for that play! I remember first thinking about it when I was a teenager. I had a reproduction of that fabulous surrealist painting by Max Ernst on my wall – you know the one of the naked woman with a bird's head wearing a cape of red feathers? That's how long I've been fantasizing about doing that show. And now that big poof Damien Whelan's doing it.'

'Hell – you always were much more culturally inclined than me. Surrealist repros on your walls? I had posters of Wham on mine.' Lola drained her wineglass. 'Shall we walk home or share a cab?' Lola and Aphrodite rented artisan cottages in adjacent streets in an area of town called Stoneybatter – also known as 'Bitterbatter' because of the number of out-of-work theatre people who lived there. At one stage they had considered sharing a house, and then decided against it. Workspace was a priority for each of them, and the west-facing spare rooms in both houses served as what they jokingly referred to as their 'studios'.

'Walk.' Aphrodite yawned and stretched. 'I need

to clear my head after all that alcohol. Thanks for treating me, Lo. I'll do the same when I get the cheque from that set-dressing job. We'll go some-where ultra-groovy.'

Just as she reached for her jacket, the waiter arrived with two glasses of champagne.

'We didn't order those,' said Lola.

'Compliments of Mr Whelan,' said the waiter, indicating the booth behind Aphrodite. Clocking the expression on Lola's face, Aphrodite looked over her shoulder. The man sitting immediately behind her turned at the same time, and raised his wineglass at them.

'Congratulations, Lola,' said Damien Whelan. 'I hear you're going to be designing *Oedipus* at the Chamber.'

'Oh – hi, Damien,' said Lola. 'Well. Um – yes, that's right. Ah. Well. Thanks very much for the champagne.'

'You're welcome. No better way to celebrate your first major gig than with a glass of bubbly.' He turned his attention to Aphrodite. 'Anything in the pipeline for you, Aphrodite?'

''Fraid not!' Aphrodite tried to sound jocular, but it wasn't easy. She had broken out in a nervous sweat.

'I wouldn't worry too much if I were you.' He gave her a reassuring smile. 'I hear you've been doing a bit of set-dressing recently. Maybe you should stick to that – there's more money in it. Plus, it doesn't tax the imagination quite as much as theatre design. Forgive me for eavesdropping and forgive me for

27

saying so, but your ideas for *The Seagull* were quite unutterably banal. *Santé*.' Raising his glass at her again, Damien returned his attention to his dining companion.

Aphrodite bit her lip and turned back to Lola, who was trying hard to look composed. They drank their champagne in silence, Aphrodite nearly choking on every gulp. At last the glasses were empty. Aphrodite burped, grabbed her jacket and bag, and started to edge along the velour banquette. She heard Damien laugh unpleasantly and say: 'Arkadina as a peacock! Trigorin as a vulture! Puh*leeze*! How undergraduate can you *get*!' His companion gave a complicitous snigger, and Ahprodite felt her face flare up as she reeled towards the door, cursing herself liberally for not having kept her lip zipped in the top theatre gossip venue in town. As she wound between the tables she abstractedly registered two men sitting in a booth, engaged in conversation.

'Mind if we join you?' Two impossibly slender, nymph-like girls with long, long golden curls had sashayed up to the booth. They were wearing identical shimmery dresses, and both had little crowns on their heads. Aphrodite knew who they were. A pair of famous Irish models who also happened to be twins.

'Sure, Morgana, Nimuë. How's it going?'

The voice was familiar. Aphrodite's focus zoomed in on the face. The man was giving one of the models the once-over with amused, sexy eyes. It was Jack Costello.

Aphrodite legged it out of the restaurant before he

could see her, leaving Lola to take care of the bill.

'Oh, fuck, Lola!' she said when Lola joined her on the pavement. 'I called Damien Whelan a gobshite!'

'So did I. He *is* a gobshite, Aphrodite. Everyone knows it. You mustn't let it worry you. There's no point. We've burned our bridges, spilt our milk and let the baby out with the bathwater. Whatever that means.'

'You mean *I* have. I called him a poof as well as a gobshite. My stunning deficiency in the political correctness department would have incensed him more than anything, probably.'

'True. But *I* didn't give out about your political incorrectness, so that makes me an accessory. Damien Whelan isn't worth wasting our breath on, so let's change the subject.' Lola linked her arm in a reassuring way. 'Hey! I've heard those twins are goers. Looks like Mister Costello's in for a stimulating evening.'

'As long as conversation's not on the agenda,' remarked Aphrodite, wondering why she was being so bitchy. For all she knew, the twins might be members of MENSA. 'Oh, Jesus, Lola. I can't *believe* I was so indiscreet! Damien Whelan could—'

'Forget it. Don't beat yourself up over him. He doesn't give a toss what our opinion of him is. We're small fry. He'll have forgotten it by tomorrow.'

It was OK for Lola to be offhand about offending the designer, thought Aphrodite. At least she had her foot on a rung of the career ladder now, with her production of *Oedipus* to look forward to. But Aphrodite could ill afford to make enemies of anyone who wielded influence in the theatre world. Especially with take-no-prisoner types like Damien Whelan. She had a mental image of the baby going down the plughole with the bathwater, and knew that the baby was a metaphor for her career. What a total klutz she had been!

They crossed the road, heading towards Temple Bar and the bridge that would take them to the north side of the city. Aphrodite listened dispiritedly as Lola filled her in on her plans for redecorating her bedroom. It had started to rain. A passing truck swished through a puddle and sprayed her with dirty water. A passing escaped-convict type sized up her potential as a mugging victim. A passing drunk barged into her and a passing suit leered at her. Aphrodite stuck her hands in her pockets. All things considered, it had not been a good day, she thought, as she trudged homeward to Stoneybatter, feeling – well – bitter.

Chapter Two

When she got home Aphrodite fed her cat, Bob, then hit the playback button on her answering machine. Her mother's distraught voice came drifting over the speaker, sounding as if she was drowning. 'Aphrodite? Phone me the minute you get home. I don't care what time it is, just call me.'

Oh God, thought Aphrodite. Another drama. Sometimes she wished she wasn't an only child. It would be nice to have a sibling who could share the awesome responsibility of looking after Thea. She made herself a cup of herbal bedtime tea which tasted disgusting but was amazingly soporific, then picked up the cordless and punched in Thea's number. The phone rang for ages before there was any response.

'Yes?' Her mother's voice on the other end sounded characteristically vague.

'Hi, Mum.'

'Who is this?'

Aphrodite sighed. 'It's your daughter Aphrodite, Mum.'

'Oh, darling! Is there something the matter? It's nearly midnight, you know.'

'Mum. You left a message on my answering

machine telling me to ring you the minute I got in, no matter what time it was.'

'Did I?' Thea sounded even vaguer. 'Oh – yes. Now I remember. Oh, God! How could I forget! Darling – listen. I've had the most *appalling* news.'

'What's wrong?'

'I've got a job.'

'But that's not appalling news. You should be delighted! You've been moaning about being out of work for ages.'

'No, no. Don't jump the gun. Just wait till you hear what it is.'

'What is it?'

Her mother let a suitably dramatic pause slide down the phone line before announcing in tragic tones: 'I've been asked to play Winnie in *Happy Days.*'

'In the Beckett festival? But, Mum – that's excellent! Winnie's a brilliant part.' It *was* a brilliant part. The play was a two-hander, but the lion's share of the dialogue was Winnie's. In fact, the play was virtually a monologue, and a fantastic showcase for an actress.

'*What?* How can you *say* that! I spend the first half of the play embedded to the waist in a mound of earth, and the second half embedded to my neck! Imagine how physically gruelling it will be, Aphrodite!' A fumbling noise came over the phone. 'Hang on a sec – just let me get a refill.' Aphrodite heard chinking sounds, and then gurgling from a bottle as Thea sloshed wine into a glass. Aphrodite pictured her mother in her childhood home reclining with her Burmese cat on her faded velvet chaise-longue, wearing her favourite faded Japanese silk kimono. There'd be a bottle of Fleurie on the table beside her, a novel within arm's length, and a dog-eared Filofax lying open at the phone number section. There might or might not be a lover skulking somewhere around the house. Her mother's voice was in her ear again. 'But that's not the worst thing, darling – of course it's not. The *worst* thing is . . . Guess.'

Aphrodite didn't need to guess. She knew what would be the worst thing for Thea. The worst thing for Thea would be the character's age. The part of Winnie had been written for a 'well-preserved' fifty-year-old, and Thea had celebrated her fortieth birthday for at least the fifth time last summer. 'The age thing,' she said.

'Yes! *How* can I do it, darling? It's so humiliating to realize that I'm at that stage of my career where I'm being considered suitable casting for a *fifty*-year-old!' She made 'fifty-year-old' sound like 'leper'. Thea had always played younger than her real age, and her CV to date had been a repertoire of seriously glamorous roles in plays by writers like Wilde and Coward. Her last role had been the Marquise in *Les Liaisons Dangereuses*, and she'd had a ball swishing round the stage in exquisite gowns of trailing silk and velvet. No wonder she didn't relish the notion of playing a garrulous old bat buried up to her neck in a sandpit.

'Have you accepted?'

'Yes. It's ages since I last worked. I can't afford to

turn it down. And Frank's late with the maintenance again.' Aphrodite's parents had divorced years ago. Her father was now living in New York with a thirty-something solicitor who looked like a cast member of *Sex and the City*. Aphrodite got a card from him once a year on or around the time of her birthday.

'I think you're right to do it, Mum. It's an amazing role. Think about it. It's a real departure from type – it could open up whole new avenues of employment for you.'

Thea sighed. 'I suppose you're right. Work's getting scarcer and scarcer, and looking at cast lists is more and more depressing these days. Did you know that work for actors is three times more abundant than work for actresses? Or is it four? And most of the parts going are for actresses younger than thirty. You'd think that women of . . . a certain age didn't exist.'

'Well, look on the bright side. At least they didn't ask you to play Nell in *Endgame*. You'd have to spend most of the evening stuck in a bin.'

'Ha! You know who's playing that role?'

'Who?'

'Ann Fitzroy.' Ann Fitzroy and Thea had been arch-enemies all their lives.

'Ann's far too young, surely? Isn't Nell meant to be ancient?'

'Have you seen La Fitzroy recently?' purred Thea happily. 'She's aged a lot. You could almost describe her as *ravaged*. She never got over David leaving her for Eva Lavery, whereas I *blossomed* after Frank left me.'

This was a good time to put the phone down, when her mother was feeling happy and secure once more. If she let her go on any longer she'd revert to the subject of fifty-year-old Winnie and get depressed again, and when she was depressed it was impossible to get her off the line. 'I've gotta go, Mum. Kiss Lucifer for me.' Lucifer was Thea's cat. 'We'll meet for a drink next week, OK?'

'All right – but not in that awful dive you frequent, please.'

'OK. Where's good for you?'

'The Merrion of course, darling.'

Aphrodite gave a wry smile as she put the phone down. Her mother had the most expensive tastes of anyone she knew, so it was just as well she did an accomplished line in wealthy consorts. Thea had never really lived in the real world, and while Aphrodite had had great fun growing up with a mother who was more of a friend than a parent, sometimes she felt as if she was the one who did most of the parenting. It hadn't helped that most of her boyfriends confessed to fancying Thea.

A photograph of the pair of them was pinned on the noticeboard in Aphrodite's tiny kitchen. She took it down and studied it. It had been taken on Thea's last birthday, and the forty-something-year-old looked like her older sister. Aphrodite didn't look too bad either. But that photograph had been taken ages ago, before her break-up with Badley. She transferred her attention to the mirror that hung beside her noticeboard. Her hair was lank and an inch of flab oozed over the circumference of her belt.

She tousled her hair a little to see if it made any difference, but it just looked ratty. 'Because I'm Not Worth It,' she intoned at her reflection. She reached for the Post-It pad that lay beside the telephone and scribbled a note to herself. BOOK A HAIR APPOINTMENT she wrote in block capitals. That was brave of her. She'd had a phobia about hair salons since a trainee had once made her look like Michael Flatley. And TAKE OUT POOL MEMBERSHIP she added for good measure. Then she underlined the words to emphasize their urgency, swigged back her disgusting herbal tea and went to bed.

*　　*　　*

She actually did book a hair appointment. But she couldn't keep it, because life did one of those things that it's prone to doing when you least expect it. It went into overdrive. Suddenly Aphrodite found herself working on commercials back to back. She was promoted from set-dresser to stylist to assistant designer, and she knew it wouldn't be long before she'd have the official union card that would allow her to work on films. Her application was to be discussed at the next Equity meeting. She was busy, she had made impact, and she was earning money at last.

But she wasn't very happy. Occasionally, if she was feeling particularly maudlin, she'd take out her portfolio and admire the designs she'd worked so hard on at college. Her favourites had been for *A*

Midsummer Night's Dream. She'd executed them when she'd been at the height of her passion for Badley, and they were unashamedly romantic. Her fairies had been real woodland fairies – not Goths or punks or rock chicks or clowns or transvestites, which were looks most of her colleagues had foisted on the play in an attempt to be different. Her tutor had given her an excellent grade. 'I am so fed up,' he'd said, 'of this endless striving for anachronism. Do you know that someone came up with an idea for a *Waiting for Godot* with the tramps as fading Hollywood starlets? Your fairies, Aphrodite, are refreshingly *fairylike.*'

Late one evening she came home to find the post still lying on the doormat. She'd left the house at seven o'clock that morning, and shooting on the commercial she'd been working on that day hadn't finished until after 8 p.m. She scooped up the envelopes and shambled into the kitchen to pour herself a glass of wine. God, she was knackered.

The answering machine was blinking at her belligerently. She turned it off. She didn't want to hear any messages – they'd all be nagging work-related ones. At least the post looked benign enough. She hadn't had any narky letters from the bank in a while, and bills weren't as unmanageable as they'd been a couple of months ago. Once she'd discarded the junk mail, there was very little else. A postcard from a friend who was on holiday in Malta, and an invitation to the opening night of the *Oedipus* that Lola was designing in the Chamber. Or Chamber Pot, as they'd taken to calling it. She'd almost forgotten about that – she'd been so up to her eyes that she hadn't spoken to Lola for ages. There was no point in phoning her at home: she was slap bang in the middle of previews – always a nightmarish time for a designer – but she could try her on the mobile. She looked at her watch. Too early. The preview wouldn't be over for at least another hour. She'd leave it till eleven o'clock.

She took the wine bottle and Bob the cat into the sitting room, turned on the television and snuggled up on the sofa while Bobcat snuggled up on her. Yet another interior design programme. How insecure people were about their own taste! she thought. She couldn't understand how anyone could allow someone else to dictate to them how their homes should look. Any time she flicked through *Hello!* magazine she could tell whether the individual featured in the photo spreads had decorated their own house, or paid someone else to do it. She was convinced that some of the tackier interiors were the result of some crackpot joker of a designer, who'd scarpered laughing up his sleeve after shafting these gullible individuals with more money than taste.

Most of her own furnishings were junk shop finds, or stuff that she'd purloined from skips outside theatres. It was amazing the stuff you'd find unceremoniously dumped the day after a show closed. On one occasion she'd helped herself to a vast expanse of midnight blue velvet, the painted figurehead of a ship, and a fake leopardskin rug complete with head, tail and paws. Lola had got a gilt throne and a set of carved library steps.

When it came to clothes, Aphrodite's preference

was for dead straightforward unpretentious stuff from places like Gap, slung together with second-hand purchases and bits and pieces that she'd made herself. Today she was wearing loose linen trousers from Penneys teamed with a low-slung, tasselled Dries van Noten belt courtesy of the Brown Thomas sale, a T-shirt with *no* slogan, antique embroidered Moroccan slippers and dangly bejewelled earrings to show that she was a 'creative' type. How silly, really, she thought, that appearances should matter. How sillier still to hazard an opinion on a person based on a first impression . . .

And for some reason she remembered Jack Costello, the photographer she'd met all those weeks ago at the IFC, and she found herself wondering what impression he'd formed of her then, and if he'd ended up in bed with one – or both – of those shimmery twins the night before he'd gone to the States, and if he still had her phone number.

Just after eleven o'clock she poured herself another large glass of wine – wondering as she did so if she was becoming a dipsomaniac like her mother – and punched in Lola's mobile number.

When the designer picked up she sounded surprisingly calm. 'Everything's cool,' she said, in response to Aphrodite's 'How are things?' 'I'm amazed that it's all gone so smoothly. I haven't even had a row with any of the actors.'

'You are one lucky bitch. I've had millions with the diva on the clingwrap ad.'

'Still stuck on kitchen sets?'

'Yup. I'm starting on a new one tomorrow. For

some new kind of pot noodle. But – da-dah! – I've been promoted to assistant designer.'

'Excellent! I hope you've raised your fee accordingly?'

'Damn right. They balked a bit, but I stood my ground. They can afford it. The kind of money they spend on commercials is unreal, Lola.'

'Wish I could say the same about theatre. You're coming to the opening?'

'Of course. Thursday, isn't it?'

'No. It's tomorrow. Didn't you get your invitation? I know they went out a bit late.'

'I just got it today. I didn't look at it properly. Shit. That means I won't be able to get my hair cut before the opening. I'm totally fed up with it, Lo. I've been going round with it in plaits for the past month because I hate it so much.' She *was* totally fed up with it, but the real reason she hadn't been near a hair salon, she knew, had as much to do with her hairdresser phobia as with her hectic schedule.

'Do it yourself,' said Lola matter-of-factly.

'What? *Cut* it myself?'

'Absolutely. Remember that fad a couple of years ago when loads of the more radical luvvies and models were cutting their own hair? I thought it looked great. It would really suit you, Aphrodite – that lovely, mussy, sexy look.'

'Seriously?'

'Seriously. Oh – I'd better go. The scenic artist's looking pissed off. She's going to be here all night if I don't give her a hand. Sorry to dash. See you tomorrow.'

'Good luck, Lola.' Aphrodite put the phone down and wandered over to the mirror above the fireplace. It was an art deco mirror with a blue and gold enamel frame that she'd picked up for a tenner in a charity shop. She'd felt guilty about bamboozling the charity shop because she knew the mirror was worth a great deal more, but Lola had told her not to be such a wuss.

Her reflection, surrounded by its blue and gold frame, looked a little peaky. Running from commercial to commercial and skipping lunch on a regular basis had shed her *avoirdupois* more effectively than swimming could have done. She wound one of her stupid-looking plaits round a finger. Did she dare to cut them off? No. That was a totally bonkers idea. She slugged back her wine and poured another glass. She shouldn't have done that, she knew. She had to be up at the crack of dawn again tomorrow. Then she unravelled first one plait, then the other. Her hair looked like a shorter version of Madonna's when she'd gone through her 'Ray of Light' phase. Aphrodite had always hated that look. She considered for a moment or two. Then she got her hairbrush from the bathroom, and her sewing shears from her work box in the studio. She positioned herself in front of the mirror again, threw her head forward and brushed her hair into a kind of upside down ponytail. For a split second she had second thoughts. Then she took a deep breath – and cut. What the hell! Any hairdo was preferable to the barnet she'd been sporting for the best part of a year.

She stood up and faced the mirror, keeping her

41

eyes shut for a minute until she found her nerve. When she did open her eyes, her mouth opened too, automatically, in surprise. Well, hey! It suited her! She'd created a kind of shaggy, choppy look, and now her hair stood out from her head in an untidy halo. She considered, then divided it into two bunches on either side of her face and cut first one, then the other to jaw length, shaking it about a bit to make it untidier still. Yeah! That was better than sticky-out plaits, or that cruddy centre parting that hadn't done anything for her at all. What nerves of steel she had!

Or what Dutch courage, she reminded herself, as she stuck the cork back in the wine bottle and headed for the bathroom. She allowed herself one last peek at her new image over her shoulder as she went, hoping she wasn't seeing herself with rose-tinted glasses. Maybe in tomorrow morning's light she'd realize that she'd made a big mistake . . .

* * *

She hadn't made a mistake. When she turned up at the Chamber Pot the following evening, all her friends remarked on how funky her hair looked. She'd swiftly gone through her wardrobe before leaving for the theatre, and had located the slinky skirt that she hadn't been able to get into for months. She'd slid into it effortlessly, wanting to cheer. And the buttons of the clingy top she liked to wear with the skirt actually buttoned up without gaping. Hey! It felt so *good* to look sexy again! How could she have allowed Badley to cramp her style for so long?

Hah! There he was now, on the other side of the foyer – *sans* his little blond boyfriend. He was posing, trying to catch her eye! Well, fuck him, she thought, as she turned away, pretending not to have seen him and sending the barman an extra-radiant smile as a kind of revenge. She leaned against the bar and cased the joint as she waited for her drink. It was heaving with familiar faces. There was Lola, deep in conversation with her director and clutching the pack of Marlboro lights that she only ever allowed herself to smoke on opening nights. There was her mother, looking glorious in Ghost. There was that poisonous toad Damien Gobshite Whelan poncing about for some social column photographer. There was David Lawless, director of *The Seagull* that was due to start rehearsal soon, with his wife, the stage and screen luminary Eva Lavery. There was . . . there was Jack Costello. It must be two months – more – since she'd last seen him. He was tanned, his dark hair was longer, he'd put on some weight. But he was still – as Lola had described him – *brutishly* sexy. And he was smiling at her. She smiled back, libido all aflutter.

'Glass of white wine?' The barman had set it down on the counter behind her. She turned and extracted a fiver from her wallet. As she waited for her change, she could see in her peripheral vision that Jack Costello had insinuated his way through the crowd at the bar and was now lounging against the counter beside her. She swallowed hard, then turned to him. 'Hi,' she said. 'How was the States?'

'Shouldn't it be "How *were* the States"? But I won't nitpick. The States was fine. How are you?'

'Fine. Busy.'

'You look very different.' She wasn't sure whether he meant it as a compliment or not. 'What are you up to?'

'This and that. Working on commercials, mostly.'

'No theatre work?'

'None, unfortunately. But at least I'm earning.'

'I might be able to put some work your way if you're interested in styling stills. I'll check it out with the editor of *Individual*, if you like.'

'Would you? I'd really appreciate that.'

There was a pause. Aphrodite refused to let herself be fazed by the way he was scrutinizing her. 'I lost that book of matches,' he said.

'Book of matches?'

'With your telephone number on.'

'Oh – no problem. I'll give you my card, shall I?' She had just that day picked up a batch of business cards from the printers, and she was thrilled by how hiply professional they looked. This was her first opportunity to show them off. She took one from her wallet and handed it to him.

'Aphrodite Delaney. Design Consultant,' he read aloud. 'Phone, mobile, e-mail . . . Well. You're eminently contactable now, aren't you?'

Shit! Her phone had started to ring in her bag. Jack Costello watched in amusement while she rummaged for it. When she located it, the display told her that the caller was the director of the commercial she was currently working on. She'd

44

have to take it. 'Excuse me,' she said. 'It's my boss. I'll be toast if I don't take this call.'

'That's cool,' he said, sliding her card into his pocket. 'But I'd turn your phone off before the show goes up, if I were you. Otherwise you'll be burnt toast. I'll leave you to it.' He inclined his head at her, then moved off through the crowd of opening-nighters, leaving Aphrodite cursing her director for having got his timing so fiendishly wrong. It was a wasted call, anyway, because her phone was breaking up and she couldn't hear a thing. She stuffed the hateful object back in her bag and stood on tiptoe, scanning the crowd for Jack Costello. There was no sign of him. She'd just have to try and catch him again at the interval.

But she didn't. At the interval she was collared by her mother and her mother's latest toyboy. Well, he wasn't exactly what you'd call a toyboy – he was somewhere in his thirties – but he was very much younger than Thea.

After introductions had been effected and Thea had admired Aphrodite's new business card ('So chic, darling! You've arrived at last!'), Aphrodite asked her how rehearsals were going for *Happy Days*.

'Splendidly,' pronounced Thea. 'I'm going to be bloody good in this. And I've got some more excellent news. I've been asked to play Arkadina in David Lawless's *Seagull* at the Phoenix!'

'Isn't Eva Lavery playing that?' Aphrodite was curious. David Lawless always cast his wife in his productions if there was a role suitable for her, and she certainly fitted the bill for Arkadina.

'She can't,' said Thea happily. 'She's off to LA to do some movie with Liam Neeson.'

'Well! Arkadina! Nice part, Mum. And you'll get to wear some gorgeous frocks, I bet.'

'Yes. I will.' Thea was like the cat who got the cream. 'I was talking to Damien earlier – he's designing. He's going to base his entire concept on birds, and I'll be wearing the most glorious peacock gowns.'

'What? What do you mean?' Aphrodite felt something unpleasant lurch in the pit of her stomach.

'Well,' said Thea even more happily, 'Arkadina's such a showy role, Damien felt that a peacock was the perfect image for her.'

The unpleasant thing in Aphrodite's stomach moved again. It felt like an octopus uncurling. 'I don't believe you, Mum!'

'Why don't you believe me? I think it's a brilliant idea. Nina will be a seagull, of course, and Konstantin a raven, and Trigorin – Finbar de Rossa's playing Trigorin – is going to be a vulture. Between you and me, Finbar's not best pleased with that idea. I suspect it's because he knows I'll upstage him easily in my glamorous peacock creations. And he has to shave all his hair off—'

Aphrodite couldn't listen to any more of this. 'I'm sorry, Mum, I've just seen someone I need to talk to urgently up at the bar. I've gotta run.'

She turned and shouldered her way through the crowd, not caring about the cross looks people were giving her. She couldn't think. She could hardly breathe. But there was one thing she knew with blinding clarity: she *hated* Damien Whelan more than she'd ever hated anyone in her life. She had never known until this moment what it was to feel murderous. She hoped to God she wouldn't run into him. She knew beyond the shadow of any doubt that if she did, she would grab the nearest glass, smash it into shards, and gouge it into his face.

She reached the bar and was lucky enough to grab the barman's attention immediately, even though she'd lost the radiant smile and was now behaving like someone suffering from Jekyll and Hyde syndrome. This time it was the look of insane anger on her face that made him jump to it. 'Brandy, please,' she said through a trap-like mouth. 'A large one.' She downed it in three gulps, grimacing at each one. The bell announced the end of the interval, and the audience started trickling back into the auditorium.

The last thing Aphrodite wanted to do was sit through the second half of *Oedipus*, but she couldn't not go in. She owed it to Lola. She sat in her bucket seat, rigid with rage and heaving with hatred. Life sucked. Damien Whelan sucked. The bloody *theatre* sucked. The business was crawling with reptiles, all of them oozing venom. She wanted no part of it. What were those actors *doing* on the stage? Who cared about Oedipus and his stinking mother? Where was its relevance to real life? The bloody *clingwrap* commercial she'd worked on was more relevant to real life. At least clingwrap was *useful*. And what were all these wankers doing sitting here in the audience, paying obeisance to a writer who'd died centuries ago? There'd more than likely be a standing ovation at the end of the evening. The design deserved it, she conceded, knowing how Lola had bust a gut to get it right (although it was a mystery to her how she had allowed the actress playing Jocasta to wear a Wonderbra). But the rest of this posturing, pretentious crap! She remembered the kind of stuff directors she'd worked for in the past had come out with, and the way the actors had nodded their heads like earnest puppets, and gone 'mm' meaningfully. She'd done it too! She'd talked in abstracts with the best of them, and come up with pet theories, and rationalized design concepts to unconvinced, insecure actors – and then bitched about them behind their backs. She was as much a culprit as anyone in this stupid, specious profession. Her lip curled. Good luck to Damien Whelan and the ideas he'd stolen from her. She never wanted to set foot in a theatre again – not even if David Lawless himself asked her. They could all fuck off with their airy-fairy ideas and their pathetic, poverty-line budgets!

The play came to its dramatic conclusion. On stage, the chorus intoned the final cheery farewell to Oedipus as he was led off stage.

'No man is privileged that is not in the grave.
The dead alone have won the reprieve from
   pain.'

There was a moment of hush, and then applause thundered out. Two people in the second row of the stalls rose to their feet, followed by four more in the

48

third row. Then half a dozen to Aphrodite's left stood, and a further half a dozen to her right. Suddenly everybody was standing, with the exception of Aphrodite and a bloke at the end of the aisle some rows further down the stalls. The applause went on and on. Aphrodite could no longer resist the sheepish urge to follow the herd. She too got to her feet as the actors trooped back onto the stage for their third curtain call. When the ovation finally petered out and the lights went up in the auditorium, she snuck a look at the maverick who hadn't succumbed to herd syndrome. Of course it was who she'd expected it to be. She remembered what he'd said the day they'd met at the cinema. '*Everybody's raving about it, so it* has *to be good.*'

She trailed out into the foyer along with the rest of the flock. Everyone was baaing about the show. Aphrodite couldn't hack it. She did a swift recce of the room, located Lola, and made a beeline. 'Your stuff was fab,' she said. 'But I have to go. I can't run the risk of bumping into Damien Whelan.'

'Aphrodite, it's a small town. You can't spend the rest of your life trying to avoid him. I told you—'

'It's not what you think, Lola. I'll call you tomorrow and fill you in. I'm telling you – if I run into that bastard this evening I won't be responsible for my actions.' She gave Lola a swift kiss on the cheek. 'Gotta go.'

On her way out of the theatre she spotted Jack Costello. She dithered momentarily over whether or not she should stop and talk to him, but the decision was taken out of her hands. 'Jack!' she heard someone call. 'I need to talk to you about arranging a sitting some time.' Damien Gobshite Whelan hove into view, and Aphrodite dived for the door.

A little later, as she fumbled in her wallet for her taxi fare, she felt a sudden overwhelming, totally irresistible urge to look at her brand-new business card. Its glossy surface gleamed in the half-light of the street lamps, and she felt a surge of something fierce. There it was. Her new career. Her new identity. Aphrodite Delaney. Design Consultant.

*   *   *

The next morning she was making her breakfast coffee when she got a call from her mother.

'Look up a phone number for me, darling, would you?'

'What's wrong with you? Glass fingers?'

'No. I've just painted my nails and don't want to ruin them by riffling through the Golden Pages.'

'What's wrong with eleven-eight-fifty?'

'I can't gossip with the girl on eleven-eight-fifty. By the way, what happened to you last night? There was someone there you really should have met.'

Aphrodite plunged her cafetière with more than usual force and black liquid splooshed out onto the work surface. 'I got a headache.' There was no point in telling her mother the truth. The fewer people who knew about the *Seagull* fiasco the better. No-one would believe that Damien Whelan had stolen her design concept, and it would just look like sour grapes on her part if she started levelling accusations at a designer as established as he was.

'I'm not surprised. So did I. That *Oedipus* was bloody awful. I can't understand how it got a standing ovation, can you?'

'No.' Aphrodite was curious, suddenly. 'Did you stand?'

'Well, of course I did. Didn't you?'

'Yes. But I'm not very proud to admit it.'

'Oh, pooh, darling. Personal integrity counts for nothing in the face of theatre politics. It's not worth running the risk of offending *anyone* in this business.'

Aphrodite reached resignedly for the phone book. 'What number are you looking for?' she asked.

'The Powerscourt Health Farm. I want to spend a whole day out in Wicklow being pampered.'

Aphrodite perused the pages. 'H, h, h, h . . . Health. P, p, p, p . . . Powerscourt. Here you are.' She relayed the number. 'Who was this person I should have met last night, incidentally?'

'Person?'

'Mother. You said there was someone at the Chamber last night that I should have met.'

'Oh, yes! Listen to this! I may have found you a job.'

'Oh?' Aphrodite felt a little fizz of anticipation. 'What kind of a job?'

'An interior design job.'

'Oh.' The fizz went 'phut'. 'Mum. I am *not* an interior designer.'

'But I'm sure you could do it if you set your mind to it, couldn't you, darling? After all, it says "design consultant" on your business card, and that covers a multitude.'

Aphrodite had chosen the words with care when she'd ordered the cards, and had decided that 'design consultant' had an impressively authoritative ring to it.

'And it's for the most *amazing* man,' resumed her mother. 'I gave him your card last night, and he said he'd get in touch.'

'Who is this *amazing* man?'

'Troy MacNally.'

'The fashion designer?'

'Yes.'

'Wow.' Troy MacNally was emerging as a force to be reckoned with in the brave new world of Irish fashion. His stuff was ingeniously cut and intricately tailored, and accolades inevitably included comparisons with the work of Hussein Chalayan in the UK. Prada devotees wouldn't be seen dead in it, but Aphrodite loved it.

'It's the most extraordinary story, Aphrodite.'

'What is?'

'The reason he wants his apartment redecorated. Listen to this. His muse – Miriam somebody, I can't remember her name –'

'Miriam de Courcy. You must have seen photographs of her, Mum. She's that angel-faced model with hair like Rapunzel.'

'I'm sure I have,' said Thea vaguely. 'Anyway, apparently this Miriam has become a total coke fiend and has disappeared off to live in South America. Their rift was *not* amicable, and Troy is not a happy man.'

'When did this happen?'

'A couple of weeks ago.'

'And what's this got to do with redecorating his apartment?'

'He wants a complete change. He says that by revamping his surroundings he can open a new chapter in his life and exorcize all the demons that are holding him back.' Thea embellished her tone with a dramatic flourish.

'Exorcize demons? He actually said that?'

'Mm-hm.'

'What a wanker. Why doesn't he look under "I" for "Interior Designer" in the Golden Pages?'

'He doesn't want to trust the job to someone who's likely to play safe and do a rehash of something out of *wallpaper**, or one of those despotic style glossies. He wants a more imaginative approach, and when I told him about you he started looking interested. It turns out he'd seen that fringe production of those Yeats plays you did – when was that?'

'Ages ago. That was the first job I got when I came back to Ireland.'

'Well, Troy MacNally went as far as to call your set design "inspirational", and said that getting hold of your card was sheer serendipity.'

Inspirational! Serend-*what*? More wankology! 'Serendipity? What's that?'

'Something felicitous that comes to you out of the blue.'

'Oh.' Aphrodite couldn't help prinking a little. Maybe he wasn't such a wanker after all.

'So. What do you think of the idea?'

Aphrodite pondered. She found the notion of meeting Troy MacNally rather intriguing. 'I suppose there's no harm in talking to him,' she said.

'Good. I'm glad to have been of assistance. Expect a call from him today – he's leaving the country in the very near future. Oh, God and horror, look at the time. I'd better run, darling, or I'll be late for rehearsal. Happy days!'

And Thea put the phone down.

Aphrodite poured a mug of coffee, wandered into her sitting room and started to riffle through a pile of old magazines. There, in a September issue of *Individual*, was a photograph of Miriam de Courcy wearing a gown from Troy MacNally's last autumn collection. She was draped around a stone angel in some overgrown graveyard, and her night-black hair floated around her exquisite face like a thundercloud. The gown was in pleated khaki lined with amethyst silk, and Miriam wore it beautifully. She gazed directly into the lens of the camera with a dreamy, rather melancholy expression on her face. Aphrodite found herself thinking how strange it was that this ravishing creature had probably been strung out on cocaine when the photograph was taken.

In the kitchen, the phone rang again. She didn't recognize the number on the display.

'Hello?'

'Aphrodite Delaney?' The voice was chocolate.

'Speaking.'

'Aphrodite. It's Troy MacNally here. I spoke with your mother last night at the Chamber theatre.'

'Oh, yes. She phoned me this morning.'

'So you know why I'm calling.' Bitter, dark chocolate.

'Yes. She told me that you're interested in having me do some work on your apartment.'

'That's right.'

Aphrodite hedged a little. She still wasn't sure about this. 'Troy – I've never done professional interior design work before, so I may not be what you're looking for.'

'A professional interior designer is exactly what I'm *not* looking for.'

'Well.' She tucked the phone into the niche between her jaw and collarbone, and reached for the pen and Post-It pad. 'Maybe we should meet up and have a talk.'

'I don't need to discuss it. I'm asking you to do it. Money's not a problem. I'll pay you very well.'

Aphrodite hated talking money. 'Well, of course I'll have no idea what to charge until I've seen the place. When can we meet?'

'We can't. I'm going away tomorrow.'

'Oh.' She tried another gambit. 'When you get back, then?'

'No. I want the place finished by the time I get back. I don't want painters or workmen hanging around the joint while I'm there.'

'I see.' This was all happening very fast. 'Maybe you could outline some specifications for me and I'll have a think.'

'There's only one specification, and that is that I want it all to be as different from the way it is now as it's possible to be.'

This wasn't just happening very fast, this was *bonkers*! 'What do you mean?'

'It's all up to you, Aphrodite. Do the room any way you want. Just as long as the change is a radical one.'

'The room? Sorry, I'm a little confused. I thought you wanted your entire apartment redone?'

'No. Just the bathroom.'

Curiouser and curiouser . . . 'Why?' she asked.

'Personal reasons,' he said. On the other end of the line Aphrodite heard someone else talking, and Troy made a sound of irritation. 'You'll have to excuse me. I must go. Are you willing to take the job on?'

'Well, yes, in principle I am–'

'Good. I'll have my PA e-mail you the relevant details. If you have any problems, talk to her. Goodbye, Aphrodite.' The phone went dead.

Well, thought Aphrodite. What the *fuck* was all that about?

Chapter Three

A little later that day Aphrodite accessed her e-mail, and found the following:

Dear Ms Delaney,

Troy MacNally asked me to send you some information.

He will be out of the country until the 3rd March. He would appreciate it if all work could be completed on the room in question before this date. Please feel free to employ plumbers, painters, carpenters, whomever you need – so long as you can be sure that they will work to your exact specification. His decorative preference is for something entirely fresh and original – you have absolute freedom to experiment as you wish.

You may pick up the keys from his studio reception any time tomorrow.

Please do not hesitate to contact me if you have any queries, and perhaps you'd e-mail me with your budgetary requirements as soon as possible.

Yours sincerely,

Polly Riordan. pp Troy MacNally

Biz*arre*!

She immediately picked up the phone and punched in Lola's number.

'What was all that about last night?' was the first thing Lola asked.

What with the weird events of the morning, Aphrodite had almost forgotten Damien Whelan's Wicked Witch of the West behaviour.

'*Bastard!*' said Lola after Aphrodite had filled her in. 'But, hey! Why do I not find it shocking? Jesus. I would have spiked the slimy git's drink with something toxic if I'd known. Which is what somebody could well have done to me, the way I'm feeling today.'

'Hungover, my dear?'

'Massively so. I don't suppose you're suffering, Ms Party-pooping Goodie Two Shoes?'

'No. I am a smug bitch. What are the reviews like?'

'I haven't seen a paper yet, but I'm told they're excellent.'

Aphrodite had suspected as much. 'I'm very glad for you, Lola mia. You deserve good press. But I will be frank with you, and say that the show stinks.'

'I know. It's a pile of shite, isn't it? But what else do you expect to find in a Chamber Pot?' Lola yawned down the phone, and then said: 'Ow! That yawn hurt my head. D'you fancy meeting somewhere for a coffee? I could do with a quadruple espresso.'

'I was just about to ask you that very question. There's something I need to run by you.'

'Oh? What?'

'It's too weird to go into on the phone. I'll tell you when I see you. Butler's? Midday?'

'Uh-oh. There's a tiled floor there, isn't there?'

'Yeah. You want to go somewhere less clackety?'

'No. Their macchiata is the best in town. I'll just have to hack the noise.'

*   *   *

Aphrodite was ordering hot chocolate for herself when Lola streeled into Butler's wearing sunglasses and a pained expression.

'I'll have a macchiata,' she said to the waitress. 'And a glass of water, please.' The water was for her Solpadeine, which she knocked back in one. 'Yeuch! This stuff'd better kick in quick. I'm doing an interview with the *Irish Times* later on this afternoon, and I'm not going to be able to string two words together. So.' She took off her sunglasses and gave Aphrodite a bloodshot blink. 'What did you want to run by me?'

'Do you know anything about Troy MacNally, Lo?'

'He's a fucking looker, I know that. He was at the show last night.'

'So I heard.'

'Why are you asking?'

Aphrodite filled her in.

'Bizarre!'

'That's exactly the word I used!'

Lola looked thoughtful. 'Although I suppose it kind of makes sense. I was talking to someone last

59

night who knows him and was pissed enough to be a little indiscreet. There's been a lot of gossip about Troy floating around since his muse Miriam upped and left.'

'Oh? Share it with me at once! What's he like?'

'Sex on legs.'

'OK. Forget about the sex thing. I need to know what he's like as a person.'

'Um. Let's see. According to this girl I was talking to, Polly—'

'Not Polly Riordan? His PA?'

'Yup.'

'She's the one who sent me that e-mail earlier.'

'Well, according to her, since he split up with Miriam he's been moody and reclusive. That broody, artistic temperament thing, you know? She's been very concerned for him. Apparently last night was the first time he's been out since the split.'

Aphrodite put her elbows on the table and leaned in closer to Lola. 'OK. Tell me more.'

'She told me that he's spent most of the past two weeks either in his bed or in his bath – can you believe that? Just lying there trying to forget Miriam, and – because he has a deadline to meet – trying to come up with ideas for his next collection. His bathroom is like his . . . um . . . what's the right word? Where do you go to escape from real life awfulness?'

'Sanctuary?' suggested Aphrodite.

'Spot on. His sanctuary. It's where he goes for inspiration. If he has a block he just floats in his bath and waits for the creative juices to start flowing.'

'So *that's* why it's so important for him to have the

place made over!' exclaimed Aphrodite. *Now* things were starting to fall into place. Aphrodite knew what it was like to have a block – all creatives did. She coped with it by walking the mile-long Pigeon House pier until she got her head together, but she knew one person who swam laps, another who plugged into recordings of ocean waves, another who spent hours staring at his fish tank. She even knew someone who did all their hand washing when hit with a block. Funny how water always seemed to be part of the equation . . . Aphrodite pondered a moment longer, and then threw Lola a horrified look. 'Hell, Lola – what if I screw up?'

'You won't,' said Lola with the assurance of which only a best friend is capable.

Aphrodite scooped the froth off the top of her hot chocolate with a teaspoon and sucked it thought-fully. 'Still – it's a massive responsibility, isn't it?'

'You don't *have* to do it,' Lola pointed out reason-ably.

'I know. But I'm kind of intrigued, now.'

'*I* know why you're intrigued, you big sheet of plate glass.'

'Why?'

'Because I said Troy MacNally was sex on legs.'

'That's *not* why!' said Aphrodite indignantly. And then: 'Hey! Is Tony busy at the moment?' Tony, Lola's brother, was a builder.

'Not as far as I know. He had a gig lined up, all right, but he mentioned something last night about it being postponed until next month.'

'So he could do with a nixer to tide him over?'

'I'm sure he'd be glad of it.'

'Will you ask him if he'd be interested in this one? I could do with having a team on board that I can trust.'

'Sure. I'll phone him tonight.'

Aphrodite had wanted to ask the next question for ages. 'Aren't you going to eat your chocolate?' she said. The coffee in Butler's always came accompanied by miniature confections in chocolate.

'Nah. The mind is willing, but the hangover ain't. You can have it.'

'Thanks. By the way, what made you allow that actress playing Jocasta last night to get away with wearing a Wonderbra?'

'I didn't. I've told her time and time again not to, but she keeps sneaking it on. I'm going to get my revenge on her tonight. I'm going to fray the straps on it with a Stanley knife before she arrives in her dressing room. Ha! What a sight it'll be to see her bosoms drop as well as her face when she goes into breast-beating mode in the second half.' Lola was peering out through the window. 'Wow, look at her.'

A stunning girl was standing on the footpath across the road, talking to an equally stunning boy. She was wearing a beautifully cut full-length black gabardine coat, which made a dramatic contrast with her shock of platinum hair.

'Do you know something, Aphrodite?' remarked Lola, looking at her friend shrewdly. 'Now that your hair is so much shorter, it would look really great that colour.'

'White blond?' said Aphrodite.

'Yeah!' Lola was nodding enthusiastically.

'A bit Kelly Osbourne meets Marilyn Monroe, don't you think? Are you sure your hangover isn't misleading you, Lo?'

'No. Absolutely not. Go for it.'

'Seriously?' Aphrodite looked at the girl again and pictured herself with white blond hair. It wasn't the kind of colour that could be worn by a coward, but Aphrodite knew that Lola was right. It would transform her brave crop from looking just great to looking maybe sensational.'

Lola was reading her mind. 'Come on,' she said, knocking back her coffee. 'I'll hold your hand. We don't even have to go to a hair salon – we'll get something from a chemist's. That means if you don't like it, it'll disappear after a few washes.'

'OK. I'll go for it,' Aphrodite said with the same sudden decision that had induced her to hack all her hair off the night before last. She took another look at the girl across the road, then grabbed her bag and got up from the table. 'But let's hit the pub first.'

'You're taking me for a cure?'

Aphrodite shook her head. 'No. I'm going to need a large vodka before I do this,' she said.

*   *   *

The next morning Aphrodite walked into Troy MacNally's studio with hair the colour of white gold. She still wasn't used to it, and was feeling self-conscious and insecure. Her insecurity was compounded by the behaviour of the hip telephone-talking receptionist who ignored her and ignored her and ignored her until Aphrodite leaned towards her and said: 'Excuse me,' quite loud.

'Excuse *me*,' said the girl with hauteur, finally relinquishing the receiver. She took in Aphrodite's threads and her ragged blond crop with an expert eye, and Aphrodite knew from her expression that on the scale of style hierarchy she was probably the sartorial equivalent of a dog turd. 'How may I help you?' She didn't even bother with a stapled smile.

'Polly Riordan said she'd leave the keys to Troy MacNally's apartment at reception. I'm doing some work on his flat.'

'Oh yes,' said the girl, reaching out a languid hand to a tray behind her and hooking a manila envelope with manicured fingers. 'You're the painter and – er – decorator, aren't you?' Aphrodite was appalled by the disparaging way she articulated the word 'decorator'. She might as well have called her the 'Dyno-rod man'. She flushed and flailed around for some smart retort, but the receptionist's attitude had fazed her badly and her defence mechanisms were down. When the phone rang and the girl started ignoring her again, Aphrodite just stuffed the envelope in her pocket and retreated through the door with a blazing face.

The *painter* and *decorator*! She was a design consultant! Why oh *why* did life's rules decree that you always came up with a smartarse response two minutes too late? Why hadn't she been able to retaliate with something like: 'Well, at least I've more interesting things to paint than my nails . . .' or: 'You could do with some advice on how to paint your face. Here's my card.'

She clenched her hand round the envelope in her pocket and pulled it out. It was addressed to her in bold black italic script, and it contained a set of keys and a card with Troy's address printed on it. She was glad to see that his apartment was on Camden Street – the new 'French Quarter' of Dublin that was within walking distance of the city centre, and not a million miles away from her own gaff. She set off fast, keen to put as much distance between her and Ms Snoot the receptionist as she could, still composing mental put-downs twenty minutes later when she arrived at the address on the card.

She was surprised to discover that the apartment was located above a not madly salubrious huckster's shop that had baskets full of tacky household items on display outside. The state of the doorway suggested that drunks returning late from the local pub might use it as a urinal, and the stairway was the kind you'd expect to see in a seedy detective film. It looked as if nobody had bothered redecorating since some time in the Forties. The apartment was three floors up worn linoleum-covered stairs. Aphrodite unlocked the scuffed wooden door with a chunky key, and let herself in.

She found herself in a corridor so long and dark she was only just able to make out a door at the far end. There were two more on either side. The light switch was located to the right of the door she had just come through. Aphrodite flicked it, but nothing happened. A floor board creaked as she made her way gingerly towards the first door on the right, keeping her hand against the wall for balance in case she encountered some unexpected step or other hazard. The door boasted an old-fashioned, elegantly wrought brass handle. She depressed it and slowly pushed the door open, registering as she did so that her heartbeat had accelerated. Then her heart seemed suddenly to stop. Aphrodite stood quite still on the threshold and stared.

It was as if she had been magically transported into the palace of some *fin-de-19th-siècle* aristocrat. The room was gorgeous: gorgeous in the true sense of the word. Silk hung on the walls, heavy velvet at the windows. There were armchairs upholstered in jewel-coloured brocades, and couches heaped with the kind of pillows that begged to be pummelled. There was a Victorian upright piano in an alcove, below a faded tapestry depicting Leda and the Swan, and what Aphrodite thought might be an Aubusson carpet glimmered on the floor. An oriental shrine in black lacquer stood against the wall, opposite a black marble fireplace above which was suspended a mirror framed in Gothic-inspired, elaborately carved mahogany. A nude ebony Venus embraced Cupid on a side table, and a half-finished chess game was frozen in cold warfare on an anthracite and marble board.

Aphrodite's heart started to beat again. She took a tentative step into the room, then another, and then she was moving from one precious object to the next, running her hands along wax-polished wood, caressing curves of smoothly sculpted ebony, rubbing inquisitive fingers over voluptuous velvets, sliding her palms across sensuous silks. She paused when she reached a glass-fronted bookcase, unsure as to whether or not it was kosher to examine the contents. Casing the joint for ambience was one thing, snooping around Troy MacNally's reading material might be overstepping her brief a bit. Still . . .

Running her eyes along the titles on the spines behind the glass, she noticed that there was a lot of poetry amongst them, mostly French. There were works by Villon and volumes of Verlaine, Apollinaire and Mallarmé. The novels of Huysmans, Zola, and Flaubert. The Marquis de Sade. Baudelaire's *Les Fleurs du Mal.* The Flowers of Evil . . . Aphrodite tensed. She was beginning to feel uncomfortable.

Back in the hall, a pair of plinths on either side of the far door supported two enormous alabaster vases that contained the strangest, most exotic flowers Aphrodite had ever seen. Some had swollen, hairy stems and huge, scarlet petals like something Georgia O'Keeffe might paint; some boasted phallic-shaped protuberances, glossy as red peppers; some had heavy, pendulous blossoms the colour of raw meat.

Les Fleurs du Mal. Aphrodite realized she had goosebumps.

The door flanked by the plinths was locked. Three other doors beckoned ominously. The first one she tried was a cupboard full of cleaning equipment, the banality of the contents somehow reassuring. The next door led to a dining room furnished in much the same style as the sitting room – if 'sitting room' wasn't too prosaic a term for the salon she'd just left. There was a dining table of polished mahogany flanked by half a dozen chairs with high, carved backs. On a sideboard rested a glass case full of stuffed birds dressed in huntsmen's outfits. One was wielding a miniature bow between its wings, and another was lying on its back on the floor of the case, an arrow buried in its tiny red breast. A banner unfurled above the heads of the participants of this macabre tableau bore the legend *Who Killed Cock Robin?* in faded Gothic script.

On the other side of the room, a swing door led into a tiny kitchen, perfunctorily equipped. Aphrodite had the impression that not very much cooking got done here.

She wouldn't have been at all surprised to have found a four-poster in the bedroom, but in fact the bed was a *bateau lit* with scrolled mahogany ends, guarded on either side by a pair of stone sphinxes. A dressing room led off the bedroom and she jumped when she came face to face with herself in an elaborately carved cheval-glass. Again that unpleasant snoopy feeling came over her as she ran a hand along the rows of suits hanging in the gentleman's (Victorian) wardrobe. Where did he keep his more casual clothes? she wondered as she gazed at the serried ranks of polished leather shoes. In that camphor wood chest by the door? Or in the carved armoire standing next to it? She didn't open either. A faint smell of sandalwood hung in the air.

The smell intensified when she opened the door that took her from the dressing room into Troy's bathroom. Light streamed into the room through a stained-glass cupola in the ceiling, throwing jewel-like patterns onto the middle of the floor. It was plain that nothing had been changed here for over a century. It was fitted with what the Victorians liked to describe as 'sanitary ware'. A throne-like lavatory with a chain dangling from the cistern. A big porcelain basin with brass taps. A cast iron bath with claw-and-ball feet. Intricately wrought sconces encrusted with dark red wax were set into the wall above the scrolled edge.

Directly opposite the bath hung a picture, shrouded in a dust sheet. Aphrodite froze. For some reason she was completely fazed by the idea of unveiling that picture. She didn't want to see it. She was beginning to wish that she'd never accepted this commission. Could she phone Polly Riordan and say she'd changed her mind? She toyed with the idea for a moment or two, and then: fuck it, she thought with decision. It would be too lucrative a gig to turn down.

Aphrodite took a deep breath, then took hold of a corner of the dust sheet like a magician doing the tablecloth trick, and pulled. She found herself gazing at the portrait of a woman, executed in passionate oils. She recognized her immediately as Miriam de Courcy, Troy MacNally's ex-muse. She was nude, lying on her stomach with her back to the painter, but with her head turned, looking back over her shoulder so that whoever viewed the painting locked eyes with her immediately before letting their gaze travel over the geography of her body. There was a manacle around her ankle with a chain attached, and there was more than a hint of sadness in her beautiful, smoky eyes. She lay on a couch draped with velvet, one arm hanging limply over the edge, the other supporting her chin. A red leather-bound volume lay on the couch by her elbow, pages splayed. Aphrodite peered at the gold-tooled lettering on the spine. *Erotica Universalis,* she read. A marmoset was playing with an opium pipe that the sitter had obviously let slip to the floor. The woman was so quintessentially *naked* that Aphrodite felt like covering her up with the dust sheet again.

Instead, she let herself out of Troy MacNally's apartment and took a taxi straight to the Pigeon House pier.

*   *   *

She walked its length not once, but twice, waiting for inspiration to strike. What was she to make of the weird scenario that lay behind the shabby front door of Troy MacNally's flat? What did it reveal about him, about the way he lived his life? His taste in décor indicated clearly that he harked back to another era: the *belle époque* when lavishness ruled, and decadence was the order of the day, the era plundered by Baz Luhrmann for *Moulin Rouge.* Aphrodite tried hard to recall what she knew of the late nineteenth century. Not much. It had been her favourite period of art history once upon a time – all that gloomy symbolism and preoccupation with artifice and sensuality had held huge appeal for a hormonal teenager – but she hadn't studied it with any great seriousness. It had been a strictly adolescent phase, and she'd moved swiftly on.

What was the first Herculean labour that faced her now? She thought very hard. She'd have to gut the bathroom – that much was staring her in the face. She'd have to rip out all that elaborate Victoriana and send it to somewhere that dealt in architectural supply and salvage. What would she have then? An empty space. *An empty space* . . . Hang on – she was getting somewhere here . . . What had he said to her on the phone yesterday? 'I want it all to be as different from the way it is now as it's possible to be . . .' Troy MacNally wanted different? An empty space was as different as it got. Yes! She would fulfil her brief to the letter.

A vision in white hung before her mind's eye. A pristine room with clean lines and Zen ambience. A place for contemplation, a place with no distractions. A sanctuary. An anchorite's retreat. An empty space.

*   *   *

When she reached home she got straight on the phone to Lola, whose brother Tony had left a message on her machine to say he'd be glad to do the building work on Troy MacNally's Bathroom.

Every time she thought of it now, and registered the enormity of the task, she automatically added that capital 'B' to the word 'bathroom'.

'Spooooky,' said Lola in a ghostie's voice when Aphrodite filled her in on what she'd found behind Troy's unprepossessing front door.

'Yes, it is a bit. But at least the next time I go I won't be on my own. Tony rang to say he'd help out.'

'So. What do you plan to do with the joint?'

'Rip it. I've got some amazing ideas, Lo. I'm getting really excited by this project.'

'Spill the beans.'

'Well. I'm going to make it an absolute model of Japanese restraint. I picked up some catalogues on my way home, and in one of them there's this bath that's just a clean oval scoop.'

'Wow. Cool.'

'It is. Mega cool. I wouldn't be able to afford anything like it in a million years.'

'What's your budget on this, Aphrodite?'

She put on a politician's voice. 'I am not at liberty to discuss my financial arrangements with Mr MacNally.'

'Smug bitch.'

'Too right. But we're talking a lot of dosh, Lo.'

'He must have some kind of private income. He's not *that* established a designer,' said Lola. 'He hasn't gone international yet, as far as I know. I wonder where the moolah comes from?'

'Mafia connections,' speculated Aphrodite blithely. Then her enthusiasm took over again. 'I'm going to have Tony build a kind of platform in the middle of the room, with steps up – directly under the stained-glass cupola I told you about. The colours in that are so fantastic, Lola–'

'You're not going to rip *that* out, are you?'

'Christ, no. It's far too beautiful. That's where I plan to sink the bath.' Aphrodite was gesticulating graphically, as she always did when she was impassioned – a habit she had picked up from her mother. 'That light shining through the stained glass onto the bath directly below will be the only splash of colour in the entire room. I'm going to make that bathroom monastic in its simplicity! I'm going to conceal all the usual paraphernalia behind plain white panels–'

'You mean like screens?'

'No. Built-in cupboards. Floor to ceiling along one entire wall. I'll even hinge the mirror in such a way that the plain white reverse side swings to face the room when it's not in use. Not even Mr MacNally's reflection will be able to distract him when he's in contemplative mode.'

'What about the sexy portrait?'

'I don't know what to do about that. Should I hang it somewhere else?'

Lola pondered. 'I'm not sure that's a good idea. Why don't you wrap it in its sheet and put it out of the way?'

'There's a store cupboard.'

'Perfect. That's the first thing you do, then. And don't let Tony see it. I can just imagine the politically incorrect remarks it would inspire. When do you start, by the way?'

'Tomorrow,' said Aphrodite.

'Yikes,' said Lola. 'Good luck.'

* * *

Four weeks later, it was finished. Having seen enough television coverage of Your Worst Nightmare Builders from Hell, Aphrodite knew she'd been lucky with her team. They'd worked so flat out to get it finished on time that she was a bit pissed off when, two days before Troy's return date, she got a message from Polly Riordan to say that the designer had prolonged his holiday by a week, and wouldn't be returning until the 10th of March.

She let the last workman out of the flat on a Saturday evening and wandered back through the rooms to have one final look at her creation. Lola had visited earlier in the day to admire the finished product. She'd left her *Irish Times* behind on the kitchen table, Aphrodite noticed, along with a copy of *wallpaper**, the style bible. Aphrodite picked the magazine up and started idly leafing through it on her way to Troy's bathroom. What pretentious shite! she thought, scanning a feature on the latest expensive, must-have accessories. Turning the page with contempt, she found a feature on must-play CDs. Oh, *sad*. She turned the page again. What she saw there made her stop dead.

It was her bathroom. OhJesusChristpleasehelpmeGod. It was, near as dammit, her bathroom. It was stark. It was white. It was Zen. A platform in the centre of the room was the focus, with a bath

74

inlaid. A clean white scoop. Tall panels to conceal bathroom junk. The only difference was that these panels featured handles. She became aware of other differences as she surveyed the photograph with a sinking heart, but they were negligible. Oh *God*! How could she have been so stupid? It was a classic bathroom concept, after all. Her single-minded determination to create an empty space had blinded her to the fact that her idea wasn't really that original. And Troy MacNally had insisted that he didn't want anything that remotely resembled the work of an interior designer. It had been his principal reason for hiring her, for Christ's sake! Aphrodite had blithely gone and blown his rationale into kingdom come. How would he feel when he came back from holiday to find that his bathroom had been transformed into some parody of a stylist's dream in *wallpaper**?

A blind panic was beginning to rise in her. Stop! she reprimanded herself. This would not *do*! Panicking was going to solve nothing. She sat down heavily on the edge of the recently Polybonded platform, not caring that she'd smudge it, and forced herself to think. Hang on, hang on, her pragmatic voice reasoned. You still have another week to do something about this. *Do?* What exactly did she think she was going to be able to *do*? She'd used up her entire budget. She couldn't hire anyone, or buy materials. She was asking for a miracle. But miracles did happen sometimes . . . A little inspiration often resulted in miracles . . .

The Pigeon House pier beckoned. But it was late, and she didn't fancy the idea of walking there alone in the dark. She cast the odious magazine aside, stood up, and started to pace. She paced the bathroom, and then she paced through the dressing room to the bedroom. Was there any clue to be found here, any inspiration? Her eyes fell on the sphinxes that flanked Troy's bed. They looked back at her with such smug inscrutability that she wanted to kick them. With hands clasped together and knuckles pressed against her mouth, Aphrodite strode down the hall until she found herself in the sitting room, brow furrowed in concentration.

What was the antithesis of the plain white space she'd created? That was easy. Colour. Colour was manageable. Paint was cheap. Should she paint Troy MacNally's bathroom in one strong colour? Vibrant orange, for instance. Oh no. Orange was *so* two seasons ago. And orange walls were meant to drive people mad. Her mother's walls were washed with saffron, which explained a lot. So. Not orange. Loads of colours then? An image of flowers suddenly projected itself in front of her mind's eye. What? Flowers in a man's bathroom? No. Not flowers. *Fleurs. Les Fleurs du Mal* . . . Where had that come from?

She had stopped in front of the glass-fronted bookcase. The volume of Baudelaire poems was on a shelf at eye level. Maybe there was something in Troy's bookcase that she could look to for inspiration? Getting to her knees, she angled her head to see what was on the lower shelves. There, in a dark corner was a big book bound in dark red leather, the title tooled in gold letters on the spine. It was the book Miriam had been reading in the portrait that had hung on the bathroom wall. The *Erotica Universalis*.

Aphrodite tried the door of the bookcase. It opened with a spooky creaking sound, and her heart started to pitter as she took the heavy volume from its shelf. She opened it, then swallowed hard. The pages were covered in illustrations of couples in coitus that, had the participants not been depicted with considerable artistic flair, would have verged on the pornographic. Aphrodite leafed randomly through the book, pausing to admire a drawing by Matisse of a reclining nude, then shut it with decision. She was letting herself be distracted here, not inspired . . .

As she slid the volume back onto its shelf, something dropped out. It was a postcard reproduction of a painting she was familiar with, a painting that had taken her breath away when she'd seen the real thing in the Museum of Modern Art in New York. It was the work of Henri Rousseau, and it depicted a dark beauty reclining on a divan in the middle of a dense green jungle, surrounded by flowers and animals. The reverse of the card was covered in a flurry of violet ink, which Aphrodite elected not to read. She'd done enough snooping. She sat down on the ottoman next to the bookcase and gazed at the painting Rousseau had called *The Dream*.

She remembered an essay she'd once done for her history of art tutor. It had been one of those 'compare and contrast' exercises, and Rousseau's name had come up several times. Compare and contrast. *Compare and contrast* . . . This celebration of nature with its fresh, exuberant naïvety was a complete contrast to the current Zen-like ambience of Troy's bathroom . . .

Oh! It hit her with blinding clarity. That bathroom was a blank canvas, a pristine sheet of white paper for her to cover in colour. The colours of nature in all their infinite hues. She had thought that an empty space was as different as it got? No, no, no! A Rousseauesque landscape would be the last thing Troy MacNally would expect to see in his bathroom . . .

But. But what if he hated it? What if it gave him more of a shock than a surprise? She was taking an audacious, last-ditch risk. And then Aphrodite's most pragmatic voice sounded scarily in her head. Well, girl, it said. You don't have much choice. And you don't have much time, either . . .

*   *   *

The next morning Aphrodite went shopping. She bought paints. She bought jungle green and heliotrope blue and sunset pink. She bought fiery red and banana yellow and mandarin orange. She bought brushes and charcoal and methylated spirits. Then she went home and fetched her painting overalls, and then – stopping off in Waterstone's on the way to buy an art book – she returned to Troy's apartment.

She sat down on the edge of the bath in the pool of jewel-like light that streamed in through the skylight, and started to leaf through the pages of glossy Rousseau reproductions. She would transform this room into a Garden of Eden – a garden populated with lions and tigers and bears. Oh, my! And jaguars and apes and elephants and snakes. Exotic birds. A naked Eve, innocently accepting the gift of a luscious fruit from a scarlet-tongued serpent . . .

Scanning the text that accompanied the illustrations, she learned that Rousseau's credo was 'full creative freedom for the artist whose inspiration is for the beautiful and the good'. The beautiful and the good . . . This was exactly what she wanted to hear! She would trash those *fleurs du mal* and paint the walls with vital, vibrant flora and fauna instead. Serendipity had struck!

She jumped to her feet, pulled on her overalls and flexed her fingers. Then she reached for a stick of charcoal, took a deep breath, and began to trace bold black outlines on the blank white walls of Troy MacNally's bathroom.

*   *   *

She found herself working flat out *again*. But – she told herself – at least it was only for one more week. And she had help in the form of Lola, who had volunteered to come in and wield a paintbrush when she was available.

As she worked, a jungle began to take root. Green tendrils unfurled in corners and crept along the walls. Palm trees sprouted and soared ceiling-high. The resprayed bath became an aquamarine pool above which gleamed a cool silver moon in a pale evening sky. Monkeys swung from eucalyptus branches and panthers lurked in a labyrinth of leaves. A serpent proffered Eve an apricot. The Garden of Eden flourished and brought forth fruit in Troy MacNally's bathroom.

And finally, very, very late on the evening before her client was due to arrive home, a knackered Aphrodite cleaned her brushes, tidied the detritus that had accumulated over the course of the past seven days, and dumped her gear in the hallway by the front door. She'd come back and pick up all her stuff first thing tomorrow; she couldn't be bothered lugging it home now. There was a party happening later – the last-night bash of Lola's show – but Aphrodite's limbs were aching, her mind was reeling, and partying was the last thing she felt like doing. Theatre parties never got going until really late, and the idea of trailing down to the theatre around midnight to drink cheap lukewarm wine out of plastic cups filled her with dreariness.

Back in the bathroom, she discarded her overalls and pulled out the mirror to get a load of how she looked. Like shite, she thought. Pale, tired, and with streaks of green paint in her hair. The cupboard behind the mirror contained a selection of seductive aromatherapy oils. Eucalyptus, musk, lavender . . . She pulled the cork on one of the purple glass bottles and the subtle scent of sandalwood slipped out. Aphrodite's eyes slid to the aquamarine scoop in the centre of the room. Would it be outrageously cheeky to help herself to a bath?

No, she decided, turning on the taps and pouring oil into the water. It *wasn't* cheeky of her. She needed to be certain that she had fulfilled her brief, after all. To find out if her creative strategy had worked. To – um, well – 'assess how her client might relate to the brand new environment she had created for him'. That was good 'Design Consultant' speak! Of course she couldn't get into Troy MacNally's mindset, but she wanted to know how it might feel to lie in a pool surrounded by a magical forest and just – think . . .

She wandered into the kitchen to fetch a glass of water, wishing she'd had the cop-on to buy herself a sandwich earlier. She hadn't eaten since lunchtime and she was starving. She looked in the freezer to see if there was anything she could nick. She'd replace it tomorrow when she came back to collect her gear. The freezer was bare. The fridge, then. The workmen might have left something salvageable. There was no food at all in the fridge – apart from a half-full carton of milk and some unidentifiable thing that had obviously passed its sell-by date weeks ago – but there were several bottles of champagne. Cristal. It would knock her back a small fortune to replace a bottle of Cristal . . . But: fuck it, she thought, grabbing one and stripping off the foil. Troy MacNally had paid her generously, and she damn well deserved a treat after working so hard.

She fetched a cut-glass flute from a cupboard and trailed back into the bathroom where she stripped off her clothes before cracking the bottle. The sound alone was enough to lift her spirits: her mother had once declared that the sound of a champagne cork popping was the best sound in the world. Aphrodite filled the flute, noticing as she did so that her nails were thickly encrusted with paint. There was a pair of nail clippers in the cupboard that housed the bath oils. She fetched it, and a file, then sat down on the edge of the bath to do her nails while she waited for it to fill. It was such a big bath that it took an age for the water to reach an acceptably luxurious level. She had time to do her toenails, too, in between sips of champagne. Finally she turned off the taps, slid into the silken water, leaned back against the smooth, aquamarine curve, closed her eyes, and gave the kind of sigh you reserve for when a moment is suddenly perfect.

After a few moments she opened her eyes again and surveyed her handiwork. She tried hard to be dispassionate about it, but it was impossible. She'd done it – she was sure of it. She had pulled it off. The scented steam that rose from the bath like mist lent her fresco even more of a tropical ambience, and she remembered the poem that had inspired Rousseau to paint his *Dream*.

Yadwigha, sleeping peacefully,
In a beautiful dream
Hears the notes of a pipe
Played by a friendly snake charmer.
While the moonlight gleams
On the flowers and verdant trees,
The tawny serpents listen
To the instrument's sweet airs.

Aphrodite lay there for an hour, lost in her enchanted landscape, just gazing and gazing. When the temperature of the bathwater dropped she topped it up with more hot, and when the level of the champagne in her glass dropped she topped it up with more fizz. The longer she lay there the more she felt her senses fuzz over with drowsiness and wine and warm water, and the more she didn't want to move.

And then she was dreaming. She was Yadwigha, asleep on her couch in the middle of a jungle, moonlight gleaming on her naked skin, hearing the charmed notes of the snake man's pipes, watched by beasts with tawny eyes . . .

But she wasn't asleep, she realized muzzily. There were pipes playing somewhere – a melody she knew and vaguely recognized as Debussy's *L'après midi d'un faune.* And she wasn't alone. Leaning against the jamb of the bathroom door, watching her with tawny eyes, was the most beautiful man she had ever seen.

Aphrodite was too confused to be shocked. She lay there for a moment looking at Troy MacNally with her mouth open, and then she reached for the towel that she'd left by the side of the bath and got slowly to her feet, holding the towel in front of her. Too much champagne on an empty stomach made her sway slightly. She was also having difficulty focusing on this god who had materialized in front of her.

'I'm – I'm sorry,' she mumbled. 'I wanted to have a go in your bath to see if it worked.' Oh God. If she'd *tried* she couldn't have sounded more dorkily inarticulate.

But he seemed to understand, because 'It works,' he said, moving towards her. He took the towel from her and let it drop to the floor. And then he took her face between his hands and kissed her.

Chapter Four

She let him. And after a couple of tentative moments she began to kiss him back. It was impossible not to. She had never before been kissed with such silky expertise. A cautionary voice in her head asked what the hell she thought she was doing, allowing herself to be kissed by a complete stranger, but she blocked her ears to it and just carried on kissing him anyway.

Troy kissed her with breathtaking languor, taking his time. God, it was sexy! It was as if he was *enjoying* her as an epicure would enjoy fine food – relishing the taste of her on his tongue. Finally he slid his lips away from her mouth and deposited a light kiss on her forehead, as though rewarding her for being a good girl. She looked up at him with a dazed expression, silently pleading with him not to stop kissing her, registering the enquiry implicit in his gaze. And when she nodded a 'yes' to his unspoken question, he simply took her face between his hands again, and put his lips to her ear. 'What's your name?' he murmured. 'Tell me it's Aphrodite.'

'It's Aphrodite,' she murmured back.

And then Troy MacNally pulled her naked, wet body hard against him and said: *'Yes!'*

* * *

Much later they lay in his carved *bateau lit*, satiated with sex.

'Aphrodite – um – who?' he asked. 'You'll have to forgive me for forgetting your surname. I was totally stressed when I spoke to you the day before I left Dublin. Your Christian name was vividly etched into my memory, though. It'd be pretty difficult to forget that particular moniker.'

'It's Aphrodite Delaney.'

He gave her a fantastic smile. 'And you'll presumably have deduced by now that I'm Troy MacNally.'

'Yes,' she said, smiling back. 'I've always prided myself on my sleuthing skills. I'm so pleased to meet you.' She extended a limp hand to him across the tousled sheet. It felt delightfully silly to be shaking hands after they'd just spent the past couple of hours having rampant, glorious sex.

'Not as pleased as I am to meet you,' he said, taking her hand and kissing the palm. 'I'd hoped the girl would live up to the name, and you haven't let me down.'

'What do you mean?'

'What could be more serendipitous than to walk into my flat to find the Goddess of Love floating in my bath? And when you stood up looking so stunningly fucking *starkers*, I knew I'd found my brand new Venus.'

'Um. Explain?'

'My brand new Venus – my muse, darling. And about bloody time, too.' He raised himself on one elbow and looked down at her, and the way he narrowed his eyes made her feel sexy again. 'Under

86

the circumstances, Aphrodite Delaney, hasn't it occurred to you that *fate* has decreed you to be my muse?'

'A muse? *Me?*' She laughed out loud.

'And as if on cue, you've given me an opportunity to trot out the little pun that you'll be hearing a lot from now on. If, that is, you will indeed do me the honour of accepting the post.'

'What's the pun?'

' "You find the idea very a-musing." The tabloids find that hilarious little play on words especially useful.'

His eyes were travelling over her body and she wondered why she didn't feel self-conscious. Badley had had a habit of making such disparaging remarks about her physique that she'd always tried to keep herself covered up around him. She smiled at Troy and said: 'Well, if I really am a serious candidate for the post as Troy MacNally's muse, you'd better fill me in on some of the practicalities. Boss.'

'Practicalities?' He pronounced the word as if he'd never heard it before.

'Yes. Such as – what does a muse *do* exactly? I've always wondered.'

'Well. The way you emerged from my bath this evening like Aphrodite emerging from the sea wasn't bad for starters. I found that pretty damn inspirational.'

Aphrodite loved the way he spoke – in a languid, velvety drawl. She remembered how she'd compared his voice to bitter chocolate when she'd first heard it on the phone. Now the bitterness was gone, it sounded more like *expensive* chocolate. The kind her mother ate. Uh-oh, she thought. She'd have to keep Troy away from *her*, in case he decided he fancied Thea, the way so many of her boyfriends had in the past.

He started tracing spirals on her belly with his middle finger. 'I watched you for a long time as you lay in my bath, picturing swathes of gossamer fabric clinging to your breasts and floating round your hips like seaweed. I hope you don't mind being the unwitting victim of a voyeur.'

She didn't mind. In fact, the idea filled her to overflowing with sexiness. His spiral completed, he brushed her nipple with his finger, then slid an arm around her so that she could spoon herself even closer against him. 'And I hope you don't think I'm an awful slut, Troy. I've honestly never done anything like this before.'

'Of course you haven't. Neither have I. That's what made it so incredibly special.' He brushed a strand of hair away from her cheek. 'You still have paint in your hair.'

'I must look like a neo-punk.'

'I rather like it. I imagine most naiads have seagreen streaks in their hair. It's inspired, by the way.'

'What is?'

'Your Rousseauesque bathroom. How did you hit upon the idea?'

'Um.' She couldn't tell him she'd been searching through his library and had found a Rousseau postcard in a volume of erotica. 'Well. You asked for contrast, right? I recognized that your taste veers very much towards – um – towards opulence.' Ow. Was she sounding critical here? 'I hope you don't mind me using the word "opulence"?' she added quickly.

'Why should I mind?'

'I dunno. Some people think it's derogatory.'

'Try telling Karl Lagerfeld that. I don't have a problem with it.'

'Good. Well, the first thing I did was to rip out your bathroom fittings – I got you a very nice price for them, by the way, from a dealer on Francis Street – and replace them with clean, unfussy lines. And then it occurred to me that the walls were crying out for someone to come and splash colour all over them.' A literal white lie! She couldn't – wouldn't – tell him that her original concept had been for a Zen bathroom *à la* last month's *wallpaper* * mag.

'You're talking about a blank canvas.'

'Exactly! That's *exactly* what came into my head.' Oh wow! They thought on the same wavelength! This was getting better and better!

'There's only one thing wrong with it,' he said, winding a strand of her hair round his finger.

His expression was so grave suddenly that she got a fright. 'Oh? What's that?'

'Your Eve. She's dark. I want you to repaint her as a blonde. A blonde with sea-green streaks in her hair. I want my *current* muse to inhabit that Garden of Eden.' He smiled at her. 'And now I'd better get back in there. I need to take a leak.'

Aphrodite winced. 'Oh, no!' she protested, flinging back the sheets. 'Let me go first, please. I've been putting it off for ages, and I'm bursting for a pee.' It wasn't customary to discuss one's lavatorial habits with people one had only just met, she knew, but then it wasn't customary to have the shag of one's life with them either. And she really did need to get into that bathroom as soon as possible. She needed to get rid of the neat little pile of toenail clippings that she'd suddenly remembered lay abandoned by the side of Troy MacNally's bath. If he spotted them, they might put him off his new muse for ever.

Humming to herself, she nipped through Troy's dressing room, following the trail of clothes that led back to the bathroom. He'd been in a tearing hurry to divest himself of them earlier. Ha! What a wheeze! she thought. What a silly joke life could be! She felt so elated she wanted to laugh out loud. She'd love to see Lola's reaction when she told her that she was Troy MacNally's new muse. She was *dying* to tell Lola!

As she peed, she studied the exotic temptress she'd painted on Troy's bathroom wall, the dark-haired beauty he wanted to turn into a Clairol blonde. What would being a muse involve? she wondered. A lot of lovemaking, probably. And lying around while Troy draped exquisite fabrics over her. Taking baths together. Wearing Troy MacNally originals, drifting through his opulent rooms, trailing silks and velvets . . .

OK, so she'd have to keep the day job. She'd still have to spend hours hanging round photo-shoots, waiting for endless Polaroids to come out, placing product 'just so' and listening to the fatuous burble of models. But she'd have a glorious man in her life, and she hadn't had one of those in a while.

In her fantasy bathroom, Aphrodite laughed out loud as she washed her hands, then danced towards the door. Something made her put the brakes on just as she overran the threshold. She performed a perfect U-turn, scooped the offending nail clippings into the palm of her hand and flushed them down the pan just as Troy rounded the corner.

*　　*　　*

Late the next morning she repainted her Eve while Troy watched from the bath. Something sexy and classical was floating out through the speakers concealed in the wall.

'Put your little mole in,' he said. 'That sweet little mole on your left buttock.'

'You think it's sweet? Yeuch. You pervert. I've always hated it.'

'It's very, very sexy. *You're* very, very sexy. I'm feeling horny just watching you paint. Take those overalls off at once and get in the bath.'

'No,' she said, laughing. 'I've spent all morning doing what I've been told. It's time I got some work done.' It was true that she had spent all morning doing as she'd been told. Troy had suggested some extremely inventive sexual techniques, and she had found herself doing things with him she would never have thought physically possible – if, that is, she'd even had the imagination to dream them up herself.

'I'm glad you're a compliant hussy,' he said. 'That

was one thing that bothered me a lot about Miriam towards the end of our relationship. She lost interest in sex. With me, at any rate.'

Aphrodite felt a flash of shock at this reference to his old muse. She did a little mental dithering, and then decided that it was perhaps judicious to pretend that she didn't know who Miriam was.

'Miriam?'

'My previous muse.'

'You don't mind talking about her?'

'Not at all. She's ancient history.' The trace of bitter chocolate that crept into his voice suggested that actually, he did mind.

Aphrodite wasn't sure whether or not to encourage him to elaborate. She felt a bit strange talking about Miriam de Courcy: she supposed it was how Jane Eyre might have felt any time Mr Rochester talked about his mad wife in the attic. But it was like trying to resist the temptation to scratch an insect bite. Impossible. 'How did you discover her?' she asked.

'I first saw her at a party in a friend's château in France.' Wow. Troy obviously had some top class friends. She hoped she wasn't going to be too out of her depth here. 'She was dressed like a Pre-Raphaelite artist's model, and she was reading Baudelaire. I found her intriguing, and of course she was very beautiful. But she lost it. Got into drugs and couldn't handle it.' He shrugged. 'What did you do with her portrait, by the way?'

'The one that was hanging in here?'

'Yeah.'

'I put it in the store cupboard.'

'Hah! She'd hate that. She was claustrophobic!' Troy's voice was redolent with bitter chocolate now. Aphrodite wondered how he could sound so vitriolic about someone who had obviously meant a great deal to him once upon a time. But he'd let drop a hint that Miriam had been unfaithful, and she supposed in that case he was allowed to be bitter and twisted about her. He submerged his head under the water and surfaced looking sleek. 'Anyway, she's part of my past, and what's important is the future. What are you doing next week?'

'Nothing.'

'No, you're not. You're coming away with me – that's what you're doing.'

'Am I? Where?'

'We're going to Kerry. I have friends who have a country house there.'

Oh, yikes. Country houses, French châteaux . . . 'Like a weekend kind of country house?'

'Yeah. They built a stunning house on the shore of a lake in a place called Coolnamaragh. It's completely off the beaten track, but it's very, very beautiful. Gareth Fitzgerald, the bloke who owns it, is an architect. He's also one of my main financial backers. He and his wife Jolie are shareholders in Troy MacNally Enterprises. They'll let us have it for as long as we like. How are you fixed for the next couple of weeks if we decide to stay on?'

'I've nothing on,' she lied. In fact she had a photo-shoot pencilled in for the week after next, but she'd find some way of getting out of it. The prospect of heading off to a romantic rural retreat with Troy MacNally was just too irresistible to turn down.

'So you'll come?'

'Sure.' She tried to sound careless, but inside she was all aflutter.

'Good. I've been lying here picturing you on some windswept beach gathering seaweed; or in a forest, wandering among lichen-covered trees; or on a cliff top, reclining naked on a couch of bracken. I mustn't forget to bring my camera.'

'You're going to take photographs of me – um – naked?'

'Of course. As long as you're cool with the idea.'

'Yeah. It's cool.' She actually wasn't that cool with the idea. She hated having her photograph taken, and she also wasn't mad about the bracken thing. Being naked on bracken would be dead uncomfortable, and she'd read somewhere that bracken released carcinogenic spores into the atmosphere.

Troy brought the flat of his hand down on the surface of the water with such force that Aphrodite was showered with droplets. 'I'm going to get so much work done!' he exulted, reaching for the book on Rousseau that was lying open beside the bath at the painting of Eve.

'You mean you're going to be *working*?' This hadn't been part of her scheme of things. Her agenda was more along the lines of log fires and *diners à-deux* in off-the-beaten-track Egon Ronay restaurants and walks along deserted beaches, playfully swatting each other with bunches of sea pinks. Uh-oh. Maybe she'd been styling too many commercials.

'Absolutely. I feel ideas coming on fast and furious. I'm way behind with my next collection, and I need to get drawings done a.s.a.p.'

'Oh.' Thinking that she probably sounded a bit unenthusiastic, Aphrodite tried to evince a little more support. 'What are your ideas?' she asked brightly, wiping her brush on a rag.

'Nature. I'm going to look to nature for inspiration. Just like Rousseau.' He was turning the pages of the book with leisurely fingers. 'It's all down to you, you inspirational minx. I've found my new direction through you.'

Aphrodite smiled at him. The nervous feeling had gone, and she was feeling flattered now, instead. He was lounging against the curve of the bath with one arm behind his head, scanning the book with lazy, honey-coloured eyes and looking so sexy that she felt very tempted indeed to discard her overalls as he'd suggested earlier, and dive back in there with him. She forced herself to tear her eyes away and concentrate on painting the green streaks into Eve's hair.

'Troy?' she asked idly. 'Do you mind me asking what's in the room with the locked door at the end of the passageway? The one that has plinths on either side?' She had often speculated about this. Any time she'd been alone in the flat she'd felt a bit like a heroine in a Gothic novel. Gothic novels always had secrets behind locked doors, skeletons in cupboards. *Skeletons in cupboards . . .* The thought of poor Miriam shut away in the cupboard suddenly produced an involuntary *frisson.*

'Oh – it's full of real life crap.'

'Real life crap?'

'Yeah. Computer, fax, phone. I only go in there if I have to.'

She had often wondered about that aspect of Troy's life. The apparent absence of any twenty-first-century paraphernalia in his home had struck her as odd from the first time she'd visited it.

He made a face. 'Pah! I suppose I'll have to face all that stuff today. There'll be about a million of those stinking little e-mail envelope icons lined up for me to open.'

'Oh! I'd love that! I love getting e-mail.'

Troy sent an interested look in her direction. 'Really? Maybe I could off-load some of it on to you?'

'I can't open your mail,' she protested.

'Of course you can. It makes perfect sense to me. I hate handling the stuff, you love it. *Ergo* – you should do it.'

Aphrodite shrugged. 'Well . . . I'd be glad to help out if you really don't mind. It's not, strictly speaking, madly ethical.'

'Ethical schmethical.'

'Why didn't you activate out-of-office auto reply before you went away?'

'Out-of-office auto reply? I wouldn't have a clue how to do that.' He tossed the book aside. 'Have you finished?'

'Nearly. You're sure you want me to put in the mole on my bum?'

'Yup.' Troy swung himself out of the bath and

wrapped a towel around his waist. He stood there for a minute or two, towelling his hair and yawning, watching while Aphrodite put the finishing touch to her self-portrait. Then he ambled over to her and kissed her lightly on the lips. 'It's perfect,' he said. 'And so are you.' He smiled down at her and she waited for him to kiss her again, but instead he stretched out a hand and opened a door in the wall that had a bird of paradise flying across it. 'Any idea where I might find my shaving gear? I'm going to have to reorientate myself to this bathroom.'

'I stowed it in here,' said Aphrodite, moving to a cupboard by the basin. If it hadn't been for the painted ivy twining round the streamlined pedestal, the basin would have passed for a font in some stark, modernist cathedral. Like the bath, it was just an oval scoop, with the taps cunningly concealed. 'It seemed the obvious place to put it, just by the mirror. I'll give you a guided tour later, if you like.'

He yawned again. 'I know what I want to find right now. My poxy phone.'

'It's on the floor in the bedroom. You left it there after you sent out for food last night.' Troy had ordered food from a French restaurant that was so prohibitively expensive Aphrodite had never crossed the threshold. They'd eaten the main course of lobster at the long mahogany table in the dining room, and taken the apricot mousse back to the bedroom. She had never tasted anything quite like it . . . 'I'll find it for you,' she said, obligingly going to fetch it. On her way through the dressing room she paused, hesitated, then gathered his discarded clothes and hung them on wooden hangers in the wardrobe.

The dessert bowls were still on the floor beside the bed, alongside an empty wine bottle. Sheets were in a state of serious disarray, and there were traces of apricot mousse on the pillowcases. Aphrodite allowed herself a little smile that held more than just a hint of the cat-who'd-got-the-cream. She located the mobile at the base of one of the sphinxes, then returned it to Troy in the bathroom.

'I'm starving,' he said, turning his phone on and entering his PIN code. 'We'll send out again, shall we?'

'*Again?*'

He looked surprised. 'Why not?'

'Troy,' she said, squatting down and putting the lid back on the last of her paint pots. 'It's very generous of you, but I can't allow you to treat me to two meals in a row. Why don't you let me cook something for you?'

'You can *cook*? Like – *proper* cooking?' Troy sounded surprised.

She nodded. 'It's hardly *haute cuisine*, but, yes, I can cook.' She'd realized at quite a tender age that if she didn't learn how to cook she'd probably end up suffering from malnutrition. Her mother's idea of cooking was to bung stuff from Tesco and Marks & Spencer into the microwave. If she remembered to buy anything at all, that is.

'Wow. I don't think I've ever met anyone who can cook before. Apart from Jolie Fitzgerald. She did a course in it.'

Aphrodite joined him by the wash basin, and smiled at his reflection in the mirror. 'You must have led a very, *very* rarefied kind of life,' she said, tapping the tip of his nose with a forefinger, 'if you don't know anyone who cooks.'

Troy gave an apologetic shrug. 'I suppose I have. I've been very lucky. I've never known what it's like to be short of money. My mother and father left me a chunky inheritance, and an ancient cousin of my grandmother's left me a load of property. This flat belonged to her. In fact, this entire building – shops, offices, everything – was hers.' He wandered over to the platform that housed the bath, and sat on its edge, looking vaguely perplexed. It was as if this was the first time he'd ever had to scrutinize the provenance of his privileged lifestyle.

'Your parents are dead?' She asked the question very gently, in case he was still hurting.

'Oh yeah. Ages ago – in a yachting accident. My aunt and a series of boarding schools brought me up.'

'Was it tough?'

He dropped his eyes and studied his hands. 'Tough. Was it tough? Losing my parents wasn't tough. I was only a baby when they died. Being sent to boarding school in England was tough.' Then he gave a bark of a laugh and looked directly at her. 'But life's never tough when you've got plenty of money, Aphrodite. Only whingers think it is. Nothing exasperates me more than self-obsessed "poor little rich kids" moaning about how crap their lives are. They should go take a hike through the slums of

Delhi if they want to see how tough real life can be.'

'Have you been there?'

'Yep. If you ever want a preview of hell, go there.' From the closed expression on his face she could tell he didn't want to talk about it.

'So this *entire* block of buildings belongs to you?'

'Yeah. I let out the retail and office space through an agent. I was going to sell it all, but when Jolie saw this gaff she told me to hang on to it.'

'Jolie? The Jolie you were talking about earlier?'

'Yeah. She was my first muse.'

'Oh.' *OK*. Don't go there.

'She fell in love with it.'

'I don't blame her.'

Troy leaned back a little further on his elbows, and the light from the stained-glass cupola above the bath fell onto his dark hair, giving him the appearance of a luminous Byzantine angel. 'It's all real, you know. It's a genuine bona fide *fin-de-siècle* apartment. My superannuated cousin was a bit of a looper. She was more entrenched in the old style of doing things than the Queen Mother. That's why I got this joint.'

'I don't understand.'

'As her last living male relative. It was held in trust for me until I came of age. She kept this place just as it had been in her childhood.'

'Wow. A real life Miss Havisham?'

'Yeah. It's a fucking museum piece. Sometimes I think I should just gut the joint.'

'Oh, Troy, no! This is the most romantic apartment I've ever been in!'

'I'm not sentimental,' he said. 'And there are a lot

100

of ghosts hanging around here who should be laid to rest.'

Something told her he wasn't talking about his ancient cousin. There was a pause, and then Aphrodite, feeling the draught from the conversational vacuum, said: 'Were you very close to your aunt? The one who brought you up?'

His face closed over again. 'I wouldn't say that,' he said. 'She was very young and very beautiful, and the last thing she needed was a child cramping her style – especially one who was bequeathed a massive inheritance she wasn't allowed to touch. Nannies saw more of me than she did. She's living in Australia now. It was as if she couldn't wait until I'd grown up so that she could put as much distance as possible between us.'

'Oh, I'm sure that's not true.'

His lip curled. 'You don't know my aunt.'

'So you're all alone in the world?'

'Yup. I'm the quintessential orphan.' He looked so little-boy-lost that Aphrodite felt compelled to take him in her arms. She moved across the floor to where he was sitting on the edge of the bath, pushed a strand of damp hair away from his eyes and sat down beside him, snaking her left arm around his waist. Just as she was about to kiss him, the phone that was still dangling from his hand gave a subdued chirrup.

Troy struck his forehead with the heel of his hand. 'Oh shit,' he said. 'Someone's actually got through. I always try and keep the bastard thing turned off.' He fumbled ineffectually with the phone for a minute, trying without success to silence it.

'Leave it if you don't want to answer it,' said Aphrodite. 'It'll ring off automatically.' But for some reason it didn't. The ringing just became more and more persistent. 'Here. Give it to me,' she said. He handed her the phone as if it was red hot. It was so high tech and minimalist in design that even Aphrodite, who was normally quite clever at these things, couldn't work out how to turn it off. 'Shall I just go ahead and answer it?' she asked.

'Jesus,' he said, with a heavy sigh. 'Please do. Hell! I suppose I'm going to have to face up to real life at some stage. I've taken a long enough break from it.'

Aphrodite pressed pick up. 'Troy MacNally's phone,' she said crisply into the receiver.

'Troy? Sorry – where *is* Troy?' The female voice on the other end sounded put out.

'I'm afraid he's not available right now,' said Aphrodite. 'May I take a message?' She reached for her sketchpad and the stick of charcoal she'd been using.

'Sorry – who *is* this?'

'I'm – er – I'm a friend of Troy's. He's asked me to take any messages that come through.' Troy was looking at her with an expression of combined amusement and admiration.

'I see.' The voice on the other end of the line sounded even more aggrieved. 'In that case, yes, please take a message. I've been trying to get through to him since yesterday evening. He has returned neither my calls nor my e-mails.'

'He arrived back in Dublin very late last night,' explained Aphrodite. 'He hasn't had time to access messages.' She turned to Troy with enquiry in her eyes to ascertain whether she was saying the right things, but he just smiled at her, then said in a low voice: 'You, sexy, sexy, *sexy* musey thing,' and started to undo the buttons on her overalls.

'Can you ask him to phone Polly as soon as possible?' the voice in her ear was saying. 'I have a new mobile and I'm going to be out of the office on business for the rest of the day. Have you a pen handy?'

'Um.' Troy had slipped a hand inside her overalls and was playing with her nipple. 'Have I a pen handy? Yes. Yes, I do.' She covered the mouthpiece again. 'Stop it!' she mouthed. 'You're distracting me!' But Troy just smiled again – that smile that contrived somehow to be boyish and gut-wrenchingly sexy at the same time – and carried on doing what he was doing.

'My new number is 086–' Polly lobbed the rest of the number at her, while Aphrodite tried wildly to concentrate. She hardly heard the fractious tones coming over the phone, so delightfully distracting were Troy's deft fingers. His other hand was moving down her body now. She felt it move from her belly to her pudenda. She tried hard to keep her legs together, but Troy was persistent. His hand slid between them, and Aphrodite found herself relaxing her thigh muscles and saying: 'Could you repeat that, please?'

'With pleasure,' he murmured, giving a low, wicked laugh.

Polly gave a little 'tch' of annoyance, and repeated

the number as if she was talking to a particularly stupid child of five. 'And there's another thing,' she said. 'Could you please ask Troy to . . .'

By the time she had finished taking down Polly's new number and had finally put the phone down some minutes later, Aphrodite was on the brink of orgasm again.

*   *   *

They spent the next day and the one after that sorting out all Troy's real-life stuff. He unlocked the door of his office, and showed Aphrodite around. Together they sifted through countless e-mails, Troy going 'Delete! Delete! Delete!', and responding only to the most urgent ones. There was a lot of mail from women wanting to know his whereabouts, and a lot of invitations to parties and weekends away in exotic places from people with exotic names.

Then Troy trawled through the myriad messages on his answering machine and made a series of phone calls. Aphrodite was impressed by the tactics he'd devised to avoid meaningful dialogue. He never agreed to be put on hold, and if he got diverted to voice mail, he simply hung up. Poor Polly got a bit of a fright when he called her.

'I'm going away, Poll.'

Aphrodite heard a shriek of '*Again?*' and then a panicky babbling.

'No worries, Polly. It's not a holiday this time, and I've a new muse to thank for that. Aphrodite Delaney. Yep. She's agreed to field my calls when

I'm working, so if a woman with a very sexy voice picks up the phone, treat her with a great deal of respect, OK? And yes, I *promise* I'll keep it turned on.'

When he finally put the phone down he turned to Aphrodite with a smile. 'There,' he said. 'It is now official. You are categorically and without question my new muse. It'll be all round town soon.'

'What do you mean?'

'Polly loves to gossip. Oh, Jesus, there's the phone *again.* Let's leave the answering machine to pick up and we'll have a bloody good snog instead.' He pulled Aphrodite to her feet and took her in his arms, and she felt her lips part automatically as he expertly coaxed a kiss from her with the tip of his tongue.

A man's voice came through the answering machine – a posh-ish voice. 'Hi, Troy – Gareth here. I just got your message about the house in Kerry.' Troy stopped kissing Aphrodite with some reluctance. 'It's cool,' continued Gareth, 'but you'll need to drop by the penthouse to pick up the keys.' The *penthouse*? thought Aphrodite. Holy schomoly! What rarefied new planet was she hurtling towards, without a map to guide her? 'The best time for me would be–'

'I'm going to have to take this. Sorry,' said Troy into her mouth. He moved to the desk and lifted the receiver. 'Gareth! Hi!' Aphrodite heard a burble of mateyness come down the line. 'Yeah? You mentioned keys? Sure. No problem. Excellent. You're a pal. Talk to you later. 'Bye.'

'That,' he said, putting the phone down and

turning back to Aphrodite, 'was Gareth Fitzgerald, the architect friend whose house we'll be staying in in Kerry. We must take him and Jolie out to dinner when we get back to say thank you. I know they'll be dying to meet you. Jolie in particular.'

'Why in particular?'

'I thought I told you? She was my muse before Miriam.'

Ow. She really didn't want to be hearing this stuff about his past muses. It was a million times worse than hearing Badley talk about his ex-girlfriends when he'd used to compare her to them – and he'd done it quite a lot. But then that curious Jane Eyre/Mr Rochester thing kicked in again, and she had to know. She was just about to ask how long Jolie had been Troy's muse when suddenly she couldn't say anything at all because he was kissing her again. And then the questions she wanted answered about Jolie Fitzgerald just weren't relevant any more.

Chapter Five

On Wednesday morning Aphrodite went home to pack for her trip to Kerry. She was running late because they'd decided it would save time if they shared a bath, which, of course, had been a big mistake . . .

She pulled open her wardrobe doors and viewed the contents with dismay. What in hell's name was she going to bring? Now that she was officially muse to one of Ireland's hottest designers, she really ought to make the effort to look the part. She wished she had time to run out and buy something new to wear, but she was to meet Troy at his studio at midday, and it was eleven o'clock now. Country stuff. OK. That should be fairly easy. She had jeans and shirts and a couple of sweaters that might just pass muster, and a rather elderly suede jacket. The sun was shining outside, but she knew how prima-donna-ish the Irish weather could be. A scarf and gloves would be essential, as would sunglasses and something rainproof. Her boots were good – a sale purchase – but they were a bit scuffed-looking. Well, she didn't have time to polish them now. She flung them in her bag as they were. What else? Troy had mentioned that they might be eating out a lot. What if they were to go somewhere posh? Her mother had stolen her prettiest Ghost dress and she'd be lucky if she ever got it back.

She lunged for the phone. 'Lola?' she said when her friend picked up. 'Lend me your little Lainey!'

'What? Are you mad? It's the most precious thing I own.'

'Please. It's an emergency.' Aphrodite filled Lola in as economically as possible.

'You're right. This *is* an emergency. I'll be right round,' said Lola. 'You'll need to borrow heels as well.'

Lola was at the door in ten minutes, with her precious Lainey Keogh shift wrapped in tissue paper, and her heels in a plastic bag. She laid the items on Aphrodite's bed as reverently as if she were laying sacrificial offerings on an altar. '*If*,' she said, her voice oily and weighty and dense with menace. It was the only word she needed to say.

'I know, I know,' said Aphrodite, who was still riffling through her wardrobe so frenziedly she looked blurred. 'If anything happens to it I am burnt toast and dead meat, up shit creek and in deep doodoo. Oh, look,' she said, delving into the bottom of the wardrobe and emerging with a crumpled mass of steel blue silk and cashmere. 'My old pashmina! I wonder if it's still banished to fashion hinterland by *Vogue*?'

'Who cares? Be a style anarchist and wear it with pride. Throw it over here and I'll run an iron over it for you.'

'Star, star, star!' Aphrodite started flinging items of

make-up into a bag she'd got free with Clinique products. 'Yuck. Some of this stuff's a bit grungy. I bet bloody Miriam de Courcy had one of those groovy cases from Make-Up Forever to cart her stuff around in. You know the ones that look as if they're full of surgical equipment?'

'They probably are. For cosmetic enhancement.'

'Or for stabbing other models in the back. Will you feed Bobcat for me, Lo? And water the plants?'

'Sure. But you know what always happens when you go away.'

Aphrodite shrugged. 'Bob gets fat and the plants get anorexia. It's still a better option than having my mother do it. Then Bob would end up anorectic too.' She pulled a little marabou feather-trimmed alpaca thing free from a tangle of wire hangers. 'Oh, good! I'd forgotten about this. It's quite sexy if you leave loads of buttons undone.'

'Why is the label cut off your pashmina?' asked Lola, examining a corner.

'I got it in Marks and Sparks.'

'Snob.'

'Unapologetically so.' Aphrodite paused and drew breath. 'Well. Wow. I think that's about it. Oh! My portfolio!' She ran into the spare room that served as her studio and came back with the portfolio she'd spent silly money on in Winsor & Newton in Covent Garden.

'Why are you bringing your portfolio?'

'Troy wants to see my stuff.'

'Ee-yeuch. It's sick-making.'

'What is?'

'The idea of you and Troy comparing your work, yakking about design concepts. Wandering around Kerry with your sketchpads, doing little watercolours of the landscape. I can just picture it.'

'I intend to spend a lot of time in bed, actually,' said Aphrodite archly.

'Ow! You bitch! That's even more sick-making. Did you pack sexy underwear?'

'Loads of it.'

'With the labels cut off?'

Aphrodite laughed. 'Not off the Agent Provocateur ones you gave me for my birthday. Hey. I'll take over the ironing now. You're earning too many Brownie points. I'll be in debt to you bigtime if I'm not careful.'

Lola smiled sweetly. 'That's the idea, sister. I'm counting on getting a few opportunities to strut my stuff in original Troy MacNally. What's he like in bed, by the way?'

Aphrodite sent her a foxy smile, and tapped her nose with an index finger. 'Let's just say I'm in love.'

'Really, Aphrodite?'

She suddenly found herself thinking about it seriously. 'Oh dear. I don't know. I don't think I've ever been in love before. Badley doesn't count. What do you think, Lo? How are you meant to know?'

'How many times did he make you come?'

'So many I lost count.'

'You're in love,' said Lola.

*　　*　　*

110

When she walked into the reception area of Troy's studio five minutes after midday, she steeled herself for the kind of disrespect she'd received from the receptionist the time she'd called in to pick up Troy's key. But, to her surprise, the girl put the phone down as soon as she saw her and stretched out her hand. 'Ms Delaney!' she said with a big smile. 'Hello. It's nice to meet you. I'm Saskia MacCann.'

Aphrodite was momentarily nonplussed by the VIP treatment. This couldn't be the same girl who had looked aghast at her appearance and treated her as if she was an undesirable tradesperson. And then the penny dropped. Polly Riordan had obviously spread word around that there was a brand new muse on the block, and Saskia MacCann was now regretting have dissed Aphrodite first time round. And she was regretting it bigtime, thought Aphrodite, for the brightness of the receptionist's smile and the firmness of her handshake hadn't succeeded in disguising her unease. Hey! Maybe she could have fun with this! Thumbing your nose at condescending receptionists and waiters and shop girls and hair stylists was one of the sweeter things in life, simply because the opportunity so seldom arose.

'Nice to meet you likewise,' she said, returning the girl's smile perfunctorily. Then she crossed the reception area, swung her bag onto the big leather-upholstered couch and sat down without waiting to be invited. 'Could you please let Troy know I'm here?' She was delighted to be able to demonstrate first-name familiarity, especially when the girl picked up the phone and said: 'Mr MacNally? Ms Delaney's here for you. Yes, I'll tell her.' She looked over at Aphrodite. 'He's on his way down to you now. Would you like anything, Ms Delaney? Tea? Coffee? Water?'

'No, thank you, Saskia,' said Aphrodite, determined to be meticulously but coolly polite. That was scarier than open hostility.

'A magazine?'

The usual swanky suspects were fanned out along the coffee table. She knew there'd be scarcely anything worth reading in those style bibles – they were just glossy excuses for advertising obscenely expensive designer labels.

'No, thank you.' Aphrodite smiled pleasantly and sat there radiating perfect, serene insouciance. The receptionist gave her an uncertain, rictus grin, then bent her head and pretended to 'do' things. Her head shot up again when a door opened and Troy came through looking edible in what had to be Helmut Lang.

'Hey!' he said when he saw Aphrodite. 'All set?'

Aphrodite prinked as he kissed her cheek. Then he slid his lips down her throat as far as her collarbone and inhaled. 'Wow,' he said. 'You still smell of sandalwood from our bath.'

'So do you,' she said, breathing him in with equal enjoyment.

'The scent of sandalwood,' he said, kissing her again, 'will from now on be in my mind synonymous with sex. And it's all your fault.' He reached for her bag, which lay on the couch. 'Let's get out of here, princess, before I'm tempted to take you on the coffee table. 'Bye, Saskia.'

Troy moved to the main door and held it open for her. As Aphrodite went through, she couldn't resist sneaking a backward glance at Saskia. She looked as if someone had just tramped all over her.

'Got your walking boots with you?' asked Troy. 'We'll be doing a lot of tramping around the countryside.'

'Sure,' said Aphrodite with a sunny smile. 'They were the first things I packed.'

*   *   *

Troy's car was a beaut: a little Mercedes convertible in pillarbox red. It was a stunning blue-sky day – surprisingly mild for March – and they drove with the soft top down, attracting covert, envious looks from other drivers. She couldn't help prinking even more. Here she was, sitting beside a breathtakingly handsome man in a groovy car, heading off to stay in a country house in one of the most beautiful counties in Ireland! How she wished Badley could see her now! Aphrodite wanted to sing with happiness, but she was too conscious of the uncool factor to attempt to harmonize with the Nat King Cole number that was sliding silkily through the speakers.

Once out of city gridlock, Troy put the boot down. Because the Merc was such a smooth ride, Aphrodite didn't realize how fast they were going until she snuck a look at the speedometer. The car was hitting ninety.

A journey that should have taken them over five hours took four. By the time they reached Killarney, Aphrodite's palms were pitted with impressions of her fingernails. The roads here were treacherous. Corkscrew bends had been blasted through mountains and along vertiginous precipices. Signs warned against hazards such as falling rocks and steep gradients and deer that might spring out in front of you at any minute, and other signs kept advising drivers to DRIVE SLOWLY. But Troy ignored their exhortations, and negotiated the sinuous roads as nonchalantly as 007. There was very little traffic on the roads, and for this she was profoundly thankful, as he took corners recklessly, veering around hairpin bends on the wrong side, admiring the scenery vociferously, and pointing out landmarks as he went. On one occasion they came face to face with an articulated truck, and Aphrodite bit down so hard on her lip at the blare of the horn that she drew blood. The surrounding scenery was glorious, but Aphrodite saw little of it because she elected to have a little snooze in the passenger seat. In fact she wasn't feeling remotely sleepy – she just wanted to shut her eyes tight and blot out as much of the journey as she could.

They stopped for a sandwich at a dingy pub perched incongruously on a mountainside. Aphrodite went straight to the loo and tried to think strategically. How could she volunteer to take over the driving without offending Troy? One thing was certain – she couldn't tell him that she was scared shitless because that would cast aspersions on his driving ability, and it is a truth universally acknowledged that *no-one* likes to have their driving skills criticized. As she was washing her hands she had a brainwave.

When she emerged from the loo he was sitting on a low stool at a table by the window, leafing through a guidebook. She sat down on a stool beside him and laid a hand on his thigh. 'Troy?' she said as disingenuously as she could. 'I've just had what I think might be a stunningly good idea. You're after inspiration on this trip, right? I mean, you're on a working holiday, and I'm really just coming along for the ride. But I'd like to make myself useful in any way I can. So . . . why don't I take over the driving? That way you can concentrate on the scenery – take notes, photographs, whatever.'

To her relief, he didn't demur for a second. 'That's a bloody good idea, Aphrodite,' he said.

'There's no problem with insurance, is there?' she asked, keeping her fingers crossed.

'No. I've comprehensive coverage.' Aphrodite smiled and uncrossed her fingers. 'In that case, I'll have a pint with my sandwich now that I've officially relinquished my chauffeur's badge to you.' He flicked back over a couple of pages of the guidebook. 'Look,' he said, sliding it towards her over the tabletop. 'I've found the most astonishing place to visit.'

' "Ilnacullin",' she read, ' "is an island garden of rare beauty. Because of its sheltered situation and the warming influence of the Gulf Stream the climate is almost subtropical." ' She turned the page. 'Wow! Get a load of those giant ferns!'

'I've got to get there,' resumed Troy, leaning over her shoulder so that he could see the photographs. 'It'll be like walking through your bathroom mural. Look, there's even an area of the garden they've called "The Jungle". With a bit of luck there'll be no-one around at this time of the year and we'll be able to find some secluded spot where we can indulge in some fantastic al fresco sex. You can be Yadwigha, naked and "sleeping peacefully, in a beautiful dream."'

'And who will you be?'

'The snake charmer, of course, who persuades you to take off all your clothes.'

The barmaid looked up suspiciously from where she was preparing their sandwiches. 'Ssh!' said Aphrodite. But the smile she gave him was provocative. She looked at her watch. 'We won't get there today anyway. It closes at five.'

'There's no hurry. We've all the time in the world.' He stretched, then sighed with pleasure. 'Hell. Look at that view!' Framed by the window, the Killarney landscape looked like a *trompe-l'oeil* painting. Under a lavender blue sky washed with wisps of snowy cloud, purple mountains plummeted to the placid pewter surface of a lake that reflected mountain and sky in all their tumbled, upside-down glory. 'It makes me feel like a wealthy man, Aphrodite.'

'You *are* a wealthy man,' she pointed out.

His lip curled. 'In material terms, yes.' He indicated the Merc parked outside, with sunlight glinting off its flashy red bonnet. 'Hey, wow, whaddya know – I'm a radical geezer with a nifty Merc and a Patek

Philippe wristwatch and designer threads and all the desirable "Lifestyle" accessories a man could want. Have you noticed, Aphrodite, that people don't live *lives* any more? They live Life*styles*. We're a generation of spiritual and emotional degenerates, eternally searching for the perfect life and not appreciating what's under our noses.'

Aphrodite remembered the array of magazines in the reception area of Troy's studio, and thought of how Lola had called her a label snob because of what she'd done to her Marks & Spencer pashmina, and she remembered the issue of *wallpaper** mag in which she'd found her 'original' Zen design for Troy's bathroom, and she thought that yes, Troy was probably right. The very concept of spirituality had been commandeered by con artists out to make a fast buck with specious mind/body/spirit merchandising. 'Are you a religious person, Troy?' she asked him now.

'No. Not at all. But I admire people who eschew materialism.'

Aphrodite tried to think of anyone she knew who eschewed materialism and couldn't. 'Such as?' she asked.

'Such as the monks in Tibet who renounce all wordly things and whose sole mission in life is to acquire spiritual knowledge. It must take a whole lot of courage to do that. I used to fantasize about it when I was younger. I'd been backpacking in Thailand, and found the temples just *awesome* – in the real sense of the word. But I soon realized that there was too much of the voluptuary in me. Living in a beach hut in Thailand sounds romantic, but you want to get a load of the sanitation there. The poverty in some areas is as chronic as in India.' He turned to her with a rueful smile. 'I'm deeply, deeply ashamed to admit it, Aphrodite, but I'm too strongly attached to the good things in life to relinquish them. I like my fast car and my cashmere suit and my expensive watch.' He brushed her mouth with his, and the narrow-eyed smile he sent her would have made her lean across and snog him there and then if it hadn't been for the arrival of the barmaid with their sandwiches. 'And I *adore* beautiful women,' he said, smiling at the charismatically challenged barmaid and making her fall in love with him immediately.

* * *

When they'd finished their horrible sandwiches, Troy drained his pint and raised his cashmere-clad arm to look at his watch. 'Time to hit the road again,' he said. 'I want us to get there before dark so you can get a load of the view.'

'Why is Patek Philippe so expensive?' asked Aphrodite, checking her own watch.

'Haven't a clue,' he said, extracting his sunglasses case from his pocket and fitting the shades to his face. He was about to put the case back in his pocket when he suddenly froze, and sat there staring at it. 'More designer fucking logos,' he said. 'They could probably feed a village in Afghanistan for a week with what I paid for these.' He turned to her, and there was something very grim about his smile. 'You asked a very good question there, Aphrodite. *Why* is Patek Philippe so expensive?'

She watched as he got to his feet abruptly and crossed the room to the far end of the bar, where an ancient mountainy man wrapped in a raincoat was nursing his pint. 'Excuse me, sir?' asked Troy. 'Do you have a watch?'

The mountainy man squinted at him with rheumy eyes before checking the watch on his wrist. 'I do,' he said. 'And the time is–'

'No, sir. I don't need to know the time. I have a perfectly good watch of my own –' Troy unstrapped the Patek Philippe '– but it hasn't made me a happy man.'

'Um. What are you on about?' asked the man, looking even more befuddled.

'I'm saying – no – I'm *proposing* that we swap.'

'Swap?'

'Yes. Watches. Look. This watch cost me some thousands of euros. But what's the point? It just tells me the time. I presume your own watch is reasonably accurate? Let's see, are our watches synchronized? Do they both say the same time?' Troy held his watch out so that the old man could see it.

The man looked from Troy's gleaming gold watch to his own on its cheap *faux*-leather strap, and back again. 'Indeed and they do,' he concurred.

'So. Do you agree to a swap?'

The man's face was alert with suspicion suddenly. 'What's wrong with it?'

'My watch?'

'Yeah.'

'Nothing. Have a look at it. It's in perfect nick. Here.' Troy handed over his watch. 'See for yourself.'

'It's real gold?'

'Yes.'

The man inspected the watch with such scrutiny that Aphrodite half expected him to test the metal between his teeth the way pawnbrokers in films did. Finally, without modifying his suspicious expression, he acceded to Troy's bizarre proposition with a grunt and a nod. He handed over his own watch and slid the Patek Philippe into the pocket of his greasy gabardine.

'Thank you, sir! Nice doing business with you,' said Troy, strapping on his new timepiece. He gave the old man a jaunty salute, then rejoined Aphrodite, who was rooted to her barstool in disbelief.

'Jesus, Troy!' she said below her breath. 'Are you completely bonkers?'

'Completely,' he agreed, giving her the benefit of his boyish grin. 'Come on. Let's get out of here.'

Still feeling gobsmacked, Aphrodite followed Troy through the door. Outside, he slung his arm round her shoulder and smiled at the expression on her face. 'Completely bonkers but happy,' he said. 'Let's hope it's made that dour old git happy too.' He was arrested suddenly by the sight of an ancient Skoda parked on the road outside the pub. 'Mm,' he said in an ominously speculative way. 'I wonder is that his car?'

'Troy!' Aphrodite looked aghast. 'You're not going to–'

This time her expression made him laugh out loud. 'Fooled you!' he said, like a schoolboy who's just pulled one over on a friend. 'I may be bonkers, but I'm not *that* bonkers. I love my car so much that if she was human I could ride the arse off her.'

'Hey!' Aphrodite stood at the driver's door, arms akimbo in mock indignation. 'You mean I'm competing with a *car* for your affections?'

'Try driving her yourself and you'll see what I mean.' Troy tossed the keys across the bonnet to her. The keys were followed by his mobile phone, for which she had to make an ungainly lunge.

'I can't answer your phone for you if I'm driving, Troy,' she protested.

'So turn it off.'

'But you promised Polly you'd keep it switched on.'

'I also told her you'd be fielding my calls. Which, as you have correctly pointed out, you won't be able to do if you're simultaneously driving my car.'

'So what do you want me to do?'

He gave her that smile again. 'Just turn the phone off and drive, bitch,' he said.

* * *

The Merc handled beautifully, and *was* a dream to drive. Behind the wheel, Aphrodite felt as if she was in the embrace of a professional dancer as she negotiated the twists and turns of the roads, and she now understood Troy's inclination for recklessness. A car like this couldn't help but instil in the driver a thrilling sense of power: the temptation to drive fast was difficult to resist and she felt a compulsion to indulge in the kind of stunts that were ordinarily the preserve of drivers in sexy auto advertisements. But sense prevailed, and she kept within the speed limits and on the right side of the road. St Patrick's Day was due to fall on the following Monday, and Aphrodite knew that next week the roads would be jammed, but today they waltzed round the Ring of Kerry without getting stuck behind a single tour bus, stopping only once in the village of Waterville to stock up on food. And after they left the main road they didn't meet another soul on the journey to Coolnamaragh.

Their route took them through inhospitable mountain terrain littered with sheep. Aphrodite wondered out loud who all the sheep belonged to because there was no sign of human habitation. They had travelled miles without seeing a single homestead.

'There!' said Troy, a little later in the drive. 'A house!'

It was the kind of old-fashioned house that children draw – four windows and a door. 'Jesus,' said Aphrodite. 'Imagine living there, with no neighbours for miles. Whoever owns it must suffer bigtime from cabin fever.'

'Or else they're congratulating themselves for having kept the human race at bay for so long. That's what I love about Coolnamaragh. Its isolation.'

'But at least you can choose to go back to real life whenever you want, Troy.'

'Sometimes I can't choose. Not when people start baying.'

They swooshed through a dark pine forest, and when they emerged from the gloom, everything seemed incandescent. Scutch grass glowed rose gold in the evening sun, and each time the road curved to the south Aphrodite made out the tinsel glitter of a lake. Troy instructed her to hang a right onto a winding road. It was little more than a track flanked by high hedgerows that obscured the surrounding landscape. It got narrower as she drove, and bumpier too, the overgrown surface pitted with potholes. As she rounded a corner the hedgerows gave way to low banks surmounted by fences – and suddenly there was the lake on her immediate right.

'Holy shomoly!' she said, putting her foot on the brake. 'What a view!'

'You'd better get used to looking at it,' said Troy. 'It's all yours for the next couple of weeks.'

'This is it? This is Coolnamaragh?'

'Yeah. The house is down there, at the bottom of the track.'

'Wow! Oh, wow!'

Where the gradient of the heather-covered mountain slid sharply into a near-vertical cliff was a broad strip of plate glass. A long low building was inset into the foot of the mountain, with a waterfall running adjacent to it and an ivy-choked deck running parallel. More ivy grew where the glass met the rock face, and because the outline of the building was slightly curved, the effect was of a cave mouth with greenery tumbling down over the entrance. It was quite gobsmackingly spectacular. The silver ribbon of the waterfall drew the eye up to the mountainous hinterland that curved around the lake like a sleeping dragon. To the west the mountains dipped just where the dragon's head came to rest upon its paw, and the late afternoon sun scattered spangles of amber light across the surface of the water.

'How on earth did your friends dream it up?' she asked when she'd overcome her initial astonishment. She took her foot off the brake and let the car trundle down the track.

'They stumbled on this place quite by accident. Gareth rounded the bend in the road and there, waiting for him at the end of the track and lying empty and available as a spurned sweetheart – as he put it – was a virgin site just waiting for someone to build on it.'

They got out of the car and Troy produced a key.

'It must have been one hell of a job,' remarked Aphrodite, following him up the front steps of the house.

'Yeah. It took a lot of effort, a lot of rows with contractors and planning department officials, and a lot of Solpadeine.' He took the four steps that led onto the deck in two easy strides. 'It was a labour of love, but they got there in the end.'

'They certainly did. It's totally stunning.' Aphrodite scanned the front of the house, noticing that the far end of the deck curved round the side of the mountain where the waterfall cascaded. 'What's around there?' she asked.

'A hot tub.'

124

'A hot tub? Oh, bliss!' She pictured herself sitting in a hot tub with Troy, listening to birdsong and the sound of spring water rushing over rocks. 'Hey!' she said as Troy unlocked the sliding front doors. 'We'll be like troglodytes.'

'Troglodytes?'

'Cave dwellers.'

He raised a sceptical eyebrow at her. 'You want to get a load of the inside, darling. Cavemen never had it so good.'

He let Aphrodite precede him into the house, and then he pressed a button and a massive expanse of indigo curtain parted to allow sunlight to flood in through the glass walls. The room she found herself in was the kind of sitting room you might find in *Elle Decoration*. The furniture was simple, Shaker style, crafted from white oak and upholstered in pale mint suede. The walls were hung with original modern paintings, the floor carpeted in rugs that were works of art in themselves. The impression was of restrained elegance – unpretentious, but unashamedly luxurious – and, thought Aphrodite, the complete antithesis to Troy's gaff. She was secretly quite relieved that this place was so quintessentially modern. She was beginning to think she'd had enough of old-world ambience recently after spending so much time in his funereal apartment with its spooky ghosts.

Beyond the sitting room were a study, a dining room and a rake of bedrooms. The beds were big as platforms draped in indigo quilts, the curtains were of heavy indigo moleskin, and the lighting flatteringly subdued – until Troy parted the drapes to showcase the view, and light bounced in off the lake. All the rooms were accessed by way of a long corridor that skirted the back of the building. It terminated in a vast kitchen where a big, porthole-shaped window had been blasted through the rock face. The wall here was a metre thick, and framed a circular view of water cascading down the mountainside right next to the hot tub.

Aphrodite leaned against one of the slate work surfaces and gazed around at the Philippe Starck inspired interior. An image came into her head of her stirring something on the stove top – a hollandaise sauce, maybe – while Troy wrapped his arms round her from behind and nuzzled the nape of her neck. She'd pretend to be cross with him for distracting her, and then she'd laugh and relent and allow herself to be kissed before sitting down to their first course at the massive white oak table and toasting each other with some splendidly flinty chilled Pouilly Fumé. In fact, she recalled now as the vision receded, that had been the scenario for an ad for packet sauces that she'd styled a year or so ago . . .

'Penny for them?' said Troy.

He'd have to pay a lot more than a penny for her to confess her kitchen fantasy scenario. Instead she said: ' "The rich are different from us." Who said that?'

'I wouldn't have a clue, darling,' he said with nonchalant candour, 'since it doesn't really apply to me.' He took her in his arms and started unbuttoning her jacket. 'Tell you what – I'll fetch the bags from the car while you get undressed. Then you can stroll on down to the lake.'

'Don't you think it might be a bit cold for a swim?'

'I wasn't thinking about swimming,' he said. 'I was thinking about an al fresco fuck.'

* * *

But they chickened out, because as soon as the sun disappeared over the horizon the temperature plummeted. Instead, after they'd unpacked and turned on gas and electricity and stocked the fridge and poured themselves some wine and eaten finger food in front of the fire, they cosied up in the hot tub. Aphrodite concluded that it would be very easy indeed to get used to such a sybaritic lifestyle – and hellishly difficult to relinquish once you did get used to it. She gazed and gazed out over Coolnamaragh Lake and thought that she had never been happier. Until Troy announced that it was time for bed, that is. That was when her happiness peaked.

* * *

The next day they drove – or rather, Aphrodite drove – to Ilnacullin, the garden island in Bantry Bay that Troy was keen to visit. Troy lounged back in the passenger seat and drank in the scenery, occasionally scribbling something in a notebook, or asking her to stop so that he could take photographs.

They were the only passengers on the ferry that serviced the island. They sat in the back of the boat relishing the salt taste of a wind that was – thankfully – still balmy. The weather was due to turn, according to the skipper – the days of this unseasonable premature summer were numbered. The ferry deposited them on a jetty, and they set off round the island, their walking boots making a satisfying thudding against the hard earth paths. Apart from this rhythmic noise, the only other sound was of boisterous birdsong. 'Listen to those birds!' remarked Aphrodite. 'They're going apeshit!'

'It's that time of year. Courtship rituals are *de rigueur*.' Troy slung an arm around her shoulders and smiled down at her. 'We've picked the best time. After St Patrick's Day the invasion of tourists starts. Every time you hit a bend in the road you run up against a tour bus.'

Ow, thought Aphrodite. Her nerves would be in flitters if Troy was behind the wheel of the car. 'Oh, look!' she exclaimed, getting down on her hunkers. 'Primroses. And violets!'

Troy crouched down beside her and ran his hand along a stone that was overgrown with moss. 'Pity we can't pick them. You would look edible wearing a coronet of wild flowers. Wow. Feel the texture of that moss,' he said. 'Can you imagine a fabric like that?'

'It's like the pelt of an animal,' said Aphrodite, stroking the moss as one would a cat, and feeling tempted to rub her cheek against it.

'And here,' said Troy, turning his attention to the bole of a tree that was thickly encrusted with lichen and rubbing some between finger and thumb. 'It's almost as if all this stuff had been hand-woven. I'll have to do some research when I get back to Dublin. Find someone who can recreate these colours and textures.'

'You'll commission someone?'

'Possibly. Although there's an amazing specialist fabric shop in Paris. I might find what I need there. Fancy spending a weekend at the Ritz?'

Oh God yes she did! 'That'd be cool,' she said.

Troy got to his feet and pulled his camera out of his case. 'Next time we go walking remind me to bring bags so I can collect samples. Photographs are useful visual mnemonics, but you can't beat the real thing.' He focused on the patch of moss and clicked a couple of times, then turned and started ambling down a path that led towards the shore. There they paused and looked out to sea. At their feet the water lapped, pellucid and inviting.

'What made you decide to become a designer, Troy?' asked Aphrodite.

'A love of women.'

'Really?'

'Really.' He smiled down at her. 'I've always found women fascinating. My aunt was extraordinarily elegant.'

'Was?'

'I think I told you. I haven't seen her for years. She's in Australia.'

Something about the tone of his voice made Aphrodite intuit that the rift had been difficult for him.

'When did you actually start building costumes?'

129

'Not long after my adolescent hormones kicked in. I started making stuff for my aunt, and then all her friends were clamouring for clothes. I adored fitting them, adored watching them wear my designs. It was the sexiest feeling in the world. Still is. I can't wait to deck you out in something fragile and diaphanous – like that seaweed. See it? Just by your foot.'

He bent down and picked up a strand of weed. It was emerald green, and when he spread it across his palm, Aphrodite could see that it comprised myriad tiny, feathery fronds.

'Look at the texture of that,' said Troy. 'It's exquisite. I'm going to make you a gown fit for a goddess, Aphrodite Delaney.' He regarded her with such flattering scrutiny that she felt a sudden urge to take his patrician head between her hands and kiss that sulky boy's mouth better.

Just then his mobile shrilled in her backpack. The noise was alien and unwelcome in this bucolic idyll. 'Hell,' said Troy with feeling. 'Real Life barges in on Paradise.'

'Don't worry. I'll send it packing,' she said blithely. Oh yeah? *How* exactly would she send real life packing? What if it was Troy's backer, or some scary person in Paris or New York demanding designs? She realized suddenly that fielding Troy's phone calls might not be such a piece of piss after all. 'Hello – Troy MacNally's phone,' she said into the receiver, hoping she sounded efficient. 'No. No, you have it wrong. Well that much is right – why don't you try substituting 087? *Vous êtes française, Madame? Alors, écoutez bien. Zéro. Huit. Sept. Oui. Oui. Ce n'est pas de problème, Madame. Au revoir.*' She depressed the 'hang-up' button and stuck the phone back in her bag.

'Hey, well done,' he said, looking at her with admiration. 'You handled that brilliantly. Who was it?'

Aphrodite looked sheepish. 'It was a wrong number,' she said. 'A French woman with very little English.'

Troy laughed. 'And there I was thinking you were fielding my calls effortlessly.'

'I wish.' She pulled her backpack open to its full extent and peered in. 'It's about time I checked my own phone for messages, come to think of it. Oh. It's not there. I must have left it back at the house. Ha! Just as well! Can you imagine what kind of sad asshole would wander around the countryside with two mobile phones vying for attention?'

'I know some people who do exactly that. They spend so much time wheeling and dealing and jabbering on their mobiles that they need a spare for when they run out of juice. The insides of their skulls must be a gourmet's dream.'

'What do you mean?'

'Don't you know that in some parts of the world scrambled monkey brains are considered a rare delicacy?'

'You're talking about humans here, Troy, not monkeys.'

'Not the ones I know,' he said, flashing her his great smile. 'Some of them are more challenged in the humane department than great apes.'

*   *   *

They spent over two hours on the small island wandering between an Italian garden and a jungle, a temple and a Martello tower. Troy announced that he wanted to climb the tower so that he could get a load of the view from the top, but Aphrodite wanted to check out the walled garden. 'I'll wait for you there,' she said. 'I've had a thing about walled gardens since I read *The Secret Garden* as a child.'

She sat on the steps for a while, enjoying the feel of the sun on her face, and wishing life was always like this. Real life with its mundane minutiae could be a million miles away. Except it wasn't of course, she registered, as Troy's phone rang again. She took a deep breath and picked up. 'Hello? Troy MacNally's phone.'

'Well that's obviously not Troy.' It was a man's voice. Cultured. Posh.

'No. I'm Aphrodite Delaney, his –' His *what*? She could hardly say: 'I'm Aphrodite Delaney, his muse', or even 'I'm Aphrodite Delaney, his assistant', or 'I'm Aphrodite Delaney, his new inamorata.' So she just said, 'I'm Aphrodite Delaney, his friend.'

'The one he's taken down to Kerry?'

'Yes.'

'I'll be meeting you soon, in that case. It's Gareth Fitzgerald here. Listen – I'm afraid we're going to have to interrupt your idyll for a while. I hadn't realized that Jolie had invited house-guests for the weekend, and she can't put them off. There'll be half a dozen of us descending on you some time tomorrow and leaving Sunday evening. Is that OK?'

Noooooo! 'Oh yes – of course!'

'Do you think you could do us a huge favour, Aphrodite, and organize a caterer somehow? Jolie's been let down by the crowd we usually use.'

'Oh! Oh, I'll certainly do my best.'

'Thanks. I'm sorry about this, but I promise we'll be out of your hair in just a couple of days. And I very much look forward to meeting you.'

'Thank you. Me too. Um. 'Bye, Gareth.'

''Bye.'

She resisted the temptation to fling the phone against a rock and then throw herself to the ground and dash her head against it. Oh, no no no! She didn't want to share her fairy tale! She wanted Troy all to herself! The prospect of all these cultivated, clever people – as they undoubtedly would be – invading her Ruritania was scary. They'd all be wearing designer threads and comparing exotic holiday destinations and talking about their latest must-have acquisitions. She'd be completely out of her depth, like a grouper stuck in a tank with a load of exotic angelfish.

Troy was strolling down the path towards her, stowing his camera back in its case. 'Come on,' he said. 'It's time to hit the jetty. The ferry should be here any minute.' Then he gave her a second look. 'What's wrong with you? Your face has gone all mopy.'

'Sorry,' she said, stapling on a smile. 'I just got a phone call. We're going to have company.'

'Company? What do you mean?' He held out a hand to her, and pulled her to her feet.

'Your friend Gareth's coming down for the weekend.'

'With Jolie?'

'Yes. And some other people.'

'Well! That might be fun. A house party.'

'Mm. But I thought the whole point of coming here was to avoid people, Troy?' She traced a little pattern in the gravel of the path with the toe of her shoe.

'To avoid the human race, yes. Not to avoid friends. Friends are a bonus – as long as they don't stay too long and stop me getting any work done. You'll like them. Honestly. Jolie's a perfect angel.'

Yikes! That made her feel even more inadequate. The image of the clumsy grouper floundering around presented itself even more vividly to her mind's eye. And then she told herself to shut up and stop being so supremely selfish. How dare she go into a sulk just because the people who were generous enough to let her stay in their little piece of paradise wanted to join them for a couple of days? She was going to come up against his friends some day, and at least she couldn't ask for a more relaxed environment in which to meet them for the first time.

'Gareth said something about organizing a caterer,' she remarked.

Troy looked blank. 'Oh. How many people are coming?'

'He said six.'

'OK. Um. Maybe you could locate someone in the

Golden Pages? We'll stop off on the way back to Coolnamaragh and check it out.'

It wasn't going to be easy, she thought as she boarded the ferry, to locate a caterer who would be willing to travel to the back of beyond at such short notice. In fact, Aphrodite strongly suspected that she would end up doing the catering herself. She started casting around for easy dinner party food, and making a mental shopping list. Hell! What had she said to herself earlier? That real life seemed a million miles away? What a joke! It seemed there was no escaping it. Unless you were Troy MacNally, that is. He was obviously a consummate escape artist. A Houdini. She turned and looked at him.

He was sitting, lost in thought, on the starboard side of the ferry. Port Out, Starboard Home. The origin of the word 'posh'. Posh people always took port cabins in liners on the way out to the East and starboard cabins on the way home because that was the side of the boat that got the sun. The sun was shining on Troy now, bestowing its rays like a privilege. He *was* privileged, she thought. A real golden boy. He was privileged to have talent, privileged to have good looks, privileged to have wealth. He shook his head suddenly, then raised a hand to take off his sunglasses.

Aphrodite looked away immediately. His face wore the kind of expression that you don't intrude upon, and one would never, ever have guessed from his eyes that he was a privileged individual. His eyes were like the eyes in that painting by Edvard Munch. When Aphrodite told Lola about the incident many

135

weeks later, she wasn't exaggerating when she described them as the eyes of a soul in torment.

When she dared to look back at him he had put his dark glasses back on and was smiling at her. 'Can we stop for ice-creams?' he said.

*   *   *

They drove back via Kenmare, stopping off in a filling station for ice-creams and then at a pub, where Aphrodite did the Golden Pages thing. Of course there was no caterer available. Gareth phoned again, and Aphrodite was relieved when he told her that one couple had had to cancel at the last minute, and that there would be only four extra people to cater for, bringing the total to a manageable six. Aphrodite felt reasonably confident that she could rustle up two decent evening meals, and Troy had already mentioned that Jolie could cook. Maybe she would help out. They sat there over a pint and a glass of Guinness while Aphrodite compiled a shopping list.

'What was the view like, by the way?' she asked.

'View?'

'Mm. From the top of the Martello tower.'

'Oh. I wimped out, I'm afraid, and took another stroll through the jungle instead.'

'Wimped out?'

'Yeah. I suffer from vertigo, embarrassingly. Once I got to the top of the steps I couldn't bring myself to look over the parapet.'

'Poor thing.' Aphrodite continued scribbling her shopping list. 'Who's the other couple who are coming down with Gareth and Jolie?' she asked as she scribbled down 'eggs, milk, coffee, loo roll . . .' They were going to have to do a massive shop.

'Another architect – Hugo O'Neill, and his wife. I've stayed in his house a couple of times and he's kosher.'

Another architect. That wasn't too scary. It wouldn't have surprised her if he'd said Sir Peregrine ffrench-Smythe.

'Is he from Dublin?'

'No, Westmeath. He restored his own house there.'

'Easier than what Gareth had to do with Coolnamaragh, I suppose.' Chicken breasts, tomatoes, beer, snacks. Pringles.

'No, actually. Restoration can be as time consuming as building from scratch, and there was a lot to be done. His is a much bigger house.'

Aphrodite's heart started to sink. 'How big?' she asked, crossing out 'Pringles' and putting in 'olives' instead. Basil, mozzarella, decent wine. Smoked salmon. Pimm's?

'He has a Georgian mansion. He inherited it.'

'I see. I suppose he inherited a title too!' This pathetic attempt at a quip was intended to conceal her increasing discomfort.

'Not quite, but he is directly descended from the High Kings of Ireland. Don't worry,' he said, registering her dropped jaw. 'He won't expect you to bow down to him.'

Aphrodite's hand scribbled faster. Champagne. Bath Olivers. Quails' eggs. She crossed the last two items out. The likelihood of finding Bath Olivers and quails' eggs in a provincial town was on a par with finding High King Hugo in McDonald's.

Beside her Troy stretched and yawned. 'I think I'll have another pint,' he said.

Chapter Six

They were sitting over lunch in the kitchen the next day listening to the wind and the rain that had descended out of yesterday's clear blue skies, when Gareth's party arrived. Troy had spent the morning in the study, sketching. Aphrodite had spent it reading a P.D. James novel in the hot tub. To sit in a hot tub listening to rain drumming on the deck and watching it pit the pewter surface of the lake beyond made her feel as if she was cheerfully thumbing her nose at the inclement weather. Lunch was goat's cheese and olives and French bread and a bottle of chilled Sauvignon blanc.

Aphrodite was just about to clear away the dishes when she heard someone coming along the corridor towards the kitchen. It was a confident stride – proprietorial. 'Hello! Troy? Are you at home?' A woman's voice – low, sexy, beautifully modulated. A smoker's voice.

Then the door opened and the owner of the voice walked into the kitchen.

'Jolie!' Troy got to his feet and crossed the room to her. 'Great to see you!' He took her in his arms and gave her a massive hug.

'It's been a while, hasn't it?' She was hugging him back, eyes closed, a radiant expression on her face.

Then she released him and turned the radiant expression on Aphrodite. 'Hi,' she said, extending a hand. 'You must be Aphrodite. I'm Jolie.'

Jolie. The French word for 'pretty'. It didn't do her justice. This woman was stunning. Her shaggy, jaw-length bob was expensively cut and highlighted with gold. Her eyes were denim-blue and heavily lidded, which lent her a slightly post-coital look – a look that contrived to be both lazy and intelligent at the same time. She was taller than Aphrodite, and slimmer, and older by some ten years. She was wearing a shirt of soft butter-coloured chamois leather, jeans, and Patrick Cox loafers that Aphrodite had seen in the sale at Brown Thomas and still hadn't been able to afford. Her jewellery comprised a simple diamond stud in each of her perfect ear lobes, and a plain gold wedding ring.

'Hi,' said Aphrodite, returning the handshake. 'Nice to meet you.'

'Likewise,' said Jolie, standing back and putting her head on one side as she assessed Troy's new muse. 'Hey! I love your hair! Who cuts it?'

'Um – I do,' said Aphrodite.

'No!' said Jolie. 'You brave thing! How clever of you! It's too absurd – I spend an absolute fortune every month to keep mine looking like I just fell out of bed.' She slung a soft leather satchel onto the kitchen table and extracted a packet of Sobranie cigarettes, helping herself to an olive before lighting up.

'You're not still smoking those vile things, are you?' remarked Troy.

140

'Sure am, sweetie,' returned Jolie, drawing in a lungful of smoke, and then exhaling it in a smooth stream. She was one of those smokers who looked so cool they made you wish you were a smoker too. 'They keep me sane. You try living with six-month-old twins some time. I guarantee you you'd go back on them.'

Aphrodite pounced on this opportunity for social dialogue. 'You have twins? How lovely! Where are they?'

Jolie sat down on a kitchen chair, swung her legs up on the one opposite and made an apologetic *moue*. 'I confess I did a shameful thing and left them at home with the nanny. I adore my boys, but I've learned that a gal needs an occasional break from motherhood.'

'Where are the others?' asked Troy, craning to see down the corridor.

'Unpacking the cars. So.' She cocked her head on one side and turned the full beam of her attention on Aphrodite. 'Polly tells me you're a theatre designer.'

'That's right.'

'That must be fascinating. I'd love to work in the theatre. Gareth's always telling me I should have been an actress. Is it madly glamorous?'

Aphrodite laughed. 'If you call being up till five o'clock in the morning supervising scenic artists glamorous. And then getting into the theatre for ten o'clock that same day to listen to some diva telling you exactly why her costume's all wrong.'

'Sounds like the fashion business,' remarked Troy.

'What made you decide to go into theatre design?' Jolie was still regarding her with a luminosity worthy of Cameron Diaz at her most incandescent.

'My mother's an actress. She introduced me to theatre at an early age. In those days it really did seem like a magical place.'

'Weren't you ever tempted to become an actress like your mother?'

'She's what put me off,' explained Aphrodite laconically.

Jolie threw back her head and gave a throaty laugh. Then she shook out her leonine hair with elegant fingers, and sighed. 'Coolnamaragh!' she crooned. 'At last! I haven't been here for a whole month. I need it like a plant needs water,' she explained to Aphrodite. 'To get away from the stinking city, to go for long walks, to sit by the fire and drink wine and read – it's my idea of absolute heaven!' She turned over the novel that Aphrodite had left lying on the table, and her smooth brow furrowed. 'Oh, Troy!' she chided. 'You're reading *thrillers*!' She invested the word with such scorn that she might as well have said: You're reading *porn*!

Aphrodite was spared a shamefaced confession by the arrival of a tall, fair-haired man who looked the way Aphrodite had always imagined Jay Gatsby to look.

'Troy!'

'Gareth! How's it going?' An exchange of backslapping, manly embraces as more people arrived. 'Hugo! Nice to see you again.' A manly handshake. 'Miranda! Hi!' Some cheek-kissing.

The big kitchen seemed terribly crowded suddenly. Aphrodite felt like running out for fresh air. Beside her Jolie flicked ash onto the lid of the plastic container the olives had come in.

'Oh!' said Aphrodite. 'Let me fetch you an ashtray.'

She started to move across the room, but Troy intercepted her. 'Aphrodite – this is Gareth, Miranda, Hugo.'

Aphrodite observed the introduction ritual. 'Nice to meet you – terrible weather! Hello, pleased to meet you. Hi – I believe you drove down from Westmeath?'

Gareth she liked immediately. He had kind eyes. Miranda O'Neill was very pretty, but her eyes had a dead look about them, and her handshake was as limp and indifferent as her husband's was cool and firm. Descended from a High King he might be, thought Aphrodite, but his eyes were those of a gypsy, and he exuded an aura of dangerous sex appeal.

'Where did you all meet up?' asked Troy.

'A pub in Waterville,' said Gareth, moving towards the table. He picked up the wine bottle and checked out the label. 'Excellent. Got any more of this?'

'You're in luck. There's some in the fridge,' said Aphrodite. She fetched another chilled bottle, handed it to Gareth along with the corkscrew, and set an ashtray down in front of Jolie. Then she fetched more glasses from the cupboard.

'Don't bother with a glass for Miranda,' said Hugo.

'Just give her her own bottle and let her swig it by the neck.'

'Droll,' drawled Miranda, giving her husband her dead-eyed look. She took a glass from Aphrodite and held it out for Gareth to pour.

'Well. You're managing admirably, darling,' continued Hugo. 'No shakes today?'

'Droller and droller, darling.' She raised her glass at him, swigged back half the contents, and walked out of the kitchen like a somnambulist.

There was a slightly awkward pause. Then: 'What's the catering situation, by the way?' asked Jolie, clearly trying to diffuse the tension.

'Couldn't manage to get anyone at such short notice, I'm afraid,' said Troy.

'We're well stocked up, though,' said Aphrodite, helpfully. 'We did a big shop in Kenmare yesterday. There's masses of food.'

'Excellent,' said Jolie, breaking off a chunk of French bread. 'I'm always starving when I come down here. I'll root through whatever you've got and fling something together for supper.

'I was going to do a beef casserole,' hazarded Aphrodite.

Jolie looked surprised. 'You managed to get organic beef in Kenmare? How extraordinary!'

'Well, no. I mean – it's not organic.'

'Uh-oh.' Jolie made that apologetic little pout again. 'I'm afraid I can't touch it then. Got any free range chicken?'

Thankfully Aphrodite had.

'I'll do my Pollo Spago. And some salad. Gareth

– remind me to soak some chickpeas overnight, will you? I'll do hummus tomorrow and make it positively *sing* with garlic.' Jolie got up and stretched as Gareth poured wine into her glass, and then she wandered over to the vegetable rack. 'Courgettes. Good. We'll have Zucchini Trifolati with the chicken.'

Aphrodite felt wildly redundant now. 'Isn't there anything I can do?' she asked.

'You can look picturesque,' said Jolie, sending her her radiant smile. 'Oh – and if you can bear to, you could load the dishwasher. I hate doing that.'

'I'll be your *commis-chef*,' said Hugo. 'I wield a mean Sabatier.' His black eyes looked more dangerous than ever.

'I'll top up your wineglass,' said Troy. 'I'm good at that.'

Hugo gave a hollow laugh. 'Don't go near Miranda in that case, or you'll end up with tennis elbow.'

Jolie gave him a playful swat on the arm on her way back to the table. 'You are horrid about her, Hugo. It's not as if she's an *aggressive* drunk. She just gets more and more like the dormouse in *Alice in Wonderland* as the evening progresses. I think it's rather sweet.' She gave her wonderful, husky laugh. 'Remember the time she started to snore at that party of Polly's, and you took her dress off? That was terribly, terribly cruel – but terribly funny all the same. She didn't bat an eyelid when she woke up. She just calmly put her dress back on as if it was the most normal thing in the world.'

'I don't remember that,' said Gareth, sounding puzzled.

'You were away somewhere on business, darling.'

'I don't remember it either,' said Troy.

'You had more pressing concerns on your plate at the time, sweetie-pie. It was during one of your emphatically anti-social phases when you were trying to persuade Miriam to go into rehab. Which is,' she said turning back to Hugo, 'what you should be doing for Miranda. No wonder she's hitting the bottle – stuck in that great big rambling mansion with nothing to do all day. Give her some babies. That'll keep her busy.'

Hugo's lip curled. 'Not possible, I'm afraid,' he said.

Jolie looked stricken. 'Oh, God. How crass of me. I *am* sorry. Can't she have any?'

'I'm sure she's perfectly fecund,' said Hugo. 'But we haven't had sex for years.'

'More wine, anyone?' said Aphrodite.

* * *

It got worse. After a rather desultory tour of the house and the grounds for Hugo's benefit, in which the two architects talked shop and Jolie linked arms with Troy, their hostess announced that she was going to cook. Her audience comprised Troy, Hugo and Aphrodite, who was actually kept too busy tidying up after the chef to do much audience participation. Gareth went for the hot tub option, and Miranda was nowhere to be seen. Aphrodite noticed that another bottle of Sauvignon blanc had gone missing from the fridge.

Jolie wrapped an expanse of white linen around her waist, French-waiter style, and started boning the chicken with a dexterity that Kay Scarpetta might have envied.

'Where did you learn how to do that?' asked Hugo admiringly.

'Switzerland. I did a cordon bleu course after I left school.'

'So did Miranda,' observed Hugo. 'But she's lost the knack of things culinary – unsurprisingly.'

After the chicken had been expertly dismembered, Jolie threw some leaves into a big bowl. 'Peel some garlic for me, Hugo, will you, while I improvise a dressing,' she said, making a face at the olive oil Aphrodite had bought. 'Oh well. It'll have to do. Beggars can't be choosers,' she remarked stoically. 'Troy – make yourself useful and chop some basil. Not too finely – rough is OK. Now, Aphrodite, what can we find for you to do?' Jolie seemed blithely unaware of the fact that Aphrodite had been scraping dishes, wiping spills, putting tops back on jars and bottles, and emptying and filling up the dishwasher. 'I know! Open a bottle of champagne, will you? Not that stuff that's in the fridge – there's a bottle of Cristal ready to go in the ice-bucket. And then maybe you could set the table?'

Aphrodite fetched champagne flutes from the cupboard and handed them round, feeling like the maid in a French farce. Jolie opened the bottle with the expertise of a sommelier, poured, and said: 'What'll we toast? Oh – I know!' She gave Aphrodite her radiant smile, and said: 'To Aphrodite, Troy's new muse. Welcome to our – oh God – welcome to what? What are we?'

'We're a bunch of debauched drunks and whore-masters,' said Hugo.

'Hugo, you'll unnerve the girl! Don't believe a word of it, Aphrodite!' Jolie shot Hugo a mock-reproving glance, and then looked thoughtful. 'I know! We're a clique, that's what we are. Welcome to our clique, Aphrodite!'

Jolie couldn't have devised a better way of making her feel left out. Her inclusion of Aphrodite in her 'clique' was so patently spurious that she had subtly achieved the very reverse effect – making Aphrodite more aware than ever of the fact that she was a rank outsider.

Their hostess set down her glass and tasted her dressing. 'Mm. Not bad,' she said after a moment's consideration. 'Pity about the oil, though. Oh – I'm going to need some parsley chopped, Troy, as well as the basil. Do you know where it grows in the garden? Good. Fetch me a big bunch, will you? I'll want some tomorrow.'

'What do you plan on cooking tomorrow?' asked Troy.

'Risotto ai Funghi,' said Jolie, unwrapping the napkin from around her waist. 'Who's going to be brave and volunteer to come on a hungover early morning mushroom hunt with me?'

'I'm on for that,' said Hugo. 'It'll be good to get the

148

day off to an early start if we're going to do the Skelligs.'

'The Skelligs? Are there boat trips out there?' asked Troy.

'Yes,' said Jolie. 'It's a fantastic experience. The trip takes over an hour, but it's worth it. The place is amazing. Have you ever been, Aphrodite?'

Aphrodite vaguely knew that the Skelligs were two uninhabited islands off the coast of Kerry, and that one of them was the site of an early monastic settlement. 'No, I haven't,' she said.

'It's a truly spiritual place. The climb is tough, but once you get to the pinnacle of the island you feel as if you're breathing pure sky. It's no wonder those monks retreated there – it's the ultimate escape. You're welcome to come with us tomorrow.'

'That's a great idea, Jolie,' said Troy. 'I've always wanted to visit that monastery.'

'Ah, but are you sure you'll be able for it, Troy – with your vertigo?' asked Jolie. 'It's a long way up.'

'I'll go as far as I can, but I'm not stupid. If I start to get panicky I'll come back down.'

'I'll never forget the time I dared you to look over the parapet at the top of the Guggenheim in New York,' said Jolie with a laugh. 'I've never seen anyone go so ashen.'

Aphrodite dreaded having to say what she knew she was going to have to say next because it would make her sound like a complete wimp. 'I won't be able to go, I'm afraid. To the Skelligs.'

'Oh?' Jolie looked surprised. 'Why ever not?'

'Well, talking of going ashen, I wouldn't last

twenty minutes in a boat – especially if the weather's like this. I suffer from chronic seasickness.'

Jolie's face was a perfect picture of sympathy. 'Oh! You poor thing! How awful for you.'

'You don't mind if I go, do you, Aphrodite?' Troy asked.

'No, no. Not at all,' she lied.

'Oops,' said Jolie. 'I feel awfully guilty abandoning you like this. But of course – you won't be all on your own. Gareth and Miranda don't want to come.'

'Miranda doesn't want to come where?' said Miranda, veering in from the hall with an empty wineglass in her hand.

'To Skellig Michael, darling, in St Finan's Bay,' said Hugo. 'It's famous for its well preserved remains of an anchorite settlement and – it goes without saying – it would be of absolutely no interest to you at all.'

Miranda teetered over to the table and sloshed Cristal into her glass so recklessly that the fizz erupted over the edge like lava out of a volcano. 'I can't conceive,' she said, picking up the glass and ignoring the champagne that was teeming over her hand, 'of a more odious odyssey.' Then she turned and veered out of the door again.

'Divorce – as you've very likely realized by now, Aphrodite,' said Hugo, raising an insouciant eyebrow at her, 'is most definitely on the agenda.'

'Let's just change the subject, will we?' said Jolie sweetly. 'Troy, you're neglecting your duties. You haven't got me my parsley yet.'

'I was hoping you'd forgotten. It's still pissing

rain out there.' But Troy obediently got to his feet and went about the knight's errand set him by the queen of Coolnamaragh. They heard him whistling as he went down the steps of the deck. Through the window Aphrodite could see Gareth still sitting in the hot tub outside, surveying the sodden landscape.

Jolie picked up her champagne flute and looked at the timer on the cooker. 'Keep an eye on that for me, Hugo, while I scoot upstairs and change. I wouldn't normally bother – we're very casual here, but pooh!' She raised an arm and sniffed. '*Je sens de la cuisine, j'en suis sûre.*'

'*Au contraire,*' said Hugo, leaning into her. '*Tu sens divine.* What scent do you use?'

'Poison.' Why wasn't Aphrodite surprised? She'd sampled Poison once, and Bobcat hadn't gone near her until she'd had her shower the next day and gone back to her usual Body Shop stuff.

Before leaving the kitchen, Jolie dipped her thumb into a bowl of something delicious she'd conjured from thin air, and sucked on it the way Nigella Lawson always did. Aphrodite remembered all the thumb-sucking that had gone on in that poxy French film *Chose de Neige* that she'd seen months ago – the one where she'd met Jack Costello – and how it had reminded her of an ad for Gucci's Envy. The way she was feeling now, Envy could become her signature scent.

She might have been mistaken, but she could have sworn that Hugo's hand grazed Jolie's buttocks as she turned round and swished out of the room. He gazed at her retreating rear as she sashayed down the corridor. 'Wow,' he said, shaking his head incredulously. 'She never ceases to amaze me. Jolie Fitzgerald is some class act.'

'She sure is,' said Aphrodite. 'Act' being the operative word. The woman could out-Oscar Halle Berry. 'Have you known her long?'

'A couple of years. I met her and Gareth at some tedious architectural conference in Berlin and we hit it off immediately.'

'Is she an architect too?' Was there any end to this woman's talents?

'No. She was just there to keep Gareth company, look gorgeous, and schmooze. She doesn't work. Or rather, she works her ass off, but she doesn't have a job, *per se.*'

'Oh? What does she do?'

'Organizes charity gigs. She's a total live wire. Imagine sitting on all those committees, entertaining Gareth's clients and raising two babies at the same time. She's even breast-feeding them still – that's why she doesn't like to abandon them for too long. She's absolutely phenomenal. Plus, she skis, rides, plays a mean fiddle, *and* she's a master scuba diver. She's even had a novel published.'

By a vanity press, thought Aphrodite bitterly. 'Oh? What's it called?'

'*Fandango in Tunis.*'

Aphrodite was surprised that it wasn't 'My Brilliant Career'. 'Did it sell well?'

Hugo laughed. 'Of course not. Only to a couple of hundred discriminating individuals. It was far too

152

esoteric to do well. Anyway, it would horrify Jolie to see her book on a bestseller list alongside a load of commercial fiction.' He invested the word 'commercial' with a great deal of scorn.

Troy came back in from the garden, shaking a bunch of wet parsley. 'Where's Jolie?' he asked.

'Gone to change for dinner.'

'Are we dressing?'

'No. She just felt that she smelt of kitchen smells.'

'Bloody delicious smells they are too,' said Troy, leaning over the cooker and inhaling. 'How does she do it? She never ceases to amaze me.' It was the second time in under a minute that someone had said that about their hostess.

I hate her, thought Aphrodite. I am a sad, vicious, nasty little human being who should be grateful to Jolie Fitzgerald for the hospitality and graciousness she has bestowed upon me. I also know that I should be in awe of her talent and her beauty and her vivacity and her warmth and her popularity and her altruism, but I can't help it. I hate her. And, hey, whaddya know? Not only am I a sad, vicious, nasty little human being, I am also an impostor. She should be the one with the name of a goddess, not me.

'Hell's bells!' came a voice from the kitchen door. 'Is Gareth still in the hot tub? His willy will be shrivelled up to the size of a pickled cucumber, and he'll be of absolutely no use at all to me later.'

Aphrodite turned to see Jolie lounging against the door jamb, empty champagne flute dangling from elegant fingers. She was wearing ankle-strapped heels and a wisp of eau-de-Nil chiffon that wouldn't have looked out of place on Gisele at London Fashion Week. And under the chiffon she was wearing a miniature thong and absolutely nothing else.

She catwalked into the room and held her glass out to Hugo. 'Top me up, darling,' she purred.

*   *   *

After a dinner that was worthy of the River Café, Jolie deftly rolled a joint while Aphrodite and Gareth cleared the table and Hugo made coffee. Troy poured brandies. Miranda had force-fed herself some morsels of chicken earlier before wafting off with her plate in one hand and her wineglass in the other.

'Let's move into the drawing room for charades,' suggested Jolie, lighting the joint and passing it to Troy. 'You're continuing to confine yourself to B-class, I trust?' she asked, putting her head on one side and gazing bluely at him. He nodded meekly at her, and then Jolie laid a hand on his arm with such manifest concern that Aphrodite felt a horrid pang of something. There was so much she didn't know about him, so much history, so much shared experience between the two of them.

And now they were going to have to play charades! Aphrodite felt as if she were looking into the maws of hell. She hated charades and had always been crap at them. She had a strong suspicion that her hostess excelled at them, however, and that she would soon be angling for her Oscar nomination. Jolie rose to her feet, brandy glass in hand, and her guests did likewise. A lot of alcohol had been consumed, but Jolie was perfectly steady on her pins as she led her fan club along the corridor, chiffon shimmering in her wake. Aphrodite was feeling a bit fuzzy. She'd definitely turn down any top-ups of brandy, but she'd better not refuse the joint in case she looked unhip.

Miranda was in the drawing room, reclining on a mint-green suede chaise-longue and trying to focus on *Harpers.* Jolie glided towards her and sank to her knees in an effortlessly graceful attitude. The chiffon settled around her like a small cloud.

'We're having a game of charades,' she said, taking hold of one of Miranda's hands. 'Will you play?'

'I don't play charades,' slurred Miranda. 'I live them.'

Jolie adopted a concerned expression. 'Are you all right, little lost one?' she asked in the kind of voice that Florence Nightingale had probably used. 'Would you like some coffee?'

'No coffee.' Miranda indicated her empty wine-glass. 'But I wouldn't say no to a refill of this.'

Jolie took the glass from Miranda's slack hand and held it out to Aphrodite. 'Aphrodite? Would you get 'Anda another glass of wine?' She adopted a confidential tone as Aphrodite obligingly took the glass from her. 'I know I shouldn't encourage her drinking,' she said, 'but she tends to get obstreperous if one refuses.'

Aphrodite couldn't imagine this poor wraith-like

individual ever having the energy to be obstreperous, but she did as she was told.

'We've drawn lots,' announced Jolie when Aphrodite returned with ''Anda's' glass. 'I'm on first, and you mustn't laugh. Hugo's given me something fiendishly difficult.' She was standing in the middle of the room surrounded by satellites. Hugo and Troy were lounging in big leather armchairs on either side of the fireplace, and Gareth was sitting beside Miranda on the chaise-longue.

'Film!' chorused Troy and Gareth as the floor show began. 'Two words! Second word! One syllable!'

Jolie described a rectangular shape in the air with her elegant hands.

'Um. Screen?'

She shook her head.

'Parcel? Present? No. It's one syllable, of course. Gift?'

Jolie shook her head again, and put a pensive finger on her lips. Then she raised an imaginary lid.

'Case?' said Gareth.

'Trunk?' hazarded Troy.

Aphrodite supposed she'd better join in, otherwise she was going to start looking like an awful party-pooper. 'Box?'

Jolie swung round, pointed a finger at Aphrodite and nodded encouragement.

'Box,' said Gareth. 'So – box is the second word. *Something* box, yes? And now you're going back to the first word. First word. Three syllables. Second syllable.'

Jolie pointed towards the door.

'Door,' said Aphrodite astutely.

'Door? Hey! Pan*dora*!' shouted Troy. 'It's *Pandora's Box*! The film with that sexy vamp – what was her name?'

'Louise Brooks,' said Aphrodite. She'd seen it during a retrospective at the IFC. It was a film about a woman who has the power to seduce anyone she wants – male or female. What an apt title for Jolie's charade, she thought. But as for it being 'fiendishly difficult' . . . She reckoned even she could have managed *Pandora's Box*.

Aphrodite successfully managed to postpone humiliation for several rounds of the game, but by the time the second joint was being rolled, she had a suspicion that she wouldn't be able to put it off for much longer.

'Aphrodite!' cried Jolie in an accusatory tone. 'You haven't done one yet! I believe you've been deliberately trying to get out of it. And nobody's allowed to get out of doing post-prandial charades except poor 'Anda because she always falls asleep.' Miranda had indeed fallen fast asleep beside Gareth on the chaise-longue. She had laid her head on his lap, and he had draped one arm protectively over her shoulders. 'Let's see,' resumed Jolie inexorably. 'I know.' She leaned into Aphrodite and whispered in her ear. '*Chose de Neige*,' she hissed, and then gave Aphrodite a cat-like smile. It was an impossible title for charades.

'But it's French!' she protested.

Jolie pounced. 'Aha! Forfeit, forfeit! You spoke.

And you gave away a big hint by letting drop that it was French. That means you *have* to do it.'

Aphrodite sent Troy a pleading look, but he just smiled and shrugged. 'That's Jolie's house rule,' he said.

Aphrodite bit the bullet. With a bit of luck somebody else present would have caught the film during its interminable run at the IFC. She got the preliminary stuff – *Film. Three words* – out of the way, and then she embarked on the charade proper. For the word *chose* she tried to mime 'shows', but her audience just looked more and more perplexed as she stood in the middle of the floor flailing around. Defeated, she moved on to *de*, making the letter 'd' with her fingers. But everyone just kept saying 'Dee. Dee, dee, dee, dee, dee,' like relentless parrots. Her *neige* was indecipherable. Finally she shrugged and gave up. 'I'm sorry,' she said. 'I give up. It's impossible to convey. I really don't see how anyone could do it.'

Hugo turned his black eyes on Jolie. 'Could you?' he asked.

She returned his challenging smile and, after a nanosecond's hesitation, resumed her position centre-stage. *First word. Sounds like.* She pointed an elegant foot in its delicate ankle-strap.

'Foot.'

'Shoe.'

She nodded and made a gesture that invited them to elaborate.

'Sounds like shoes, plural?'

Another nod. *Third word. Rhymes with.* Jolie moved

to the chair where Hugo was sitting and laid a languid hand on his arm, rubbing the rich fabric of his beige shirt between finger and thumb.

'Rhymes with shirt.'

She shook her head.

'Rhymes with arm?'

Another negative.

'Rhymes with – um – beige?'

A triumphant nod.

'Beige. Jays. Kays,' enunciated Troy.

'Jays and kays don't rhyme with beige,' pointed out Hugo. 'And what are "kays" anyway?'

'Isn't that how Americans pronounce "quays"?'

'Mm.' A pause while the players speculated what else it might be.

Then Gareth said: 'Neige! It's *Chose de Neige* – that French film we saw at the IFC!'

'You're bang on, darling!' Jolie stalked across the floor and gave her husband a big kiss on the lips.

Oh, God. Not only had Jolie succeeded in winning the game, thought a beyond-glum Aphrodite. She had done it in just a fraction of the time it had taken *her* to fail so ignominiously.

'I didn't see that film,' said Hugo. 'But I heard it was terrific.'

'It was,' said Jolie, 'an absolute masterpiece. A revelation. Did you see it, Aphrodite?'

'Er – yes.'

'What did you think of it?'

Aphrodite didn't want to become part of the religion that was Jolie, but if she was going to hang out with Troy she would have to find some way of

159

gaining credibility with his friends. She remembered what Jack Costello had said to her on the way out of the cinema after sitting through *Chose de Neige*. *A load of crap, wasn't it?* And then she heard herself take a deep breath.

'I agree,' she said. 'I thought that it was absolutely stunning.'

*   *   *

It was much later. Everyone was by now the worse for wear except Jolie, who obviously had a remarkable capacity for putting away alcohol. She was playing Scott Joplin extremely proficiently on the piano, having the pages of her sheet music turned by Hugo, who was leaning against the instrument watching her. Aphrodite had noticed that his eyes had got even more dangerously glittery as the evening wore on.

The music must have jangled Miranda out of her hibernation because she suddenly stood up, yawned, stretched, and swayed towards the door. But just as she reached out a hand to open it she turned and bestowed a beatific smile on her husband. 'By the way, darling, there's something you ought to know,' she said. 'I am with child.'

Hugo didn't bat an eyelid. 'Who's the lucky father?' he asked, with a saturnine smile worthy of Clark Gable in *Gone with the Wind*.

'*Très droll*,' replied Miranda in her automatic pilot's voice. And then the door shut behind her. Gareth slipped quietly after her.

'Is she really pregnant?' asked Jolie carelessly.

'I don't have a clue. She's pulled this stunt on me before. But I can assure you that if she is, I had absolutely nothing to do with it.'

'Why did you bring her with you?' Jolie stopped playing and lit up a Sobranie. 'She's simply too boring for words when she's like this.'

'You may recall that the last time I left her behind she tried to burn the house down. I have no intention of being deprived of my ancestral home by a crazed pyromaniac. Until I get her committed I have to watch my back.'

Aphrodite wanted out of there. The evening had disintegrated beyond repair. Troy had consumed so much Rémy Martin that he could very well have replaced the comatose Miranda on the chaise. It was time to wind things up.

Somehow, she managed to get Troy out of the drawing room without either Jolie or Hugo appearing to notice that they'd gone. In the bedroom she stripped off first his clothes and then her own, and then she lay down beside him, quite unable to sleep and positively buzzing with nervy energy. Whatever had been in those joints had made her feel very speedy. She was also dying of thirst.

She slid out of bed and into her kimono, and padded on soundless feet into the kitchen to fetch a glass of water. A steel-coloured mesh blind had been drawn over the big porthole window, and now a pale light lent it a silver sheen, and she saw that it must be nearly dawn. How beautiful to watch the sun rise over the mountains of Coolnamaragh! Quietly she moved down the corridor, into the sitting room, and out onto the deck. She wasn't the only person who was awake she realized, on hearing voices coming from the far end, where the hot tub was housed. She could tell by the thrum of the engine that drove the water jets that someone was using the tub, but she couldn't see who it was because the bend in the deck had been designed to afford bathers a degree of privacy.

'Anyway I'm glad he's found a surrogate.' The drawl was unmistakable. 'Aphrodite will do very nicely. She's biddable, and that's more than can be said for Miriam towards the end. I made a huge mistake in procuring her.'

'Procuring? She wasn't a hooker, was she?' Aphrodite found herself creeping closer to where the deck curved to the left. She couldn't help herself.

'No. I mean procuring her as Troy's muse. I spotted her wandering around the National Gallery and I knew he wouldn't be able to resist that smouldering Pre-Raphaelite look – he's a wildly romantic boy at heart. So I engage her in conversation and she agrees to join a house party Bianca was giving in her gaff in France. I furnish her with the correct props–'

'Props?'

'Yeah. I made sure she was reading a volume of French poetry when I introduced her to Troy – and abracadabra: Troy is smitten, the designs keep coming and we're all happy bunnies. If I hadn't found a substitute for me he might not have hacked it.'

'You're a clever woman, Jolie.'

'You need to have your wits about you to be a muse. You have to learn fast how to kick professional ass. If you don't, you're just asking to be trampled on. Most people in the fashion industry know more about cutting throats than about cutting patterns. No wonder Miriam failed so spectacularly.'

'How long were you his muse?'

'For nearly seven years. He was devastated when I told him I was going to marry Gareth. That's why I moved like a flash to get Miriam on board. I knew that Troy was going to have huge problems delivering the goods if he had no muse working on his case, and when you've invested the kind of money that Gareth and I have sunk into the business you want to keep your creative happy. A little more pressure there, darling. Oh, God yes – that feels divine. You have the cleverest fingers of anyone I know.'

A low laugh and a pause, and then Hugo spoke again. 'How did he find Aphrodite?'

'She found him. The clever girl seduced him by making sure that the first time he laid eyes on her she was looking as provocative as possible.'

'Oh? How did she manage that?'

'She was lying stark naked in his bath, darling. Troy told me, and Polly confirmed it. Of course, his version of the story is madly romantic, but Polly told me Aphrodite knew the exact date and time of Troy's arrival back from holiday.' That's not fair! thought Aphrodite. No-one had taken the time lag factor into account when they'd told her his flight schedule. There'd been a nine-hour difference. If she'd known about that, of *course* she'd have legged

163

it out of there and would never have dreamed of lolling around in Troy's bath. 'She should have been well out of his apartment by the time he came back – she timed it perfectly, the astute minx. There's a lot more going on under that obliging exterior than you'd think, angel. She's perfect muse material. Al*though* –' she drawled the word, giving it a ruminative flavour '– although I think we're going to have to do a little work on her image. I'm going to have to persuade her out of those threads she favours into something a little more *au courant.* It would never do for Troy MacNally's muse to be seen looking like some reject from a thrift shop. It astonishes me the number of people who don't realize that most people actually *do* judge a book by its cover. To continue the analogy, if Aphrodite were a book, she'd be in the remaindered department of Easons.'

'She's a very pretty girl. I'd give her one.'

'Your libido never ceases to amaze me. Is there anyone on the face of this planet to whom you wouldn't "give one", as you so charmingly put it?'

'My wife.'

'No more than she'd give *you* one. Anyway, I wasn't talking about Ms Delaney's personal pulchritude, darling. I was talking about her style. Or lack of same.' Aphrodite heard Jolie suck in her breath sharply, and then let it out in a long hiss. 'Oh – God, yes! Diviner and diviner, darling. Don't stop.'

'Take off your thong. Let me in. I've been nursing a hard-on all evening admiring your tits bouncing around under that little see-through number.'

'I am not fucking you in the hot tub, Hugo.'

'Jesus, Jolie – why not? Feel just how badly I want you.'

A little purr of appreciation preceded her response. 'Hygiene reasons, pure and simple. Other people use the tub.'

'Get out, then. Sit up on the rail and spread your legs.'

'Darling – you forget my husband is in another part of the house and may chance upon us any minute. Also, it will be extremely cold out of the tub.'

'Forget about the cold, and listen to this.' Hugo's voice took on a menacingly lubricious tone as he carefully articulated the following words. 'I am so hot for you, baby, that I do not intend to take things at a *leisurely* pace, I warn you. There is no possibility in the world that you will catch cold out there. Do it now, bitch. Get out of the tub.'

A throaty laugh. 'How could I refuse such a masterful inducement?'

There was the sound of water surging and plashing, immediately followed by the sounds of extremely urgent shagging – sounds that wouldn't sound out of place in a soft porn movie. The dialogue was worthy of *Austin Powers*, with lots of exhortations from both parties to 'do it to me, baby'.

Aphrodite stood with her glass clutched tightly in her hand and her face flaming, rigid with the need for revenge. She felt like running into Gareth's room and waking him to tell him exactly what his wife was up to on the deck with his good mate Hugo. She felt like warning Miranda that her 'concerned' hostess had a two-sided cat face. She felt like ripping to

165

shreds the entire cosy cobweb of intrigue that had been so carefully constructed for the smooth running of Jolie's 'clique', and she felt like crushing underfoot the black widow spider who had woven it.

She turned and legged it back to her bedroom, trying to erase the memory of the soundtrack of that duplicitous, lurid lovemaking. And there was another quandary seething in her mind. Should she tell Troy about what she had just seen and heard? Should she warn him that Jolie was poisonous? She didn't think so. Some small pragmatic voice told her he wouldn't believe her. Oh, God. Maybe she should leave him now – get out of this untenable relationship before she became too irrevocably smitten? The very thought made her want to weep hot tears. They'd only just found each other!

He was sitting up in bed with the side light on. 'Where were you, Aphrodite?' he asked, sounding very dopey. 'I dreamed that you'd left me like all the others, and when I woke up you were gone.'

She had never seen him looking so incredibly vulnerable. Her heart went all wobbly with love, and she knew she'd left it too late to effect an escape from him. She *was* irrevocably smitten. There was no going back now.

'It's all right,' she said, sitting down beside him and pushing a wing of silky black hair away from where it fell over his face. 'I just went to get a glass of water. What woke you up?'

'Your phone was ringing.'

At this hour in the morning? 'Oh? Who was it?'

'I don't know. It rang off before I could pick up.'

Curious, Aphrodite picked up the phone. The display told her there was a new message in her mailbox. She pressed the relevant access numbers, and Lola's voice came over the line. 'Aphrodite? I'm sorry to ring you so late, but I need to talk to you a.s.a.p. I'm afraid I have bad news. I just got back from a party and dropped in to feed Bobcat. You've been broken into. I'm really sorry to have to tell you this, but they've trashed the joint. You're going to have to come home.'

Chapter Seven

Gareth offered to drive her to the station in Killarney early the next morning. Troy had wanted to do it, but Aphrodite insisted that he stick to his original plan to visit Skellig Michael with Jolie and Hugo.

'I feel guilty, abandoning you,' he protested, taking her in his arms in the driveway of Cool-namaragh and stroking her hair. 'Are you sure you don't want me to drive you up?'

The prospect of being driven anywhere by Troy made her knees turn to mush. Her state of mind was precarious enough after the grim gavotte that had been so macabrely choreographed the previous evening. 'No, no,' she reassured him. 'Lola will be there to hold my hand. There's no point in you cutting your stay here short.' Lola had gone into very little detail about the break-in, but had reassured her that it looked worse than it actually was, and there didn't seem to be much missing – although the CD rack appeared a bit depleted.

'Will you come back down?' asked Troy.

'I really don't know. It depends on how much clearing up there is to be done.'

'We'd better get going, Aphrodite, if we're going to make that train.' Gareth was already behind the wheel of his Land Rover, and the engine was running.

'Coming.' Aphrodite raised her face to Troy's for one last kiss, and then swung her bag into the back seat.

'Call me as soon as you get there,' he said. 'Good luck, darling. I hope it's not too hellish for you.'

As the Land Rover swept through the gates, Jolie and Hugo came into view, strolling along the road. Jolie was wearing a cream knit cowl-necked sweater and a near ankle-length skirt constructed from acres of rust-coloured linen that billowed and swirled as she walked. Her hair was piled on top of her head with loads of sexy tendrils escaping, her face was bare of make-up, and she had a picturesque wicker basket heaped with field mushrooms hooked over her left arm. She looked the picture of robust, rustic good health, as if she'd just stepped out of some bucolic lifestyle feature in a glossy magazine. Aphrodite could hardly believe that this was the same siren who'd prowled around in diaphanous chiffon the night before, knocking back litres of champagne and committing adultery all over the place. At least Hugo had the decency to look a bit rough. He was unshaven, and the eyes that had glittered so dangerously only hours earlier were bloodshot and tired. Aphrodite noticed a small cut on his bottom lip, as if he'd been bitten there.

'Morning!' sang Jolie, as Gareth pulled up alongside them. 'Where are you two off to? Just look at these glorious mushrooms! We're going to breakfast like princes!'

Gareth briefly filled Jolie in on Aphrodite's predicament.

'Oh, how awful!' Jolie's expression was one of aghast concern. 'If there's anything we can do to help – anything at all, Aphrodite, you must phone at once. D'you promise me you will?'

'Of course she will,' said Gareth. 'By the way, darling, what on earth were your shoes doing on the deck this morning?'

The faintest flash of alarm flitted over Jolie's beautiful face before she widened her eyes disingenuously. 'And what, pray, is wrong with leaving my shoes on the deck? My feet were killing me, darling, after all that prancing about doing charades.'

'It's not the fact that you left your shoes on the deck, darling,' returned Gareth. 'It's the fact that they were full of Pollo Spago.'

Now Jolie had the decency to look genuinely alarmed. '*What?* Someone put chicken in my Jimmy Choos?'

'So it would appear.'

Jolie now looked so outraged that Aphrodite felt compelled to say: 'It wasn't me.'

'Ha ha ha,' went Jolie. 'Of course it wasn't you, Aphrodite. You're far too grown up to pull a silly stunt like that. It must have been Miranda. She was so out of it last night that she'd have been capable of anything.' The bright smile she gave was a big crack in the porcelain of her face, and Aphrodite felt like cheering for Miranda.

Gareth slid the Land Rover into gear. 'Anyway, they're still there on the deck.' He glanced at his Rolex. 'We gotta go – we're running late. Be sure to save some of those mushrooms for me.' They took off up the road, and as Aphrodite watched the image of Jolie waving a fond farewell getting smaller and smaller in the passenger-side wing mirror, she wished she'd dreamed up the idea of putting leftover chicken in her Jimmy Choos. Beneath the unprepossessing façade, Miranda was clearly a warrior princess.

After Gareth had packed her onto the train, reminding her that he'd be glad to help out in any way he could, Aphrodite got her phone out of her bag. She wanted to call Troy to let him know she'd made it in time. She punched in the number and heard the ringing tone. Across from her, a fellow passenger's phone was ringing, too. It rang and rang, and eventually Aphrodite leaned across the table that separated them and said: 'Excuse me. D'you realize your phone is ringing?'

'It's not mine,' said the man. 'I don't have a mobile.'

Aphrodite looked at the backpack she'd dumped on the tabletop between them, and the penny dropped. She delved inside the bag. There, at the very bottom, was Troy's tiny little silver Nokia, bleating at her piteously.

*   *   *

It rang twice on the journey. The first caller was a journalist, phoning to ask if Troy was available for a comment on some fashion *faux pas* made by a famous politician's mistress. Aphrodite didn't know the number in Coolnamaragh, and, even if she had known it, she wasn't sure whether or not it was kosher to give it out. In the end she suggested that the caller contact Polly Riordan.

The next caller was Polly herself. 'What's the problem?' she asked.

'Sorry about this, Polly. I was in a hurry to get back to town, and completely forgot that I still had Troy's phone. Maybe you could give me the phone number in Coolnamaragh so that I can at least call him and let him know?'

'I can't give out that number to anyone, I'm afraid,' said Polly crisply. 'It's ex-directory. *I* will call him.'

Oh, lighten up! Aphrodite wanted to say, but didn't.

Within minutes Troy was on the phone. People in the train carriage were starting to give her dirty looks, and she felt embarrassed when she remembered what she'd said to Troy about sad assholes who spend their entire lives with mobile phones clamped to their ears. She squeezed past the person sitting next to her and scampered down the aisle to the very end of the carriage where she could take the call without all the passengers earwigging.

He laughed out loud when she apologized for unintentionally filching his mobile. 'That's the best news I've had in ages. You know how much I hate the bastard thing. If you don't mind carrying on fielding my calls for me, then I'm tickled pink for you to have it.'

'But I feel like a total impostor! What authority do I have to take calls for you, Troy?'

'Mine. As my muse.'

Aphrodite cringed a bit. 'But I can't very well say "Oh, *I* decide on who talks to Troy MacNally because I am his muse, so there."' She put on a superior tone, not unlike the one Polly had adopted earlier.

'You don't have to. Just say you're Aphrodite Delaney. You don't have to explain yourself to anyone – the bush telegraph will have done that by now. I read Polly the riot act by the way, when I realized she'd refused to give you the number here. I think you'll find she'll be more obliging in future.'

'I don't want to make any enemies, Troy.'

He laughed down the line again, but this time it was a short bark of a laugh. 'Polly will do as she's told, darling. I have no truck with negative vibes.' In the background Aphrodite could hear Jolie's honeyed tones calling him. 'I'd better go,' he said. 'We're off on our trip to the Skelligs. Jolie's had the bright idea of bringing her fiddle with her.'

I bet, thought Aphrodite bitterly. An image flashed in front of her mind's eye of Jolie Fitzgerald sitting in the prow of a boat as it beat its way over the white horses of St Finan's Bay, fiddling more proficiently than Sharon Corr, golden hair wind-ruffled, laughing over her shoulder as she shared a joke with her 'boys', being eyed lasciviously by a boatman in a báinín sweater. She stuffed Troy's phone in her bag and made her way back down the train, apologizing as she went to the surly Saturday morning commuters she kept being jolted against. Not once was her apology acknowledged.

*   *   *

Lola was waiting for her in the little house in Stoneybatter. Aphrodite could see her at the window as she paid off her cab, and before she could slide her key into the lock, her friend was there at the front door. She held up her hands, palms upward. 'Better take a deep breath, babe. I did what I could to minimize the mess, but those boys were party animals, I'm afraid. "Animals" being the operative word.'

Aphrodite stepped into her sitting room. 'Oh, fuck,' she said, dropping to her hunkers and covering her mouth with her hands. Lola had been right when she said they'd trashed the joint. They'd had a can of spray paint which they'd used liberally on the walls. To judge by their graffiti they had the IQ of pond life, but the gist of what they wanted to convey was plain enough.

'Are you going to get sick?' asked Lola anxiously.

Aphrodite thought seriously about it for a moment or two, then shook her head.

'I tidied as much as I could after the guards got here. I had to bin some stuff, I'm afraid. The detective took fingerprints, but he was honest enough to admit that it's unlikely they'll find the bastards. They did poor old Miss Gibson's house next door, too. She was away staying overnight with her sister. Just as well.'

'Bastards,' said Aphrodite fiercely. 'Fucking bastards.' She got to her feet slowly and moved across the room. 'What was the *point*? All for a few CDs?'

174

'The bedroom's worse, I'm afraid. They went through your wardrobe and your drawers. I had to trash a lot of your clothes.'

Aphrodite gave Lola a questioning look.

'They – um. They urinated on them.'

Aphrodite shut her eyes for a beat or two, and then opened them again. 'Yeah,' she said dully. 'I suppose I expected something like that.'

Lola took Aphrodite's hand in hers. 'It could have been a lot worse, you know. At least there's nothing valuable missing, and everything's replaceable. I nipped into the Garda station earlier and picked up a form for you to fill in.'

'You're a doll, Lo.'

'No problem. You'd do the same for me. You'll need to get the detective to sign it. He's cute, by the way. Black leather jacket, great ass, amazing eyes.'

Aphrodite gave Lola a wan smile, and just then a vile thought struck her. 'Bob! He's OK, isn't he?'

But before Lola could answer Aphrodite heard the familiar thwack of the cat flap, and Bobcat came marching in from the kitchen with his tail held high in the air. He greeted his mistress with a growl, and she swung him up into her arms and buried her face in his marmalade fur.

'At least you've buckets of paint,' said Lola, surveying the graffiti on Aphrodite's walls. 'For your new redecoration project.'

'What do you mean?'

'All the stuff that's left over from the work you did on Troy's joint.' She indicated the tins of paint that Aphrodite had dumped in her hallway before heading south. 'It's just as well your visitors brought their own spray cans, otherwise they might have been tempted to use your paint to indulge their artistic impulses. This place was due a facelift, anyway. We could start straight away, if you feel up to it.' Lola gave her a shrewd look. 'How *are* you feeling, babe? Patrick warned me that you might feel kinda violated.'

'Who's Patrick?'

'The detective. He's in next door with Miss Gibson now, interviewing her and waiting for a ban garda to come and hold her hand. The poor thing's nerves are so shot that she's talking about moving in with her sister permanently.'

'How am I feeling?' Aphrodite repeated Lola's original question in a stupid voice, shifting Bob onto her shoulder and looking around at her desecrated home. 'How am I *feeling*? I'm not quite sure *how* I feel, Lo. I'm not really feeling anything at all. Numb just about sums it up. I suppose I'm still in a state of shock.' The cat's loud purring in her ear was comforting. She clutched him tighter. 'But I'm *not* going to allow those bastards to get to me. They're scum. I'm bigger and better and stronger than they are. And,' she said, nodding towards a drawing of an erect penis that had been crudely executed on the wall above her couch, 'I'm a much more talented artist than they are, too.'

Her friend gave her a look of mock surprise. 'Ooh,' she said. 'When was the last time you did a drawing of a penis?' Aphrodite attempted a laugh and tapped her nose with her forefinger. 'It's so long since I've seen one that I've almost forgotten what they look like,' came Lola's mournful rejoinder.

Just then the doorbell rang. Aphrodite noticed that Lola went a bit pink. She shot her a look of enquiry. 'Are you expecting someone?' she asked.

'The detective. I told him he'd be welcome to drop in for a cup of coffee when he finished next door.'

Aphrodite raised an eyebrow. 'Then you'd better put the kettle on,' she said, heading towards the hallway.

The detective *was* cute, with eyes bluer than Aidan Quinn's and an unseasonable tan. He introduced himself as Patrick Larkin, and then he walked into the middle of the room and stood there looking vaguely uncomfortable. Aphrodite felt a bit uncomfortable too. It would have been difficult not to, surrounded as they were by such lurid graffiti. No wonder elderly Miss Gibson next door needed her hand holding by a ban garda. The raciest stuff *she* read was by Barbara Cartland. However, when Lola emerged from the kitchen, Patrick Larkin relaxed visibly and a lop-sided smile spread across his face. Aphrodite noticed that Lola had fluffed out her hair, that she smelt suspiciously of freshly sprayed Gaultier, and that she'd undone another button on her shirt.

'Will we have coffee in the kitchen?' she said, holding the door open. 'I think I've feasted my eyes sufficiently on the work of these inspired disciples of Basquiat.'

Aphrodite looked sideways at Patrick to see if he'd understood Lola's jokey reference to the famous

New York graffiti artist, and was glad to see an answering gleam of recognition in his eye. 'Maybe you should invite some of the more avant-garde gallery owners round and ask them if they're interested in an astonishing new installation,' he said. 'You could stand to make a few bob out of this, Aphrodite.'

'The form you've to fill out is on the table, by the way,' said Lola, following them through into the kitchen. She started spooning coffee into the cafetière. 'You must have witnessed thousands of these scenarios, Patrick. Can Aphrodite claim for her clothes?'

'For sure,' he said. 'Although they weren't actually stolen, they were still damaged enough for you to have to fork out for replacements.'

Aphrodite sat down at the kitchen table and ran her eyes down the insurance form. 'At least this won't take long to fill in,' she said. 'A dozen CDs and a bunch of clothes that weren't worth a whole heap of money. Thank God I'd taken my best stuff away with me.'

'A dozen CDs?' said Patrick. 'You surprise me. I would have thought that was a pretty accurate assessment, to judge by the gaps on your CD rack.'

'It *is* accurate. So why are you surprised?'

'Most people would claim for at least twice that amount. Are you sure there's nothing else missing?'

'Absolutely. I had to make an inventory for the insurance people recently. I'm really lucky I was covered at all. I'd put off doing it for ages.'

'Well. You're a remarkably honest person, Aphrodite Delaney.'

'I know,' she admitted. 'I have a pathological fear of authority figures. I think it's something to do with a dread of being found out.'

'Yeah?'

'Yeah. When I was a little girl I blushed every time I told a lie. It was an instant giveaway. I soon realized that if I just told the truth I wouldn't get half as much flak, and as a result I'm sick-makingly honest. I'd make an appalling politician.'

'Aphrodite's probably one of the most law-abiding people you're ever likely to come up against,' said Lola, sending Patrick her best smile.

'What about you?' He raised an eyebrow at her. 'Are you a good girl, too?'

'Well, you know what Mae West said. "When I'm good, I'm very, very good, but when I'm bad, I'm better."'

'I like the sound of that. Maybe you could elaborate over dinner some time?'

'Maybe.'

'When might you be free?'

'If I say let me consult my diary I'd be doing you no favours.'

'Why?'

' "Because only good girls keep diaries. Bad girls don't have the time." Tallulah Bankhead. You may have noticed that I do a mean line in quotes. It's less taxing on the brain than trying to dream up something original.'

Aphrodite felt like a spectator at Wimbledon for Flirts, what with all the arch looks and coquettish smiles that were being lobbed about her kitchen.

'But I happen to know I'm free tonight,' added Lola carelessly. 'Does that make me look too keen?'

'No. It makes you look like the kind of gal who doesn't waste time playing games.'

'And what kind of gal is that?'

'My kind,' said Patrick Larkin.

O-K. Aphrodite decided it was time to go back into the sitting room and phone Troy. In Coolnamaragh, Gareth picked up the phone.

'Hi, Aphrodite. What's the damage?'

'Not a lot was taken, but the place is a mess.'

'Shit. I *am* sorry. You'll want to talk to Troy – he's not back from their Skelligs trip yet. I can give you Jolie's number if you like?'

'No! I mean, no – it's OK. Just ask him to ring me later, will you?'

When she put the phone down, the sound of loud laughter was coming from the kitchen. She was just about to rejoin Lola and Patrick, when something made her change her mind. The laughter had stopped suddenly, to be replaced by a profound silence that could only mean one thing. When the silence finally stopped, Aphrodite plucked up the nerve to go back in. Lola and Patrick were sitting at opposite ends of the kitchen table, looking ostentatiously casual. But there were two new things about them. Lola's face was flushed, and Patrick had a faint smudge of lipstick on his chin that certainly hadn't been there before.

*   *   *

Troy rang around midnight.

'Darling! How grim for you. Why don't you just put it all out of your head, leave things the way they are for the time being and come back down to Coolnamaragh?'

'Troy – that's hardly what I'd call responsible behaviour. That's the kind of thing my mother would do.' It was also – obviously – the kind of thing Troy would do, too, she realized with a slight twinge of dismay. 'I really can't put it on the long finger. The place is a shambles. I'll have to repaint and everything.'

'Couldn't you get someone in to do it for you?' he pleaded with her. 'The weather's set to improve down here, and you know how fantastic it can be.'

'I can't, Troy. I can't afford to get a painter in. I won't be getting my insurance money for ages, and I really need the place sorted now. Anyway, I'm easily as experienced as a professional. I've spent a lot of time wielding a paintbrush lately.'

'I wish there was something I could do for you. I feel like a complete cad.'

Aphrodite laughed at the old-fashioned word. 'You're not a cad, darling. Did you get any work done today, by the way?'

'Not a thing. But Jolie and the gang are due to leave tomorrow, so I'll get into some kind of routine then.'

'How was Skellig Michael?'

'We never got there. The boats are still in for the

winter. We just stood on the cliffs on Bolus Head for ages, staring out to sea. They were like something you'd see in a dream – shrouded in mist with just the pinnacles showing. But I'll definitely do it another time. Now that I've seen them, I'm determined to get there.'

'Where did you go instead?'

'We drove on to Valencia and ran into a mutual friend, as it happens.'

'Oh? Who?'

'Jack Costello. He has a house on Valencia island.'

'The photographer?'

'Yeah. Your name came up, and he said he knew you.'

'We're really just acquaintances.'

'He's a top bloke, Jack.'

'How do you know him?'

'He's a friend of Gareth. And he's done a few photo-shoots for me. He was responsible for my last diffusion range spring catalogue. Jolie came up with a brilliant idea by the way.' Of course she did, Aphrodite didn't say. 'When she heard what had happened to your clothes she suggested you go down to the studio and get yourself kitted out in samples.'

'Samples?'

'Yeah – you know – the outfits that get made up but don't get the green light to go into production. They're once-offs, try-outs. I'd be happy for you to help yourself to anything from my daywear stuff. And Jolie reckons that, as my new muse, you ought to be wearing Troy MacNally anyway. She's right, you know – but I just hope *you* don't mind. I'd hate for you to wear anything you didn't feel comfortable in. Clothes don't look sexy on women who are uncomfortable wearing them.'

'Oh, Troy, I'd love to get decked out in your threads. I really would, but I *am* strapped for cash right now and–'

'Come off it, Aphrodite. I'm not going to charge you for samples. I'll ring Polly in the morning and tell her to look out some stuff that'll suit you. Run down and see her on Monday.'

'Are you sure?' *She* wasn't sure, she realized. She also remembered what Jolie had said to Hugo the night before, when she'd eavesdropped on their conversation in the hot tub. *I'm going to have to persuade her out of those threads she favours into something a little more* au courant. *It would never do for Troy MacNally's muse to be seen looking like some reject from a thrift shop* . . . If she allowed Troy to do this, it meant that Jolie's first stratagem in the subliminal game of warfare that was being played between the two women had succeeded. And the idea of being kitted out in a brand new wardrobe by her brand new lover made her feel a bit like . . . like a *concubine* or something. Like a kept woman. The image of Troy's former muse, sad-eyed, manacled Miriam, swam before her mind's eye.

'Am I sure?' Troy said now. 'Princess, I am absolutely sure. Be sure to phone me and tell me what you've chosen. That means I can lie in bed tomorrow night and picture exactly how I'm going to undress you. I know every hook and eye and

183

button and buttonhole on those samples. I can strip you naked in my mind's eye, inch by delectable inch.' He gave that low laugh she loved so much.

And suddenly Miriam swam before her eyes again, naked and vulnerable, lying on her tummy on a velvet couch, looking back at the painter with clouds in her eyes.

A sudden, ominous thought struck her. 'By the way, Troy – I always meant to ask you this. Who painted that portrait of Miriam that used to hang in your bathroom?'

'Jolie did,' he said.

*   *   *

Aphrodite stayed up late that night slinging paint onto her walls. She wanted to obliterate the obscenities that had been daubed there as fast as possible. She had also volunteered to do Miss Gibson's place for her, which was rash, because the next day she got a call checking out her availability for a styling gig later in the week.

'I'm so sorry,' she said down the phone to Miss Gibson. 'But I can recommend someone else who can do it. There's a scenic artist who—'

'Don't worry, Aphrodite. My nephew has already said he'll do the job. You're a good girl, and kind. I'm very lucky to have you as a neighbour.'

As soon as she put the phone down, it rang again. Phones had been going off all over the place. Troy's mobile rang incessantly and every time it did, she automatically parroted Polly Riordan's number and told the caller to try her instead. Lola had rung to say she was in love, her mother had rung to commiserate about the break-in and to winkle out any gossipy nuggets she could about Troy MacNally, and advertising people had phoned with *urgent!* details that had to be sorted *a.s.a.p.!* because things were getting *critical!* This time she picked up the phone to a harassed-sounding Polly.

'Troy tells me I'm to kit you out in some samples,' she said, sounding peremptory. 'When can you come in?'

As soon as possible, as far as Aphrodite was concerned. She wanted to surrender Troy's phone to Polly and escape the onus of fielding his bloody calls. 'This afternoon?' she ventured.

'Four o'clock,' said Polly.

* * *

Aphrodite wandered into the studio at the appointed time, after throwing another coat of paint at her walls, and was shown into an office by an unctuously smiling Saskia. Polly Riordan rose from her desk to greet her. She was small, blonde, and formidably efficient looking. She stuck out her hand and said: 'We meet at last,' making the words sound as if it was somehow Aphrodite's fault that they hadn't met till then. 'Pleased to make your acquaintance,' she added. Actually, she didn't look at all pleased, and Aphrodite didn't blame her. It must be grim, looking after all Troy's business affairs. And now poor hard-done-by Polly had a new muse to kit out on top

185

of everything else. 'Come this way,' she said, after raking her eyes perfunctorily over Aphrodite. 'I've looked out some stuff for you.'

She led the way through to a larger room beyond. Here organized confusion reigned. Costume rails crammed with clothes were ranked alongside towers constructed from bales of fabric. Piles of magazines and books covered every inch of shelf space that had not been colonized by countless glass jars containing buttons and buckles and beads. Paperwork proliferated on desktops, and pin boards bristled with magazine cuttings, sketches, and swatches of sample fabric. Here and there partially dressed tailor's dummies stood sentinel, reflected in the huge gilt-framed mirror that was bolted to the wall.

For Aphrodite this was an Aladdin's cave crammed with treasure. Even the brown paper patterns that hung from the ceiling had an emotional resonance for her. Feeling like someone living in a black-and-white film that's just been restored to glorious Technicolor, her eyes feasted on the rich textures and jewel-like colours and panels of exquisite silks and sequined embroidery. It had been a long time since she'd been in a costume shop as sexy and theatrical as this. The most luxurious item of clothing she'd handled in her recent professional past had been a cashmere cardigan worn by the star of that cling-film commercial. Here were the *real* tools of her trade! God, how she missed them! She longed to rummage and explore, but she didn't want Polly to think she was snooping.

Polly was scrutinizing her now with narrow eyes.

She had moved to a costume rail where a mini collection of samples was hanging. 'This stuff's from the diffusion line – Troy suggested a good capsule wardrobe that you can play around with. He also told me you were a size ten,' she said, 'but since his samples are cut with models in mind, you may have trouble getting into some of the more close-fitting stuff. This won't go near you.' She relegated a suit to another rail with an eloquent flourish, then proceeded to check out the other garments, inspecting each one, then slanting a look of assessment at Aphrodite. Occasionally she'd go 'tch, tch', and swish the item in question onto another rail. Every time she did it, Aphrodite felt as if she'd gone up another dress size. 'Tch!' went Polly for about the sixth time, and Aphrodite turned away.

Oh! This was intolerable! But even with her back turned, she could still feel Polly's eyes upon her. 'Who's this?' she asked finally, in a last ditch attempt to deflect attention from herself as she heard 'tch!' number seven. The 'this' in question referred to a black-and-white portrait of a slender woman that was hanging on the wall. The pose was an arrogant one: the woman's head was held high, her hair was scraped back off a face that boasted amazing sculpted cheekbones, there was a chenille stole swathed theatrically around her shoulders and her mouth was a dramatic gash in her face. Elaborate amber earrings hung from her ear lobes.

'Oh,' said Polly, 'that's Troy's aunt.' She answered in the carefully careless tones of someone who is privileged to have insider knowledge.

'The one who brought him up?'

'Yes. She was his first muse.'

'I thought Jolie Fitzgerald was.'

'No.' Polly gave her a look in which pity and contempt were mixed. 'He started designing for his aunt and her coterie of friends while he was still in his teens. Before Jolie.'

'I knew that,' said Aphrodite, despising herself for this pathetic attempt to regain ground.

Polly culled two more outfits before turning back to Aphrodite and saying: 'Check this stuff out.' By this stage, a scant half-dozen garments were hanging on the depleted rail. A phone sounded in the other room. 'I'd better take that. I'll leave you to it.' And Polly disappeared back into her own office.

Aphrodite managed to send a dagger zinging between her shoulder blades as the door swung behind her. Then she moved to the costume rail and ran her eyes along the garments on display. She wasn't sure that they were really *her*. Troy's diffusion label stuff was beautifully cut and tailored with painstaking attention to detail, but it wasn't as original as his evening creations. He'd told her that his daywear collections were only there to please the shareholders, and that if he had total autonomy he'd never design anything to be worn before eight o'clock at night. The evening gowns on the adjacent rail were more to her taste: romantic and sexy, Edwardian lady transposed to the twenty-first century. Of course it made sense to produce daywear that was wearable – anything too idiosyncratic would be commercially unviable – but the shops were full of clothes like this, the kind of clothes that the people who worked in the advertising agencies that employed her might wear.

Still, Troy had made an effort to stamp his signature on most of these sample pieces by including small, unobtrusive details – curiously wrought buttons, or unusual colours in lining materials, or delicate lacing where you might have expected a zip, or an unexpected choice of fabric. That's what differentiated his stuff from the other lookalikes that swung off the shop rails onto the streets every minute of every day.

She tried on three dresses, a handful of tops, some funky harem pants, and a quirky jacket in soft green pleated leather. Then she found her eyes sliding to a suit that Polly had relegated to the sartorial no-go area, the one she'd said wouldn't 'go near' Aphrodite. She'd never owned a suit before, and something told her that maybe it was about time she did. Feeling like a guilty child, she quickly tried it on. It fitted – just. The way it was cut flattered her figure, but it was so neatly tailored she felt constricted by it. She remembered what Troy had said on the phone the previous evening. *Clothes don't look sexy on women who are uncomfortable wearing them . . .*

Suddenly something made her feel as if she was being scrutinized again – but this time it wasn't Polly. There was something unnerving in the way Troy's aunt was regarding her from her vantage point on the wall. Aphrodite quickly stripped off Troy's threads and got back into her own street clothes, realizing as she gathered up the garments she'd selected that she would be the envy of any reader of any glossy that deserved the name.

Still, she couldn't help sending longing looks towards the rail where the furbelows and the flounces and the sexily distressed sateens sang their siren song to her as she backed through the door into Polly's office with Troy MacNally's cutting-edge samples spilling out of her arms. Carefully she set them down over the arm of a sofa.

'How did you get on?' Polly was giving her the once-over, bigtime. Aphrodite remembered how Troy had warned her that she was addicted to gossip, and something told her that she'd have to tread carefully around this woman.

'The stuff is beautiful. Thanks for looking it out for me.'

'It's worth a small fortune. You're a very lucky girl.'

Aphrodite didn't like being condescended to. Nor did she like the implication that she was gold-digging. She'd better set this woman straight. 'I wouldn't call having my house broken into and half my wardrobe destroyed being "lucky",' she said with a smile. 'But I *am* lucky to have a designer boyfriend to kit me out.'

Polly flinched when Aphrodite used the 'b' word. Uh-oh, thought Aphrodite. Is this woman jealous? This could be getting dangerous.

'He kitted out his last muse too. It's fairly standard practice.' Now she was being vicious! 'And of course, Jolie Fitzgerald never appears in public wearing anything other than Troy MacNally.' The phone rang. 'Hello? Troy MacNally's office? Troy! Hi!' The timbre of Polly's voice changed at once. She practically gushed down the phone, and Aphrodite saw that she'd pinkened. She *was* jealous! Now things started to make sense. Polly Riordan had the hots for her boss. 'Mm-hm. Mm-hm. Yes. Actually, she's here now – she's just finished helping herself.' Helping herself! How crass that sounded! 'Hang on a sec.' Polly put her hand over the receiver and said: 'He wants to speak with his new *muse*.' She invested the word with such contempt that she might as well have substituted the word 'whore'.

Aphrodite took the phone from her. 'Hi, darling.' Polly looked away at once and pretended to busy herself with the desk diary, but Aphrodite could tell that she was earwigging shamelessly. 'Yes. Thank you so much. They're beautiful. No. No – there was no evening dress. Will you? Are you sure, Troy? Wow. You are an angel. Yes. Well, thank you.' She laughed at what he said next, a low, husky, intimate laugh that she knew would get right up Polly Riordan's nose. The bitch deserved to feel a little pain. 'Oh, yes, I still have it, but I was going to leave it with Polly. Oh. Are you sure? Well – OK – if you feel you can trust me to sweet-talk for you.' Another laugh. 'Sure. Talk to you later. Bye, darling.' Then: 'Oh, Troy! I just remembered – I left my portfolio in our bedroom in Coolnamaragh.' She noticed with pleasure that Polly's expression contorted at the word 'our'. 'Will you bring it back with you, when you're coming? Thanks, darling.' She put the phone down and then said – in a voice that she very carefully kept free of any trace of accusation – 'Troy said he'd asked you to look out some evening stuff for me.'

'Did he?' Polly sounded unconcerned.

'Yes. For any functions that come up. It's quite important, apparently.'

'Well!' She was on the defensive now. 'I suppose I'm entitled to slip up sometimes. I'm kept extremely busy here, and looking out clothes for Troy's current girlfriend wasn't hugely high on my list of priorities, as you can imagine.' Jesus! This woman was as poisonous as Jolie Fitzgerald. 'I'll get round to it some time.'

'Don't bother,' retorted Aphrodite. 'He said he'd do it himself.'

The land line rang again. 'You'll need a few bags for your spoils, won't you?' said Polly before picking up. She nodded her head towards what appeared to be a broom cupboard. 'You'll find some old plastic carriers in there. Hello? Troy MacNally's office? Yes? Yes. OK, just let me make a note of that.' She reached for a pen and started making notes in a desk diary with ruthless efficiency.

Aphrodite turned to the door Polly had indicated. It did indeed open into a broom cupboard. Between the Hoover and a broken ironing board was a cardboard box containing a load of crumpled Tesco bags. She felt a sense of profound humiliation as she crouched down, preparing to help herself to half a dozen. Then she reconsidered. What was she *doing*, allowing herself to be treated like this? She'd fucking well *had* it with Troy's female cohorts treating her with such arrant disrespect! She stuffed the plastic bags back into the box, shut the door of the cupboard and sat down opposite Polly, who gave her an impatient look, as if she wished that Aphrodite would just go away and stop annoying her.

Aphrodite looked back, level and icy. She was going to have to start calling some shots around here, otherwise her life would be made miserable by Troy MacNally's associates. She'd done it with Saskia downstairs – she could bloody well do it with Polly Riordan. Jolie was a more formidable adversary, but she'd cross that particular bridge when she came to it.

'OK,' said Polly into the phone. 'Yes, that makes sense. Yep. Talk to you later. Bye.' She put the phone down. 'What's the problem?' she said, leaning back in her chair and treating Aphrodite to a disdainful look. 'Can't hack the ignominy of walking down the street like a bag lady?' She said it in a jokey voice, but Aphrodite knew that the jokey voice was adopted to camouflage the seething contempt this woman had for her. She didn't care if word got back to Troy: she was going to have to kick ass.

She deliberately mirrored Polly's body language, leaning back in her chair and laying languid forearms on the arm rests. 'Polly,' she said, in a tone of casual menace. 'I don't give a shit what kind of bags I walk down the street with. I'm just beyond appalled that you suggest I sling Troy's creations into plastic carriers, and I suspect Troy would be beyond appalled also – *if* he were told. Please pack these clothes properly, and have them delivered to my house later. This should cover the delivery charge.' She extracted her wallet from her backpack, slid a twenty out of it, and dropped the banknote on Polly's desk.

Just as she was about to stand up, Troy's mobile went off. She withdrew it from her pocket, and Polly stretched a hand out for it. Aphrodite noticed that the hand was a little shaky. 'Sorry,' she said pleasantly to the other woman. 'Troy wants me to man his mobile.' She gave the PA a sweet smile, pressed 'talk', and answered Troy's phone with an assurance bred of bravado. 'No. I'm afraid he's not available, but perhaps I can help you. Aphrodite Delaney. Yes. He should be back by then. Let's see.' She reached for the diary that lay between her and Polly on the desktop. 'Sorry. He has an engagement that afternoon, but the next day is clear. I will put you down in very heavy pencil.' A friendly laugh. 'Nice to talk to you, likewise. Oh? How lovely! I'll look forward to that. Goodbye.'

She scribbled something in the diary, feeling as she did so like a smug cat marking another feline's territory. Then she returned the phone to her pocket, and looked back at Polly Riordan. 'I had hoped that you might like me, Polly, but that's obviously not the case, and frankly, I can't be bothered worrying any more about whether you like me or not. But the fact is that we're likely to be seeing quite a lot of each other in the future, and it's in both our interests if we get along. So if you're prepared to help me out a little, I'd appreciate it. Incidentally, I suspect that I am made of much tougher stuff than Miriam de

Courcy was. I think it's only fair to warn you.' She rose to her feet. 'Enjoy the rest of your day. Oh – and Troy expressed a desire not to be disturbed for the next week or so. Please feel free to contact me if you need anything run by him. Don't worry – I know that ex-directory number off by heart now.'

And then Aphrodite turned on her heel and strode out of the door, with her head held high and her heart pumping with nervous adrenalin.

Once on the street, heading for the bus stop, the adrenalin metabolized into just nervousness. The confrontation with Polly had unsettled her a lot more than she would've liked to let on. Beneath her carapace of cool she'd felt as quivery as Jodie Foster in *Panic Room*. She'd never done anything like that in her life before. She'd never found herself in a situation where she'd *had* to.

What had it all been about? A pecking order thing, she supposed. Polly Riordan perceived herself as Troy's right-hand woman, and it was presumably something she felt strongly enough about to lock horns with anyone who looked like a contender for her position. Except Jolie Fitzgerald, of course. Polly would never dream of talking to Jolie the way she'd talked to Aphrodite. Nobody on the face of the planet would.

Jesus Christ! The more Aphrodite learned about the people who inhabited the new stratosphere she was entering, the more certain she became of the importance of watching her back. It looked like guerrilla warfare was as epidemic in the fashion industry as it was in the theatre industry, and it was more than likely that there would be further battles to be waged. Aphrodite bit her lip as she boarded the bus. The round she'd just fought may have won her respect, but she'd made a serious enemy. Had she done the right thing? It was impossible to know.

She knew later that she had done the right thing when she ran the story by Lola. When she got to the bit about answering Troy's phone, Lola spat red wine all over the kitchen table, and when she'd finally stopped choking with delighted incredulity, Lola had just said: 'You go, girl!'

Chapter Eight

The following week Aphrodite spent redecorating, singing tunelessly along to her love song compilation CD as she slapped paint onto the walls, trying to decide which song was hers and Troy's. She also spent a lot of time fielding Troy's calls and relaying information to Polly Riordan. Initially, she wasn't sure how she'd hack having to talk to Polly, but she found that she loved being able to pick up the phone to her and be put straight through as if she was the President. Once she'd been asked if she could hold, but even though she had just finished painting her nails and could have held for the eternity it took them to dry she just said 'no', and she was put through without further preamble.

'Hi, Polly!' she'd say in her best singsongy voice, making sure to use loads of exclamation marks. 'Isn't it a beautiful day! Here's yet *another* entry for Troy's diary! Goodness! What a busy time we're in for when he gets back! His engagement book must be crammed fuller than Nicky Haslam's in *Hello!*'

And every day Polly rang her, to run by her all the invites that had been mailed to the studio. There were parties and launches and lunches and charity gigs and film premières and exhibition openings and scary formal dinners to be attended. Everyone wanted a piece of him, because the presence of Troy MacNally at any of these events enhanced the social standing of the individual concerned or endorsed whatever product they were desperate to push, or – in some truly sad cases – simply validated their existence.

One day Polly phoned to tell Aphrodite that Troy had received an invitation to the hottest theatrical opening of the year, which was none other than David Lawless's production of *The Seagull*, starring Thea Delaney, and designed by Damien Gobshite Whelan. Would they be attending?

Aphrodite's first reaction was to say 'no'. The prospect of turning up at an opening night and running into Damien Whelan with his alligator smile was about as appealing as committing hara-kiri with her dressmaking shears. And then Polly said something that made Aphrodite stop up short. She said: 'I also received a charming letter from the designer of the show, Damien Whelan, asking if Troy would be interested in doing costume designs for an upcoming David Lawless production of *Antony and Cleopatra*. Will you run the idea by Troy when you're next speaking to him, Aphrodite?'

Aphrodite was only half listening. She was too busy thinking. She'd obviously let an ominous silence fall, because the next thing she heard Polly say in her ear was: 'Please.'

'Absolutely, Polly. I'm sure Troy will be very flattered that a theatre designer as eminent as Damien Whelan is interested in collaborating with him. And will you RSVP in the affirmative to the invitation to the opening of *The Seagull*? We'd *love* to go.'

'Certainly, Aphrodite. And may I ask –' there was a hint of anxiety creeping into Polly's voice now, the merest soupçon of gratifying desperation. 'May I ask how Troy's autumn designs are coming along?'

'I'm delighted to be able to tell you, Polly,' pronounced Aphrodite in the manner of a benefactress distributing largesse, 'that the designs are finished. And that Troy is coming back to Dublin tomorrow.'

'Oh! That's excellent news, Aphrodite!'

'Yes. He's been working flat out. He rang me at three o'clock this morning to tell me that he'd just finished, and that he was cracking a bottle of champagne to celebrate.'

'Oh! Poor Troy, working such punishing hours! Oh, he really shouldn't do that to himself! He'll burn himself out if he's not careful!'

'Don't worry, Polly. I'll take care of him once he gets back. I'll make sure he's tucked up in bed well before midnight every night this week.' Aphrodite's solicitous tones were belied by the expression on her face, which was one of unabashedly triumphant glee. And when she put the phone down to Polly, she finally allowed herself the luxury of laughing out loud.

*   *   *

The next evening Troy took her out to dinner to celebrate the fact that he'd finally finished his autumn collection. 'Thanks to you,' he said, raising his glass to her. Then he sat back in his chair and surveyed the room. 'Ha! Look at the expressions on their faces.'

'Whose faces?'

'Our fellow diners'. The men want to touch you as much as I do, and the women are all jealous. I can't say I blame them. You wear Troy MacNally extremely well, even though I can put my hand on my heart and say that you look even better with nothing on at all.'

She was wearing her favourite this evening – a little grey mercerized cotton with a drop waist and a pale pink tulle petticoat. She'd discovered that while the tulle was very pretty to look at, it was quite scratchy to wear. She supposed that was the reason this particular sample had never made it to the production stage.

'Well, you've a treat in store for later, then. I think we should share a bath when we get back to your gaff. Speaking of later, when am I going to get to see your new designs?'

'In bed tonight,' Troy told her. 'After I've rogered you rotten.'

'Goodie.'

'Goodie to the designs or to the rogering?'

'Both.' She gave a cat-who-got-the-cream smile, and then said: 'Oh! I nearly forgot!'

'What?'

'Damien Whelan wants to know if you'd be interested in designing costumes for *Antony and Cleopatra*. David Lawless is directing an all-star

200

production, and Damien's doing the set.'

'David Lawless? Wow. Top class director. I'm not sure about Whelan, though. His stuff's a bit derivative.'

'Tell me about it.'

'What do you mean?'

'Oh. I'm not sure I should tell you this.' She focused the full beam of her attention on him and said, in a carefully categorical voice: 'You see, Troy, I have very strong personal feelings about the man, and I wouldn't want to run the risk of prejudicing you against him.'

'Oh, go on. I know he's a vicious queen, so I'm prejudiced anyway.'

'I – Oh God. I haven't told anyone about this apart from my friend, Lola. I just know that no-one else would believe me – it's such a preposterous claim to make against anyone . . .'

'*What*, Aphrodite?'

She took a deep breath and launched into the story about the awful night in the Trocadero, when Damien Whelan had eavesdropped on her design concept for *The Seagull*, and how her mother had told her that he was using her ideas for the current production. She bit her lip when she finished. 'Do you believe me?' she asked.

'The bastard! Damn right I believe you. Hell – I'm not even that surprised. And I'm very *glad* you told me, because it's made my mind up. It'll give me great pleasure now to be able to tell Damien Whelan to stuff his job offer.'

Aphrodite gave him a complicitous look. 'We've

been invited to the opening of the show on Thursday night.'

'Good. In that case I'll be able to tell him to his face.'

'You won't tell him the reason, will you?'

'Of course not. But when he sees you with me I'm sure he'll hazard a pretty accurate guess.'

Aphrodite smiled at the waiter who was just setting her plate down in front of her. It was a remarkably radiant smile. And later, on her way to the loo she tried the same smile out on an elderly gentleman who was dining solo at an adjacent table. She was practising. She was practising the kind of smile she was going to send Damien Whelan on Thursday night when Troy MacNally told him that he wasn't remotely interested in working with him on this – or any other – project.

*   *   *

She was doing rather a lot of smiling these days, she realized, as she lay beside Troy in his big mahogany bed much later. He'd insisted on undressing her himself as soon as he'd shut the front door behind him, and it had been the sexiest thing he had yet done to her. His hands had moved with languid assurance as he'd located fasteners and buttons and zips, encouraging her to raise a co-operative arm here, bend an obliging knee there, so that he could strip her even more expertly, brushing deft fingers over erogenous zones as more items of clothing dematerialized. With maddening slowness he'd slid fingers down over her breasts, her belly, her pudenda, applying pressure there with the heel of his hand, and then he'd finally crooked a finger inside the elastic of her pants and slid it inside her. She'd heard a murmur of approval as he manipulated her with a silky dexterity that took her breath away. 'Good girl,' he'd said. 'All ready for me. Shall we take that bath now?'

But Aphrodite hadn't been able to wait for the bath. She'd come there and then, pressed up against the hard wood of Troy MacNally's front door.

Now they were lying in drowsy post-orgasmic bliss, Troy with his head resting on her belly. He was humming something she knew, but she couldn't quite place it. Then: 'I know!' she said. 'It's the tune from that ad for that super groovy new car.'

'Is it? I wouldn't know. I never watch television. It's actually the chorus from *Aida*.'

'Oh. How I hate the way advertisers do that!'

'What?'

'Steal classical tunes so that when you hear them, instead of being uplifted by the music, all that comes into your head is an image of the product they're bombarding you with. All I can see in my mind's eye now is that car whizzing along through the beauty of nature.'

'So they're stealing the beauty of nature now, as well?' asked Troy in a bantering voice.

'Yeah! Bastards.'

'But I do that, too.'

'What do you mean?'

'I just spent the past two weeks plundering nature for my designs.'

'But that's different, Troy. You're an artist.'

'I bet the bloke responsible for putting that ad together considers himself to be an artist, too.'

Aphrodite pulled a scathing face. 'Probably. I worked with a guy recently who thought he was the greatest artist since da Vinci. I was styling an ad for "traditional" gravy granules—'

'Does such an anomaly exist?'

'Believe it or not,' said Aphrodite in her best spooky voice. 'The world out there is pretty scary, Troy. Anyway, I had to set the table up to look like something out of Dickens, and the way the director instructed me to place product, you'd think I was some acolyte setting up items of worship on an altar. When I'd finished he stood there looking at it with his hands pressed against his mouth, like this –' Aphrodite demonstrated '– and then he raised his arm in this big theatrical gesture and said: "Cobwebs!"'

'Cobwebs?'

'Yeah. I had to go to inordinate lengths to get hold of fake cobweb to drape over the bottle of claret on the table, so that it looked like it had just emerged from a wine cellar.'

'Did it work?'

'No. It just looked really stupid sitting next to all the polished glasses and cutlery. It took me ages to persuade him to lose it. He knew it looked stupid, but he didn't want to admit it because it had been his idea.'

Troy imitated the stance she'd mimicked and repeated the word 'Cobwebs!' in a pompous voice. 'Yes, indeed! Cobwebs!'

'What on earth are you on about?'

'I'm going to say that every time I come up with a brilliant idea. I've just had one.'

'Share it with me.'

'I want you to direct the shoot for the autumn catalogue.'

'Seriously?'

'Seriously.'

'Well. Um – wow. I'd love to.' Aphrodite felt incredibly flattered to have been asked. 'Is this another part of my brief as muse?'

'Yeah. It's not that uncommon for muses to take that kind of artistic control, you know. Think of Amanda Harlech and Galliano. Think of Donatella – the powerhouse behind Versace. She was hugely instrumental in his success story before she became a big star in her own right. See her as your role model.'

'I'm really not a big Versace fan.'

'It doesn't matter. Look at the broader picture, look at what you might achieve.' Troy laughed, and swung himself out of bed suddenly. 'Cobwebs!' he proclaimed.

'What bright idea have you had now?' she asked.

'I'm going to fetch my portfolio,' he said. 'I want you to take a look at my new stuff.'

He went out into the hall and came back with his portfolio under his arm. Getting back into bed beside Aphrodite, he undid the cords that fastened it, and drew out a sheaf of paper.

'Oh!' said Aphrodite, looking at the topmost drawing. 'It really is cobwebs!'

'Yeah,' said Troy. 'Remember I took a load of photographs of that extraordinary cobweb on that magnolia tree in Ilnacullin? That's what inspired this design.' Then: 'Well? What do you think?' he asked.

'Oh, Troy! They're really, really beautiful.'

And they were. Aphrodite leafed through page after page of the quite exquisite drawings Troy had done in Coolnamaragh. The garments were magical – like something wood nymphs might wear. The fabrics depicted were gossamer: fragile and diaphanous as the spider's web from which he'd drawn inspiration. Most of the colours were autumnal, reminiscent of the landscape around Coolnamaragh – the gold of wind-dried grass, the russet of last year's fallen leaves, the purple of the heather that had carpeted the mountains . . . He truly had plundered the wealth of nature.

Because he'd worked so hard, he'd actually got ahead of himself: there was even a handful of designs for next spring's collection. These drawings were inspired by the stirrings of new life that they'd seen emerging in rural Kerry – tentative leaf greens, palest daffodil yellows, with an occasional vibrant flash of the hot pink or blood red that they'd seen amongst the exotica in Ilnacullin.

'A mermaid's dress!' said Aphrodite, lighting upon a slinky green number.

'Yeah. I got the idea for that the afternoon I went to Valencia with Jolie and Hugo. We were on a stretch of deserted beach, and I found this fantastic skein of seaweed. I told Jolie that I wished you were there, so I could drape you in it –' Aphrodite thanked God for small mercies – 'but Jolie very obligingly volunteered to stand in for you.'

Aphrodite froze in her perusal of the designs. 'What? What do you mean?'

'She stripped off so that I could experiment with the stuff on her.'

Oh! The sense of outrage she felt shocked her. *She* was Troy's muse! How *dare* Jolie Fitzgerald impersonate her! She struggled hard with her feelings as she leafed through the remaining drawings with numb fingers and unseeing eyes, trying to tamp down the volcano that was threatening to erupt inside her. She felt almost as violated as she'd done when she'd returned to Dublin from Coolnamaragh to find her house trashed. Jolie Fitzgerald had overstepped the mark, and Aphrodite was damn sure she wasn't going to allow her to pull a stunt like that ever, ever again.

'I'd been thinking along the lines of tropical island,' Troy was saying now, 'but we won't have a huge budget, so the locations won't be madly glamorous.'

'Sorry? Sorry, Troy – I wasn't listening. I was too gobsmacked by your drawings. They really are fabulous.' She boxed the pages neatly, then put them back into Troy's portfolio. 'What were you saying?'

'I was talking about the location for the autumn catalogue shoot. Jolie suggested that there might be a nice irony in photographing models in building sites or factories. She rather liked the idea of juxtaposing such aspirational clothes against a background of grim industrial banality – the antithesis of the natural world that inspired them.'

'Oh?' Aphrodite was completely focused now, and thinking furiously. 'Don't you think that's a bit London Fashion Week Y2K?' she said. 'Remember when they staged shows in car parks and other vaguely seedy locations?'

Troy looked uncertain. 'Oh, yeah. Maybe you're right,' he said. 'Maybe it *is* a bit of a hackneyed idea.' Aphrodite resisted the urge to crow. 'Where would you suggest?' he asked.

She thought even more furiously. 'Well,' she said, 'it's interesting that Damien Whelan should have approached you about designing costumes for the theatre. Don't you think the dividing line between fashion and theatre is becoming more and more blurred, Troy?'

'I guess. Catwalk shows are definitely getting stagier, that's for sure.'

'So how about this? How about approaching a really old-fashioned theatre like the Gaiety, and asking if you could stage a shoot there? All that ornate gilt and plush would act as a kind of visual contrapunto to the simplicity and fragility of your designs. Um. It would be a way of showing nature juxtaposed against the artifice that's implicit in the very word "theatre".' She was thinking on her feet here, winging it wildly. She didn't think the idea was particularly inspired or clever, but she wanted to see whose idea he'd buy – hers or Jolie's.

'That's good,' said Troy, the slow smile that was spreading across his face reflecting the one on hers. 'I like it.'

'Think: models framed by the parameters of the private boxes – you know the ones that are practically on top of the stage? Think: models against that vast expanse of faded plush curtain. Think: models on stage under a spotlight, with dust motes drifting round them. Imagine the wonderful, grainy, soft-focus effects you could achieve.'

She could tell Troy was impressed. 'Well, Aphrodite Delaney,' he said. 'You have come up with one of the most original ideas ever hatched by a muse of mine.' He pushed her back against the pillows and looked down at her. 'What a fantastic fucking team we're going to make! You deserve a reward for coming up with that!'

And as he began to trail kisses over her breasts and down her belly, and as she wriggled with pleasure, Aphrodite was thinking: Ha! Round two to me, Jolie Fitzgerald! And then what Troy had said to her earlier about Donatella came back to her. Donatella. The powerhouse behind Versace. She dared to try it out: Aphrodite. The powerhouse behind Troy MacNally. It sounded good. The final thought that struck her as she surrendered herself to the lovely muzzy sexy feeling Troy was conjuring up in her was: Aphrodite Delaney. The power behind the throne . . .

*   *   *

The next day Troy took himself off to his studio to have serious consultations with his pattern cutter and machinists. And Polly, of course. He was under pressure to have toiles – prototypes in calico – of his designs made up as soon as possible. Aphrodite joined him around five o'clock. He had told her he wanted to look out something stunning for her to wear at tomorrow night's glitzy opening in the Phoenix theatre.

She was shown up to the machine room by a deferential Saskia. The room was buzzing with the noise of sewing machines, and loud pop music blared from the radio. Aphrodite recognized the 98FM jingle. Troy was lounging against the vast pattern-cutting table, staring into space, seemingly oblivious to the din.

'I wouldn't have thought you were a 98FM fan,' she remarked as she joined him.

'I'm not,' said Troy. 'But the machinists are.' He kissed her on the tip of her nose, and Aphrodite was aware that she was being covertly scrutinized by the women operating the sewing machines. A flutter of gossip ran round the room, making Aphrodite feel suddenly self-conscious. She felt even more self-conscious when Troy took her by the hand and led her through Polly's office into his. Polly was on the phone, but she covered the mouthpiece with her hand and gave Aphrodite a bright: 'Hi there!' as she passed. Aphrodite wiggled her fingers at her and twinkled 'Hi there!' back.

'OK,' said Troy, indicating the costume rail where last season's *faux*-genteel Edwardiana languished. 'Let's kit you out.' He ran appraising eyes over her, and immediately Aphrodite felt that overwhelming urge to take all her clothes off again. He turned to the rail and selected a full-length costume with a bustle skirt in cream calico.

'Oh, yes!' said Aphrodite. 'I want it!'

Troy slid the gown off its hanger, held it out at arm's length, shoulder to shoulder with Aphrodite, and assessed the look with analytical eyes. 'No,' he said. 'Wrong colour. Green is more you.' He returned the dress to the rail, and rummaged for something else, finally producing a similarly cut gown in a subtle shade of sage green. 'Try this one,' he said.

Aphrodite lost her street threads and slid into the sage-green costume. It took ages to do up all the little buttons that ran from the high neck to just below the waist. There were buttons, too, on the tight-fitting sleeves. If there hadn't been, she would never have been able to get her hands through the cuffs. Troy took a step back, folded his arms and narrowed his eyes, giving her that analytical look again. 'Good,' he said. 'Very good. Muss your hair more. Yeah. Now – wait a sec.' He reached into a wicker skip and did some more rummaging, finally producing the kind of velveteen riding hat an Edwardian lady would have worn. 'Let's see. Gloves would be good. And

211

boots. Little lace-up ankle boots. I'll send Polly out for some. Take a look at yourself, princess.'

Aphrodite turned to face the big gilt mirror on the wall behind her. If it wasn't for her anachronistic messy blond crop and the fact that Troy had invested the gown with his trademark quirkiness, she could have walked straight out of a BBC period drama. The tight-fitting bodice made her waist look tiny, and the way it constricted her bosom actually made her feel pretty damn sexy.

'Oh! Thank you, thank you, thank you!' She turned back to him, eyes shining, and planted a big kiss on his mouth, then turned back to the mirror and executed a twirl, relishing the satisfying swish of the skirt against her bare legs.

'You look like some very lucky schoolboy's governess,' said Troy. 'Only less strict. A very fuck-able governess indeed.' He nodded in the direction of his desk. 'Sit up there for me, darling, and lift your skirt.'

She sent a cautious look towards the door. 'Polly might come in.'

'Polly,' he said, 'knows very much better than to disturb me when I'm fitting a muse.'

'OK,' she said meekly, slanting him a smile. 'You're the boss.' She sat up on the table and took hold of the hem of the dress. 'I suppose you want to make some alterations to the length?' she asked with a disingenuous look.

'No,' he said. 'I just have a sudden burning urge to reacquaint myself with your inside leg measure-ments.'

* * *

The opening night of *The Seagull* was seriously glitzy. Eva Lavery had flown in from LA to be at her husband's side. Gabriel Byrne was there, chatting to Seamus Heaney and the Taoiseach. Bono and the Edge were there with their wives, Bob Geldof was at the bar buying drinks for Rory McDonagh and Deirdre O'Dare, and film star Sophie Burke was posing for an *Irish Times* photographer alongside Ireland's answer to Tara Palmer-Tomkinson. Those model twins she'd seen chatting up Jack Costello in the Troc were there, wearing practically nothing.

As Aphrodite wandered back into the heaving foyer after a trip to the loo, she heard her mobile whimper from the little beaded handbag she'd picked up in a second-hand shop. It was Lola, clearly pissed.

'Hey, Aphrodite! Patrick persuaded me to ring you. I told him you'd be hanging with a bunch of famous people tonight, and he wants all the insider gen. Who's all there? Is the weathergirl there?'

'Jesus, Lola!' Aphrodite had to laugh. 'Yes she is, as a matter of fact.'

'Wow. The weathergirl's there, Patrick! How high does she score on the celebrity point scale? Pah! A mere *deux points*, Aphrodite, according to Patrick. You can do better than that!'

'OK. How's this?' Aphrodite reeled out a litany of A-list celebrity names. When she got to Bono, Lola cheered.

'Yay! Ten out of ten for Bono and the Edge! Ha!

Who'd have thought a year ago that you'd have hooked up with the Celtic tiger superstar set, Aphrodite?'

'And tigresses. That scary person Jolie Fitzgerald has just prowled in. There's some serious air-kissing going on.'

'I dare you to kick the Taoiseach up the arse,' said Lola. 'That would get your picture in the papers.'

Aphrodite laughed again. 'Stop being so irreverent, Lo. I'm going to have to go and sit through some serious art in ten minutes' time. Oh – wow! I've just spotted Ronan Keating, and I'm sure that's a Corr over there.'

'Sure, isn't it blessed we are to be Oirish,' said Lola. 'Sure, aren't we the trendiest nation on earth? Begorrah, *céad míle fáilte, ceol agus craic* and *póg mo thóin.* Go pose, Aphrodite!'

'Bye, Lola.' Aphrodite tucked the phone back in her tiny bag, a wry smile on her face. When she next looked up, steeling herself against the excitement of seeing yet another celebrity, she found Jack Costello's amused eyes upon her.

'What a consummate chameleon you are,' he said.

Aphrodite felt her face going pink. 'What do you mean?' she asked.

'You look different every time I see you.' He raised his glass to her, then knocked back the remaining red wine that was in it. 'I hear we may be working together in the near future,' he said, setting the empty glass down on a nearby table.

'You're shooting a commercial?'

'No. I just ran into Troy. He tells me you're

directing the shoot for his autumn catalogue. I'm photographing it.'

'Oh. Great. Well. Maybe we should meet up some time and trade ideas?'

'Sure. I'll call you.'

A woman's voice came from somewhere to his right. 'Jack! How's it going?' An elegant arm serpented with bangles was waving at him above the heads of the surrounding crowd.

'Oh, hi, um –' said Jack vaguely. 'Sorry – can't stop to talk.' He turned back to Aphrodite. 'Excuse me. I've got to get out of this joint.'

'Aren't you staying for the show?'

'No. I'm here in a work capacity.'

'Oh? Publicity shots?'

'No. I'm doing a series of portraits of actors. I wanted to get candid backstage shots. Your mother is Thea Delaney, isn't she?'

'Yes.'

'I got a fantastic shot of her doing her pre-show vocal warm-up.'

Uh-oh, thought Aphrodite. She knew that the cast would have done their warm-up before getting into make-up. She was reasonably sure that Thea wouldn't thank Jack Costello for taking a shot of her without her face on, and with her mouth stretched wide going 'Mee mee mee', the way actors did during vocal sessions.

Aphrodite cast around for further conversation, but she needn't have bothered because Jack Costello just said, 'Enjoy your evening,' and was gone.

Aphrodite watched his retreating back. His big,

shambling figure in its battered sheepskin jacket looked very out of place here as he made his way laboriously through the crowd, clearly trying to avoid catching people's eyes. She noticed that they tried to catch his, though. Sheaves of slender arms were waved at him during his progress and a chorus of fluty female voices harmonized in greeting.

Troy was talking to Jolie when Aphrodite rejoined him. Jolie looked glorious in indigo Troy MacNally.

'Aphrodite! You look divine! Doesn't Troy suit you!' The two women observed the air-kissing ritual, and as Aphrodite inhaled the scent of Poison, she realized that flashbulbs were going off.

'Jolie! How are you this evening? Looking forward to the show?' A woman was standing by her elbow with a biro poised over a notebook. Aphrodite recognized her as Andrea Mooney, the social diarist of a popular daily newspaper. So many reputations had been incinerated on the pyre of her gossip column that it was colloquially known as 'Andrea's Ashes'. The photographer with her had lowered his camera and was looking round for further quarry.

'Hi, Andrea,' returned Jolie with an incandescent smile. 'Absolutely am I looking forward to it. And I imagine Aphrodite is, too.' Jolie included Aphrodite in the conversation by snaking an arm around her waist. 'Her mother's playing Arkadina.'

'Oh?' Andrea turned an expression of polite interest on Aphrodite. 'And you are . . . ?'

'Aphrodite Delaney. My mother is Thea Delaney.'

Andrea started scribbling in her notebook. 'And are you an actress too?'

'No,' said Aphrodite. 'I'm a – a design consultant.'

'She's also Troy MacNally's new muse,' put in Jolie helpfully. 'Isn't she, Troy?'

Troy cleared his throat. 'Yes,' he said. 'Aphrodite and I have discovered that we share a great – er – rapport.'

'Really?' Andrea's interested expression became even more interested. 'So you two are an item?'

'Er – yes,' said Troy.

'Since when?'

Troy was clearly so uncomfortable discussing his private life with this woman that Aphrodite felt compelled to help him out. 'It all happened very fast,' she provided. 'Troy commissioned me to do some work on his apartment recently, and it's kind of taken off since then.'

'Is that Troy MacNally you're wearing now?'

'Yes.'

'And doesn't she wear it well!' sang Jolie for the second time that evening. 'By the way, Andrea – did you know that Troy is to be Ireland's newest hot fashion expert? He's had orders from Saks Fifth Avenue, and the Japanese are taking an interest as well.'

'Going international? Congratulations, Troy!' Scribble, scribble, scribble. 'Well! I suppose you'll be wearing threads by Troy MacNally for the fore-seeable future, Aphrodite?'

Aphrodite laughed. 'I don't have much choice. Virtually my entire wardrobe was destroyed in an accident recently, and Troy was generous enough to kit me out.'

Andrea put her head on one side and gave Aphrodite an enquiring look. 'How does it feel being a muse?'

'Um. A bit bemusing, to be perfectly honest!'

'Very good!' The woman laughed at the awful pun and scribbled harder. Then: 'Thank you,' she said. 'D'you know, I'd love to do a full-length feature on designers' muses. Would you be interested in doing an interview with me some time, Aphrodite?'

Aphrodite looked uncertain. There was a beat or two of uneasy silence as she and Troy exchanged looks. Then suddenly she heard Jolie say: 'Hey! What a compliment, Aphrodite! No-one expressed any interest in interviewing *me* when I was Troy's muse in the days before I became a plain old housewife and mother! Could muses be the new rock stars?'

'What a great idea for headline copy, Jolie,' remarked Andrea. 'You'll do it, Aphrodite, won't you?'

'Um. Sure,' said Aphrodite, feeling anything but. She slid her business card out of her evening purse. 'Here's my card.'

'Cheers! I'll be in touch,' promised Andrea before negotiating her way through the crowd to where her colleague was flashing away with his camera.

Jolie gave Aphrodite her catlike smile. 'Nice little publicity coup, Aphrodite,' she said smoothly. 'You handled that beautifully. Didn't she, Troy?'

'Hell, yes,' he said, sounding relieved. 'Much

better than I would have done, that's for sure. I always get tongue-tied and inarticulate when I have to talk to the press.'

'Maybe you should allow Aphrodite to be your official spokesperson, then. Take some of the weight off Polly's shoulders. Oh! There's Sophie Burke!' The expression that crossed Jolie's face reminded Aphrodite of a hunter readjusting his sights. The film star was fluttering into view in what had to be Versace. 'Sophie!' cooed Jolie. 'Come and meet Troy's new muse!'

Chapter Nine

Aphrodite had to admit that Damien Gobshite Whelan's – or rather, *her* plagiarized design for *The Seagull* worked like a dream. Rage had been seething away inside her since the curtain went up, and it hit flash point when her mother swished onto the stage as the glamorous Arkadina in her peacock frock. People actually gasped out loud, making Aphrodite want to hiss and boo. She was tempted to run down the central aisle, leap onto the stage and denounce Damien Whelan in front of the glittering, chittering celebrity audience as they rose at the end of the play to give their standing ovation.

There was a party after the show. Troy hadn't much wanted to go, but Aphrodite felt obliged to, for her mother's sake. She needn't have worried about her mother. The only thing Thea had said to her was: 'What did you think of my frocks?' before she was headhunted and carried off like a trophy by someone effecting celebrity introductions.

Not very many of the truly stellar celebrities had bothered attending. Aphrodite presumed it was because they had lives they felt like living the following day. The weathergirl had turned up, and the Tara Palmer-Tomkinson clone, and the model twins, and Damien Gobshite Whelan. Sophie Burke was the biggest star who showed – apart from Eva Lavery, of course, who had to be there for her husband. But David Lawless was looking tired, and the celebrated couple made their exit quite early on in the proceedings.

Jolie introduced Aphrodite to loads of people as Troy's new muse, and she wasn't sure whether she felt chuffed or embarrassed. However, she couldn't help prinking smugly at the aghast look that appeared on Damien Whelan's face when he over-heard Jolie introducing her to the model twins. The model twins looked suspicious and glared at her a bit when they heard the muse news, but they went smiley again when Troy told them he wanted them to do his autumn catalogue. The highlight of the evening for Aphrodite was when Damien tried to lure Troy into a corner, and he wouldn't go. 'Let's just say I've too much on my plate already, Damien,' Aphrodite heard him say, and she found herself going 'hee hee hee' like a six-year-old.

However, the next morning's hangover made her feel about ninety. It wasn't helped by the fact that she'd had very little sleep, and what little she'd had had been fitful. Troy had been restless during the night, tossing and turning a lot. Around dawn she'd thought that he wanted to make love, but when she'd opened her sleepy eyes and focused on his face, she saw that he was still very much asleep. The other thing she saw was that his face was wet with tears. 'Troy?' she'd said, stroking his hair. 'Troy?' But he hadn't woken up.

When they surfaced, she decided not to mention

the incident to him. She always hated it when people told her about things she'd done in her sleep: she didn't like the way it made her feel so *exposed*. 'Are you going into the studio today?' she asked him now as she shambled from the kitchen to the bedroom bearing a tray laden with orange juice, bagels and coffee. The Jewish bakery nearby did the best ones in town, and on her way back to Troy's apartment she'd picked up any papers that were likely to carry reviews of last night's show.

'No. Everything's under control. I don't really need to go in again until the toiles are ready.'

'Here's the post.'

'Yeuch. Brown envelopes.' Troy dived back under the duvet. 'Will you handle them, Aphrodite? Just make the cheque out to whoever and I'll sign. D'you mind? I really couldn't hack the idea of dealing with all that tortuous bill-paying stuff with a hangover. Jolie always used to do it for me.'

'Sure I'll do it.' If Jolie Fitzgerald could do it, so could she. Hell, she could pay bills for the Olympics – she'd been doing it for her mother for years. When she'd come back to Dublin after her years spent in London, the sheriff had been banging on Thea's door, and Aphrodite had had to sort out one of the most complex tax liabilities since the former disgraced Taoiseach's. This partnership could work out quite well, she thought, as she plunged the cafetière. She wouldn't mind accepting Troy's gifts of glorious dressing-up clothes if there was something useful she could do for him in return. She had a suspicion that she'd start to feel

222

unpleasantly like a kept woman if he continued showering her with gifts of dresses, as he'd announced was his intention.

Aphrodite poured coffee, and started to butter bagels. 'Come out from under there,' she said, 'and help me trawl through the papers for reviews. You'll feel better when you've had some coffee. What kind of coffee is this, anyway? It smells fantastic.'

'It's Jamaican Blue Mountain,' said Troy, emerging reluctantly from underneath the duvet and taking the cup and the copy of the *Irish Times* Aphrodite was holding out to him.

Aphrodite's jaw nearly hit the deck. 'Jamaican Blue Mountain?' she said. Her mother had bought some recently on a whim. It had set her back thirty euros for half a pound. 'Wow. It's the most expensive coffee in the world, isn't it?'

'I dunno. Jolie put me on to it.' He blew on his coffee, and turned to the arts page. 'Well. There's an excellent review in the *Irish Times*,' said Troy, scanning column inches. 'Your designs get a great mention.' Troy and Aphrodite had started to refer to Damien Whelan's plagiarized designs as 'hers'. 'Listen to this: "The characters' personalities are further delineated and made manifest in Damien Whelan's fiendishly clever and visually delightful costume designs."'

'Bastard! Bastard! Fucking, fucking bastard!' Aphrodite jabbed the knife repeatedly into the bagel she was buttering. ' "Fiendish" being the operative word. Does he say anything about Mum?'

'Yep. Here we go. "Thea Delaney lives up to her

name, playing Arkadina as a sexy, pampered goddess, and the crucial second act scene with Konstantin is almost incestuous in its intense physicality."'

'Oh, Christ. Mum'll be unbearable now. I'd better ring her to congratulate her.'

Troy handed her the phone, then turned to the crossword page and idly started filling in the cryptic one. Aphrodite was impressed. Sometimes she couldn't even manage the Simplex.

Thea purred down the receiver when she finally picked up. 'Thank you, darling. Sorry I didn't get a chance to talk to you properly last night.'

'Are all the reviews good?'

'Yes. Except that bitch in the *Independent* didn't mention me. Jealous, I suppose. What did you think of it? It's quite a raunchy production, isn't it?'

'Yes. Whose idea was it that you should get your tits out, Mum? I don't suppose it had anything to do with the fact that you fancy the arse off the actor playing Konstantin.'

The quasi-incestuous scene referred to by the *Irish Times* had involved Thea suckling her grown-up son, in order to comfort him. It had had huge shock value, as she must have known it would. Aphrodite knew that her mother had a keen knack of pulling scene-stealing stunts out of the bag when it suited her. She'd get miles of column inches out of this particular one.

'Oh, darling! Do you have to put it quite so crudely?' Thea sounded only mildly offended. 'And no – it has nothing to do with the fact that I "fancy"

– as you put it – Jason. It was a collaborative decision that evolved in the rehearsal room. I think it works brilliantly, don't you?'

'Yes. It does,' conceded Aphrodite. 'You actually managed to get two gasps from the audience last night, and I bet all the papers will mention the incestuous stuff. Down there for dancing, Mum.'

'Thank you, darling. Incidentally, you got some nice press, too.'

'What?'

'Yes. In Andrea's Ashes.'

'Oh, God. I didn't think I'd be newsworthy enough to be included, what with all the luminaries that were floating around last night. I'd better check it out. Bye, Mum. Talk to you later.'

'Mm. Oh, by the way, darling. I'm so glad you've hooked up with that Troy boy. He's absolutely *edible*.'

'Hands off, Mum.' Aphrodite realized as she put the phone down that she'd sounded terser than she'd meant to. As if her own *mother* posed a threat to her! But then, she supposed, she'd had so many confrontations lately with predatory females that it was understandable that she should be on the defensive.

She reached for the relevant paper and leafed through it until she came to Andrea's Ashes. An entire half-page was devoted to the opening night of *The Seagull.* 'Oh, God,' she said. 'We're in.' She folded the paper in half and angled it so that Troy could read it as well.

This was how the piece went, under a photograph of her and Jolie embracing:

Up and coming design consultant **Aphrodite Delaney**, daughter to the actress **Thea Delaney**, was highly a-mused by her latest assignment. When **Troy MacNally** – who, Andrea can exclusively reveal, is set to be Ireland's latest fashion export to the international market – needed a new look for his apartment, he commissioned Aphrodite. The couple hit it off so well that Aphrodite has become the designer's latest muse. Now Aphrodite's laughing, although she confesses to being still a little bewildered by how fast it's all happened. 'I wear nothing but Troy MacNally now,' she smilingly confided in me last night. Andrea says: I wish we could all afford to be in your shoes, Aphrodite!

The flush of shame Aphrodite felt made her bite down hard on her lip. 'Oh,' she said. 'Oh, fuck. I sound like a total bimbo. "*I wear nothing but Troy MacNally now,*"' she parroted in an air-head's voice.

Troy shrugged and inserted the word 'venality' in his distinctive black print in 10 down. 'Don't worry,' he said. 'It honestly could be worse. You should see some of the quotes that have been attributed to me in newspaper interviews. It's like signing a pact with Mephistopheles when you talk to the press – a double-edged sword thing. You're dependent on them for the publicity, and they're dependent on you for copy. It's part and parcel of being in the public eye. You just have to keep your fingers crossed and hope they won't say anything too unpleasant.'

Aphrodite's mobile rang. She picked it up and said, 'Yeah?'

Lola's voice came down the phone. '"I wear nothing but Troy MacNally now,"' she mimicked. 'What the fuck were you *on*, Aphrodite?'

Aphrodite didn't want to be hearing this. 'Oh, piss off, Lola,' she said, 'I didn't *say* it like that!' She flung the phone onto the floor, pulled Troy MacNally's duvet over her head and sought solace in sex.

* * *

The next few weeks were pretty quiet work-wise, but frantic socially. Aphrodite and Troy made frequent appearances in gossip columns and in the society pages of the glossies. Aphrodite was careful not to say anything too gushing to the reporters who sought her out, but she found it difficult to keep a tight rein on her tongue after a couple of glasses of wine – especially when she was feeling pretty damn cheerful to be kitted out in Troy MacNally and standing hand in hand with the gorgeous dude himself. And they were so *interested* to talk to her and *delighted* to meet her, and so very, very seductive. 'You're obviously very happy, aren't you, Aphrodite?' remarked one young man with an engagingly frank expression. She felt sorry for him. It was his first assignment, he'd told her, and he was very nervous. So Aphrodite had responded, 'Yes, I am – *very* happy, thank you – and good luck!' The following Sunday she'd opened the paper to discover that she'd actually been 'smiling smugly', and looking 'inordinately pleased with herself'.

So Aphrodite developed a carapace of cool, tried hard not to smile, and tried even harder not to care what was written about her. Whereupon she immediately started attracting adjectives like 'scowling' and 'snooty'. Hell's teeth! You just couldn't win! Here she was, having her cake and trying to eat it and not being allowed to enjoy it.

Still, she learned to accentuate the positive by viewing their relentless carping as a foil for her happiness. Fuck the begrudgers for whom she was providing precious column inches of meretricious crap! Imagine earning your living by being nasty about people. She *had* to be happier than them with their sneering and backbiting and penchant for all things dark and negative. Whatever happened to the 'all things bright and beautiful' she'd sung about at school?

One day two things happened. She got a phone call from Andrea Mooney asking when it would be convenient to do an 'in depth' interview (Aphrodite's heart sank at the words 'in depth') and she got a phone call from the editor of *Individual* magazine asking if she'd be interested in writing a regular style column for them. She obliged Andrea by naming a time and place, and told the *Individual* editor she'd get back to her.

'What kind of thing do they have in mind?' asked Troy when she told him about the second phone call over the dinner of poached salmon she'd cooked for him. They were in her tiny kitchen, and Troy was feeding morsels of salmon to Bobcat. Aphrodite hadn't spent as much time at his flat as he'd have liked latterly, because she needed to be at home for the cat. She couldn't rely on Lola to scoot in from time to time and feed Bob and water the plants because she hadn't spoken to her since the day she'd put the phone down on her. Aphrodite kept meaning to call her friend, but it seemed that every time she resolved to pick up the phone and end the stalemate there'd be another mention of her in some paper's social column, or a photograph of her posing with Troy, and Aphrodite just couldn't hack the idea of Lola crowing at her again.

Troy sneezed, and dropped another salmon flake onto the floor. 'Stop spoiling the cat, Troy. He'll never go back to Whiskas if you keep feeding him fresh salmon. Um. Let's see. What kind of thing do they have in mind?' She repeated his question and then made a face. 'A "what's so this month, what's so last month" type of thing. It's bonkers! As if *I'd* know.'

'You're as well qualified for the job as anyone. Better.'

'Why? Just because I'm muse to Troy MacNally?'

He sloshed Chablis into both their glasses. 'Well, that's obviously the prestige angle that they're after. But your real qualification, Aphrodite, is that you have an excellent eye. I think you should do it. It would be really invaluable publicity for us.' He sneezed again, and said: 'Sorry about this. I must be coming down with a cold.'

'Oh, God, Troy. I'd feel a right arse telling

people what this month's happening accessory is.'

He leaned back in his chair and smiled. 'You could have fun. "Wearing your bra over your little strappy top is *de rigueur* this season".'

Aphrodite laughed. 'Yeah! Try 40 denier American tan tights in shiny, shiny, shiny Lycra. They look especially fantastic with sandals!'

'Strut your stuff in sockettes!'

'What on earth are sockettes?'

'Those totally grotesque little flesh-coloured nylon socks that some women wear with bare legs and shoes.'

'Eeyoo. Why?'

'I have never been able to fathom that particular sartorial phenomenon. I think it's to protect their feet from getting blisters.'

'I'd rather sport the blisters, thanks.' Aphrodite took a gulp of wine. 'Hey, Troy! I needn't confine myself to sartorial affairs. I could infiltrate all sorts of other areas. "Chardonnay is *so* last season. Serve Blue Nun at your next dinner party".'

Troy sneezed again. 'Except the dinner party is dead, according to *Harpers & Queen.* It lost favour with the fashion monarchy around the same time as the pashmina.'

Aphrodite leaned her elbows on the table and rested her chin on her knuckles. 'Well, eat my sockettes,' she said in a tone plangent with incomprehension. 'People really *do* obey the style police, don't they?' She gave a shrug of indecision. 'Shall I do it, Troy? Should I take them up on their offer?'

'Go for it. You could call your column "The Style Shepherdess".'

Aphrodite clapped her hands and laughed out loud. 'Excellent! Because I'm writing it for sheep?'

'Absolutely.' He leaned over and kissed her.

'Maybe you're right. Maybe I could have myself a little subversive fun here.' She looked pensive for a moment, then got to her feet and started clearing away the dishes. Bobcat twined himself around her ankles. 'Oh, all right, Bob. You can have the leftovers.' She scraped salmon into his bowl and rubbed his ears.

'When are you doing the Andrea Mooney interview?' Troy asked.

'Next week. I'll have to exercise some caution round her, I think.'

'Mm.' Troy considered. 'Don't be too cautious, though. It makes for very dull reading. You know why so many of those *Vanity Fair* celebrity interviews are so incredibly dull? It's because A-list celebs like Madonna and Warren Beatty have veto over the copy. They're hagiographies, not interviews.' Suddenly he sneezed again. And again. And again. After about the ninth sneeze he turned to her and said: 'D'you know something, Aphrodite? I think I'm allergic to your cat.'

* * *

The following week Aphrodite found herself sitting in the lobby of the Merrion Hotel sipping a flute of champagne courtesy of Andrea Mooney. A little tape recorder was on the table between them. They were halfway through their interview, and so far the questions had been innocuous enough. Aphrodite had filled the journalist in on her unconventional childhood, her years in London, and her decision to abandon theatre design for the more lucrative world of commercial styling. She refrained from mentioning that the catalyst that had propelled her away from theatre was Damien Gobshite Whelan.

Andrea signalled to the waiter to bring them two more glasses of champagne. 'Now,' she said, when the drinks arrived on a tray. 'I'd like to hear more about how you and Troy met. I know you were redesigning his apartment—'

'Well, more specifically, his bathroom,' Aphrodite amended. 'It's Troy's favourite place. It's his sanctuary, really – where he goes for inspiration.'

Andrea cocked her head to one side and raised an inquisitive eyebrow. 'And a little bird tells me he got it in spadefuls when he met you first. In his bathroom.'

Aphrodite faltered. 'What do you mean?' she asked.

The smile Andrea gave her was complicitous. 'Aphrodite rising naked from the waves? I heard the story of how you happened to be taking a bath when Troy arrived back unexpectedly from holiday. How you took one look and fell into each other's arms. It's breathtakingly romantic.'

'How – how did you hear that?'

'It's a small town.'

To say that Aphrodite was disconcerted would be

equivalent to saying that Bill Clinton was slightly put out by Monica Lewinsky's allegations. She had absolutely no idea how to respond. Should she deny it outright? State categorically that it wasn't true? But if she did that she'd be rubbing Andrea up the wrong way, and she didn't want to make an enemy of this woman. She didn't want to end up like a suttee widow on the funeral pyre of her own reputation. Andrea was quite capable of doing a hatchet job on her, she knew that. Aphrodite decided to hedge.

'What makes you think it's true? Not all rumours you hear are substantiated in fact.'

'Of course they're not. But what if some tabloid got hold of this one and really went to town?' Andrea looked at her carefully, and then very deliberately pressed the 'off' button on her tape recorder. 'You can trust me, Aphrodite. I don't want to write some salacious little piece of dirt-dishing. I want to write something uplifting – a true love story. It's the stuff of *Hello!* magazine fantasy land, and my brief is to feed the readers' appetite for fantasy, not stuff more seedy sex scandal down their throats. There'll be no references to "temptress Aphrodite" or "sexy siren spills the beans". Nothing like that. I give you my word.'

Aphrodite thought on her feet. 'Will you allow me copy approval?'

'I'm afraid not. That's my prerogative.' Aphrodite remembered what Troy had said, about anodyne interviews with stars who demanded ultimate control over what was written about them. 'The decision is yours, Aphrodite,' said Andrea. 'I could throw you to the lions – i.e. let the tabloids know about the bathroom incident, and let them interpret your behaviour whatever way they like within the limits of the libel laws, or I could do a beautiful, rose-tinted version of how Troy MacNally met his muse.'

Aphrodite swigged back more champagne and did some more swift thinking. She couldn't phone Troy and ask his opinion because he simply wouldn't pick up the phone. She really knew she had no alternative. 'OK,' she said. 'I'm prepared to tell you the story if you tell me who your source was.'

'Fair enough,' said Andrea. 'It was Jolie Fitzgerald who told me. She thought it would make excellent copy, and she was right.'

Jolie! Of course it was Jolie.

'All right, Aphrodite?' Andrea raisd an eyebrow, her finger poised above the 'record' button. 'Are we ready to continue?'

Aphrodite took another swig of champagne, and gave her interlocuter a taut smile. 'Ready,' she said, as Andrea Mooney switched the machine back on.

*   *   *

A week later she heard from the journalist again. 'My editor loves it,' she said. 'He wants to put it on the cover of the Sunday supplement, along with a photograph of you. He intends to commission a portrait by Jack Costello. Do you know him?'

'Yes.'

'Well then, you know he's top class.' There was a beat, and then Andrea said: 'There's only one slightly sensitive issue involved, though. My editor asked me if I'd run it by you. He thinks it would be a glorious idea to have a portrait of you naked.'

'On the cover of the supplement? Are you mad?'

'Listen, listen, Aphrodite.' Andrea's voice was reassuring. 'The portrait would reflect the tone of the piece I've written. There would be nothing – absolutely nothing – prurient about it. I want to emphasize that. I mean – when was the last time you saw a salacious portrait by Jack Costello? His stuff is hardly likely to end up on page three, is it? Whatever pose you adopt will reveal nothing you don't want to be revealed. You've seen the kind of thing before – celebrities do it all the time. I mean – think of those wonderfully erotic shots of a stark naked Kate Moss where she's posed so that nothing – and I mean nothing – is revealed. It can be done quite easily with the clever use of light and shadow, and your own arms and hands can, of course, conceal a multitude.'

Oh, Christ. Aphrodite wished she'd never met Andrea Mooney. Never been sweet-talked into doing an interview. It was all Jolie Fitz-bloody-gerald's fault. She gave a heavy sigh down the phone. 'Look, Andrea. You've got to give me time to think about this. I should run it by Troy, for starters. He may not like the idea.'

'Sure. But get back to me as soon as possible, can you? I'll need to get moving on this soon.'

When she put down the phone, Aphrodite reached for a packet of chocolate digestives and rang Troy.

Of course he approved. 'Fantastic!' he said. 'Shots

by Jack Costello! You should be seriously chuffed.'

'I'm not seriously chuffed by the thought of strutting my stark naked stuff all over a Sunday supplement,' she said. Or in front of Jack Costello in his studio, she could have added.

But Troy just argued all the pros for the case in much the same way as Andrea had, and actually succeeded in making her feel so uncoolly prudish that she finally relented and rang Andrea back with an affirmative.

'Excellent!' said the journalist. 'You won't regret it. I'll get on to Jack right away.'

He phoned Aphrodite later that afternoon when she was halfway through her seventh chocolate digestive. 'I believe you're sitting for me, Ms Delaney?' he said. 'I'll look forward to that.'

'Likewise,' said Aphrodite listlessly.

'How about aiming for a session some time towards the middle of the week? Would that suit? I have Wednesday morning free.'

'Sure.'

'Say eleven o'clock?'

'Eleven o'clock's fine.'

'My assistant will do a make-up job on you. I'd prefer you barefaced, but I know how self-conscious most women are at the idea of not having a mask to hide behind, so I'll ask her to do something light. Don't wear anything tight on the day or you'll have tread marks on your body.'

Yeah, yeah, yeah, thought Aphrodite despondently as she put down the phone. What had she let herself in for? A can of worms had been opened and they were slithering round all over the place. Aphrodite wished they'd turn into snakes and go and slither nearer Jolie. She was just about to go into the kitchen and put the chocolate digestives firmly back in the cupboard when the doorbell rang. She opened the door to her mother, who flapped a glossy magazine in her face.

'Hello, darling! I just read your piece in *Individual*. What fun!' Thea glided into Aphrodite's sitting room and sank down on a sofa.

'Oh, Christ,' said Aphrodite, feeling another flutter of nervous anticipation. 'Is that out already? Show me.'

The magazine was folded open at the relevant page. 'This month Aphrodite Delaney, muse to fashion designer Troy MacNally, writes the first of what we hope will become a regular column telling us what we should be seen in, where we should be seen, and what we shouldn't be seen dead in.'

'Oh, Christ,' groaned Aphrodite, wondering how many of her friends had picked up this month's *Individual*.

'It *is* fun, isn't it?' said Thea, kicking off her shoes and reaching for the packet of biscuits Aphrodite had left on her coffee table. 'Except I wish you hadn't put in that bit about angora jumpers being passé,' she added petulantly. 'I've just bought one.'

'Maybe you should take it back to the shop, then,' returned Aphrodite sarcastically.

To her horror, her mother said, *actually said* – without the faintest trace of irony – 'Oh! Good idea! I could exchange it for . . .' She took the magazine from Aphrodite and scanned the column. 'What's your recommendation? Ah, yes. Here it is. "Something in softest merino".' Thea put the magazine down and gave Aphrodite an anxious look. 'I'd better do it soon. There's going to be a big run on merino now.'

*   *   *

On Wednesday morning at eleven o'clock Aphrodite rang the doorbell of Jack Costello's elegant Georgian house. His assistant, a very pretty blonde girl who introduced herself as Perdita, answered, and led Aphrodite along a high-ceilinged white-painted hall, through a side door, and down a wildly beautiful garden.

'Wow,' said Aphrodite. 'I didn't know gardens like this existed so close to the city centre. Who looks after it for him? My mother's looking for someone to remedy the mess she's made of hers.'

'He does it himself,' said Perdita, pushing open the door to what had once been a mews cottage.

Aphrodite found herself in a space awash with light flooding through massive Velux windows and bouncing off white walls. Jack Costello was sprawled in an armchair at one end of the room, studying a sheet of black-and-white contacts, and nursing what looked like a glass of tomato juice. He was wearing loose cotton trousers and a baggy white T-shirt. More contact sheets lay scattered on the white floor at his bare feet. Amongst the usual photographic paraphernalia comprising lamps, tripods, rolls of backdrop and silver cases, Aphrodite's eyes took in mugs and a carton of milk on a desktop alongside a cafetière with dregs in. A couple of empty wine bottles and glasses with lees. An ashtray with spent roll-ups. A pedal bin overflowing with cartons bearing the logo of an upmarket delicatessen. In a sink beneath one of the Veluxes, dishes were piled.

Jack looked up when Perdita shut the door behind Aphrodite, and got to his feet rather shambolically. 'How's it going?' he said, crossing the room and taking Aphrodite's hand. 'I've just realized I've seen more of you between the covers of magazines than in the flesh lately.'

The only thing she could think of to say back was 'Hi.'

He released her hand, then moved back across the floor, put down his tomato juice and picked up the contact sheets, boxing them deftly into a neat sheaf before sliding them into a desk drawer. 'Forgive the mess,' he said, and turned to his assistant. 'It's pretty superficial, you know, Perdie. You'll have it sorted in no time.' He yawned and stretched, then glanced at Aphrodite. 'Yes. I am hungover, if that's what you're thinking.' He reached for his glass again, and saw her looking. 'And, no, unfortunately there is no vodka in my tomato juice. There's some in the fridge, though, if you want a shot of Dutch courage. A lot of sitters need a snifter before they do nude shots.'

'I'll manage.' Aphrodite gave a pallid smile that became even more pallid when she spotted a copy of this months's wretched *Individual* lying on the

239

draining board. Jack had been responsible for the cover shot. Again he saw her looking.

'I note you've become a card-carrying member of the style police,' he said with a smile. 'I'm glad I'm wearing my white T-shirt today.' Aphrodite remembered she'd said something positive about white T-shirts in her column. 'But I'll confess that trashing my collection of angora jumpers will bring tears to my eyes. I became very partial to angora after seeing Johnny Depp in that film.'

She was about to assay a smart retort when the phone went. 'Excuse me,' said Jack, stretching out a paw for it. 'Perdita, would you take Aphrodite through to the dressing room? Thanks.'

In the dressing room Aphrodite undressed and slipped into a loose cotton kimono that Perdita had hung on the back of the door. Then she sat down at the make-up mirror. Perdita worked quickly and silently on her face, humming to herself as she juggled her brushes. 'Nice,' she said, viewing the final result in the mirror. 'There's a lovely, dewy glow to your skin.'

That was probably down to all the sex she'd been indulging in recently. But the make-up job *was* a good one, Aphrodite conceded. Some make-up artists she knew were heavy-handed, but this girl had gone easy with the powder puff, and had just brushed her skin with a little shimmer. 'Are you a professional?' she asked.

'No. But I did do a course. It's a useful skill to have when you're an apprentice photographer. I want to set up on my own some time, or in partnership with

Sam, my boyfriend.' She handed Aphrodite a hair-brush, and then reconsidered, standing back with her head on one side. 'No,' she said. 'Don't bother. It looks better messy. How are you feeling? OK?'

'OK,' replied Aphrodite. 'A little shaky, of course. I've never posed nude before.'

'It's natural to feel a bit shaky. Even the professionals do. Are you sure you don't want a drink? There's champagne in the fridge as well as vodka.'

'No thanks. I'd love a cup of coffee, though.'

'I'll bring you one while Jack sets up. Anything else? I can run out for bagels or something if you're hungry.'

'No thanks.' Aphrodite was too nervous to eat.

'OK. I'll be back in a tick. Help yourself to a magazine.' She indicated the pile of glossies that lay on the make-up counter, and then she was gone.

Aphrodite ignored the magazines and instead picked up a coffee-table book of photographs by Jack Costello. They were portraits, all in black and white, all nudes. There were young subjects and old ones, black subjects and white, men and women – and Aphrodite found it infinitely comforting that there was, as Andrea Mooney had assured her, absolutely nothing salacious about these photographs. Her attention was drawn more to the eyes than to any other part of the anatomy: the souls of the subjects shone out of them.

When Perdita finally came to fetch her, she knew that she could trust Jack Costello with her nakedness. She even felt that she might trust him with her soul. By the end of the session, because it went so smoothly, so effortlessly, she actually felt tempted to trust him with her heart. If she hadn't already given her heart to someone else, that is.

* * *

Jack directed her in the kind of low, level voice she'd heard her vet use to soothe a nervous Bobcat. His instructions were precise, and easy to follow. It was amazing how, by adjusting the angle of her chin by a mere millimetre, a shot could suddenly go from being 'good' to 'superb!' How, by simply shifting the focus of her gaze, the reaction produced was not just 'yes', but a murmured 'God, yes!'

And the adjectives he used! He called her beautiful, exquisite and perfect. He called her gorgeous, lissom, lovely. He called her radiant as the goddess she was named after. Aphrodite blushed at how compliant she was in response to his outrageous compliments. She'd fallen for his flattery and it had made her malleable as putty in his hands. She also blushed at how aroused she became during the session. She felt like taking a cab straight to Troy's studio so that she could indulge her sudden urgent and voracious craving for sex.

'That's the one,' he said, after an hour of shooting. As soon as he lowered his camera he turned his back on her and a swift-footed Perdita was there with her kimono. Aphrodite felt very strange. It was as if she'd engaged with him to the point of fairly advanced foreplay, and suddenly he'd changed his mind.

She tried to force herself into a more businesslike

mode. 'Will you send the contacts to Andrea or to me?' she asked.

'To Andrea. But I'm sure they'll give you the final say.' He turned round and gave her a perfunctory smile, and then he moved to the fridge and opened the door. 'You've earned at least a glass of champagne, don't you think?' he said, producing a bottle.

Aphrodite dithered momentarily, and then said: 'Yes, please. I would like a glass.'

He reached into a cupboard for flutes. One. Two. She realized she had rather a stupid smile on her face. Three. Three? The smile faltered.

'Perdita!' called Jack, as he pulled the cork. 'Come and get it!'

The little blonde put her head round the door and looked quizzical. 'Champagne?' she said. 'Isn't it a bit early in the day to be indulging?'

'Not when it's a special occasion,' said Jack, pouring fizz into flutes. 'Happy birthday, Perdie.'

Perdita gave her boss a surprised smile. 'How did you know it was my birthday?' she demanded, feigning indignation.

'Sam told me.'

'Well, he shouldn't have. I knew you'd do something extravagant if you found out. Vintage champagne at half-past twelve on a working day! You're incorrigible, Costello!'

'And here's your present.' Jack forced a badly gift-wrapped parcel into the girl's protesting hands. 'Open it,' he said with an authority that Aphrodite sensed he'd adopted to conceal embarrassment.

243

Inside was a framed photograph of Perdita with her arms around a strikingly beautiful boy who was as blond as she was. The couple were quite clearly so absorbed in each other that they'd been totally unaware of the photographer who had aimed his lens at them.

'Oh, Jack!' Perdita set the photograph aside and gave him a big hug. 'What a beautiful, beautiful present!' She kissed his cheek, then picked up the photograph again. 'When did you take it?'

'At that beach barbecue Sara threw.'

'Oh, yes! That was such an amazing day!'

Aphrodite was beginning to feel seriously *de trop*. She was delighted when an excuse to get out of there was afforded by the ringing tone of Troy's mobile, which she'd left in the dressing room and had forgotten to turn off. 'Excuse me. I'd better take that,' she said, shimmying towards the door. The caller rang off before she got there. As she waited for the message icon to appear on the screen, she got back into her street clothes. If, she thought absently, *anything* by Troy MacNally could accurately be prefixed by such a pedestrian adjective as 'street'.

Because Jack had requested that she avoid anything tight, today she was wearing her dove grey drop-waisted number. She regarded herself in the mirror, standing there in her cutting-edge designer gear, with what the papers had taken to calling her 'signature' blond crop looking all sexy and tousled, champagne flute in her right hand – and she knew that she bore absolutely no resemblance to the girl that Jack Costello had met at the IFC all those months ago when they'd gleefully trashed *Chose de Neige*. She remembered what she'd heard an artist's model say in a documentary once: 'You don't reveal anything at all when you take your clothes off. But you reveal an awful lot when you put them on.'

In the studio she heard him laugh at something Perdita had said. Troy's phone bleeped at her in an irritating, querulous fashion. She heard a doorbell, and then the sound of girlish voices and more laughter. The laid-back jazz that had been playing during her session with Jack was changed for something a little more upbeat. Finally Aphrodite swigged back her champagne and accessed the message. It was from a PR person she knew, 'just checking' that she and Troy had received their invitation to the launch of some new alcoholic beverage. It was to be held in a swanky restaurant, the opening of which they'd attended only last week.

Aphrodite tucked the phone back into her bag, and slid back into Jack Costello's studio. There were two women there, both dressed in casual clothes – jeans and T-shirts. Their hair was long and glossy, they wore a mere soupçon of discreet make-up, and there was a new, faint trace of some scent Aphrodite couldn't identify in the air. It smelt expensive. They turned as she came into the room, and Jack Costello said, 'Are you off, Aphrodite?'

'Yes,' she said. 'Thanks for the session.'

'Sorry it took so long.' Oh, God. She'd thought the session had gone so well! 'But we got there in the end. I'm sure I'll get a couple of great shots out of that lot.' A couple? He'd gone through three rolls of film!

'Hi.' One of the women came towards her and held out her hand. 'I'm sure I know you from somewhere. Haven't we met before? I'm Rebecca Henry.'

'Esther McDermott,' said the other woman, holding out her hand too. 'You know, I'm sure I've met you too.'

'I don't think so,' said Aphrodite, wildly relieved that Jack hadn't volunteered the information that they probably knew her as Troy MacNally's muse who'd had her mugshot plastered all over the society pages recently.

She knew who *they* were, though. One of them was an accomplished cellist, the other a composer. They'd been in the news recently, too, because of some collaboration they were working on.

'OK, photogenic ladies,' said Jack, looking at his watch. 'I know you're both under pressure, so let's get you out of here as soon as possible. It shouldn't take more than half an hour. By the way, Aphrodite,' he added, shooting a look at her from under his brows. 'Your idea for the photo-shoot in the Gaiety is great, but you'd better get your finger out and book the session soon. I'm going away next month.'

Aphrodite knew she was colouring. 'Oh – sorry – I did mean to let you know about that, but I've been busy. Who told you?'

'Polly Riordan filled me in.'

'Oh.' *She* should have done it. Polly's taking the initiative meant that Aphrodite's authority had been undermined. 'I thought you were going to phone me so that we could meet up and discuss the idea?'

'I did try phoning you,' said Jack. 'Many times. But

your phone was always engaged. And because I like to talk to people directly, I never leave messages. Maybe you should invest in a second phone.'

When Perdita showed her to the front door, Aphrodite's face was scarlet. Oh! How could she have got him so *wrong*? That special relationship – that *vibe* she thought they'd got going between them – was simply the rapport that any professional photographer worth his salt learns to establish between artist and sitter. She'd seen enough photographers at work in her line of business to know that! She'd even heard – and nearly got sick at – that classic bad line: *Make love to the camera, baby!* How had she not recognized his way with words for what it was – sheer professional expertise? Relaxing a model was the first trick a portrait photographer learned – it was the oldest trick in the photography bible – and even the most inept practitioner of people skills should know that everyone everywhere in the world responds to flattery every time.

But no amount of berating by the rational little voice in her head could stem the searing sense of betrayal she felt.

She strode along the pavement, starting to seethe. Fuck Jack Costello! How dare he make her feel like this! And when she tried to analyse *why* she was feeling the way she was feeling, she realized that she'd only ever felt this particular strain of betrayal once before in her life, when she'd indulged in an extremely ill-advised and majorly humiliating one-night stand. And for some horrible reason, that was the way she was feeling now.

Chapter Ten

She did get her finger out about the shoot in the Gaiety theatre. The real reason she hadn't been in touch with Jack Costello sooner had been because Troy had left it so late to deliver the goods. His team was working round the clock to get frocks constructed in time.

Finally they were ready, and the session began to take shape. Models and hair and make-up artists were booked, and assistants and gofers. Aphrodite hired her own favourite trainee stylist, a girl called Nell who was keen to learn, had flair and imagination and – even more importantly – possessed an irreverent sense of humour that had saved Aphrodite from going round the twist on numerous occasions.

She and Troy met up with Jack so they could recce the theatre and decide where to set up shots. Aphrodite spent much of the recce taking notes, very glad indeed of an excuse not to meet Jack's eye. She wondered if he had sussed the fact that she had felt so erotically charged during their photo session together, and the thought that he might have done made her want to curl up and die.

Just as they finished, Troy's mobile shrilled from her pocket, closely followed by her own from her bag. She spent a couple of minutes juggling and fielding calls while Troy and Jack continued to work on the game plan for the shoot. The calls were really pissing her off. She would have switched the phones off, but there was something urgent in the pipeline that required an immediate response from Troy, and she couldn't afford the luxury of doing that. Finally she heard herself say: 'Excuse me, I have a call waiting. I'll get back to you later,' and as she pressed the relevant buttons she noticed that Jack Costello's eyes had slid in her direction. Hell's teeth! She was performing the very social manoeuvre he'd once told her he despised! Constructing a telephone call hierarchy! But she had no choice. She knew the incoming call was from Polly, and Troy simply *had* to talk to her. He'd been procrastinating about making a decision on the offer from Japan – he couldn't put it off any longer. 'Troy?' she said. 'I'm sorry to interrupt, but Polly needs to talk to you. It's urgent.'

He sighed, and the expression on his face was stoical as he took the phone from Aphrodite and slunk off to take the call.

'I'm glad to see you took my advice and got yourself another phone,' said Jack, just as she'd suspected he might. Insufferable git!

'One of them's Troy's,' she said. 'I screen his calls for him.'

'All part and parcel of being a muse, I suppose.' There was a beat, then: 'I read your interview,' he said.

Oh, God. For some reason she found the idea profoundly embarrassing. If a salacious feature had appeared in the tabloids, at least he'd have known to take it with a hearty pinch of salt (although she doubted that Jack Costello touched the tabloids). But Andrea Mooney had been true to her word and had concocted a piece so flattering it verged on hagiography. It was as if she had repented of all her past spleen and was now determined to make up for it by waxing positive as some contributor to *Oprah* magazine. After describing in rather purple prose how they had met ('Aphrodite emerged naked from the water and – shazam! *Coup de foudre* struck them both simultaneously. The couple spent the next three days in bed'), she had made reference to Aphrodite's charm, talent and 'idiosyncratic' beauty, and described her relationship with Troy as 'the stuff of fairy tales'. She had concluded the interview with the following words: 'Life really is a dream come true for this girl with the name of a goddess, this gifted girl with the dreamy smile and the faraway eyes.'

Aphrodite had imagined Lola reading it, and cringed. She knew she could never pick up the phone to her friend again. She'd simply never be able to live this one down. Lola wouldn't know that she had adopted a dreamy smile and vague expression expressly to disguise the fact that behind the enigmatic mask she was performing mental acrobatics, determined not to say anything that could be construed as undiplomatic about her relationship with Troy's former muse Jolie Fitzgerald (Andrea had asked some probing questions about that), or about how Troy's staff had welcomed her into the flock, or about the whole poisonous seething snake pit that was the fashion industry. The image she'd projected of herself may have been of the swan gliding effortlessly over the lake, but beneath the surface the swan that was Aphrodite had been paddling like fuck.

'You just can't win with the press, can you?' remarked Jack. 'They either love you or they loathe you.'

'What's their slant on you?' asked Aphrodite.

'I'm one of the luckier ones. Their attitude is one of supreme indifference. They couldn't give a shit about me.'

'That surprises me. You're top in your field.'

'That may be. But unlike you I don't photograph well. What did you think of the pic, by the way? I thought it was bloody gorgeous.' He continued without waiting for her to reply, 'Nor do I play the social round, nor do I dish dirt.'

Aphrodite was indignant. 'Neither do I!'

'Not about other people, I'm sure. But you spilled a lot of beans about your own private life in that particular interview. Forgive me for saying so, but it smacks a little of hubris to assume that other people are interested in your sex life.'

Aphrodite had never wanted to hit someone so badly in her life. 'You,' she said, almost trembling with the exertion her self-control was costing her, 'you are – a–'

'Pig?' he hazarded.

The fact that the word 'pig' *had* actually been the first one to spring to her mind, coupled with the fact that he'd second-guessed her, caused her to clench her right fist even tighter. 'I wasn't going to use such a juvenile term as "pig",' she lied.

'Oh? I'm intrigued. What were you going to call me?' Now his smile made her hate him even more.

She racked her brains. 'I was going to call you a churlish ruffian and blackguard.' Churlish ruffian and blackguard! Where had *that* come from? But at least, she reassured herself, it was a modicum more dignified than 'pig'.

He looked impressed. '"Churlish ruffian and blackguard!" Wow. That *is* a first.' Narrowing his eyes, he gave her a look of consideration she would have described as flattering if it had come from any man on the planet apart from Jack Costello. 'Well. I have to say it makes me feel pretty damn sexy to be called a churlish ruffian and blackguard. Sorry about that. That's presumably not the effect you intended.'

She was spared the effort of dreaming up some smart-arsed response by the return of Troy.

'That's sorted, you'll be glad to hear,' he said, slinging an arm around her shoulders.

'Good,' she said shortly.

'Troy?' said Jack Costello. 'Have you ever been called a churlish ruffian and blackguard?'

Troy looked puzzled. 'No,' he said. 'Why do you ask?'

'Well, with a bit of luck, one day you will be.'

'What? Why?'

'When a dame tells you you're a churlish ruffian and blackguard it makes you feel kind of – er – *manly*, for some perverse reason.'

'You know something, Costello? You're a difficult

man to figure out, sometimes.'

Jack laughed. 'Yeah? I like to keep people guessing. It's more interesting than baring your soul to all and sundry, I find.'

Aphrodite knew he was making an oblique reference to her 'in depth' interview with Andrea Mooney. She wouldn't have been surprised if he'd added 'And baring your body' to 'baring your soul'. She showered him with mental abuse in which the word 'pig' was predominant.

Jack looked at his watch. 'Gotta go,' he said. 'See you next week. Enjoy your weekend. Oh, and Aphrodite?'

She looked at him coldly.

'What's with all this dreamy, fairy tale, faraway stuff? You look much more beautiful when you're angry, Ms Delaney.' And then turned on his heel and strolled out through the glass doors of the theatre.

'What was all that about?' asked Troy curiously. 'Was he flirting with you?'

'Christ, no,' said Aphrodite with more vehemence than she intended. 'I'm not his type at all.'

'What makes you say that? You're an eminently fanciable woman. And you've posed nude for the guy. It wouldn't surprise me if he did fancy you.'

'Troy. Jack Costello categorically does not fancy me, OK?' She looked at her watch. 'Now let's make tracks. You're needed in the studio a.s.a.p.'

As they headed towards the car park Aphrodite found herself replaying extracts from her dust-up with Jack Costello. '*It smacks a little of hubris to assume that other people are interested in your sex life . . . What's*

*with all this dreamy, fairy tale, faraway stuff? . . . I have
to say it makes me feel pretty damn sexy to be called a
churlish ruffian and blackguard.* Now she wished she
hadn't called him that. She wished she'd followed
her initial impulse to call him what he really was.
Jack Costello was, quite simply, a pig.

* * *

On the morning of the shoot, Aphrodite got her
period. She also got a call from Nell, her assistant.
'I'm sick!' the trainee wailed down the phone. 'I'm
really, really sorry, Aphrodite – I've been throwing
up all night.'

'Oh, Nell – poor lamb!' said Aphrodite. 'Have you
someone to look after you?'

'Yeah. I'm at my mum's house. She's been spoon-
feeding me Dioralyte, but I can't keep anything solid
down. I feel awful messing you about like this – and
I was so looking forward to it. Imagine getting a
chance to work with someone like Jack Costello and
blowing it!'

'Never fear,' said Aphrodite, thinking on her feet.
She was getting so good at it these days that she
suspected she might soon develop little wings on her
ankles like Hermes. 'I'll make a few phone calls.
There's always someone available.'

There was – but only just. After making half a
dozen panicky calls Aphrodite ended up doing
something she would never have done in normal
circumstances. She hired someone she had never
worked with before.

The first warning sign came when the girl arrived late, bleating into a mobile and tittering. Aphrodite wasn't sure that she'd ever met anyone before who actually *tittered*. She was wearing a string top whose straps looked as if they might snap any minute under the strain, baggy hipsters slung way too low on her pert ass, and she had lips like Jordan's. She had a tattoo on the bit of her belly that was exposed. She had body piercing. This girl was training to be a *stylist*? 'Hey, Aphrodite!' she said with alarming mateyness when she finally ended the call she was on. 'It is *so* cool to get a chance to work with you.' She elongated the 'so' in a way that made Aphrodite's heart sink. 'And Troy, of course. Hey, Troy! And Jack.' She looked around for him, but at least she couldn't say 'Hey, Jack!' because Jack Costello wasn't due to arrive for another hour. She tittered again, and Aphrodite and Troy exchanged glances. 'I'm Imogen, by the way.'

'Imogen. Hi. Nice to meet you.' Aphrodite shook hands in a perfunctory way, and Troy backed off into the stalls of the theatre where he threw himself onto a seat in the back row and pulled his jacket up around his head. He'd had another restless night, which meant that Aphrodite had, too. More and more frequently, she'd wake to find Troy in a state of distress. Last night had been a killer. She'd only just got off when the alarm had woken her with its merciless electronic beeping. She took a deep breath. 'OK, Imogen. The first thing I want you to do is to run out and buy me some Anadin. Then you can get started on the ironing. The board's in the upstairs bar. That's where make-up and changing facilities have been set up.'

'Sure.' Imogen popped a stick of chewing gum into her mouth, and offered some to Aphrodite. Aphrodite shook her head and felt an ominous feeling begin to swell like a bilious bubble in her belly as Imogen's phone went off again on one of the more obnoxious settings.

'Hey!' said Imogen into her phone as she strutted across the theatre foyer heading towards the stairs. 'How's it going? Yeah. I'm on a shoot.'

*   *   *

A little over an hour later the session slid into foreplay mode. Perdita had set up lights on the grand staircase of the theatre, where it had been decided to stage the first shots. Aphrodite wanted the model twins sitting on the steps in identical day dresses, holding hands. They descended the steps together with downcast eyes, looking fragile as china dolls, little taffeta skirts rustling. Their complexions had been painted porcelain pale, they had spots of rouge on their cheeks, and their lips were Geisha red. They curved their mouths into demure smiles when they saw Jack, and just stood there, eyes still downcast, waiting for the fracas of compliments their beauty commanded. Jack did not fail to oblige.

He spread his hands in a gesture redolent of speechlessness, smiled at them and shrugged his shoulders. 'Gemini!' he said. 'What can I say? Come here and let me air-kiss you. I know you deserve something more robust than that, but the thought of bruising those rosepetal lips sends shivers down my spine.'

The twins prinked and simpered and came forward to be made a fuss over.

'Look, but don't touch,' warned Maggie the make-up artist. 'That little work of artifice took me over an hour.'

'Actually,' Jack was assessing the twins with eyes that were suddenly narrow, 'the mouths might look good a little bruised later on. Smudged, you know?' He clicked his fingers once, twice, three times as he thought harder and his eyes got even greener. 'OK. Listen to this. What if we were to take a series of shots of the girls in a state of progressive disarray? Like this. You open the catalogue and on the first page they're china doll perfect – like two little maids from school. Then, as you turn the pages, you begin to notice the veneer of perfection slipping.'

The twins opened their mouths in identical little 'O's of fearful apprehension.

'No worries, my babies,' said Jack with a laugh. 'You may not look picture-book perfect, but you'll still look out-of-this-world sexy. You know you can depend on me for that.' The smiles returned to the twin faces. 'What do you think, Troy? Aphrodite? Look at it this way. On page two of the catalogue you notice the lipstick is smudged. On page three one of the girls is minus a shoe, and her legs are maybe a little akimbo. On page four we might have a breast exposed. You get the picture? That very painted look will sit nicely with the more structured daywear, but by the end of the shoot, when we get on to those distressed, gauzy things, the girls will have let their hair down. Literally. They'll have lost a lot of that – what did you call it, Maggie? – artifice? – and have morphed into more abandoned creatures.' He raised an eyebrow at Aphrodite. 'It's only an idea. You're the one calling the shots after all.'

Troy gave Aphrodite a questioning look.

'Do you mean to suggest,' she said to Jack, 'that they've been indulging in some kind of sexual activity between shots?'

'Absolutely,' said Jack. 'Having your picture taken can be a pretty damn sexy experience, you know.'

Aphrodite was glad that her cheeks were flushed already by the glare of the arc lamps. She considered. She had to admit that it was a rather lovely idea. She wished she'd thought of it. 'Yeah,' she said. 'Let's go for it. If Troy agrees. What do you think, Troy?'

He nodded. 'It's good. But you know I'll defer to you on this kind of stuff. I only design the frocks.'

'Excuse me,' said one of the twins in a baby voice. 'We need to know our motivation. Who are we meant to be having all this sex with? The photographer?'

'No,' said Jack with a laugh. 'With each other. You're making love to yourselves, darlings.'

The twins looked delighted by this idea and squeaked a bit.

'Now,' said Jack. 'What music do you two lovelies want to strut your stuff to today? Something mellow and sexy? How about Marley? Yeah? And I'm sure someone has been prescient enough to furnish you already with your recreational drug of choice? Yes?'

'Grass and Moët,' supplied Aphrodite. She'd sent out for chilled champagne and had several joints stashed away in a silver antique cigarette case Troy had given her.

'Clever girl.' He gave her a shrewd look. 'Coke?'

'I drew the line at that.'

'Hah! I'm a sucker for bad puns, too. That's actually quite a good one to start a session with. I warn you, the longer the shoot, the worse they get.' The smile he gave her coaxed a reluctant one from her in return, but she noticed that the twins hadn't batted a beautiful eyelash at the banter. For some reason Aphrodite found herself wondering if either of them had ever called Jack a pig.

'Let's do it.' He redirected his attention to the business in hand. 'Film, please, Perdita.' Perdita jumped to it, and Jack started loading film into his camera the way a gunslinger might load bullets into his weapon. 'OK, girls. Places, please.' A pause while he considered. 'Beautiful, *beautiful*. Whoah – not so sexy, Morgana. I know you can't help it, but try saving the smouldering for later. We're only on the first Polaroid, you delectable morsel of condensed sex appeal.' Click. 'Beautiful.'

* * *

Aphrodite had her work cut out for her. The girl Imogen was worse than inept. Aphrodite decided very early on that she couldn't even trust her with the ironing. She couldn't run the risk of getting scorch marks on the garments: she'd spotted Imogen ironing with her mobile clamped between jaw and shoulder, and had performed a stunt worthy of Pierce Brosnan as 007 in order to wrest the iron from her. The last straw was when Imogen's chewing gum somehow ended up welded into the hem of one of Troy's Ilnacullin-inspired gossamer wisps. Aphrodite was so up to ninety with stress at this stage that she'd screamed to the girl to fuck off, and not to come back.

Jack Costello shot her a warning look when she returned to where they'd set up a shot in the dress circle.

'You're upsetting the girls,' he said. 'They need a mellow vibe if they're to stay relaxed for the shoot.'

Fuck the girls, she wanted to say, but didn't. The twins were pouting sulkily, their arms wrapped round each other in a protective attitude. 'I had to lose that assistant, I'm afraid,' Aphrodite explained. 'It'll work out better if I look after things myself.'

'Fair enough,' remarked Jack, with irritating equanimity. 'Do something about that earring of Morgana's then, please, while I play around with the light? Thanks.'

Aphrodite stepped forward and helped the model hook on an earring, then pulled her bodice tighter, securing it at the back with a bulldog clip.

'Looks good,' said Jack. 'Lose some more buttons, please, Aphrodite. I want your breast exposed here.' He rewarded Morgana with a smile that had something complicitous about it.

'Excuse me,' muttered Aphrodite, unbuttoning the girl's frock as far as her waist, and pulling the fabric aside.

'A little rouge on the nipple, don't you think? And maybe a dusting of blush on the décolletage – and the ear lobes as well. That's always a post-coital give-away. See to that, Maggie, will you? No, Aphrodite – too much breast. Let's just have the nipple peeking out. The subtler, the sexier.'

He flexed his shoulders like a prize fighter preparing to enter the ring, then took a look at the test shot Perdita was proffering. 'OK. The Polaroid's looking good. And, wow – you girls look edible.' Aphrodite and Maggie backed out of the shot, and Jack focused the full beam of his attention on the twins, crouching low over his camera. 'Hold it – that's lovely. Yes. Just like that. Come to me. Come to me –' (choreographing the pose with a coaxing gesture of his fingers). The identical faces responded, turning towards Jack's lens like flowers turning to the sun. 'Hold it right there. Straight to me. Ever so slightly incline your eyebrow, Nimuë. Give me a knowing look.'

'Knowing? Knowing what?' asked Nimuë.

'It doesn't matter. Knowing anything. Lose that piece of lint, Aphrodite, please. See it? There on Morgana's shoulder.' Aphrodite skipped into shot, lost the lint, and then skipped back out again. 'Beautiful. You're so *beautiful*.' Click. 'Legs a little akimbo, Nimuë. Ah. That's *very* nice. Yes. Ha! This is the one they'll never use – the one I love the best.' Click. 'A little glint, Nimuë?' A throaty laugh. 'Too much of a glint, darling. Yes. That's the one. We're done. Relax. OK, Aphrodite.' Jack straightened up from the camera, stretched, and yawned. 'Where do you want the next shot set up?'

*   *   *

By the time the session ended many hours later, Aphrodite calculated that she had never heard the word 'beautiful' bandied around so frequently and with such manifest sincerity in her life before. The twins were like succubi, feeding on the compliments that came their way in Jack's voice in a constant, reassuring stream. They seemed to derive genuine spiritual nourishment from the murmured blandishments. Between set-ups they'd look bored, sip champagne – leaving blood-red lipstick smears on the flutes – and pay frequent visits to the loo, where Aphrodite suspected much covert powdering of noses went on.

She was sitting in the second row of the stalls with the palms of her hands pressed against her belly and her legs dangling over the seat in front when Jack finally ran out of film. He'd ordered more to be couriered round, but it hadn't arrived yet. Aphrodite was glad of the enforced break. She'd had to take more Anadin for her period pains.

'Will you let me try something?' he asked. 'I've an idea for those goldy dresses.'

She was curious to see what he'd come up with. 'Sure,' she said. 'What do you need?'

'Come with me.' He led her up onto the stage and

262

then off into the dim recesses of the wings. In a corner lay a heap of crumpled, faded green plush. It was covered in dust, and when Jack lifted a corner of its heavy mass, spiders scuttled out. Between them they dragged it out of the wings, and spread it centre stage. Aphrodite sneezed as the dust billowed around them, and picked off the bits of cobweb that had accumulated on her sleeves.

'I'll borrow a Hoover,' she said. 'There looks like there could be a century's worth of dust on this stuff.'

'Don't,' said Jack, laying a restraining hand on her arm as she made to go. 'Leave it just the way it is, cobwebs and all.'

'Hang on. You're going to ask the girls to lie on this, aren't you?'

'That's the general idea.'

'Get real, Jack. They'll never do it.'

'I can be very persuasive.'

'I don't think you could persuade even Spider-woman to lounge around on that.'

His brow furrowed, and she could hear his fingers clicking. 'I will tell them,' he said, after a second's deliberation, 'that the cobwebs are those fake ones that posers buy to drape over their wine racks.'

Cobwebs! Aphrodite smiled, then gave him a dubious look. 'Do you think they'll buy it?'

'Those twins, as you may have noticed, have very little acumen when it comes to differentiating between what's real and what's not. Although,' he added as an afterthought, 'I wouldn't like to try fobbing them off with *méthode champenoise* instead of vintage. If one bubble of fake fizz should hit those perfectly arched little nostrils, they would positively flare with exquisite indignation.'

Jack pulled at a corner of the velvet, and then stood gazing at it and rubbing his chin. 'It's good,' he said. 'But I'm going to need a stepladder. And maybe we could have access to the prop room? We might find something there we could have fun with.'

They did. They unearthed a box full of autumn leaves made of delicate gold foil. 'Perfect,' said Jack and Aphrodite simultaneously. They also found a big pile of totally hideous macramé satchels lying in a corner – obviously props intended for medieval peasant characters, Synge extras, or hippy-esque characters from some old Ayckbourn play. The little voice of anarchy in Aphrodite's head that had become increasingly vociferous of late dared her to present them to Morgana and Nimuë as Troy's latest hot accessories.

'Hey,' said Jack, holding one up. 'You could do a piece on these for your next style column. Something along the lines of: "Forget Vuitton. The homespun look makes a comeback".'

'I'd just been thinking something quite similar.' This time he wrested a laugh from her as well as a smile. Hell. She just couldn't figure this man out. One minute he had her seething with humiliation and rage, the next he'd tuned into her mindset with uncanny accuracy. He'd been perfectly right when he'd told her earlier that he liked to keep people guessing. 'Troy's new stuff's a bit of a departure, isn't it?' he remarked as he slung the satchel back in the corner.. 'How will Troy MacNally aficionados feel when they get a load of all this unstructured stuff? Don't they expect a certain signature look from him?'

'I really don't think he cares. He felt it was time for a change, especially after Miriam left him.'

'Poor Miriam.'

'You knew her?'

'Oh yeah.'

Aphrodite couldn't stop herself. 'What was she like?' she asked.

'She was stunningly beautiful,' Ow! 'but very naïve. I wasn't surprised that she descended into drug hell. She was every pusher's dream pushover. And the drugs just made her sadder. She lost it, in the end. Fucked off with her dealer the way sad girls do. I have an inkling that you'd beat her hands down in a table quiz, Aphrodite Delaney. I have you sussed as a fairly sharp cookie.'

Why did he make it not sound like a compliment?

The last shot was finally set up. The rumpled green velvet became a bed of moss for the girls to disport themselves on, and Aphrodite had to acknowledge that Jack's idea had been inspired. She'd scattered the velvet with the filigree leaves and broken down and redistributed patches of the denser cobweb – she'd done this with supremely confident fingers in order to convince the twins that the stuff *had* to be fake – before Jack persuaded the two beauties to sprawl provocatively across the drape. They made faces on account of the dust, but then, having ascertained that there was a power shower in the star dressing room, they swigged back their champagne stoically and did as he asked without being too vocal about their distaste. Aphrodite had noticed how docile and biddable they were around Jack – they had a reputation for being legendary divas on shoots. Now they just lay there whispering and fiddling with each other's hair – much to the consternation of the hair stylist – as Aphrodite adjusted the folds of the translucent pale gold dresses, spreading out metres of cobwebby fabric, arranging hems just so to display yards of lissom amber-hued limbs, and sliding wispy straps down over svelte, satiny shoulders. The garments looked ethereal, juxtaposed with the heavy velvet and when Troy finally rolled up again, accompanied by Gareth Fitzgerald and Hugo O'Neill, the twins' performance peaked. Playing to the gallery, they were in their element.

Gareth and Hugo – who, Aphrodite learned, had run into Troy on the street outside the theatre – had been invited in for a sneak preview. Hugo was vociferous in his appreciation of the twins until a glance from Jack warned him to shut up, whereupon he just lolled in the stalls and drooled at them.

Aphrodite tried to keep her profile low. She knew she must look like Mrs Mop by comparison with Morgana and Nimuë, having spent the entire day working her ass off ironing and tacking makeshift hems and tweaking at garments until they were set off to their best advantage on the beautiful (that word again!), slender bodies of their wearers. There were damp patches under her arms, the little make-up she'd been wearing had melted away under the lights, and while a delicate glow was most becoming on the twins, a livid flush did nothing for her. Muse, my arse! she thought, as she started packing up in anticipation of the wrap being announced.

Troy caught up with her as she was folding a camisole in bubblewrap at the back of the stalls. 'Hey,' he said. 'You and Jack have a real rapport, haven't you? You tuned into each other's mindsets beautifully on this shoot.'

Aphrodite was astonished. 'What?' she said, giving him an 'as if' look. 'To be perfectly honest, Troy, I don't much like the man. I find him blunt to the point of rudeness.'

Troy shrugged. 'He's *direct*. He doesn't bullshit – except when he has to. The case in point being a good example.'

On the stage, Jack was crouching precariously on the top step of an A-frame ladder, focusing down on his models and crooning at them in a low, throaty voice. Morgana and Nimuë were responding as if under hypnosis. Maybe they *were* hypnotized: they were still evidently oblivious to the colony of spiders that Aphrodite had noticed reclaiming their territory. Aphrodite kept expecting a scream to rend the air at any moment.

Troy grabbed her arm. 'Wow. Look at them now,' he said, nodding in the direction of the stage. Nimuë was leaning in to Morgana, wiping carmine off her twin's mouth with a swatch of green velvet. 'Christ, that's sexy. But it's kinda sweet, too.'

Nimuë suddenly raised herself onto her hands and knees and turned to Jack. Her face had been rubbed almost clean of the theatrical whiteface that had been so carefully painted on and powdered hours earlier, and under the traces that remained her skin was dewy and slightly flushed. Aphrodite noticed that her eyes were ever so slightly unfocused, and that the pupils were very black. Her long, long golden hair was all over the place and her mouth was swollen. She looked incredibly sexy – a little *fauve* in the forest. 'Would you like us to actually *kiss*, Jack?' she asked.

'Jesus!' There was an involuntary groan of pure lust from Hugo O'Neill in the stalls, and Nimuë's lips curved in a tiny smile.

'Uh-uh,' said Jack. 'This is nice the way it is. A kiss would be too *Penthouse*, darling. The vibe you have going between you now is spot on. You remind me of that fairy tale by the Brothers Grimm. The – um –' he clicked his fingers in that characteristically impatient way he had when he was thinking hard '– the one about the kids who get lost in the forest. The – er . . .'

'Babes in the Wood,' Aphrodite heard herself saying.

'Spot on.' Jack gave her a smile before crouching back over the lens of his camera.

'See what I mean?' said Troy in an undertone. 'You *do* understand each other. Hell, this is good.'

'What, exactly, is good?' said Aphrodite, peeling off another length of bubblewrap. She suddenly just wanted to get out of there.

'The three of us. We make a fucking great team.'

Suddenly an earth-shattering scream came from

the stage. 'Spiders, Nimuë! There are spiders in your hair!'

'It's a wrap,' announced Jack, lowering his lens.

Troy dropped a kiss on her cheek before striding off down the aisle to comfort and congratulate his house models. 'You're such a *clever* girl,' he said.

Aphrodite recalled how the concept of staging the shoot in the theatre had first come to her, how she hadn't thought the idea particularly inspired or clever, and how she'd really only come up with it to cock a snook at Jolie Fitzgerald. But Troy had bought it. And so, presumably, would the thousands of women who'd soon be forking out hard cash for his frocks.

What a silly, silly, silly world it was. How much sillier still was the world of fashion? But the silliest thing of all, she thought as she slid scissors through plastic, was that in this particular world – this planet she'd landed on where style ruled supreme – she, Aphrodite Delaney, was the butterfly in the rain forest – the one who was making things happen . . .

Chapter Eleven

'We're banjaxed. Polly's leaving.' Troy's expression was terminally troubled.

'What? You mean she's *resigned*?'

'Yes.'

Aphrodite had met up with him at lunchtime in St Stephen's Green. It was a beautiful, sunshiny day, and Aphrodite had suggested sandwiches al fresco. She'd spent the last three days styling an ad for a mobile phone company, and she was banjaxed, too. The prospect of lunch in Stephen's Green with her lover had kept her going all morning. She shouldn't even have taken a lunch break – there was stacks still to be done – but she'd had it up to here with myriad phone tones going off all over the place, and she was desperate to clear her head.

'Has she had a better offer elsewhere?'

'No. She says she can't take the pressure any more, especially with the autumn/winter show to be organized.'

'*Pressure?* Jesus, her job's a cakewalk compared to what I've had to contend with lately.' Aphrodite secretly suspected that *she* was the reason Polly had resigned. As Troy had come to turn to his muse more and more for practical as well as creative contribution, Polly's input into the day to day running of

Troy's affairs had declined correspondingly, and she had been looking increasingly peaky, sullen and put out. Aphrodite felt a twinge of guilt. OK, so there was no love lost between them, but that didn't mean she wanted to see the woman out of a job. 'How many weeks' notice has she given?'

'Four.'

'Will it be easy to find a replacement?'

'I don't know. Probably not. She's been with us from the start. She knows Troy MacNally Enterprises better than anybody.'

Something about the way he was regarding her made her wary. 'Why are you looking at me like that, Troy?'

'You know why.'

'Um. No. I don't.'

'You do, Aphrodite. The answer's staring us in the face. You're the obvious replacement for Polly.'

'Me? I'm not qualified for PA work, Troy!'

'But you're naturally brilliant at it.'

'But it's not what I *am*, Troy! You of all people should understand that. I'm a creative, not a suit!'

'So's Donatella. Your role model.'

It had been Troy who'd hit upon that notion, not her. *Was* Donatella her role model? Aphrodite wasn't sure of anything in her life right now. She rolled over on the grass on her belly, turning away from him.

'Wouldn't you even think about it, Aphrodite?' he pleaded. 'You wouldn't have to do it on a nine-to-five basis, you know. We could be really flexible – and I could hire a part-time PA for you to delegate to.'

A PA! Oh! She found the idea of having her own personal assistant rather chuff-making.

'You're the obvious choice, you *know* you are,' he continued, trailing a finger down the nape of her neck. His voice was oozing chocolate now, seducing her. 'Polly may have been a model of efficiency, but she had no artistic savvy whatsoever. You'd be invaluable in that respect. We can devise concepts together, realize visions. We can recce locations together, hire models, make sure the look's dead on for the show. We think the same way, Aphrodite, you and I. And I know that together we can achieve the ultimate aspirational collection. Just look at the way we worked so well together on the photo-shoot.' Aphrodite remembered how hard she'd worked that day spent with the intolerable twins in the Gaiety theatre. Working with Troy would be no picnic – but then, she conceded, nor was styling commercials. 'What do you say, darling? It could work so well. You're the first truly creative person I've met who's savvy with it.' He kissed her ear. 'I wonder where that pragmatic streak came from?'

Well, it hadn't come naturally, Aphrodite felt like telling him. It had evolved through sheer bloody awful necessity. How she'd love the luxury of being a ditsy creative who relied on agents and lawyers and accountants and PAs to handle their real life stuff for them! But, having realized from an early age that she'd have to be all those professions rolled into one in order to make sure that her mother's – and, by definition, her own – life ran smoothly, being an organizational wizard was second nature to her now.

'Come on, Aphrodite.' Troy's voice was even more cajoling now. 'It'll be a lot more fun than styling commercials, you know it will.' He was right. At least she'd have some outlet for her creativity if she agreed to Troy's proposal. 'And I'll pay you a bloody good salary. I know we haven't put a figure on the work you did on the photo-shoot, but I'd say your input was worth around – what? A grand? Does that sound all right to you? Actually – we should stick on a couple of hundred more for the fact that you had to cover for that trainee stylist.' Aphrodite wanted to laugh out loud and hug Troy for his naïvety. A trainee stylist would fall on her neck and embrace her like a long-lost love if offered a couple of hundred euros for a day's work. 'And what about making you a shareholder in the business? How about if I gifted you half my shares? I–'

'Troy! That's absurd. I'm not worth that!'

'Listen. Listen to me. I have more money than I could ever need or want, and if I do that – let you have half my shares – it means we're partners in every sense of the word. Will you do it, Aphrodite? Think about it, at least?'

She averted her face again and allowed her mind to work overtime. If she accepted his offer, it would mean that she and Troy would have controlling shares in the company. Jolie Fitzgerald would have less influence over him. The idea of having sway – both artistically and financially – over Jolie appealed to Aphrodite far more than she cared to admit. But the bottom line was that she would be there for Troy, not simply in some nebulous capacity as 'muse', but in a copper-bottomed legal capacity also. She'd be there to protect him from the machinations and wiles of that unscrupulous Machiavella.

'OK,' she said, with decision. 'I'll do it. But I'll need Polly to show me the ropes.'

Troy turned her to face him, and she felt a rush of love when she saw the expression of relief and gratitude on his face. He looked so vulnerable, so *appealing*! And when he took her face between his hands and smiled at her – that ridiculously boyish smile – she knew she'd done the right thing. 'Christ! Look at you!' he said, pushing her back onto the grass and kissing her full on the mouth. Well, hell! There was absolutely *nothing* boyish about that kiss. When he finally lifted his mouth from hers, there on the green velvet grass of Stephen's Green, he was quite clearly all man. 'Come back with me to the studio,' he said, urgently.

Much as Aphrodite would have loved to oblige, she had to get back to her stinking mobile phone gig. In a week or two, she thought, in a week or two she could turn her back on all that commercial styling crap and allow herself the luxury of working with her lover. In a week or two she would be known as – as what? Um. Official paid muse to Troy MacNally? PA to Troy MacNally? Co-director of Troy MacNally Enterprises?

'I can't come back with you, sweetheart,' she said, disengaging herself from his embrace. 'I really have to get back to work. We'll just have to wait until this evening. Will I cook us something?'

'Would you? Yes, please.' He touched his hand

to her face. 'But not in your gaff, Aphrodite.'

'What's wrong with my gaff?'

'Nothing at all. I love your gaff. But unless you get rid of your cat, I'm not going to be able to visit, and I don't reckon you'll get rid of your cat just because it makes me sneeze.'

'Bob's a "he", not an "it",' said Aphrodite indignantly. 'You couldn't possibly call a cat who exudes such levels of testosterone an "it".'

Troy laughed. 'I'd hate to think who you'd choose if it came to deciding between him or me.'

'Don't go there,' she warned him, with an ominous smile. She got to her feet and started clearing away the remains of their picnic lunch. 'By the way, Troy. What's my new job description going to be?'

'Um. Well – you're my muse.'

'Jesus, Troy – I can hardly put "muse" down if I need to fill out a census or a passport renewal form, can I?'

'OK. Let's give you a totally outrageous handle. How about *Chargée d'affaires sartorieuses*?'

Aphrodite laughed. 'And you're really going to let me have my own PA?'

'Aphrodite, I'll let you have anything you want. You don't know how much it means to me to have you on board.'

And then Aphrodite thought of all the logistics that would be involved in getting the autumn/winter show off the ground, and she thought about how she was going to have to brown-nose Polly Riordan in order to persuade her to hand over the baton with reasonably good grace, and she knew that for the foreseeable future, she'd have her work cut out for her. She remembered an interview she'd read in a Sunday supplement: a high priestess of fashion stylists had remarked on how she'd collaborated with designers who knew how to cut cloth like a dream, but wouldn't know how to put together a look to save their lives. And she wondered for the first time how much of a true collaboration her work with Troy would be. Who would bear the lion's share of the pressure, the stress and the hard work? And who would take the kudos?

Something struck her rather unpleasantly. She thought of how Damien Whelan had taken all the kudos for her bird-inspired designs for *The Seagull* (she'd found out only last week that he'd won an *award* for them!), and another bird analogy came into her consciousness. If she was still the swan, paddling like fuck, what did that make Troy? The peacock, the ultimate *flâneur*? Or the cuckoo, the ultimate abrogator of responsibility? And as for Jolie fucking Fitzgerald – what rank did she have in the ornithological scheme of things? She didn't need to rack her brains on that count. Troy would see Jolie as a golden eagle, no doubt about it.

But Aphrodite had a very different vision. She remembered what Jolie had said to Hugo in the hot tub at Coolnamaragh: *When you've invested the kind of money that Gareth and I have sunk into the business you want to keep your creative happy* . . . Jolie and her cohort Polly Riordan had done that all right. They'd created a fantasy world for their creative princeling to inhabit – a Cloud-cuckoo-land full of fabulous sensory delights. Beautiful women, opulent surroundings, the best food and drink money could buy, amusements and diversions and *no worries* – all designed to keep the tap of Troy's inspiration flowing. This poor little rich boy sitting at the feast didn't realize that he was surrounded by rapacious harpies, all gorging on him. A *harpy*. That was exactly what Jolie Fitzgerald was – a monster with the face and body of a beautiful woman, but the fearsome wings and claws of a raptor.

Aphrodite looked down at Troy, who was still sitting on the grass. He had hunched up and wrapped his arms around his knees – presumably to camouflage the fact that he was still nursing an erection after their kiss – and it made him look so vulnerable that her protective instinct flared again. In that instant she vowed that she would do all in her power to help him.

Power. Oh! She had never known what it was like to have power within her grasp. Once acquired, she knew, power was difficult to relinquish. You had to fight like hell to hold on to it, and there were legions of contenders out there who'd be happy to take her on. And suddenly Aphrodite Delaney wasn't sure whether the kind of power she'd be wielding as a major shareholder in Troy MacNally Enterprises scared her shitless, or thrilled her skinny.

*   *   *

The contact sheets for the photo-shoot arrived the next day. Jack had X-ed the shots he considered the best, but had enclosed a note to the effect that the final say rested with her and Troy. Troy gave the contact sheets a cursory scan, then: 'Yeah,' he said, returning his attention to a sketch he was working on. 'They're great. Your discretion, Aphrodite.'

She hesitated. She was beginning to find his indifference towards such matters seriously baffling. 'Troy?' she asked. 'You do know that the way the catalogue looks is incredibly important? How come you take so little interest in this kind of stuff?'

'I dunno.' He shrugged. 'It's like I always say – I just design the threads.' He was looking very boyish today, in a cashmere poloneck. His hair needed cutting, and a lock kept flopping across his forehead. Aphrodite leaned across the desk and tucked it behind his ear.

'I just find it astonishing that you can pass the buck with such – what's the word I'm looking for? – such *insouciance.* If these were my designs I'd be up to ninety about the way they look.'

He put his pencil down, smiled at her, leaned back in his chair, and started slowly swivelling it from side to side. 'I think I told you once, Aphrodite, that the reason I started designing clothes was because it proved an excellent way of getting my greens from my aunt's friends.'

'Your greens?'

'A quaint way of saying "getting laid".'

She remembered how he'd told her that a gaggle of women had started pestering him to make clothes for them once they'd got a load of the stuff he'd dreamed up for his aunt.

'You mean you actually slept with them?' she asked.

'Oh yeah. I lost my virginity when I was fifteen to a thirty-something woman.'

Oh! No wonder he was such an inventive lover! He'd obviously had plenty of experience. But the idea of his sexual initiation at such an early age gave Aphrodite a slightly unpleasant feeling, and she was more than a little nonplussed. 'Sorry, Troy,' she said now, trying to sound casual. 'I'm not sure I make the connection. What's getting laid got to do with your attitude towards your designs?'

'Well, once I got the woman into bed I didn't much care what happened to the dress. The first time she wore it, it ceased to be mine. I suppose it's a bit like being a painter who doesn't care what happens to his painting once he's sold it. What's the point in being precious about my designs, for fuck's sake? Being a fashion designer is hardly what I'd call a vocation. We're talking frocks, not major works of art.'

'Some people might argue otherwise. You're becoming collectable, Troy.'

'Sod that.' He gave her a wry smile. 'As I said, I only started making frocks so's I could kiss the girls—'

'And make them cry?'

'Sometimes. Not always. Sometimes it was the other way round.' His face closed over suddenly, and he looked back at the drawing he was working on. 'It's ironic, isn't it? Getting laid was my sole incentive for getting caught up in the fashion industry. Now I'm a bona fide purveyor of the kind of tat that women fork out silly money for.'

She'd never heard him talk like this before. 'You're really quite cynical about the whole thing, aren't you?' she said.

There was a pause while Troy looked thoughtful. Then: 'No,' he said. 'I'm not cynical about women and their beauty. There is nothing on earth so sexy as dressing women. What I *am* cynical about is the razzmatazz, the palaver – all that hype that's part and parcel of what I do.'

'Then why do it?'

He sighed. 'I do it for Jolie.' Ow! Aphrodite didn't want to be hearing this. 'Troy MacNally Enterprises was her brainchild. She's the one responsible for its success. She even took a course in marketing just so we could get the business up and running. This was way back, when she and I were lovers, when she was my muse. She's taken more of a back seat now that we've become a profit-making venture – and of course, she has Gareth and the twins to look after. She'll be thrilled to know that you've come on board in an administrative as well as an artistic capacity.' He picked up his pencil and resumed work on his sketch.

Aphrodite wasn't so sure about that. She looked down at the contact sheet that lay between them on the desk. But she wasn't really studying it. She was thinking that Jolie would be pretty pissed off when she heard that Aphrodite had staked a claim in the business she'd been responsible for setting up.

Feeling insecure, she picked up the contact sheet again, and then Troy's mobile rang, and no sooner had she finished dealing with that caller than her own mobile rang, and it was her mother. 'Darling,' said Thea breathlessly down the phone. 'Can you come round this evening and fill in that horrible tax form for me? I got a stinking letter from the Revenue Commissioner today, and he's actually threatening to take me to court. I can scarcely believe the nerve of the man!'

Aphrodite was just mustering the formidable patience it required to engage in any kind of dialogue – meaningful or otherwise – with her mother when something caught her eye. Across the table, Troy had exchanged his pencil for a thick, black marker, and was obliterating the design he'd been working on with a random, spiralling pattern.

'Hang on, Mum, I just need to–' started Aphrodite. She didn't finish. Troy had set down the marker. Then he covered his face with his hands, and laid his head on the desktop. 'Mum. I'll call you back.' She depressed 'end call', and stretched a tentative hand across the desk. 'Troy?' she said, touching his hair. '*Troy?* Are you all right?'

For a minute he remained motionless. Then he drew in his breath in a curious, shuddering sigh, and raised his head.

'What's wrong, darling?' she asked, feeling very scared and trying not to show it.

Troy smiled at her, his engaging, careless smile, and said: 'Nothing's wrong, Aphrodite. Absolutely nothing.' He looked down at the drawing he'd been working on, and seemed half surprised, half resigned when he registered the spiralling inky blots that defaced it. 'Oh, well,' he said, in an oddly detached voice. 'That drawing was shite, anyway.'

The finished catalogue was stunning. Aphrodite was so wowed by the way it looked that the minute it arrived she grabbed the phone and dialled Jack Costello's number. She wanted to thank him for doing such a fantastic job. As she waited for him to pick up, she studied the final shot – the one of the twins lying on the faded moss-green plush with their glorious limbs all entwined – with a smile. There, in the very top right-hand corner of the photograph, so unobtrusive you'd hardly notice it, lurked a little silver spider.

For some reason she felt absurdly disappointed when Perdita picked up the phone and said: 'Oh, I'm afraid he's not here, Aphrodite.' And then she felt relieved. She'd picked up the phone on an impulse, and she realized that if Jack had answered she wouldn't have known quite what to say to him. Since it would be impossible to predict whether he'd be in caustic or friendly mode, she'd probably find herself dithering over whether it wasn't a better idea to be professionally polite rather than breathlessly buzzy, and she'd just make a haims of the call. 'He's gone off down to his house in Valencia for a break,' continued Perdita, 'but I'll pass on your kind words about the catalogue – if he ever surfaces, that is. It seems to me that he spends half his time in Valencia underwater. It's virtually impossible to get him on the phone.'

'Underwater?'

'Yeah. He dives. Underwater photography's his passion. It's not something I've ever wanted to get into, I have to say. The idea of diving in the freezing Atlantic has little appeal for a wimp like me, but I suppose Jack's made of sterner stuff.'

When Aphrodite put the phone down an idea was starting to glimmer in the very back of her mind. She grabbed her notebook and Troy's car keys and went into Polly's office. 'Polly?' she said, adopting the half-friendly, half-peremptory tone she'd learned to use when she spoke to the woman. 'If Troy calls, will you tell him he can get me on my mobile?' He'd opted to work from home today. 'I'm going for a walk down the Pigeon House pier.'

'A walk?' Polly looked as disapproving as she dared, which was, these days, not very. 'There's rather a lot of work to be done today, Aphrodite, and I wanted to familiarize you with my filing system . . .'

'This *is* work,' said Aphrodite.

She parked the car at the end of the pier, and she walked and she walked, and she thought and she thought. The designs for spring/summer that Troy had started work on were from the other end of the spectrum to the russets and golds of his autumn collection – they were palest leaf-greens and aqua-marines, they shimmered and gleamed like . . . like the water that was dancing now on her left and on her right. They were *naiad* gowns. That was how Troy himself had described them.

And she thought: how glorious, how utterly glorious it would be to see those gowns in the element that had inspired them, in the water, swathes of gossamer fabric clinging to breasts and floating round hips like seaweed, the way Troy had pictured her as she'd reposed, drowsily oblivious to his gaze, the very first time he'd ever laid eyes on her – just before she'd risen from the foam in his Rousseauesque bathroom, Aphrodite rising from the sea . . .

Underwater shots of Troy's newest creations. The idea was inspired! A fashion shoot beneath the sea . . . she'd seen shots in expensive glossies like *Vogue* of models wandering ankle-deep in waves, trailing Valentino or Romeo Gigli or Ben de Lisi behind them on Bounty bar perfect, talcum powder beaches, and her head had reeled at the thought of so much priceless stuff being irretrievably ruined. But Troy's stuff didn't cost thousands, like those couture numbers. Troy MacNally Enterprises could afford to write off a couple of dresses for the sake of the mother and father of all PR stunts.

She hugged herself, laughed out loud, and then she made a decision. She wouldn't tell anyone yet about her concept. The spring collection was still a long way away – they hadn't even got autumn over yet. She didn't want word getting out before the event, not to anyone. She'd learned that lesson the hard way, courtesy of Damien Gobshite Whelan. No. She would hug her inspired idea to herself, and until the forthcoming show was over, she wouldn't tell anyone. Not even Troy – he was scatty enough to inadvertently let word slip. There was only one person she could trust to keep absolutely shtum, but she wasn't speaking to that person any more – hadn't for more than a couple of months now, she calculated. That person was Lola.

*   *   *

Aphrodite knew from long and bitter experience how tough theatrical opening nights could be. On one occasion, when she was about twelve years old, her mother had begged her to push her down the stairs so she might break an ankle rather than have to walk out onto the stage. Aphrodite, ever practical, had prescribed Kalms and Rescue Remedy instead.

She wished she had some now, as she looked around her at the vision of hell that was the dress rehearsal for Troy's autumn/winter show. The opening night of her worst nightmares would be a cakewalk compared to this: this grim fandango, this circus of misrule that she'd been working flat out for weeks to organize. Costume rails, overburdened with garments, were coming adrift, accessories were free-floating, models were backbiting and hiding things from each other like toddlers in playgroup. And Aphrodite's brief was to create order from this chaos. At least God had had six days. She had six hours maximum. She thought of the outrageous job description Troy had dreamed up for her. *Chargée d'affaires sartorieuses!* Pah! Factotum might be more accurate. Thank heaven for Nell, her angel trainee stylist, who'd come on board to help. And even thank heaven for Polly Riordan, who most uncharacteristically had volunteered to stay on to lend a hand, even though the four weeks' notice she'd given Troy MacNally Enterprises had expired last week. A measure indeed of how

285

besotted she was with her boss, thought Aphrodite.

Aphrodite had hit upon the idea of staging the show in an old public swimming baths. They had two days to move in, give the place a cursory clean-up, and construct a catwalk over the pool area. The baths were housed in a listed Victorian building owned by Dublin Corporation, which had been lying derelict for years. It badly needed a facelift, but its down-at-heel appearance was, for Aphrodite, part of its charm. The building had once had a glass roof, but now the vaulted timbers of the cupola that steepled skyward were open to the elements, and birds were nesting in the carved wooden arabesques that carpenters had fashioned over a century ago. The veneer of decrepitude – the cracked wooden panelling, the peeling paintwork, the rusting wrought iron – could not disguise the quintessential elegance of that bygone era: an era when refinement had been commonplace.

As had courtesy. Aphrodite had spent most of the past thirty-six hours honing her people skills and attempting to placate the Corporation official who was there to ensure no damage was done. 'Ah, yez can't be doing that, now!' was his favourite refrain, closely followed by 'Yez've to be out of here when the minute hand of me watch hits twelve!' Aphrodite found herself fantasizing about pushing him into the empty pool and releasing Rotweilers on him, the way the baddie had done in a recent *Prime Suspect* rerun.

She'd asked Lola's brother Tony to build the catwalk. She wanted to surround herself with as many people she could trust as possible. 'Why don't you give Lola a buzz?' he'd suggested. 'I'm sure she'd be glad to come in and give you a hand.' Aphrodite couldn't tell him that she and Lola were playing silly bugger relationship games, so she just said: 'I'll manage.'

But the next day, when it was patently obvious that she *wasn't* going to manage, Tony must have put in the call for her, because Lola arrived just as the dress rehearsal got under way. Aphrodite had escaped for two minutes' very necessary breathing space after a run-in involving Morgana, Nimuë and an irate make-up artist, and was sitting on the steps outside the baths with her head in her hands wishing she smoked and understanding now exactly why her predecessor Miriam had turned to drugs, when Lola materialized in front of her with her emergency dress rehearsal satchel slung over her shoulder. 'Hi,' she announced. 'I'm your *deus ex machina*, if you'll have me.'

'Oh, Lo!' Aphrodite managed, struggling to her feet and falling into Lola's outstretched arms. 'Oh, Lo – I'm so sorry. I've been so stupid – I should have phoned you ages ago and apologized for being such a jerk, it's just that–'

'Enough, already,' said Lola. 'We don't have time to do girly weepy shit now. We'll do it some time over many bottles of wine.'

'Tonight?' said Aphrodite hopefully. She couldn't think of a better way to end the day than by doing girly stuff with Lo in the quietest corner of the post-show piss-up they could find.

'Sorry. I'll have to take a raincheck. I have a hot date with Patrick. It's his birthday and I have recklessly volunteered to cook him dinner in my small but charming and oozing with character artisan dwelling. I'll have to beat it after the dress, I'm afraid, if I'm going to get to the supermarket on time. Now. Let's go kick some skinny model ass, Aphrodite Delaney. I have here my trusty emergency kit containing all the jazz we'll need to get this show safely on the road including – da dah!' She opened her satchel and pulled out a hip flask. 'V. good VSOP. OK. Let's make like Thelma and Louise, darling.' She proceeded up the stairs, trailing Aphrodite by the hand. 'Is it really that bad?' she said, giving Aphrodite a backward glance. 'Models can't be any worse than actresses, can they?'

Aphrodite refrained from comment. She didn't want her unlikely knight in shining armour beating a premature retreat.

She couldn't have done it without Lola. The dress rehearsal was running nail-to-the-quick-bitingly late. Aphrodite was practically pushing models out through the drapes onto the catwalk in order to keep the show up and running, trying to ignore the tussles and the tears over the running order. In the end she just wanted to savage the stapled pages into tiny little pieces with her teeth. Any time she peeked out between the drapes she would catch a glimpse of Troy sitting at the end of the catwalk, slumped white-faced in his seat. She looked at her watch. There was no way they were going to find time to stage the finale, where Troy would walk down the catwalk flanked by Morgana and Nimuë and followed by a retinue of proud, hollow-cheeked beauties. No matter. Troy and his two pet house models could wing it. They'd done it before. The less experienced girls would simply have to follow suit. She remembered what some wag of a director was reputed to have said to a cerebrally challenged actor. *All you have to do is say your lines and try not to bump into the furniture.* Hell. These girls not only didn't *have* any lines – there wasn't even any furniture to bump into. Nothing could go wrong.

When the last model finally sashayed through the curtains, Aphrodite called them all to attention. 'OK,' she said. 'Thank you all very, very much indeed. You all did the best you could under less than ideal circumstances. If you were able to get through *that,* the show this evening will be a piece of piss. Thanks again. And I might ask you all to make final checks yourselves, and reconvene for hair and make-up in half an hour.' Outraged squeaks and gasps met this last request. 'I know it's not a long enough break, but we just don't have time. Sorry about that, and thanks again. OK. Take thirty.'

Aphrodite staggered through the drapes and slumped into one of the plastic bucket seats that flanked the catwalk. An assistant was putting 'press only' stickers on all the seats in the front row. Troy was nowhere to be seen. Aphrodite thought he might be off getting sick somewhere, but then she remembered that he had a radio interview scheduled around now with some social diarist.

'Well.' Lola sat down beside her. 'What a fucking

joke! Avids, all of them.' 'Avid' had been their code for 'diva' any time they'd worked together in the past. 'How do you hack it, Aphrodite?'

'I delegate as much as I can. But there aren't that many people to delegate to, sadly.' A PA had been acquired for her, but she could only manage part time. That was all Troy MacNally Enterprises could run to right now. Apparently Troy had had a rare spat with Jolie over his decision to employ more staff without consulting her.

The gofer who was doing the seating arrangements moved past, and Aphrodite noticed that the sticker he put on the seat directly in front of her read 'Jolie Fitzgerald'. She hadn't seen La Fitzgerald for ages. She wasn't sure she could handle her tonight of all nights. There was to be a party at the POD club after the show, and Aphrodite knew she'd have to attend for Troy's sake.

'Where's Troy?' asked Lola.

'He's got an interview with a vampire.'

'You must be able to do that kind of stuff on automatic pilot now. You've become a seasoned celebrity since we last saw each other. How long *has* it been, d'you think?'

'I dunno. Oh, Lola – I'm sorry I didn't get in touch, I–'

'Yeah yeah yeah yeah yeah,' said Lola, in her let's-not-talk-about-it-now voice. 'I said we'd get all that crap out of the way some other time, didn't I?' She stretched, then threw back her head and laughed. 'Jesus! I cannot *believe* those models. Those fucking twins are priceless! D'you know what their real names are? Polly told me, and made me promise not to tell.'

'You mean they're not really called Nimuë and Morgana?'

'Hell, no. They took those names because Nimuë and Morgana were seemingly some kind of Arthurian sorceresses. Their real names are Krystle and Alexis after the *Dynasty* soap opera divas. Apparently they go apeshit if anyone calls them that.'

'I'm not surprised. Krystle and Alexis are even worse monikers than mine.'

'I got some brilliant eavesdropping in,' continued Lola. 'They actually *do* talk about nothing but clothes and diets. I thought that would have been too much of a cliché, but it's true. I heard one girl say to that glorious redhead: "I'm too lazy to exercise, but I'm careful to limit my calorie intake to around a thousand a day." Hell. I think I'm being temperate if I limit my consumption of *alcohol* to a thousand.'

Aphrodite suddenly felt a sense of joyous relief that Lola and she were friends again. They had so much to catch up on! 'What was the redhead's response?' she asked.

Lola put on a smug voice. ' "Oh, I'd hate that! I can eat and drink as much as I like, you know, but I *do* do a hundred lengths of the pool every day, just to stay toned." '

Aphrodite gave Lola an interested look. 'Really? That redhead's a swimmer?'

Lola shrugged. 'That's what she said. Why are you so interested?'

'I'll talk to you about it another time. It's to do with a project further down the line.'

Lola sniggered. 'You know what their nickname for you is?'

'Yeah. Musey.' Aphrodite managed a mirthless smile. 'It's better than Aphrodite, anyway.'

'Who dreamed it up?'

'Polly Riordan, probably. And as you've gathered by now, being a muse isn't a bundle of laughs.' She looked at her watch. 'Ouch. It's countdown time and I've still ten thousand million things to do.'

'Jesus, Aphrodite. You've done all you can. You look absolutely knackered, you know. You should start taking things easier, or you'll give yourself an ulcer.' The thought had occurred to her with increasing frequency. 'Look. Let me run out and get you a sandwich before I abandon you for the evening.'

'They've been ordered.'

'Yeah. But not the one I have in mind. Extra mayo, extra pesto, double decker with cream cheese and bacon and chocolate sauce and marshmallow bits, and more calories than a supermodel could shift in a week.'

'You are a total, total chum, Lo.'

'Yeah. Remember that, why don't you, the next time you put the phone down on me in a snit because of what some fuckwit of a gossip columnist's written about you.'

Aphrodite gave Lola a pained smile.

'I'll be back in two shakes, *with* two shakes. What flavour?'

'Whichever best matches my outfit, of course, darling.' Aphrodite was wearing jeans and a white T-shirt. 'Vanilla, I suppose.'

Lola saluted her and vaulted onto the boards that covered the pool. 'Hey – this feels so *cool*,' she said, putting a hand on her hip and sashaying its length. 'I reckon I could strut my stuff with the best of them. What d'you think, sweetie-pie?' And with that she executed a graceless pirouette, jumped off the end of the catwalk and was gone.

Aphrodite envied her friend her energy. She closed her eyes, laid her head on the back of the seat for a count of ten, then took a deep breath, preparing to summon the courage to get up and get on with it. But when she opened her eyes, she saw that someone was picking up an O'Brien's sandwich shop bag from where it had been left at her feet, and was sliding into the seat next to her. It was Polly Riordan. She looked blearily at the ex-PA, and then something made her look at her watch. Holy fuck! Twenty minutes had gone by! How had *that* happened?

'Aphrodite?' Polly was saying gently. 'Don't you think it's time you went backstage and got changed? Don't worry –' this when she took in the shell-shocked expression on Aphrodite's face '– everything's under control. Jolie's backstage finalizing things, and when I looked out and saw you comatose I thought it was just as well to let her take over for a while so's you could get some rest. You really do look terribly tired.'

Aphrodite slammed the heel of her hand against her forehead. 'Oh, shit, Polly – I didn't bring anything with me to change into. How stupid of me! For some insane reason I thought I'd have time to run home and have a shower before the show.' Aphrodite bit her lip. She was going to have to live with the very uncool T-shirt and jeans she'd slung on that morning. She'd just have to dash home directly afterwards and throw on some of Troy's gear. It would never do for the designer's muse to be seen sporting two-seasons-old stuff from Penney's at the showing of his autumn collection.

'Don't worry,' said Polly. 'I made sure to set aside something for you when I saw the way the day was shaping up. I've earmarked that rather sexy full-length amber silk for you. And, yes, don't *worry* –' she scolded, laying a reassuring hand on Aphrodite's arm when she caught her looking aghast at the trainers she'd slid into this morning '– there are shoes.'

Aphrodite looked dubious. 'The top on that amber silk's very see-through . . .'

'No problem. Sling one of those chenille stoles around your shoulders.' Polly put her head on one side, considering. 'And I'll look out some lovely dangly amber earrings to go with it. That colour will look divine on you under the lights. Oh, you'll be glad to know that the lighting designer can do that mirror-ball effect for the finale, by the way.'

What? 'What?' said Aphrodite, feeling as if she'd just been poked somewhere in the region of her gut with a cattle prod. 'What lights? What do you mean, the finale?'

'Aphrodite,' said Polly, even more gently, as if she

was a nurse talking to a geriatric patient. 'You have to take the stage at the finale. As Troy's muse it's expected of you. It's tradition.'

'*What!* No-one ever said anything to me about this, Polly! I'm not going *near* that fucking catwalk, no way!'

'Oh.' Polly sounded crestfallen. In fact, she sounded more than that – she sounded confused and upset. 'Oh. Well. I'd better go back to Troy and tell him. He probably just presumed you knew it was common practice. It was stupid of me not to have mentioned it earlier, but because we never got a chance to go over the finale in the dress rehearsal . . . Oh, God. He'll be very upset . . .' Polly's voice trailed off.

Aphrodite felt awful. Polly had been so good, after all, coming in to help when she wasn't obliged to. 'Look, Polly, I'm sorry I erupted like that, but I'm just not that kind of person, you know? The kind of person who swans along catwalks and enjoys applause. I'd feel like a total impostor and eejit if I were to do it.'

'But *all* Troy's muses have done it up till now! Please, Aphrodite, don't let him down. It means so much to him, and it's such an easy thing for you to give him – that gesture of support, of solidarity! It shows the world you're a team.'

Aphrodite sighed. 'Look, Polly, it may have been an easy thing for Miriam to do. She was his house model, after all. But I'm *not* a model, and–'

'Neither was Jolie.'

'What?'

'Neither was Jolie. *She* wasn't a model, and she did it for him.'

'Oh.' Oh, hell. Why did it always come back to Jolie? This was *so* unfair. She wished she could talk to Troy, ask him if there was any way out, but she knew it would be totally out of order to dump her insecurities on him at this juncture. He had enough to contend with this evening, without his muse suddenly coming on like some woozy shrinking violet type. And she couldn't bear the idea of Jolie curling her lip at her when she learned she'd wimped out.

Polly was looking at her now with assessment in her eyes. But there was more than that. There was a hint of contempt there, too. Oh, God. She supposed it *was* such a small thing to give. And *everybody* had been giving today. There may have been tantrums and sulks and invective hurled, but everybody today had worked their ass off for Troy, including Polly. And now even Jolie Fitzgerald had clearly rolled up and mucked in . . .

OK. She'd do it. She'd do it with lowered eyes and crimson cheeks and a little help from Lola's hip flask, but Polly was right. She should do it for Troy.

Chapter Twelve

The amber silk dress that Polly had set aside for Aphrodite was a stunner, especially when teamed with the dramatic flourish of a chenille stole. Aphrodite knew that if she was going to do this thing, she'd have to do it with a degree of chutzpah.

After she'd changed she manoeuvred her way through the crowd of chain-smoking models, dressers, and gofers delivering bouquets to where Troy was performing ego massage on Morgana. Aphrodite figured that Morgana was the last person who needed it. She waited till he'd finished and then touched him lightly on the arm. But before she had time to ask him if he approved of what she was going to wear for his finale, Polly grabbed her by the hand and said: 'Quick! Quick! Come with me!' Thinking there was some kind of emergency surgery to be performed on a frock, Aphrodite let herself be trailed back through the crowd towards where the make-up artists were gilding the lilies.

'What's the problem, Polly?' asked Aphrodite.

'There's no problem,' said Polly. 'I just wanted to be sure you got the best make-up girl going. Maggie's just finished her quota. She'll be glad to do you. Incidentally – I suggested that she concentrate on your mouth rather than your eyes. She won't have time to do anything dramatic with eye make-up, so a big, bold, beautiful mouth in a porcelain pale face will more than compensate.'

'Oh.' Aphrodite hadn't thought about make-up, but she realized it made sense. She'd look completely washed out under the lights if she didn't wear any. 'Oh, that's a bloody good idea, Polly. Thanks. I know I must look pretty damn peaky.'

'There isn't time to do anything to your hair, so I suggest you just keep it simple and slick it back.' Polly flashed her a friendly smile as she dashed off to busy herself elsewhere.

Maggie – the girl who'd been on the catalogue shoot – handed her a rubber cape to protect her dress. 'Sit down,' she said, sorting through little tubes of colour. 'Polly tells me you prefer the silent treatment?'

'What do you mean?' Aphrodite fastened the Velcro on the make-up cape and slid into a chair in front of the mirror.

'Well, some people like to prattle when they're nervous, and some would rather keep absolutely quiet.'

'Oh. Polly's right. Normally I'd probably like to prattle like anything, but right now I think I need some head space.'

'Fair enough,' said Maggie. 'I could do with a break from the interminable fashion-mag speak I've been obliged to listen to up till now.' The two women shared a smile, and then Aphrodite shut her eyes and gave herself over to Maggie's expert brush-strokes. It only took fifteen minutes to transform her from an extra from the *Night of the Living Dead* into a not unattractive human person. 'You've lost weight since we did that photo-shoot, you know,' said Maggie. 'Look at those cheekbones! Have you been dieting?'

'No,' said Aphrodite. 'I'd put it down to stress.'

'Do be careful. It wouldn't suit you to lose any more.' She handed Aphrodite a tube of Phytoplage and a comb. 'You can do your own hair. This stuff's the business.' She was right. In less than a minute the job was done, and Aphrodite's 'signature' blond crop was slicked back against her scalp. She leaned forward to check out her reflection, and was relieved to see that she looked a *lot* more presentable than she had for ages. The image she conveyed was one of careless, grown-up sophistication.

'I suppose you'll want to be made up for the party at some stage, too, Polly?' Maggie remarked to the passing PA. 'I should be able to fit you in later, if I don't have too much retouching to do.'

'Thanks, Maggie. I'll buy you a drink in return.'

'Damn right you will. You too, Delaney.'

'Oh. Sure.'

Maggie was peering at her own reflection in the make-up mirror. 'I could do with some *maquillage* too. Not that you really need make-up at the POD, the lighting's so subdued. But a bit of slap works wonders for a gal's confidence.'

'Thanks a lot, Maggie.' Aphrodite stood up and went to give the make-up artist a kiss on the cheek, but Maggie made a warding-off-vampires sign of the cross.

'No kissing anyone till after the show,' she said.

'Even with fixative you're going to leave marks. And if you mark a model's make-up you're dead meat. Good luck, Aphrodite.'

Aphrodite made her way back across the changing area to Troy, who was doing last-minute checks. As she passed a girl struggling to lace up the back of a frock between the protruding shoulder blades of one of the models, she heard the model's petulant voice say: 'What's bloody Musey doing hogging Maggie? She should know that make-up's far too busy with us to be bothering with her. I've been waiting to be retouched for the past half-hour now.'

The dresser gave Aphrodite a sideways look, but she just pretended not to have heard and continued on. Jesus *Christ*, she'd be glad when this night was over!

Troy was still white-faced. He gave her an abstracted once-over when he saw her. 'You look great,' he said, planting a quick kiss on her collar-bone before returning his attention to the task he'd been absorbed in when she'd approached him. He stood back, assessed, and then glanced at his watch. 'Fuck,' he said. 'It's time.'

There was a further flurry of activity before the DJ launched into Moby, and then, a few frantic moments later, the first of the models hit the catwalk. It was Morgana, who only seconds before had been scowling and gesticulating at a put-upon Nell. Now she was all composed elegance as she prowled down the catwalk with effortless, fluid grace, allowing her gaze to drift lazily over the upturned faces of the audience, occasionally rewarding an individual with a private smile which translated as 'Look at Me! I'm *So Sexy!*'

For the next forty minutes or so, Aphrodite worked on automatic pilot. It was as if the models were on a conveyor belt and she was a production line worker. No sooner had she hissed 'Go!' to one girl than there was another waiting to take her place. Aphrodite would rake expert eyes over the ensemble, tweak a strap here, pull at a hem there, expose a little more flesh with frantic fingers before sending the girl gliding out into the wall of light that lay beyond the black drapes. Occasionally she caught a glimpse of the audience – a journo scribbling in a notebook in the front row, a celebrity leaning over the wrought-iron railings of the viewing gallery above, Jolie and Gareth Fitzgerald sitting elegantly at ease in their VIP seats.

Then suddenly it was all over and it was time for the finale. She realized with a wave of despair that she wasn't at all clued in. Where, for instance, was she meant to be in relation to Troy? By his side? But no – the twins took pride of place in that hierarchy. She waved frantically towards where he was standing on the other side of the entrance, but he was absorbed in fixing an abalone shell choker that had come adrift from around Nimuë's neck, and didn't see her. Thank goodness, thank *goodness* – there was Polly Riordan coming towards her with her stole, stubbornly shouldering her way through the crowd of Amazonian models. She reached for Polly's arm just as, in the corner of her eye, she saw Troy part the curtains and stride out onto the catwalk, holding a twin's hand in each of his. The decibel level of the applause crescendoed immediately.

'Will I just forget about it, Polly?' said Aphrodite, clutching at straws. 'It's too late, and I haven't a clue what to do.'

'No, do it!' hissed Polly with passionate urgency, clipping dangly amber earrings onto Aphrodite's ear lobes and slinging the stole around her shoulders. 'All you have to do is stay a couple of paces behind Troy, turn when he turns, and follow him back up the catwalk. Go!'

She didn't even have time to draw breath. Polly was holding the curtain aside, and Aphrodite felt the pressure of her insistent hand on the small of her back, pushing her forward. The last thing she saw as she started to move was the poster she'd pinned up just by the entrance to the ramp, the glaring directives to the models exhorting them to be SEXY, SEDUCTIVE, SENSUAL, SPIRITUAL, SOPHIS-TICATED, SERENE, STRONG, SOULFUL. And she knew she was just going to look STUPID. Suddenly she was on the catwalk, blinking in the glare of the multicoloured lights that were swirling around her. She was aware of faces staring up at her, but she kept her eyes firmly fixed on Troy's tall figure moving in front of her, flanked by the willowy twins, whose progress was as synchronized as the Russian *corps de ballet*. She held herself as erect as she possibly could, but still felt clumsy and ridiculous by comparison to the twins – and by comparison to the other models who she knew were now sashaying along behind her. When Troy hit the end of the catwalk, Aphrodite dithered as applause swelled again and the models all joined in, holding aloft hands delicate as white butterflies to pitter-patter them at the man who had created the glorious garments they were showing off. Aphrodite followed suit, aware that some of the girls were giving her curious sideways looks.

Troy spent many moments acknowledging the tribute from the audience – moments which to Aphrodite seemed the longest in her life. She felt herself flushing under the hot lights, felt sweat breaking out under her armpits – how she prayed that it wouldn't stain her frock! – felt the thumping bass from the sound system pulsing through her, making her feel unsteady on her vertiginous heels. Flashbulbs were going off all round them, photographers urging Troy to turn to them so they could get a decent shot, along with calls of 'Morgana – over here!' and 'Nimuë – this way, please!' As Troy turned to proceed back up the catwalk, she heard a cry of 'Aphrodite! How about a smile?' – and she found herself stapling a rictus, fearful grin on her face that she knew must make her look like a death's head.

Aphrodite never forgot the look in his eyes when Troy saw her. It was as if he'd just walked into a wall. He hesitated for a beat, and then, with what looked like a huge effort, pulled on an impassive expression as he leaned forward to kiss her on the cheek. Cue: more flashbulbs. She felt his breath hot in her ear, and then his voice as he hissed: 'What the fuck do you think you're *doing*?'

Aphrodite was now so covered in confusion that she backed away from him a step, stumbling as she did so, and as he passed her by, still clasping the hands of his two house models, she noticed abstractedly that his knuckles were white. The other models parted like the Red Sea to let him pass, then reformed to surge back up the catwalk in his wake, Aphrodite shuffling along in their midst, feeling like the puniest member of a chain gang.

She knew immediately what had happened – it was agonizingly, grotesquely self-evident from Troy's reaction. Polly Riordan had set her up. The former PA had been determined to commit a final act of vengeful sabotage before bowing out of Troy MacNally Enterprises and relinquishing control to the pretender to the throne that was Aphrodite Delaney. It was obviously *not* common practice for a muse to join a designer on a catwalk. What she had just done had been completely out of line.

Oh, God! Oh, horror! Oh, help me, someone! she thought as she waited for the endless file of models to slink through the black drapes at the end of the catwalk. What must she have *looked* like? She must have appeared like some crazed megalomaniac as she'd stumped along the catwalk after Troy and the twins. What must people have thought? What would they think tomorrow if those wretched photographs hit the papers? What must the models have thought as they'd witnessed Musey parading along with her nose in the air, obviously imagining she could strut her stuff as well as they could? What would that mistress of *savoir-faire*, Jolie Fitzgerald, who had never thought much of her in the first place, think of her now? What – oh *God* – what was *Troy* thinking now?

She couldn't bear it. She couldn't bear the humiliation that would descend on her like a giant tidal wave the second she stepped backstage. As the last of the models shimmied through the drapes, Aphrodite thought fast. How to become the missing link in this chichi-est of chain gangs? Simple. She stepped to one side and then slid off the catwalk and into one of the wooden changing cubicles that flanked the old swimming pool. It was a half-doored construction – the head and feet of any bather who had changed there would have been visible from the poolside – so Aphrodite got onto the slatted wooden bench inside the cubicle, bent her knees up and laid her head on them. She felt like a small child who's committed some misdemeanour and is determined not to be found until the brouhaha has died down. But she was grown up enough to know that she was going to have to come out and face the music at some stage.

Not tonight. She couldn't do it tonight. She'd sidle out of the building along with the tail-end of the audience, flag down a cab, get home and take the phone off the hook. Christ! What a *bitch* of a day it had been! She felt so tired, so ashamed, so *injured* that she wanted to weep. But she couldn't yet. She'd wait until she'd closed the front door of her little house behind her.

She did all those things on automatic pilot. She put her stole over her head, concealing as much of her face as she could within its velvet folds, and sped through the building on fast feet, ignoring the officious Corporation man when he started his usual bellicose bellowing about clearing up and getting out of there before the minute hand of his watch hit twelve. Someone else could handle him. She ran down the street, managed to hail a cab, and tersely instructed the driver to take her to Bitter – sorry – *Stoney*batter. She thought with wry amusement that right now she was probably the bitterest of its inhabitants, and she hated Polly Riordan even more for making her feel this way.

How proficiently she'd been humiliated! How consummately she'd been gulled! She almost had to admire the way Polly had stage-managed her plan with such ruthless efficiency, and with such conviction. In the back of the taxi she reran mental footage of the way Polly had professed to be upset for Troy if 'Musey' didn't participate in the finale, the way she'd organized wardrobe and make-up for her, and the lengths she'd gone to to keep her away from Troy before the show began. Polly Riordan had made her exit from Troy MacNally Enterprises with all guns blazing, and an 'Up Yours, Delaney' executed larger than if she'd hired a plane to do sky-writing.

As the cab pulled up outside her house, Aphrodite realized with a flash of cold dread that she had no money on her. Her wallet was in her backpack in the models' changing area, along with her phone, her Filofax, her keys, her– Oh, God! There was no point in compiling a list of all her missing possessions. She'd just have to hope that someone had the cop-on to hang on to her bag for her. But what was she to do in the meantime? How was she to pay her cab, get into her house? The last thing she wanted to do was disturb Lola's romantic *diner à deux* – but she had absolutely no choice. The only alternative was to carry on to her mother's house and wait on the doorstep for her to come home after the show – and knowing her mother that might not be until four o'clock in the morning. Anyway, Thea was the last person she needed on her case right now.

She asked the driver to carry on to Lola's house, then hopped out and pressed the bell, hoping she wasn't interrupting anything more meaningful than the after-dinner mints.

Lola answered, and her jaw nearly hit the deck when she saw Aphrodite. 'What are *you* doing here?' she said. 'You should be moving and shaking with the *crème* of Irish café society at the POD right now, shouldn't you?'

'I'll explain in a minute,' said Aphrodite hurriedly. 'But in the meantime can you root out my spare key for me and lend me money to pay off my cab, Lo? It's an emergency.'

'Sure.' Lola never dithered. She disappeared and returned with a tenner, and then said, after Aphrodite had paid her cab fare: 'Come in right away and tell me about it. If you don't, I have a feeling that you're going to let yourself into your little house and slit your wrists, and it is my duty as a responsible citizen to do my utmost to dissuade you.'

'I can't come in, Lo,' said Aphrodite. She was starting to shiver in her thin silk gown. 'I don't want to disturb you and Patrick.'

'You won't be disturbing anything, darlin'. We had to postpone. Patrick got called out to do some sleuthing. It's no more a bundle of laughs being a detective's moll than it is being a muse, you know.' Lola held the door open and followed Aphrodite through into the sitting room where a fire was going and there were flowers on the mantelpiece and where Bobcat – who had clearly been visiting – was curled up on the hearthrug, and there was a glorious smell of basil in the air and an open bottle of Chablis in a cooler.

'OK,' said Lola authoritatively. 'Sit down, sweetie, and tell it like it is.'

And Aphrodite did.

'Well,' said Lola when she'd finished. 'The first thing you're going to have to do is tell Troy that you made a genuine mistake, and that Polly bumsteered you. What a poisonous, *poisonous* thing to do!'

'I can't phone him,' said Aphrodite despondently. 'His mobile's in my handbag.'

Lola considered. 'I'm not altogether certain that you should *phone* him,' she said. 'You can't have a conversation like that over the phone. It's better to do it face to face.'

'Oh, God, Lo! I won't be able to look him in the eye! I feel so fucking *ashamed*. He's going to think–'

'Aphrodite. It's not your fault. What happened is *not your fault*. If Troy's half the guy you say he is, he'll understand that.'

Aphrodite swigged back a load of Chablis, then put her head in her hands. 'Oh, Jesus, Lo – it's not just Troy I'm not going to be able to face. I won't be able to appear in public ever again. People will be slagging me off all round town.'

'Maybe they won't. Not everyone is privy to the arcane rituals observed by *couture*. If someone had told me it was traditional for a muse to accompany a designer along the catwalk at the end of the show I'd have no reason not to believe them. Loads of people won't see anything wrong with it. They may even be impressed by it. Hey – *Individual* might commission you to do a whole page of that "Elegantarium" garbage instead of just a half.'

Aphrodite shot her friend a sham basilisk look. 'Shut up about that column.'

'I think it's brilliant. I think you should start being an undercover sartorial saboteur and issue seriously misleading style directives every month.'

'Troy and I already thought of that.' She thought with nostalgia of the times they'd spent giggling over the kind of daft dictates Aphrodite could lay down in her style police column.

Oh, God. Troy. What to do? If she wasn't going to phone him, *when* would she talk to him? The sooner the better, obviously, but she hadn't a clue what time he was likely to get in from the POD – it could be all hours. She'd have to leave it till the morning. And then she remembered that she had his spare key. It was hanging on the back of her kitchen door. So. What if she let herself into his flat and waited there for him? She wouldn't bother staying up till he got back – she could get into his bed and warm it for him. It might be an idea to have a bottle of champagne on ice, or a joint to relax him. He'd be tired after the fraught day he'd had, and in need of comfort and maybe some special sex. The oldest trick in the book for repairing lovers' tiffs, she knew, but often the one that worked best. That's what she'd do. She'd dash home, have a quick shower, rub herself with that sandalwood body lotion he loved the smell of and then slip into his apartment and into his bed.

'Listen, Lo!' She explained her plan to Lola, who pronounced it excellent, clapped her hands and handed her a small wad of banknotes before seeing her to the door.

Aphrodite looked at it, surprised. 'The taxi won't cost me that much, you know.'

'It's not just your taxi fare – vintage champagne doesn't come cheap, honeybun. When you're forking out for ammo, you know it makes sense to buy the best. Which is Mr MacNally's tipple of choice?'

'Cristal. His fridge is usually coming down with the stuff, but we cleared it out this morning to keep the models happy backstage.'

'Mm. I don't imagine our local off-licence runs to Cristal. But it's the thought that counts. Stock up on some sexy finger food while you're at it. He'll be touched that you made the effort.'

On the other side of Lola's front door was Patrick, frozen in the action of ringing the bell.

'Is that a gun in your pocket, or are you just pleased to see me?' purred Lola.

Patrick bent down to kiss her lightly on the lips. 'It's a gun,' he said. 'But I *am* pleased to see you. I

310

could have done without that little wobbly to sort out, tonight of all nights. Hi, Aphrodite. Long time no see.'

'Hi. I'm on my way out,' she added reassuringly. 'Happy birthday, Patrick.' She stood on tiptoe to give him a kiss on the cheek, and then, with a 'thankyouthankyouthankyou, my very best chum' to Lola, she stepped out onto the pavement.

'Hey!' called Lola after her as she legged it down the road, 'good luck, Musey!'

*   *   *

She was showered and scented and on her way to Troy's in a taxi with a couple of carrier bags at her feet. The local Spar wasn't exactly the best place to shop for sexy finger food, but she'd managed to find asparagus tips (tinned – she imagined how aghast Jolie Fitzgerald would be at the notion of tinned asparagus), almond-stuffed olives, a reasonably ripe Brie and a baguette. The off-licence had supplied her with a bottle of Veuve Clicquot.

'Celebrating something?' the man serving her had asked.

'I hope so,' she'd replied with a smile.

She negotiated the scuffed street door and the three flights of stairs that led to Troy's apartment, and let herself in.

Almost immediately she knew he wasn't alone. A scent of Sobranie cigarettes came to her on the air, and then a woman's voice. Low, husky, inimitable – and unmistakable. Jolie Fitzgerald. Oh,

God! Aphrodite's mind started spinning. Were they in bed together? But the voice was coming from the sitting room, not the bedroom. Aphrodite slipped off the flat shoes she'd changed into and crept towards the half-open door, praying that she'd manage to avoid the creaking board that lay somewhere between the hall door and the polished wooden threshold of the sitting room.

Eavesdropping usually gave her an unpleasant feeling, but this time she felt no qualms, and no guilt. She and Jolie Fitzgerald were at war – ergo spying on the enemy was morally justifiable.

'You need her, Troy,' she heard her potential nemesis say. 'I – *you* made a mistake with Miriam, but Aphrodite's good for you. Yes, it was supremely arrogant of her to do what she did this evening, but I'm sure we can persuade her back on the right track without too much difficulty.'

Aphrodite had reached the door of the sitting room. She positioned herself side-on to the door jamb, then leaned forward fractionally so that she could see into the room. Jolie was sitting in an armchair with her profile to Aphrodite; Troy was on the rug at her feet. The room was in virtual darkness, the only light coming from a lamp on the side table where the anthracite and marble chessboard stood, its pieces still in roughly the exact same formation as when Aphrodite had first seen it all those months ago. Troy had told her that the game – which had been between Jolie and Miriam – had lasted only ten minutes before Jolie's black queen had taken Miriam's white and effected effortless checkmate.

'Why do you think she did it?' asked Troy.

'I honestly don't know. Perhaps she thought it was standard practice? She must have known that Miriam did it—'

'But that was different! Miriam was my house model. Jesus, Jolie – I got such a shock when I saw her there, with her mouth all lipsticked exactly the way my aunt's was in that photograph, and her hair back from her face, and that chenille stole swathed round her shoulders. She was even wearing virtually identical amber earrings. I don't know what went through my head when I went to kiss her. I actually wanted to lash out at her.'

'I know, I know – but you're calm now.' There was a pause. Jolie started to stroke his hair. 'Maybe it's time you lost that photograph, Troy? Relegated it to the past where it belongs. I've never understood why you feel the need to hang on to a reminder of someone who mind-fucked you so mercilessly.'

'It wasn't her fault. I come from a long line of messed-up minds, Jolie – as you well know. Auntie dearest was fucked up before I came along, and being saddled with me simply fucked her up even more.'

'So why have you hung on to her portrait?'

'Because she was my original muse, I suppose. It's a kind of shamanistic thing, isn't it? I'd be scared that if I trashed it I'd be hexing myself. But you're right. It's time to lay some ghosts to rest. I'll get rid of it tomorrow.'

'I think that's wise.' There was a beat, then: 'Do you love her, Troy?' asked Jolie. She put the question

313

matter-of-factly, as if she was asking him to fill in a questionnaire.

'Aphrodite? Yes. At least I think so. I'm becoming so unsure about everything these days, Jolie. Everything's confused. And the nightmares have started again.'

'Maybe you should take a break. You're very fragile. You've been under so much pressure lately, and people are going to start clamouring for the spring designs before you've time to turn round – *and* you've to have frocks ready for that Christmas charity gig. Coolnamaragh's all yours, Troy. For as long as you want. Aphrodite could go down and join you at weekends.'

'I'd rather she was there all the time.' He sounded petulant.

'That's not possible, darling. Not now she's running the shop up here. We can't train someone else in *again*. Polly's only just left – it would be a disaster.'

There was another pause before Jolie spoke again. It seemed to Aphrodite that there was something very calculated about these pauses. It was as if they were being gauged to the precise nanosecond. 'The nightmares – they're the same ones, are they? About your mother?'

'Yes. Only they're worse. I try to latch on with my mouth, searching for her breast, but she pulls away. She won't feed me.'

There was another long pause, and then, finally, a pensive sigh. 'I know what you want,' said Jolie.

'You've wanted it since you saw Aphrodite's mother on stage at the Phoenix. I'm right, aren't I?'

What? Could it be true? Could Troy have the hots for her mother? Aphrodite clamped both her hands over her mouth to stem the whimper she felt rising within her, and then she watched as Troy got to his knees and gazed up at Jolie. In the light from the lamp she saw that his face was contorted by a kind of needy longing. 'Would you? Oh, God, oh, God – would you, Jolie?'

Jolie reached out a hand to touch Troy's face. 'Why not? We'll try it, shall we? You know I care nothing for taboos. And I'm the only person who can give you what you crave.'

'How did you guess,' said Troy, 'that that's what I crave?' He had started to undo the buttons on the bodice of Jolie's dress.

'I know you so well, my darling. I know you as well as if you were my own child.'

Jolie's bodice was gaping open now. She smiled down at him, serene as a Madonna by da Vinci, and then she did something completely shocking. She slid one strap of her dress down over her shoulder and then she opened the front of her baby blue lace-trimmed bra. 'Here you are, darling,' she said proffering him her breast. 'Let's see if this helps.'

Aphrodite watched in a state of shock as Troy MacNally crawled into Jolie Fitzgerald's lap, and took her nipple in his mouth. Oh God. Oh *God*! Her knees nearly buckled, and she reached for the door jamb to steady herself. The sudden movement

315

must have registered in Jolie's peripheral vision, because she turned her head. There was an appalling moment when the two adversaries regarded each other unblinkingly, like lionesses meeting unexpectedly on uncharted territory. Then Aphrodite took a deep breath, steadied herself, and made ready to attack. But something Jolie did made her stop short. The other woman narrowed her eyes in warning. Then she slowly raised an index finger to her lips. The message was clear. Aphrodite was not to interfere – she was not to interrupt this bizarre ritual. They stared at each other for a long time until, resisting with superhuman strength the impulse to yowl like a cat, Aphrodite drew herself up to her full height, curled a contemptuous lip at her rival, and backed out of Troy's apartment on silent feet.

* * *

She didn't bother to take a cab home. She wanted to walk, to clear her head. It didn't work. No matter how hard she tried, she couldn't erase the image of Jolie and Troy from the screen of her mind's eye. The mental footage of Troy latching on to Jolie's breast reran itself over and over on a loop, tormenting her. Oh, God! The knowledge that Jolie could provide Troy with the kind of succour that Aphrodite couldn't was agonizing. She remembered how she'd compared Jolie to a harpy, gorging on Troy. It was evidently a reciprocal thing. And how wildly, hideously ironic that her own mother was the

316

one responsible for putting the idea into Jolie's head when, as Arkadina, she'd nursed her 'son' on the stage of the Phoenix theatre.

Jolie's words came back to her. *I know you as well as if you were my own child* . . . And she remembered the first time she'd seen them together all those months ago at Coolnamaragh, and the searing jealousy she'd felt when Jolie had annexed Troy. And now, all this time later there was still so much she didn't know about him, still so much secret history. She felt more than jealous now – she felt bereft. She felt as if some goblin had crawled onto her shoulder and whispered in her ear that Troy MacNally would never belong to her the way he belonged to Jolie Fitzgerald.

But that couldn't be! She loved Troy, she wanted him still. She couldn't let Jolie destroy what they had going between them. Oh, God! Her heart bled for the poor, messed-up creature who was her lover. And suddenly an image came into her mind of the anthracite checkmate. If Miriam was the defeated queen and Jolie the victorious one, what did that make Troy? A king, or a pawn?

It was after two o'clock in the morning when she finally reached home, but Aphrodite still wasn't tired. Before she went to bed she took the phone off the hook and knocked back a hefty dose of her disgusting homeopathic sleeping remedy. She suspected that her head would be an all-night arena for mental gymnastics of the most contorted kind if she didn't. Just before she fell asleep, she had a disquietingly lucid sneak preview of the dreams that would come to her tonight. And of course, she was right. She spent most of the night like Alice in Looking-glass Land, stumbling across a giant chess-board trying to ward off enemies, the most formidable of whom was the Black Queen.

Chapter Thirteen

She delayed for a civilized three hours before ringing Lola the next morning. As it was Saturday, an early morning call might have set them spiralling back down the slippery relationship slope they'd just negotiated. Her timing was bang on. When she phoned at midday, Patrick had just left.

'Lo – I'm sorry. I'm going to have to borrow your ears again.'

'I'd make a fortune as a shrink.'

'I know. Tell you what – I'll reward you with vintage Veuve Clicquot. How does that sound?'

'A tad ominous. I deduce from that that you didn't get to drink it last night?'

'No – and I'll tell you why when I see you. Have you had breakfast?'

'Yes. But all the feasting on flesh I've done since has left me ravenous. If I'm going to let you avail of my counselling services I want eggs, mushrooms, and tomatoes on toast. And lashings of Lavazza.'

'Deal. But I've no mushrooms.'

'I have. I'll bring them.'

Lola arrived fifteen minutes later, looking shambolic, and yawning.

'You look fucked,' remarked Aphrodite, slinging butter into a pan.

'I was. By an expert. What about you?'

'Sadly, no.'

'What happened? Did he not show?'

'He was already there.'

And for the second time in twenty-four hours, Aphrodite bent Lola's ear. How had she survived so many weeks without her?

'Oh, Jesus, Aphrodite,' said Lola when she'd finished. She had pressed her hands against her mouth and her eyes were huge. 'What are you going to do?'

'I don't know.' Aphrodite was grateful that Lola hadn't gone: 'Gross!' or 'Ee-yoo!' or – what she was dreading most – 'Dump him!' 'The funny thing is, Lo, although I'm shook-up and angry and all those things, I really don't feel I can level with him.'

'Has it put you off him?'

'No. It's funny. If anything, it's made me more protective of him. I know this sounds weird, but I reckon if I'd caught them *in flagrante delicto*, it might have been easier.'

'*Easier?* Are you serious?'

'Yes. You see, that would have been a cut and dried case of betrayal and I would have had every right to demand a showdown. But there was nothing *sexual* about what he was doing last night, I'm convinced of it.'

'Er – sorry to be so brutal, but how do you know?'

'I just do. I've done nothing but think of it and analyse it since. That's why I'm so kind of – well – *rational* about the whole thing now. If I'd come to you any earlier I'd have been a gibbering idiot.' It was true. The numbness of shock had worn off overnight, and when Aphrodite had woken this morning the first thing she'd done had been to wail so loudly that Bobcat had leapt from the bed and gone off to find somewhere more peaceful to catnap. Now she fixed Lola with a steady gaze. 'Look at it this way, Lo – if there had been a sexual element to it, Jolie would never have warned me off like that. Even she would have had the decency to look guilty. You know when they say that looks speak volumes?'

'Mm-hm.'

'Well, from the way she looked at me I could tell that she was sending me a message in block capitals, saying: "This has nothing to do with sex. Don't interfere." She was asking me to *allow* Troy this indulgence.'

Lola raised an eyebrow. 'Um. She was *asking* you?'

'Well. OK. Telling me.'

'And you acceded.'

'Yes. God! It's so difficult to explain. I did it for Troy, really. Can you understand, Lo?'

'I suppose.' Lola looked thoughtful. 'It's textbook stuff, isn't it? A mother fixation.'

'Yeah. It starts to make sense when you look at it that way. Remember that Jolie was his first real muse – the first person since he was a baby responsible for looking after him, encouraging him and all that. His aunt was a basket case, apparently. That's why Miriam de Courcy didn't last long – she turned into a basket case, too.'

'So then you come along and you're perfect muse

321

material because of your mumsy skills, and Jolie's delighted because she's found another Wendy for her Peter Pan.'

'I suppose. And hey – it's not *just* because of my "mumsy" skills, Lo. We have a damn fine sex life too, I'll have you know. But I can't give him the kind of emotional pampering Jolie can.' Aphrodite bit her lip.

'You've obviously been doing a lot of thinking,' said Lola.

'You reckon my theory's sound, then?'

'I dunno, darling. I just think you should stop thinking so hard. When you answered the door your forehead was all puckered, and it still is. You're going to need to invest in a Botox job and a tub of Crème de la Mer if you're not careful.'

'But I *can't* stop! I'm even analysing my relationship with Jolie from a new perspective.'

'Explain.'

'Well, it's weird, you know? But since last night something's definitely shifted in the balance there.'

'Explain.'

'I'm not sure I can. It's as if by conniving–'

'Explain.'

'Conniving? Um – it means kind of conspiring. Turning a blind eye to. And that's exactly what I did last night. I *connived* at Jolie's behaviour. I could have stormed into that room and thrown a wobbly, but I didn't. And because I didn't, I'm kind of in collusion with her now. I'm a – a what d'you call them? – an *accessory* to the crime.'

'And what, exactly, *is* the crime?'

'Oh, you know! This whole *danse macabre* that Jolie Fitzgerald's been choreographing to keep Troy happy.'

'I'm actually not sure that it *is* a crime to ensure that someone you care for is happy.'

'But not the way she's doing it! She's just doing it for the money. She's just doing it because she knows that if Troy isn't happy his inspiration will dry up. I heard her say as much to Hugo O'Neill that night in Coolnamaragh when she was in the hot tub with him, the night before I had to come back to clean up after the break-in.'

'So. Tell me this, friend.' Lola cocked her head to one side and gave Aphrodite a searching look. 'Are you in love with Troy, or are you just doggedly determined to rub Jolie Fitzgerald's nose in it?'

Aphrodite flushed. 'What do you mean?'

'I *mean*, I think, that I know you quite well. The whole Jolie thing has obviously become a huge issue for you. It's assumed fight to the death proportions, hasn't it?'

Aphrodite got up from the kitchen table and started pottering around with breakfast things. She needed to do something to cover her confusion. She sometimes wished that Lola wasn't so astute. Her friend very often knew things about her that she didn't even know herself. *Was* her involvement with Troy motivated as much by her feelings of rivalry towards Jolie as it was by her feelings for him? Aphrodite wished she hadn't asked Lola for her opinion, now. She didn't much like what she was learning about herself.

'Are you happy with him, Aphrodite?'

'*Yes!*' She gave the word loads of emphasis to prove how much she meant it. 'He's sexy, and he's generous, and he's fun – when he's not stressed out, that is.'

'Nobody's fun when they're stressed. You've been under a lot of pressure yourself, lately. You're shouldering way too many responsibilities, Aphrodite.'

'Well, I'm paid to do that now, and, hey!' – with a mock snooty toss of the head – 'Are you implying that *I'm* not fun?'

'Well, yesterday wasn't much fun, was it? When I saw you bawling Nell out, I thought to myself, "Yikes. Delaney's losing the plot."'

Aphrodite flushed for the second time in as many minutes. 'Did I bawl Nell out?' She'd certainly never done *that* before – Nell was such a doll she'd never had to. But she'd been so hyped up yesterday that she couldn't remember now who exactly had been on the receiving end of her invective.

'Yeah. Over some lace mittens that had gone missing. You said something like: "Next time, why don't you try attaching them to a cord around your neck the way they do in kindergarten, for fuck's sake."'

Aphrodite put her hand over her mouth. 'Oh. Did I say that?' Lola raised her eyebrows at her, and a sudden image flashed across her mind's eye of Nell's shocked face turning away from her as if she'd been slapped, and she realized she *had* said it. She sat back down at the kitchen table and put her head in her hands, then said in a very small voice, 'D'you know something, Lo? I'm scared. I'm scared that I'm becoming a horrible person.'

'What do you mean?'

'Ever since Damien Whelan stole my designs I've found myself thinking the most horrific, *murderous* thoughts. Not just about him – about Jolie and Polly and Jack Costello and virtually every single model I've ever met. I can't seem to think nice thoughts about anybody any more. And I've become really mistrustful around everyone I meet. I immediately think the worst of them rather than giving them the benefit of the doubt. I just automatically assume that they're out to get me.'

'It's a dog eat dog world out there.'

'Bitch eat bitch, you mean. All the people I hate most are women.'

'Damien Whelan isn't a woman.'

'He's still a bitch.'

'Jack Costello?'

'Did I say Jack Costello?'

'Yep. And I would have thought that he's *all* man.'

'He's a fucking cynic.'

'Yeah. But there's a world of difference between healthy cynicism and the malignant kind. I would have thought that he's a pretty robust individual.'

'How do you know that?'

'I approached him about taking shots of my last set design for my portfolio. He's a top bloke. And while he may be a cynic, he never resorts to sarcasm.'

Next time, why don't you try attaching them to a cord

around your neck the way they do in kindergarten, for fuck's sake. The pathetic sarcasm she'd used on Nell resounded in her ears in a kind of echo effect. 'Oh, *God*! *How* could I have been so awful to Nell, Lola? Do you think I really *could* be turning into a horrible person? A bitter and twisted type? I always thought of myself as being a rather sunny individual.'

'Listen, darling.' Lola put her elbows on the table and leaned towards her. '*Anyone* confronted with grotesques like Damien Whelan and Jolie Fitzgerald and Polly Riordan would feel exactly the same way as you. Most people behave badly when they're stressed – like you did with Nell yesterday. The only advice I can give you is textbook. Keep away from stressful situations, and try to avoid poisonous viper-type individuals like the aforementioned three. They've actually taught you a valuable life lesson.'

'Oh?'

'Yeah. You've suddenly discovered that not everyone in the world is made of such sunny stuff as you. There are a lot of malignant saddos out there, who, surprisingly enough, don't have your best interests at heart.'

'Right.' Aphrodite thumped the worktop for effect, then turned on the tap and started sluicing out the cafetière. 'From now on I am going to work at being a much better human being. I am going to remind myself on a regular basis that I'm actually quite a nice person, and I am *not* going to let the bastards get to me. I'm going to turn off the television every time those awful ads come on that push product by cynically appealing to your inner selfishness–'

'Which ads?'

'Oh, you know – those really dodgy ones. Like the one with the mother stealing her kid's yoghurt, and one with the woman hiding her husband's false teeth so she can stuff her face with Jaffa cakes. And that totally gross one with the geezer ripping the last Rolo out of his girlfriend's gullet so's he can offer it to the sexier babe who just came in. I stopped buying Jaffa cakes and Rolos when those ads came out. I couldn't help thinking of the young advertising turks who were responsible for them all sitting around think-tanking in Prada.'

'Do advertising people really think-tank in Prada?'

'Trust me. I've been there. Ha! If anyone offers me a styling job on an ad like that in future I think I'll take the moral high ground and tell them to stuff it. We're turning into a nation of selfish, ugly fucks, Lo. Whatever happened to loving someone enough to give them your last Rolo?'

'I think you should save your last Rolo for Nell, Aphrodite. She more than earned it yesterday.'

'I will. *And* I'll send her a card to apologize for bawling her out. And I'll start buying *Oprah* mag and doing affirmations. I am a nice person. I am a nice person. I am a nice person. More coffee?' she asked, flicking the switch on the kettle.

'You said it. You *are* a nice person, Aphrodite. You wouldn't be my friend if you weren't.' A loud popping noise from behind made Aphrodite jump and turn in the air with an agility that David Beckham might have envied. Lola was standing holding the bottle of chilled Veuve Clicquot in her left hand, and the champagne cork in her right.

'What are we celebrating?' asked Aphrodite.

'Our newfound friendship,' said Lola.

*   *   *

Some ninety minutes later, Lola and Aphrodite had finished the champagne and were three-quarters-way down a cheap and cheerful supermarket Chardonnay. They had filled each other in on any major life-changing events that had occurred since they'd last seen each other, and had such fun kissing and making up that they were determined to have another row some time soon so that they could do it all over again.

Lola had fallen wildly, abandonedly in love with her detective. 'He packs a mean pistol *and* he sings in a band in his spare time! I'm having a fling with a real, live singing detective!' A couple of days into their relationship he had whisked her off to France for a holiday. They'd spent the first week in a madly romantic *gîte* in Provence, then hit the posher bits of France, including Paris, Biarritz and (Lola was almost embarrassed to admit it) Cannes. 'It sucks,' she said. 'We only went to laugh at the posers. And then we came home and I expected to find at least *one* message on my answering machine from you, and I was very miffed indeed when there was nothing.'

'I'm sorry, Lo,' said Aphrodite. 'I was awash with paranoia, thinking you thought *I'd* turned into some awful posey person. Those bloody social columns did my head in. Hey – I've got a brill idea. Why don't we open another bottle?'

'OK. And don't you think you should put the phone back on the hook?'

'Oh. Oh, no. I don't think I have the nerve, Lo.'

'Go on, go *on*!' insisted Lola. 'You've loads of Dutch courage inside you now. You're going to have to talk to him soon.' Lola drained her glass. 'Uh-oh. I've just remembered where I first laid eyes on him.'

'Troy?'

'Yeah. This is getting v. spooky, Aphrodite.'

'How? Why?'

'The first time I saw him was at the opening night of that *Oedipus* I designed for the Chamber Pot. And Polly Riordan told me it was the first time he'd been out since Miriam de What's-her-name left him.'

'So?'

'He comes out of self-imposed social exile to see a production of *Oedipus*? Think about it.'

'Oh!' Aphrodite slumped. 'What is it with me and men, Lola? First bloody Badley leaves me for another man, and now I discover that the love of my life is suffering from a classic Oedipus complex.'

'Mm. It's a bummer, all right.' Lola frowned and nodded sagely, and then she looked down at the table, and then she looked back at Aphrodite, and suddenly they were both laughing.

And Aphrodite laughed and laughed until the tears ran down her cheeks. 'Oh, Lola!' she said when she could finally talk again. 'How could I get through life without you? Maybe we should just shack up together and be lesbians.'

'Oo-er. No way, sister. I have all the loving I need from my new man. And having one lesbian in the family's quite enough, thanks. My sister's talking about coming out at last.'

'Rosita?'

'Yeah. It's bloody brave of her. My mum will disown her. Now, talking of being brave, let's get serious again. You've got to put the phone back on the hook, Aphrodite. You *have* to talk to Troy some time before Monday. You're going to see him at work then, so you'll have to get this sorted before–'

'*Work!* Fuck, Lola – I completely forgot about my column for *Individual*! My deadline's Monday!' Aphrodite leapt to her feet, teetered into her studio and accessed her computer.

'Yay!' said Lola, teetering after her with the bottle. 'Let me help. How many words?'

'Around five hundred.'

'OK. How's this?' Lola settled herself down in front of the screen and started to type. 'If you happen to be passing through Barcelona (currently Europe's hippest city, as I shouldn't need to remind you), check out the totally crucial exhibition in the Magicà Gallery in Gran Via. Among the many thought-provoking installations on display, Prada Simone's "Barbie Bush" stands out. Simone has uprooted a massive dead hydrangea and planted it in a hot pink plastic urn. Where blossoms once grew, the artist has been inspired to graft on the decapitated heads of hundreds of Barbie dolls, complete with lustrous locks, lipsticked grins and hair accessories. Makes you look twice – and, more importantly, makes you think twice about the consumer culture that envelops us so totally we scarcely notice it any more, let alone question its sinister ethos.'

Aphrodite looked at Lola in open-mouthed astonishment. 'You didn't tell me you'd been to Barcelona as well as Paris and Biarritz and Cannes!'

'I didn't. Go to Barcelona, that is.'

'So how come you know about this Simone dame and her Barbie Bush?'

'I don't,' said Lola. 'I made it up. Prada Simone doesn't exist, and neither to my reasonably certain knowledge does the Magicà Gallery. But I'd be prepared to bet that someone somewhere is, as we speak, painstakingly constructing a Barbie Bush.'

A great big bubble of laughter escaped Aphrodite. 'Oh, Lola – I love you! It's brilliant!'

Lola flashed her a wicked smile, and returned her attention to the screen. 'What else can we put?'

'We could bring back the pashmina. That was the single most sensible accessory ever invented. Apart from ten-denier lace-topped stay-ups.'

'No. Bringing back the pashmina is way too rational for a style arbiter. D'you know what Rachel Hunter once said about them?'

'What did she say?'

'She said she wanted to vomit over them. It conjures up an image of her going into pashmina shops and puking up all over piles of them. Can you imagine the reaction of the sales staff?'

'They could market them as pashminas inspired by Jackson Pollock. OK,' said Aphrodite. 'Bollocks to pashminas. Put in something about awful

Seventies macramé satchels instead. I was going to fob a load of them off on Morgan– sorry – I mean Krystle and Alexis, once, and make out that they were Troy's latest hip accessories.'

'Macramé satchels? But they *are* hip again.'

'Oh. Are they?'

Lola gave her a pitying look. 'Didn't you *know*, darling? Tut tut. And you a chief inspector in the Style Police. I saw a designer one featured in *Vogue* for over a thousand quid.'

'Hey! We should break into the Gaiety and raid their props room! There's loads of macramé satchels in there. We could stand to make a fortune on the black market, Lo. We could customize them with "witty" stuff.'

'Such as?'

'Um. I dunno. I can't think of anything witty right now. My head's too fuzzy.'

'But this is urgent, Aphrodite! If we don't get your column in before its deadline, nobody will know what to wear next month, or what to talk about at dinner parties.'

'Dinner parties are *so* twentieth century, Lo.'

'OK, then. Soirées. Salons. Whatever.' Lola returned her attention to the screen. 'Let's see. How's this?'

She started typing again, while Aphrodite hung over her shoulder, avid to see what her style guru would dream up. ' "Count yourself lucky," she read, "if your mother or aunt owned an Eighties puffball skirt, and raid the back of her wardrobe for the hottest look of the season. Yes, dear reader, puffballs are in the news again, bigger, brighter and brasher than ever. And if you *dare* go to the extreme cutting edge, try trimming the hem yourself with tassels, tinsel, spangles and sequins. Go gaudy like Gaudi – hit your nearest craft shop for what I predict is going to become a runaway bestseller for Maureen Mackenzie, author of *Frippery, Frills and Furbelows One Thousand Ways with Trimmings.*" '

Aphrodite was doubled up with laughter. 'Stop it, Lo! I'm going to wet myself!'

'How many words is that?' said Lola. 'Probably not enough. You'll have to put in some serious stuff as well – "seen on the catwalk at Dries van Noten's autumn show, blah blah blah" – if you're not going to blow your cover.'

'Do I dare?' asked Aphrodite. 'E-mail it, I mean?'

Lola sloshed more wine into their glasses. 'Go for it, Musey. Style subversion rules. "It" girls go home.' Chardonnay overflowed onto the desktop, and Lola looked surprised. 'That's funny. I usually only do that when I'm pissed,' she said, leaning forward to sip out of the brimful glass. Then: 'Hey, Aphrodite, if you promise to make a habit out of sneaking stuff like that into your column every month, I will take out a subscription to *Individual* straight away. As long as you let me contribute anonymously from time to time.'

'Done deal,' said Aphrodite, squinting at the copy on the screen. 'But look here, Lola – about the Barbie Bush. Shouldn't it be "dismembered heads" instead of "decapitated heads"? Isn't that tautology? Ooh. Come to think of it, "dismembered heads" sounds a bit funny too.'

'What are you on about? Tautology, schmology! Do you really think the kind of person who takes this stuff seriously is going to notice mistakes in the grammar?'

'You're right again. Hey! Maybe I could introduce groovy new phrases into the English language while I'm at it. I could write stuff like: "The newest hip buzzword to be heard quoting is" – um. What could it be? Think of something that sounds really horrible, Lola. What words do you hate most?'

'Complacency.'

'No, Lo – I mean words that *sound* horrible.'

'Um. Nostril, grunt, snort. And gusset.'

Aphrodite considered. 'No. None of them will do. How about "throb"? As in: "Donatella's latest shrunk organza is totally throbbing"? Yeah! I think I'll– Yikes.' The doorbell was ringing, quite persistently. Aphrodite scooted to the window and peeked out. There on the doorstep was Troy, with an *Evening Herald* in one hand, and the most enormous bouquet of long-stemmed ivory roses she had ever seen in the other.

She opened the door and he opened his arms and dropped the roses and she fell into them. His arms, that is, not the roses. She wasn't *that* pissed.

'I am definitely *de trop*,' murmured Lola as she slid past them through the front door. 'This situation has the potential to become seriously throbbing. Catch you later, Aphrodite.'

As soon as the door shut behind Lola, Aphrodite and Troy went straight to bed and spent quite a long time there. And while Troy's lovemaking was as silky and imaginative and orgasmic as ever, Aphrodite couldn't help noticing that, while he kissed every other inch of her, he avoided kissing her breasts.

*   *   *

Later they slung their clothes back on – well, Troy did; Aphrodite only bothered with a kimono – and went into the kitchen to rustle up something to eat. Aphrodite stuck bread in the toaster and started arranging the roses he'd brought her. They were beautiful, elegant, but scentless. It was time to talk. Troy took the initiative.

'Where did you get to last night? You didn't show up at the POD.'

Aphrodite hesitated before saying: 'No. I was deadbeat, and – it has to be said – more than a little upset. I just wanted to go home on my own. Was it a good party?'

'I don't know. I really only went to show my face. I split before midnight and went . . .' now it was his turn to hesitate '– for something to eat with Jolie. And Gareth, too, of course. I tried ringing you, but your mobile was on divert, and your land line just rang engaged all the time. Is it out of order?'

'No,' said Aphrodite. 'I took it off the hook.' She realized now that it was still off the hook, and went to put the receiver back on its cradle. 'I didn't feel like talking to anyone.'

Troy looked at her intently and in silence for a long minute. Then he said: 'What made you do it, Aphrodite? What on earth possessed you to come out on the catwalk like that? You must have known that it would look as if you were taking credit for my designs.'

She was furious suddenly. Furious with Polly, who had so cunningly engineered her humiliation, furious with Jolie, who made Machiavelli look like a halfwit, furious with Troy for allowing himself to be so adroitly manipulated, and furious with herself for having been so gullible as to have trusted Polly in the first place. 'You probably won't believe me,' she said, trying to keep her voice level, emotionless, 'but Polly Riordan, who has always hated me, set me up. She told me it was traditional for a muse to accompany a designer down a catwalk, and because I didn't know any better, I believed her.'

'What do you mean Polly hates you? She's never had anything but good things to say about you. And why would she tell you such a thing? It doesn't make sense.'

'Oh, Troy! You don't live in the real world! You don't see half of what's going on around you! She knew it would be a very clever way of publicly humiliating me.' The toast popped. 'What do you want on your toast?' she asked automatically, shooshing Bobcat, who had just returned from hunting, back out through the cat flap. As she blocked it, she heard an indignant feline protest.

'Got any Patum Peperium?' said Troy in his privileged drawl.

She gave a ragged little bark of a laugh. 'You see what I mean? What makes you think someone like me would have Patum Peperium in my fridge?'

'Jolie always has some.'

'But I'm *not* Jolie, Troy!' Abruptly she sat down at the table, feeling defeated. It had been ages since she'd eaten, and the buzz from all the booze she'd consumed earlier had fizzled out, leaving her with a nasty, flat feeling. Now that her hangover was kicking in, she was aware that her brain was starting to hurt, too. She folded her arms on the tabletop and laid her forehead on them.

There was silence for a while, and then she felt Troy's hands on her head. 'Hey. Let's forget about it. It's not that important – and anyway, it may even have done some good in terms of publicity for the show. In fact, it already has.' He went into the sitting room and returned with his copy of the *Evening Herald*.

'Have a look at this,' he said, spreading it out on the table in front of her. There on the second page was a photograph of Aphrodite and Troy, taken when he'd kissed her last night on the catwalk. His head was angled away from the camera, so you couldn't see his expression, but the look on Aphrodite's face was that of a startled fawn. With her hair slicked back her face was so exposed that she looked extraordinarily vulnerable and little-girl-lost. Her eyes were wide and shining with uncertainty, and her perfectly painted lips were parted as if she was just about to ask *'Why is this happening to me?'* It was a truly beautiful photograph.

Aphrodite turned her attention to the copy that accompanied it. 'Aphrodite Delaney, muse to Troy MacNally, accepts a kiss from the designer on the catwalk at the showing of his autumn/winter collection last night. Since Ms Delaney has an uncanny knack in foreseeing trends, we confidently predict that muses will feature on the catwalks of other designers in future.'

Well, she thought absently, Polly's dastardly plan backfired, didn't it? She'd be laughing on the other side of her face when she got a load of this picture, and it'd serve the poisonous bitch right. 'Who's credited?' she asked, scanning the page for the identity of the photographer.

'Jack Costello,' said Troy.

'Jack *Costello*? Why didn't they use a staff photographer?'

'The picture editor's a pal, apparently. He asked Jack to do an exclusive.'

And as she located the words: 'Exclusive pictures by Jack Costello' she found herself thinking that no, Polly Riordan's plan had not backfired. The flush of humiliation she felt at the knowledge that Jack Costello had been there last night to witness her triumphant procession along the catwalk was an indication of just how well Polly had, in fact, succeeded.

Chapter Fourteen

They were taking a bath together some days later, reclining at opposite ends of that aquamarine scoop with wineglasses to hand when he told her that he was going to Coolnamaragh, to the house by the lake to work. As he told her of his plans, her eyes wandered to the figure of the naked Eve on his wall, the figure that he'd asked her to reinvent as a blonde, and she noticed that the features had become slightly blurred. Why should that be? she wondered. And then she remembered that, in the excitement of that halcyon time when she and Troy had first become lovers and spent three whole days in bed, she had forgotten to Polybond her self-portrait. It stood to reason that it would disintegrate. She really ought to do a touch-up job on it and seal it properly.

'I spent four hours in here yesterday,' Troy told her now. 'I was like a prune when I got out. But it paid off. Ideas just walked into my head, one after another.'

'I hope you made notes.'

'Of course. The entire collection's in my imagination, ready to take shape on paper. All I need now is the peace and quiet of Coolnamaragh.'

'I hate to put pressure on you, Troy, but will we have frocks ready for the charity gig in the Point?'

Troy had been approached about taking part in a highly prestigious charity fashion show, which was to take place in the Point theatre shortly before Christmas. 'Sure. December's ages away.'

'But we need advance stuff for photographs for the programme. You do know that? They've been giving me grief about it. We'll have to set up a shoot a.s.a.p.'

'Any ideas on how it should look?'

'Yes,' she said. 'I've actually had what I think is a rather audaciously brilliant idea. The downside is that it would mean destroying your prototypes.'

Troy shrugged. 'Run it by me.'

'Well. It's to do with the elemental theme of your new stuff. I thought—'

'That we could set fire to the twins? Sorry. Bad joke.'

'Ha. The good news is that I don't want to use the twins this time round. I want to use that redhead from your last show. I think her name was Anna.'

'Yeah? Why Anna?'

'Because I hear she's an excellent swimmer, and I want to get shots of your new stuff —' she took a deep breath before dropping the bombshell '— underwater. Remember you described your spring designs as being inspired by the idea of naiads? Just think how remarkable they'd look in the sea.'

He narrowed his eyes at her, and a slow smile spread across his face. 'It's a fucking wonderful idea, Aphrodite. How on earth did you come up with it?'

She was just about to tell him how she'd dreamed

up the idea the day Perdita had told her that one of Jack Costello's passions was underwater photography, and how she'd tramped the Pigeon House pier to fuel her inspiration, when Troy pre-empted her.

'*I* know!' he said. 'It must have come to you after I told you about that time Jolie and Hugo and I visited that remote beach in Kerry. That time you had to go back up to Dublin.'

'What?'

'Remember I told you that Jolie stripped to the buff so that I could drape her in seaweed? It was bloody plucky of her – it wasn't warm that day. I'm sure I have photographs somewhere. I'll look them out when we're out of the bath.'

'Don't bother.' She felt a real sense of outrage. This was *her* idea. It had nothing – *nothing* – to do with Jolie fucking Fitzgerald.

'What's wrong?'

'Nothing.' She answered him like a sullen child, and then shook herself free of the bad thoughts that crowded her mind when Jolie was mentioned, and forced herself back into businesslike mode. 'Anyway, Troy – do you think it's worth running the idea by Jack and Anna?'

'Absolutely I do. It's a stroke of genius.'

'Well. If it's workable. Jack might decide that it would be more practical to stage the shoot in a pool for instance–'

'No! Those frocks were inspired by *nature.* If we're going to go for this, we stage the shoot in a natural environment. A pool would be a complete cop-out.

We need *movement* – waves and currents – and sunlight bouncing off the water's surface, and underwater vegetation swaying around. We'd get none of that in a pool. A pool isn't an option, Aphrodite.'

She knew he was right. 'Fair enough,' she said. 'But we'll have to think about the right location. I've heard the West Coast is meant to have some wonderful dive sites, but I haven't a clue how – *plucky* – Anna might be. She might not warm to the idea of contracting hypothermia.' Now there, she thought, was a pun worthy of Jack Costello on a seriously boring shoot. 'And I'll need to ask Jack loads of questions and–'

'You've your heart set on Jack, have you?'

'What? What do you mean?'

'I'm just saying that he's probably not the man for the job. Underwater photography's a specialized skill, you know.'

'I've already checked out his credentials. He's kosher.'

'He dives?'

'To a pretty high standard, apparently. It's his passion.'

'Like Jolie. She might be interested in going along on this shoot.'

No! Aphrodite pretended to think about it. 'It's probably not worth her while. The chill factor will mean it'll be the shortest shoot ever.'

'A short shoot! My idea of heaven.'

'So I've definitely got the go-ahead?'

'Absolutely.'

'OK. I'll make sure the thing's feasible first, and

then I'll do a costing. The budget will have to cover hotel accommodation and—'

'Aphrodite?'

'Yes?'

'Hush, hush, sweetie-pie. These are things I do not want to hear. These are things that pertain to the real world, and as I think you told me once before, I don't go there.'

She drew in her breath in a sigh of exasperation, then let it out in a laugh. 'D'you know something, Troy?' she said, reaching for the soap. 'You are a spoilt brat.'

'I know,' he said, without a hint of either guilt or complacency. It was a fact of life, after all. She could just as well have said: 'Grass is green', 'Elephants are big', or 'Jolie Fitzgerald is a poisonous bitch'. But somehow she suspected that he wouldn't have acknowledged the veracity of this last fact of life. He wouldn't have acknowledged it at all.

'And while I may be a spoilt brat,' he added, looking at her meaningfully, '*you* are a dirty little girl. You are so very dirty, Aphrodite Delaney, that I think you deserve to be punished. Pass me that bar of soap this minute. I'm going to lather every last inch of you until you squeak with cleanliness.'

And with an obligingly complicit smile, Aphrodite did as she was told.

* * *

A couple of days later he phoned to say he'd arrived safely in Coolnamaragh. He had left at an ungodly

343

hour in the morning to avoid the traffic, and had done the journey in record time. Aphrodite had felt sick as she'd waved goodbye to him, watching him take off down the deserted street at 60 in a 30 m.p.h. zone. Now she said thank you to Whoever Was Up There who had watched over him as he drove.

'It's beautiful here this morning,' he said. 'Very still. It was raining earlier, but it's just made everything glow. There's a blackbird singing in the garden.' She could hear it, just. 'But I miss you. I feel lonely.' Oh! Her heart went out to him. 'Can't you come down and join me, Aphrodite? Even for a weekend?'

'You know I can't. There's too much to be done here. And I've still got to get that photo-shoot organized.'

'Have you run the idea by Jack yet?'

'No.' She'd been procrastinating over that. She should really do it this morning, but she didn't want to disturb him while he was working. She'd do it this evening.

Troy sighed over the phone. 'I'm blue, for some reason. Maybe I'm just tired after the drive, but I'm blue because – well, because . . .' There was a long silence, and suddenly he said: 'Do you ever wonder what it's all about, Aphrodite? Sometimes I look at my designs and I think: "What's the point?" Some rich dame is going to swan into a première or an exhibition opening or a swanky party wearing what I'm looking at on the page, and I don't think it's such a good idea any more. And I don't even like what I'm looking at, or the ethic it promotes, and I'm tempted to take the drawing and shred it. Do you know what I mean? It all seems so *pointless*.'

'I do know what you mean,' she said. 'After that bastard Whelan stole my ideas for *The Seagull*, I felt like ripping up every drawing I'd ever done. And I'm sorry you're lonely, and I wish I could be there for you. Oh!' She gave a little laugh down the phone. 'We're *yearning*!'

'Yes. We are.' She could hear the reciprocal smile in his voice. Then: 'Hang on a sec,' he said. 'Just let me top up my coffee.'

She pictured him in that house in Coolnamaragh with that view behind him, pouring Jamaican Blue Mountain into one of Jolie Fitzgerald's porcelain cups, like the privileged princeling he was.

'Hi. I'm back.'

'Hello again, you. Will you start work today, Troy, d'you think?'

'No. I'm going to take it easy on my first day here. I might think about doing that trip to the Skelligs. The weather's perfect for it.'

'I wouldn't call *that* taking it easy. Remember what Jolie said about it? It's a long way up.'

'Ah – but you forget that my vertigo will mean that I probably won't get much beyond the halfway point. If I don't do it today, it might never happen, Aphrodite. I'll get too involved in work to bother. You know what I'm like once I get started. I'll be working every waking hour of the day.'

'Troy. You are not to burn yourself out.'

'Hey. Talking of burnout, I was listening to a radio programme on the way down about Jack Kerouac.

345

As far as he was concerned, the only people who counted were the people who burn, the mad ones. He compared them to Roman candles. Gave me a great idea for a frock. Shit. The gardener's just materialized in the view and waved at me. I'd better go, Aphrodite – Jolie gave me a list a mile long of things she wanted him to do.'

'All right. Enjoy the Skelligs if you do decide to go. And blow kisses all around that glorious landscape from me.'

'Will do. Bye, you. Love you.'

'Love you too.'

She put the phone down and switched on the radio, and then she smiled like a sap. 'Their' song was soaring out over the speaker. Hugging herself and humming along, Aphrodite performed dance steps.

*　　*　　*

Later that day Bobcat stalked in, looking very snitty. She didn't blame him. Since she'd started staying overnight at Troy's two or three times a week, she knew that Bob had taken to spending more and more time at Lola's. Aphrodite missed him like mad, but because of Troy's cat allergy there wasn't a whole lot she could do about it. How awful to have an allergy to cats! But then, Bob was such a supercilious individual, she sometimes wondered if he didn't have an allergy to human beings. She and Lola were the only two in the world he tolerated. Thank God there was no ChildLine for cats, she thought, as she lavished majorly overdue TLC on him, before pouring herself a glass of wine.

Then she hummed and hawed for ten minutes about ringing Jack Costello. His assistant would be gone by now. That meant if Jack was in, he'd pick up himself unless his answering machine was on. She drifted around the vicinity of the phone, lifted the receiver a couple of times, put it down again, poured herself another glass of wine, and then went for it. The promptness with which he picked up almost made her jump.

'Jack Costello.'

'Jack! Oh, hi!'

'That's not Hilary.'

'No. It's Aphrodite Delaney.'

'You need hardly bother with the surname. You're the only Aphrodite I know.'

'Um. Can you talk?'

'No. I'm expecting a call from my massage person. I'm in agony.'

'Oh,' said Aphrodite, feeling stupidly relieved for an excuse not to have a conversation with him. 'Well, I'll get off the phone at once, then.'

'If you need to talk I'll be going into town later. We could meet up.'

'Oh. OK. Where?'

'Frères Jacques, nine o'clock. Hah! Call waiting at last. Gotta go. Is that cool?'

'It's cool,' she said, putting the phone down quickly so that he could access call waiting. She looked at her watch. This was bonkers. She hadn't intended going anywhere tonight: there was loads on the telly that she wanted to watch. The mirror beckoned. Oh, no, no! She couldn't go anywhere looking the way she did – especially not to Frères Jacques, which was quite an upmarket joint. A quick shower would be essential. A little make-up – not too much. Outfit? She didn't want to look as if she was trying too hard – and it would make quite a nice change not to have to. She always felt as if she had to look her best when she went anywhere with Troy. Would she get away with clean jeans and a T-shirt in Frères Jacques? Of course she would. Celebrities – even such a minor one as she was – could get away with loads.

Before Aphrodite hit the street she made sure there was food in Bobcat's dish in case he decided to stay home tonight. Feeling another pang of remorse at the way she was neglecting him, she served up a generous portion of his favourite 'luxury' Scottish salmon in jelly, wondering if there'd be salmon on the menu at Frères Jacques. She hadn't eaten since the breakfast bash she'd attended in the Morrison Hotel that morning, where details of the Christmas charity gig at the Point depot had been announced to the press. It was shaping up to be a seriously glitzy event, the kind of showcase money can't buy: supermodels, celebrities, television coverage – the works.

She strolled down to the bus stop with her beautiful Troy MacNally leather jacket slung over her shoulder. It was a balmy August night, and she pictured just how beautiful it must be now in Coolnamaragh. She thought of Troy there on his own, and of how content he must be, far from the stinking exhaust fumes and the stress and the noise of the city, and even as she thought these thoughts, she heard the raucous blaring of a siren, and an unmarked police car pulled up outside Lola's house.

Oh! What could have happened? Had Lo been burgled? Assaulted? Was she being arrested for something? She relaxed as Patrick emerged, looking unconcerned and cool as a cucumber. He had a bottle of wine in his right hand, and was swinging an arrangement of the most exquisite orchids Aphrodite had ever seen in his left. He flushed a little when he saw her.

'Must be one hell of an emergency,' she said, raising an eyebrow.

'I've never done it before,' he explained sheepishly. 'But there's been an oil spillage on this side of the quays and the traffic's a bitch. You'll be waiting there for a bus till tomorrow.'

'Oh, shit!' said Aphrodite. What with the shower and the little bit of primping she'd allowed herself before leaving the house, she was cutting it fine as it was. And she knew Jack had no mobile, so she couldn't phone him to explain. She couldn't leave him sitting on his own in Frères Jacques. It would look insufferably arrogant of her if she swanned in late. And something told her that Jack Costello wouldn't hang around for too long, waiting.

She bit her lip, then gave Patrick a smile which translated as pleasepleasepleasepleaseplease . . .

Which is how she ended up pulling up outside Frères Jacques ten minutes later in a police car.

Through the window she could see Jack sitting at

349

a table, nursing what looked like a glass of bourbon. She took care to switch off her phone before pushing open the door to the restaurant. She had no intention of being the recipient of more of his scathing remarks. 'I'm impressed,' he said, as she was shown into the seat opposite, 'that your fame has already reached such epic proportions that you require a police escort.'

'Ha ha,' said Aphrodite.

'Champagne for the lady,' said Jack to the waiter.

'How did you know I liked champagne?'

'I guessed.' He stood up to kiss her on the cheek, and then sat down again immediately. 'Ow,' he said, taking a large swig of bourbon.

'Did your masseuse get through? I presumed that must have been her on call waiting.'

'Him. Hilary's a he, and built like a brick shithouse. I need brute force, I'm afraid, not girly aromatherapy stuff to sort out my back. I would rather go through ten rounds with Mike Tyson.'

'It's that bad?'

'Yes. But it's necessary. And it works. Once this bourbon has kicked in I'll feel like a new man.' He drained the remaining whiskey in his glass and indicated to a passing waiter to bring him another. It was neat bourbon, Aphrodite noticed, but he had knocked it back with such insouciance it could have been tap water. He saw her looking. 'I don't indulge my penchant for hard liquor every day,' he remarked. 'Please be assured that this is purely medicinal. One more large one and I'll be chipper again.'

'Back problems must be a real pain in the neck.'

He raised his empty glass at her and said: 'Nice one.' Aphrodite acknowledged his tribute to her pun with a nod and a smile. 'Yeah. It's a bummer, my spinal column. It fucks up on me once or twice a year. Hilary's the only person who can do anything for it.'

'What sets it off?'

'It depends. This time round I was in too much of a hurry to shift a tank.'

'A tank?'

'Of compressed air. I dive.'

'I know.'

'I was lucky. If it had happened any later Hilary would have been winging his way off to his holiday in the Bahamas and I'd have been on my back in bed for a fortnight.'

'You poor thing!'

'It has its advantages. I'm the kind of lazy bollocks who's quite glad of an excuse to let the girl do all the work.'

It took a couple of seconds before she realized that he was referring to matters carnal rather than culinary or domestic, and in order to fill the conversational vacuum that followed, Aphrodite found herself saying – for the sake of saying *something* – 'I noticed you'd installed "call waiting" on your phone. I thought you never used it?' Wow! What an inspired invitation to dialogue!

'Call waiting saved my life tonight, but will be banished from my telecommunications system by the morning. Believe me, if you were depending on a call the way I was depending on that one earlier on this evening you would make yourself more available than Tracey Emin.'

'You've lost me.'

'Remember her "Sensation" installation? The tent papered with the names of all the people she'd ever slept with? It ran to hundreds. Not quite as original as Prada Simone and her Barbie Bush, of course.' He shot her a smile. 'I've become quite a devotee of your "Elegantarium" rubbish. So, I imagine, has she.'

Aphrodite followed the direction of his gaze. A young woman had just walked into the restaurant wearing a hideous white puffball skirt trimmed with glittery bits.

'Ha!' Aphrodite clapped her hands to her mouth and gazed back at Jack with big, incredulous eyes. She knew she'd gone pink, but she was smiling broadly behind her hands.

He smiled back. 'Has anyone else copped on yet?' he asked. 'Or are they all too busy admiring the Emperor's new threads to realize how obligingly malleable they're being? You're a wickeder woman than I thought, Ms Delaney. Thanks –' this to the waitress who'd arrived with Aphrodite's champagne and his bourbon. He indicated the menu. 'I already know what I'm going to order. How about you?'

'Um. I think so.' She quickly scanned the menu. 'I'll have the marinated salmon, please. And noisettes of lamb.'

'Glad to see you're a girl with a healthy appetite. Most people in your line of work seem to exist on nothing but champagne and frilly lettuce with exotic names. Duck confit and lobster for me, please. And a bottle of Sauvignon blanc.' The smile he gave the waitress made her dimple and go a bit simpery. It also made Aphrodite want him to smile like that at her too. He turned back to her, lost the smile and raised an interrogative eyebrow. 'What did you want to talk to me about?'

She decided not to bother giving him the smile she had been preparing for him. This was business, after all. 'OK,' she said in a matter-of-fact voice. 'This could be a totally bonkers plan. But you should be able to tell me immediately whether it's a viable one or not.' And she proceeded to run her idea for the underwater photo-shoot by him.

'I don't think your plan is bonkers at all,' he said when she'd finished. 'I think it's a great idea, and yes, I'd love to do it. There's only one problem, and it could be major.'

'What's that?'

'You're going to need a model who is comfortable in water.'

Aphrodite nodded. 'I'm aware of that. I've been told that Anna Boland's an excellent swimmer.'

'But will she be able to hack the temperature? I'm working on the assumption that your budget doesn't include flights to the Caribbean. We are talking temperatures that a sea-lion with layers of sub-cutaneous blubber would consider tropical, but that a stick thin model might find more than passing frigid.'

'I'm hoping that the prestige of landing a gig like this will be enough to persuade her. It'll be in-valuable in terms of kudos.'

'You could be right. Appeal to her higher instincts. Topmost among which for a model is, of course, vanity. Although,' he said, looking thoughtful, 'I have to say that Anna's the least vain person I know. She's a top girl.'

'So I've picked the right one to work with?'

'Damn right.'

Their starters arrived. Aphrodite fell on hers with the ferocity of Bobcat at his most ravenous.

'Have you given any thought to a location?' asked Jack. Noticing that Aphrodite's mouth was so full of food that she was in no position to answer, he continued: 'It'll have to be somewhere on the West Coast. Visibility's not great on the East, and obviously that's a priority when you're taking underwater shots.'

Aphrodite shook her head, chewed and swallowed delicious salmon before answering. 'I haven't thought too hard about it, actually. I was hoping you'd be able to recommend somewhere. I know you have a house on Valencia Island, and I remember Perdita mentioning that it was an underwater photographer's paradise.'

He laughed. 'It is. But if you're hoping for shots of a beautiful girl against a backdrop of rose coral surrounded by starfish and velvet crabs, hope on. I'm not sure Troy would like the idea of his frocks accessorized with weight belts and breathing apparatus. You're talking depths of thirty feet and more for backgrounds like that.' He narrowed his eyes again. Aphrodite remembered that his eyes were the first thing she'd noticed about him the first time they'd met. And then she remembered that those eyes had seen her naked, and she felt herself starting to blush. To make the blush go away, she forced herself to listen harder to what he was saying.

'Anyway,' he resumed, 'since the focus is to be on the frocks, it's as well not to have anything too distracting in the background – and, of course, the shallower the water, the better the visibility. There's a site by Valencia Bridge which would be dead on for our purposes. It's sheltered: even in a westerly force eight it's clear and calm there.'

Aphrodite nodded sagely, even though she hadn't a clue about westerlies and force eights and all that seafaring stuff.

'As long as nobody faffs about too much with styling shit between shots – make-up and hair and all that jazz,' added Jack. 'We'll have to work fast, otherwise Anna will get too cold to work. Lots of soup and hot drinks, blankets, puffa coats. And a hip flask goes without saying.'

'There won't be much point in the usual faffing around,' Aphrodite pointed out. 'Once Anna's underwater her hair will be all over the place, anyway. And I'll just have to trust you that the clothes work. I'm not going to be down there with you to keep an eye on how our girl is looking.'

'It'll work. Trust me. You can achieve the most extraordinary effects underwater without recourse to any of the usual trickery.'

'Will you need artificial light?' She hoped not. She wanted this shoot to be as straightforward and uncluttered as possible.

'No. The most beautiful effects are achieved with natural light. I'll shoot her from below so she'll be haloed in sunburst, and you'll see fantastic patterns made by light dancing on the surface of the water above her.'

'It sounds perfect.' Aphrodite finished her salmon, took a gulp of the wine the waiter had discreetly poured for her and wiped her mouth with her napkin. 'How will you stage-manage it? Will it be madly complicated?'

'It doesn't have to be. I'll simply drop down a couple of metres, ask Anna to wait for a count of one hundred, then dive down to me. It's going to be much tougher on her than on me, but she's a complete pro. I'm very glad you're using her and not the twins.'

'The twins wouldn't do it.'

'They wouldn't do it in Valencia. If we could afford somewhere like Mustique or Necker they'd be delighted to oblige. Where will you put the crew up, by the way?'

'Parknasilla sounds good.'

'I'd volunteer to accommodate some people, but I haven't got round to doing up my spare rooms yet.'

'Do you get down there a lot?'

'As often as I can, which is not often enough. I intend to cut back my workload next year so that I can spend more time there. I love it.'

'That doesn't surprise me. It's a beautiful part of the world. I was down there in March.'

'That's right. I remember running into Troy and

your friends – Jolie Fitzgerald and some architect. What was his name?'

'Hugo O'Neill. And I don't really consider him to be a friend. Or her, for that matter.' Why was she saying this? Was it the wine? For some reason she felt ashamed that he associated her with that . . . that *clique*.

He looked at her carefully. 'I suppose it's only natural for one muse to be suspicious of another.'

Oh, God. How petty it made her sound! She was just about to explain that it wasn't mere jealousy that made her mistrust Jolie when, as if on cue, the woman herself slinked into the restaurant wearing vintage Troy MacNally, accompanied by Gareth. Noooo! thought Aphrodite as the couple homed in on their table like Cruise missiles. She supposed that was the disadvantage of eating in classy joints. You ran the risk of bumping into dangerous people like her. The next time she ate out she'd go for a much safer option. The canteen in Mountjoy jail might be good.

'Hi, Jack,' said Jolie in a voice that sounded like the lowest, sweetest rasping notes of a rare flute. Then she turned the blue spotlight of her gaze on her opponent. 'And Aphrodite! May we join you?'

'Of course.' As Jack rose to his feet and inclined his head politely, Aphrodite wished there was an executioner's axe handy. They exchanged glances, and she thought she noticed the wry ghost of a smile in his eyes.

Place settings were magicked for Jolie and Gareth,

and Jolie slid into the one next to Jack, managing to show off an expanse of slender golden thigh as she did so. 'It's our wedding anniversary,' she fluted. 'And since this is the first restaurant we ever dined in as a couple, we decided to indulge in a little nostalgia.'

'How romantic!' volunteered Aphrodite. 'But in that case wouldn't you rather dine *à deux*?'

'Good God, no. We can do that any night of the week. It's much more amusing to dine with congenial types. What brings you two here?'

'Business,' said Jack. 'We were discussing ideas for the programme for the Point gig.'

'Oh? And what have you come up with?'

'We can't really say too much about it until we get a positive reaction from the model we're after. She may balk at the idea, in which case our plans will be well and truly scuppered and we'll have to go back to the drawing board.'

Aphrodite was relieved that Jack had chosen not to discuss the underwater shoot with Jolie. She had the feeling that Jolie might pooh-pooh the idea, or – even worse – come up with a better one herself.

Jolie attracted the attention of the head waiter with the merest suggestion of a gesture. 'Champagne, *s'il vous plaît*, Sylvain. The usual. Thanks.' And then she said something that made Aphrodite's ears prick up. She said: 'Actually, on second thoughts, make that a vodka martini.' She turned back to the table and smiled. 'I haven't had one since before I was pregnant with the twins. Now that they're weaned at last I can indulge my weakness for martinis again.'

'It didn't ever stop you from indulging your taste in champagne, darling,' Gareth pointed out. 'I'd say what you were feeding them was comprised fifty-fifty of champagne and breast milk.'

'Champagne never seemed to bother them. The only time they had a hangover was when I drank red wine. Feeding hungover twin boys is not the best way for a gal to start her day, I soon found.' She clasped her hands together at bosom level and gave Jack the smile of a wolverine, and Aphrodite couldn't help noticing that her beautiful, creamy breasts were practically spilling out over her décolletage. She also found herself speculating on the likelihood of Jolie's twin boys being called Romulus and Remus. 'Have you spoken to Troy recently, Aphrodite?' she asked now, slanting her an electric blue glance. The stuff that was unspoken between them shimmered so intensely that Aphrodite was almost surprised that it didn't manifest itself like ectoplasm.

'Just this morning,' said Aphrodite. 'He said the weather was so gorgeous down there that he thought he might take in Skellig Michael today.'

'Lucky bastard,' said Jack.

'Do you know the Skelligs, Jack?' asked Gareth.

'Very well. There's some great diving there.'

'You dive?' said Jolie. 'I didn't know that. Where, mostly, in Ireland?'

'Valencia.'

'Of course. You have a house there, don't you? I had an amazing drift dive there last year. I . . .' Oh, God. Aphrodite recalled now that Jolie included scuba diving among her myriad accomplishments.

Now she was going to monopolize Jack with scuba stories.

Gareth obviously realized that he and Aphrodite would be excluded from the conversation for the foreseeable future. He turned to her with a smile and said, 'I don't dive. The very idea of it scares the shit out of me. I'm more into climbing.'

'So you'd rather climb the Skelligs than dive them?'

'Damn right. That monastery on the precipice is the eighth wonder of the world.'

'Oh? How high is it?'

'Five hundred feet above sea level. Someone once described it as "God's hostile refuge, built virtually on air". It rates comparison with monasteries I've visited in the Himalayas.'

'Christ. I wonder if Troy will be able to hack it.'

'What do you mean?'

'He suffers from vertigo.'

'In that case it's unlikely that he'll manage more than the first few feet. Someone who'd been there recently told me that they'd had to abort the climb halfway up and inch their way back down on their bum with their eyes closed, clinging to a friend's hand for dear life. The island's dedicated to the saint of high places for a good reason. It's easy to imagine what a refuge it must have been to holy men.'

The ultimate escape. Who had described it as that? Jolie.

'Those first settlers must have had nerves of steel,' continued Gareth. 'Can you imagine making that crossing in currachs and coracles that could have been smashed like eggshells against the rocks?' He brought his hand down hard on the table in a graphic gesture.

'No.' Aphrodite didn't like to contemplate that at all. Her stomach somersaulted at the mere idea of being stuck on heaving water in a flimsy craft, but Gareth was obviously warming to his subject.

'It never ceases to amaze me when I think of how the monks ferried the stone that built their church all the way from Valencia. And then they had to cart the stuff to the top! There are two thousand, three hundred steps in all. Their architectural skills were little short of miraculous. D'you know, they managed to—'

'Oh, God, darling!' Jolie's voice interrupted him. 'You mustn't bore poor Aphrodite to death with statistics. Not everyone's interested in the architecture of stone *cloghans*, you know. Let's order.' Jolie's eyes assumed their lodestone gleam as she scanned the restaurant for the waiter, but before she could locate him, her phone went off. 'Oh. Please excuse me,' she said. 'I know it's incredibly anti-social to answer one's phone when in company, but I have to keep it switched on in case the nanny needs to contact me urgently.' She depressed the 'answer' button on her minuscule gold phone, and, as she listened to the person on the other end, her expression became increasingly concerned. 'OK, OK. Just give me a minute. I'm going to take you outside. It's noisy here, and I can't hear you properly. Excuse me,' she said to the table. 'I'll be back when I've finished sorting this out.'

'Not the twins?' asked Gareth.

'No, darling. Order the chilled gazpacho to start for me, will you, please?'

Jolie rose gracefully to her feet, and moved between the tables of the crowded restaurant and out through the door. She looked like a goddess floating on a cloud.

Aphrodite couldn't help speculating as to the identity of the caller. Was it Hugo O'Neill, phoning to arrange another liaison? Or did she have more than one lover? She could have a whole stable full of obliging studs all in a lather to be led by the nose by Jolie Fitzgerald. Or – and this last thought struck her a blow somewhere in the region of her solar plexus – could it have been Troy? Her mind went into an unpleasant free fall as she automatically smiled at the waiter who was refilling her glass, and automatically answered Gareth's enquiry as to what the marinated salmon was like, and automatically responded with a mild sexual *frisson* when Jack's sleeve accidentally brushed against the downy hairs on her forearm. What? What sexual *frisson*? It was the wine: she had imagined it. Before she could analyse her peculiar response to Jack's touch, Jolie was back, looking uncharacteristically anxious and holding the phone out to Aphrodite.

'It's Troy,' she said. 'He's in a bit of a state. He's been trying to get through to you, but says your phone's powered off. He needs to speak to you urgently, and I'd take it outside, if I were you.'

The notion that he'd had an accident on Skellig Michael suddenly occurred to her and she was outside the door in seconds. 'Troy?' she said into Jolie's tiny Fabergé egg of a phone. 'What's wrong? What's happened? Did you have an accident?'

'No. No, Aphrodite. No accident. An epiphany! I had an epiphany!' He laughed, and his voice over the phone sounded strange, hyper, ever so slightly unhinged – as if he were on something.

'What? What are you talking about? What epiphany?'

'A revelation. A moment of pure, blinding spiritual enlightenment. It was an out-of-body experience, you know? I swear to God I entered into the highest state of consciousness that it's possible for a human being to achieve.'

Aphrodite tried her hardest to sound conversational. 'Oh? And where did this – um – epiphany happen?'

'In the monastery on Skellig Michael.'

'The monastery? But I thought the monastery was on the summit?'

'It is. I stood there at the top, Aphrodite, poised between heaven and earth, watching the waves crash onto the rocks below, knowing how vulnerable I was, knowing how insignificant I really am in the scheme of things, how *unworthy*, and–'

Aphrodite had to interrupt him. 'But, Troy, what about your vertigo? How did you manage the climb?'

'This sounds crazy, I know, but you'll have to believe me. The ghosts of all those souls who drowned there guided me up – the ghosts of the drowned anchorites, the ghosts of all those pilgrims who drowned searching for enlightenment. All the dead voices – they *spoke* to me! But – and this is the most beautiful part of it – there was one ghost who meant more to me than all the others, whose voice murmured encouragement to me all the way to the very top. Who, Aphrodite? Whose voice do you think it was?'

'I think,' said Aphrodite, sensing something sinister, something ominous clog the air. She felt the words might suffocate her as she articulated them. 'I think that maybe it was your mother's voice.'

'Yes!' said Troy, and she heard him draw in a long, ragged sob of a breath before he spoke again. 'You're right. It was my mother's voice. She came at last. She came to show me the right way.'

* * *

When Aphrodite returned to the table, Jolie gave her an appraising look. 'Well,' she said. 'What did you make of that?'

Aphrodite sat down and thought for a couple of beats, and then she looked Jolie directly in the eye. It was the first time she'd ever felt she could engage the woman on a one-to-one level, without some competitive or confrontational vibe clouding the agenda. The men, immediately aware that they were superfluous, turned to each other and engaged in some boy's stuff conversation about the comparative performance of SUVs.

'I don't know,' said Aphrodite. 'At first I thought he must be on something, and then I realized that

that couldn't be the case because no boatman with an ounce of cop-on would allow somebody who looked even remotely strung out on board their craft, and then let them loose on Skellig Michael. Troy was totally *compos mentis* when he made that climb. Well, he may have been feeling high,' (oh, God! What a bad, bad pun! The thought skittered through Aphrodite's mind and then vanished), 'but it wasn't a chemically engineered high.'

'He told you about his mother?'

'Yes. And then he started to cry.'

Jolie considered. 'It *is* an astonishing experience, you know, Skellig Michael. It really could have triggered some kind of emotional catharsis in him. It may even have done him some good. You're probably aware by now that there's an extremely tortured individual behind the urbane veneer.'

'Yes.'

'I do what I can to help.' Her words were weighty with meaning.

And so, when they came, were Aphrodite's. 'I know.'

'He can be difficult to live with sometimes, I'm aware of that. I supported him for nearly seven years. Miriam couldn't hack one. You're doing well, I think. But he could be at crisis point.'

'What do you mean?'

'I mean, he's been walking an emotional tightrope for years. He could topple either way. I just hope you'll still be around to pick up the pieces if he goes over the precipice. If you need my help, call me. I know you mistrust me, and I can't blame you. But

I don't want Troy to fall apart any more than you do.'

Of course you don't, thought Aphrodite. There's too much money riding on him. And then she thought back to what Troy had said after she'd consoled him, after he'd stopped weeping down the phone. 'Why don't you come home now?' she'd suggested. 'You can work equally well here if I make sure nobody disturbs you. Come home and we'll spend a lazy evening in the bath together.

'No,' he'd said with decision. 'I'm not ready to come home. I've a lot of thinking to do.' And then he'd paused and taken a deep breath. 'And another thing, Aphrodite? I hope you don't mind me saying this, after all the hard work you put into it, but I may want to rethink the bathroom.'

Oh, God! 'Redecorate, you mean?'

'Yes.'

She tried hard, but she couldn't keep the hurt out of her voice. 'What had you in mind?' she asked.

'I think it would look wonderful if it were white. All white. Like the cell of an anchorite,' he said.

Chapter Fifteen

Aphrodite spent the next couple of weeks organizing the photo-shoot for the charity gig. The handful of designs that Troy had worked on the last time he'd been down in Coolnamaragh were to be included in the spring/summer collection, and the prototypes were looking good. These were to be the frocks they'd shoot underwater at Valencia. She decided she'd phone him with a progress report.

She picked up the phone, keeping the fingers of her right hand crossed. This had become a habit ever since the night of his Skelligs 'epiphany'. She was full of an awful foreboding that he might bring up the subject of his bathroom again, and Aphrodite knew that it would break her heart to have to paint over the mural she'd worked so hard on. So far, he hadn't made any further reference to it, but she suspected it was just a question of time.

The first thing he said was: 'I'm coming home tomorrow.'

'Oh. Don't you think that's a bit daft, Troy? The Valencia shoot's set up for next Monday. Why don't you just stay where you are until then instead of travelling all the way back to Dublin and down again?'

'Why do I need to be there for the shoot?' he asked, sounding genuinely perplexed.

'You don't want to supervise it?'

'Nah. You can do that. I'm really not interested, Aphrodite.' Now his voice had reverted to laid-back mode, and Aphrodite felt a sudden stab of irritation. She'd been working her ass off on his behalf, and this was how he thanked her! She was just about to give him a verbal slap on the wrist when his voice came back down the line.

'It's done me so much good, being down here, but it's time to move on. I feel so kind of – what's the right word? – *unencumbered*, Aphrodite. I really believe that I'm beginning to find my direction in life. I've been so *aimless* up till now.'

Still feeling miffed, Aphrodite just resisted the temptation to say: In that case, why don't you set yourself the goal of supervising your own fucking photo-shoot? Instead she bit down hard on her lip and said nothing. He'd been volatile on the phone lately; she didn't want him losing the plot again.

'I've been doing a lot of thinking, a lot of walking, a lot of reading . . .'

His voice trailed off vaguely, and Aphrodite felt a flash of panic. 'But you *have* been getting some work done, Troy, haven't you? We'll really need to get our finger out – the Point people—'

'Aphrodite? Relax. We're talking about a bunch of frocks, not a life or death situation. Don't waste energy getting stressed about it.'

Panic clutched her again, and she heard her voice go up a pitch. 'Troy, *I'm* the one who's going to have people breathing down my neck and tightening the thumbscrews if the stuff isn't ready in time, not you.'

'Hey, hey, sweetheart. Take it easy.' There was no corresponding edge of anxiety in his voice. 'If they wanted daywear as well then, yeah, sure we'd be up against it. But there's easily enough aspirational stuff for the show.' He was right. It was only the evening wear they need be concerned about. The daywear could wait a while longer. 'And the prototypes you'll be using on Monday are finished, aren't they?'

'Yes. Anna came in for the final fitting last week. She's a dream to work with compared to the twins, by the way. There's absolutely no bullshit about her.'

'Yeah. Everyone loves Anna. How do the frocks look?'

'They look terrific. I told the machinists they didn't have to be perfectionist, so they had time to run up half a dozen.'

'Sorry – am I missing something here? Why did you tell them they didn't have to be perfectionist?'

'The water will do weird and wonderful things to the frocks, Troy. I don't imagine anyone's going to take a magnifying glass to the pics and say: "Ooh – look how cunningly they've been constructed". We're selling dramatic appeal here, not attention to detail.'

'Oh, yeah. Sorry. I'd forgotten you were shooting them underwater.'

He'd *forgotten*! Only a few weeks ago he'd described her idea as a stroke of genius!

'Shame they're passé already, those frocks. I'm moving on.'

'What? What do you mean?'

'The stuff I've been working on down here is too

369

frivolous. Every time I finish a drawing, I want to rip it up.'

Oh, God! 'You haven't – have you?'

'No. But all that nature-inspired malarkey!' His voice dripped disdain now. 'Remember that garden in Ilnacullin with its so-called "jungle" and its forced hothouse exotica? That was the work of *man*, not nature, Aphrodite. In future I'll leave nature to Lainey. She does it so much better.'

'Troy! Stop it! You're not being fair on yourself. Those designs you did in Coolnamaragh were inspired.'

'You'll be happy with the new stuff, then. I've churned out more of the same.'

But Aphrodite didn't feel happy. How could he talk about his exquisite, gossamer creations in such negative terms? What did he mean, he'd 'churned' out more of the same? What had happened to the man who'd enthused about all things bright and beautiful? Oh, Christ, oh, Christ – how *tired* she felt, suddenly! She put her head in her hands, knowing she wouldn't be able to speak without sounding snitty or tearful or both. There was a long pause over the phone, and then Troy said: 'You know something? Nature isn't lush and bountiful and fertile. I've seen its real face, Aphrodite.'

'So tell me about it,' she said. She knew she sounded lacklustre, but she wasn't sure that she wanted to hear what he had to say. There was something profoundly dispiriting about this change of heart.

Troy took a deep breath before continuing: 'It's a

place of inhospitable stone, where nothing grows. *Nothing.* Do you know how those men lived, Aphrodite – those monks on Skellig Michael? They eked out a hand to mouth existence trying to coax a pathetic harvest of peas and beans out of a *scrape* of soil and seaweed. Just think what it must be like. To live on a rockface, miles from so-called civilization, hearing nothing all day but screaming gulls above and crashing waves below. *That's* elemental! *That's* nature for you!' The laidback, Zen-like timbre that had been in his voice earlier had gone. He sounded now as he had done the night he'd described his trip to the Skelligs – urgent, hyper, febrile.

Aphrodite took a deep breath and tried to adopt the kind of reasonable tone a chairman might use in an impassioned debate. 'But those men *chose* to live that way, Troy, they–'

He interrupted her. 'And how do *I* choose to live, Aphrodite? I dine in the best restaurants, I stay in the best hotels, I surround myself with luxury. I'm cosseted and protected and shielded from real life. I'm a *fucking sybarite*!'

'Ssh, now, darling, calm–'

But he wasn't listening to her. 'And when someone asks me what I do for a living,' he continued, 'I tell them I'm in the fashion industry. The fucking *fashion* industry!' His voice didn't just drip disdain now, it was pouring scorn. 'An industry which is at its lowest level dependent on the slave labour of five-year-old children in Asian sweatshops, and at its highest upon the vagaries of maybe a half-dozen spoilt divas on the planet who can afford to wear *haute couture.*'

'Jesus, Troy, we all have to make a living somehow. At least we're not loan sharks or drug dealers or con artists–'

'Oh, but we are, Aphrodite. That's exactly what we are. We're *con* artists.'

'But there are manipulative, Machiavellian types in *every* walk of life.' She thought of her style column, and gave a little 'ouch' of self-recognition. 'And you're not one of them, Troy. You're different – special. You know you are.'

'How am I different?'

'Because you don't do trendy. You don't design for fashion victims. You diversify. That's why you're a *great* designer, Troy MacNally. You don't pay lip service to anything so mundane as this season's lengths or next season's cut.'

A silence ensued, and then he gave a brittle laugh. 'Ha! Do you know what I read in the paper yesterday? I read that the "Impoverished look' is in fashion this season. How sick is that? Oscar Wilde had it right. He said "Fashion is something so ghastly that it has to be changed every six months." And here's another quote for you. "Away with silks, away with lawn, I'll have no scenes or curtains drawn." '

'What *are* you on about?'

'That's from a poem by Robert Herrick.'

'How does the rest of it go?' asked Aphrodite.

'"Give me my mistress as she is,
Dressed in her naked simplicities:
For as my heart, even so mine eye
Is won with flesh, not drapery." '

'Oh!' said Aphrodite, feeling herself topple head over heels in love with him all over again. 'How sweet! How *romantic*!' How Troy MacNally.

* * *

She made his flat ready for his homecoming. There was champagne and finger food in the fridge, she had bathed and massaged herself all over with sandalwood body lotion, she had scattered rosepetals on starched linen sheets (a whimsical notion she'd learned from her mother), and under the stunning Japanese kimono she'd bought the previous day in a vintage clothing shop, she was naked. When he called her from his car phone to say he'd be there in ten minutes, she lit candles all over the flat and an incense burner in the bedroom, then went into the bathroom to run a bath for him.

She felt almost shy about seeing him again. Would they talk first, and eat? Drink a little celebratory champagne? Or would they just throw themselves on each other and fall into bed? She checked out her reflection, put in some blue eye drops to make the whites of her eyes whiter, cleaned her teeth and gargled with the mouthwash he liked the taste of. As she sluiced mouthwash into the basin that she'd installed all those months ago, she heard the door to the flat open. She fluffed out her hair with nervy fingers, took one last look in the mirror, then turned away.

He was standing there, just as he'd stood the first time she'd ever seen him, leaning against the jamb of the bathroom door, watching her. She had thought him the most beautiful man she had ever seen. He still was. Except there were two very different things about him. One was the expression in his eyes. When she'd first seen him his eyes had been eloquent – it would have been impossible to deny the sexual hunger she'd seen in them. Now those eyes held an expression that was curiously detached. The other thing that was different about him was his hair. He had shaved it all off.

'Troy!' She tried to erase the gobsmacked expression she knew she'd assumed, but she wasn't fast enough. He'd registered it.

'A big change, isn't it? Sorry to have taken you by surprise like this. Maybe I should have warned you. Don't you like it?'

'No. I mean, no, I don't *not* like it. I *do* like it.' She smiled. 'I mean it. It suits you. You have the cheekbones to carry it off.' He certainly did. His cheekbones were more prominent than ever, and now she looked more closely at him, she saw that he'd lost a lot of weight. 'Hey!' she said in an admonishing voice. 'You haven't been eating properly. I *knew* if I wasn't around to look after you you'd start neglecting yourself. You can't afford to lose weight, Troy. Come into the dining room at once. I've stocked the fridge full of goodies.' She moved towards him, pausing when she reached him, expecting him to take her in his arms. But he didn't, so, feeling a bit uncertain, she just continued on past him into the hall.

In the dining room she busied herself with

fetching plates and glasses from the sideboard and dashing in and out of the tiny kitchen, setting little dishes of sushi on the table. Troy watched her. There was something curious about his expression as he sat in the high-backed dining chair, with his hands in his lap. Usually he lounged indolently in his chair, or leaned forward with his elbows on the table. Now he was sitting with a straight back – not exactly ramrod straight, but there was something . . . well, *symmetrical* about him. He looked centred, focused, assured. Different.

She pulled the cork on the champagne and went to pour, but he put a hand over his glass. 'None for me, thanks. I haven't touched alcohol for over a fortnight.'

'Oh. Well,' she said, feeling deflated. 'I hope you don't mind if I have some. It's been a bitch of a day, and I need the hit.'

'Of course I don't mind.'

She poured, taking her time and thinking. Something had changed. Since his 'epiphany' on Skellig Michael, something had shifted in the melting pot of their relationship. It was as if an invisible chef with a giant spoon had intervened and stirred things round without asking permission. She sat down opposite him. Should they talk? No. She didn't want to. Not yet. 'Have something to eat,' she said, pushing the dish of sushi towards him.

He studied the dish for many moments before finally selecting a few morsels of raw fish and rice. 'Come on, Troy,' she cajoled. 'That's not enough. You should be on a weight-gain programme. I'm going to have to get in Complan.' She was only half joking. The lighting in the dining room had carved huge shadows under his cheekbones, and she noticed that his eyes were ringed with purple.

He shook his head. 'I don't want to introduce too much rich food into my diet just yet. It'd be a major upset to my system. I've been fasting, you see.'

'What? Why?'

'I wanted to match some of my experience to that of the monks on the–'

'Jesus Christ, Troy!' She got down on her knees beside him and took his hand in hers. 'What has the place done to you? Come on, come on – cop *on*! You're back in Dublin now, you're back in the real world. This is how things *are*, Troy. Count yourself fortunate. Look! Champagne! Good food! A naked woman!' She parted the lapels of her kimono.

He smiled down at her. 'Thank you, Aphrodite. You've stage-managed this homecoming beautifully, and you mustn't think I'm not grateful. But something has happened in my life that hasn't happened in yours, and it's not going to be easy for you to understand.'

Oh, God! She was desperate suddenly for some reassurance that he still found her attractive, that he desired and loved her still. She took his hand and guided it to her breast. 'Come to bed, Troy,' she said, in her best, cajoling voice. She rose to her feet and bent to give him the lightest of butterfly kisses, and then she took hold of his other hand and led him down the passageway into the bedroom. Once there she started to undress him, noticing with concern that his ribs were showing.

On the rosepetal-strewn bed she invited him into her mouth and began to do to him all the things she knew he adored. But arousing him was hard work, and as she kissed and caressed him, it struck her with hellish force that she had never before used the words 'hard work' to describe lovemaking. What was wrong? What was going on inside her lover's head? *Why* didn't he find her a turn-on any more? And she knew that yet another blow had been dealt to the dynamic of their relationship, and that it needed remedial work bigtime. Suddenly his hands were on her head, indicating to her that he wanted her to stop. He held her motionless for one awful moment, and her heart somersaulted down towards her stomach in slow motion. He *didn't* want her.

Then: 'Listen,' he said, in a low voice. 'Listen and do as I tell you. I want to teach you something new.' And as Troy started to direct the proceedings in a low, very level voice, murmuring encouragement as she followed his instructions, he gradually hardened. 'Good. Blow again – very gently, very slowly. And again – fifteen more times.' Aphrodite knew better than to ask questions now. She'd leave them till afterwards. After a count of fifteen Troy said: 'Now. The other direction. Eighteen times.' Again she complied. 'A little more to the left,' said Troy. 'And now, right. Oh, God! Yes – that's it, that's good.'

He was obviously finding this a huge turn-on, but

Aphrodite had to confess that it wasn't doing much for her. Then a big thought hit her. Where had he learned all this new stuff? Had he found a bit on the side in Kerry? Had he been unfaithful to her? Had he acquired a new muse? She recalled the detachment that had been in his eyes when he'd studied her in the bathroom earlier, and the big thought started spiralling round her head in ever-increasing circles, like the ripple effect when you drop a stone into a still pond. And all the time she was having these thoughts she was aware of Troy's voice trickling on in her ear like honey, directing her to count.

And as Aphrodite started doing mental arithmetic again, she found herself thinking anxious thoughts, and imagining worst-case scenarios, and wondering abstractedly exactly how much longer the countdown to blast-off was going to take.

* * *

Her turn finally came an hour or so later, but, even though Troy was as skilful and dextrous as ever, she was so aware that he was counting inwardly that she couldn't come. He smoothed the soles of her feet, he sucked her toes, he blew along her forearms, he caressed her calves, and licked behind her knees. He even stroked her fingers and the creases of her elbows. When he got down to serious business though, she ended up faking her orgasm.

'Oh, *God*!' she said, finally, obligingly, flinging herself back against the pillows, trying to sound blissed out, and feeling miserable.

When she opened her eyes, Troy was lying propped up on an elbow, watching her and smiling. 'Good, isn't it? Welcome to your first Tantric orgasm, darling.'

'So *that's* what this was all about!' she said, trying to sound enthusiastic and hating herself for being a total fraud. She was physically wrecked, too. She had an appalling crick in her neck, her mouth was a real pain in her face, and she was buzzing with unbearable, unreleased sexual energy. Aphrodite crawled into her lover's arms, glad of the opportunity to assume a genuine expression now that he couldn't see her face. She'd been doing so much acting over the course of the past couple of hours that she'd soon be practised enough to take Jolie Fitzgerald on at charades. She started to stroke his forearm – then stopped abruptly when she realized she was counting the strokes. 'Where . . . er, *how* did you find out about this Tantric stuff, Troy?'

'I told you I'd been doing a lot of reading when I was down at Coolnamaragh?'

'Yes.'

'Well, one of the books I picked up was on sex and spirituality. I remember Jolie reading it when she was researching her novel.'

Oh, *God*! she thought, with a great deal more passion than when she'd uttered the word as she'd celebrated her fake orgasm. All that unrelieved sexual tension had left her feeling extremely cranky.

'I learned a lot, Aphrodite. I learned that sex is more to do with the mind than the body. Sex is pure *chi*. That's what we just exchanged. Not just bodily fluids. We exchanged *chi*.' Ha. There was a *cheep* joke there somewhere, but she couldn't think of it, and she had a feeling that Troy wouldn't appreciate it even if she did. She had a suspicion that he was treating this Tantric thing pretty damn seriously: she had never heard him talk quite so earnestly about anything. 'You see, we didn't just "have sex" there. We didn't just "fuck" or "make love". We "mind fucked" in the best possible sense of the word. It's all to do with Yin and Yang and . . .'

Aphrodite heard Troy, but she didn't listen to him. She was so tired (it *had* been a bitch of a day: she'd had the model twins on her case maintaining that, as Troy's house models, *they* should be the ones featured in the charity gig programme), she was hungry, and she hadn't even managed a sip of the champagne she'd bought to celebrate. And Troy's harping on about Tao and *chi* and Yin and Yang made him sound as if he was talking in a foreign language. How eagerly she'd looked forward to this evening! She'd pictured them making love in the bath by candlelight and having finger food in bed. She'd tried so hard to make everything just right, and now here she was feeling as deflated as a punctured PVC doll. Above her, Troy's beautiful voice droned on and on, and Aphrodite's eyelids got heavier and heavier . . .

And when she woke up the bed was empty. This had happened before: she knew where she'd find him.

Troy was lying in the bath in his usual relaxed fashion: arms laid out along the edge, head supported by a bath pillow. But he was wearing something strange around his head – a silk scarf knotted bandanna-fashion. And as Aphrodite stepped forward to check whether or not he was asleep, she saw that it wasn't a bandanna that Troy was wearing. It was a blindfold.

*　　*　　*

After many hours lying awake, waiting for Troy to return to bed, Aphrodite had finally fallen asleep at around five o'clock in the morning. Ten o'clock found her running late for a conference call, skeetering through Troy's flat trying to pull on her clothes, peel rosepetals off her skin, and clean her teeth at the same time. His portfolio was propped up against the wall by the front door, and she cursed herself for not having gone through the new designs with him last night. A meeting was scheduled with the pattern cutter that afternoon; she'd just have to wait until then. 'I'll talk to you later, darling,' she called into the bedroom where her lover still lay slumbering like a handsome prince in a fairy tale. 'I'll give you a buzz around lunchtime.' She didn't even know if he was listening. The ormolu clock in the drawing room chimed ten, and she seized her bag. 'Oh, fuck!' she said with feeling. 'I'm just going to have to reschedule.'

On the street she tried to hail a cab without success. One cab, then two, then a third went lumbering by without acknowledging her. So irate, frantic and stressed was Aphrodite Delaney that it took several minutes before the small internal voice of reason that had been quietly asking for her attention finally managed to make itself heard. 'Walk,' it said. 'Or take the bus.'

There was a bus just pulling up at an adjacent stop. Yes. A bus was a good idea. She could spend the journey consulting her diary and trying to make sense of the day. She leapt aboard, accessed her Filofax and ran an eye down the list of things she had pencilled in to do after her conference call. More phone calls, mostly, all morning. Lots of them. Then nothing until the meeting with the pattern cutter in the afternoon. Sitting back, she assessed her schedule. It looked clear-cut enough, but there were always loads of unscheduled chores clamouring for attention in the back of her mind. Problems and chores and more problems.

But one problem loomed larger than any of the others, and it wasn't a professional one. It was personal, and it was about Troy. What on earth was she going to do about this Tantric thing? Troy was clearly a convert, and while she was always happy enough to experiment with new and unusual ways of making love, the Tantric thing last night had been disastrous for her. Last night had been the first time she'd ever faked an orgasm with Troy, and she hated herself for it. She tried to persuade herself that maybe it was just a passing phase, the way the bondage thing had been – but she'd quite enjoyed that, and at least *that* hadn't required a degree in pure maths to get results. Oh, God, there had to be *some* kind of compromise, some kind of solution to this new problem. Where could she find the answers?

Ah-ha! The answer was staring her in the face in the shape of the phone that was ringing in her bag. There in the centre of the display she read the name LOLA in reassuring capitals.

'Oh, Lo!' she said into the phone. 'Thank God it's you! I really need–'

'To talk?' came the laconic response.

'Yes!'

'Hey! Why does that not surprise me? Aphrodite, has it ever occurred to you that *I* might need counselling too, from time to time?'

'Are you still seeing Patrick?'

'Yes.'

'And you're still both besotted?'

'Yes.'

'And he's still bringing you presents?'

'Yes.'

'Then you don't need counselling. Lunch?'

'Fitzers'?'

'Half-past one?'

'See you there. Oh – by the way, Aphrodite. Have you checked out this week's *Hello!*?'

'No. Why?'

'Rachel Hunter's in it.'

'So what?'

'She's wearing a pashmina.'

*   *   *

On her way to lunch in Fitzers' after a morning spent juggling calls and fielding calls and resisting the temptation to slam the phone down on people, Aphrodite passed a second-hand bookshop. A title screamed at her from the display in the window. *Tantric Sex*, it proclaimed in wavy blue print: *The Ultimate Spiritual Guide*. Fishing her wallet out of her bag, she sidetracked into the shop, surreptitiously scooped the book out of the window, and prayed that no-one she knew was passing.

Now she was sitting at a window table, waiting for Lola and leafing through the pages of her brand new second-hand *Spiritual Guide*, taking care that the cover was doubled back on itself so that no-one could see the title. Yikes, she thought, as she read about *chi*, *tan tiens*, and *ni wan peaks*, and studied the diagrams of energy forces zinging madly around bodies. So *that's* why he'd stroked each joint of her fingers eighteen times. It was meant to send the warm *chi* energy zooming up into her head to go bouncing off her brain and back down to her loins. Aphrodite could think of a less roundabout way of achieving roughly the same effect.

'*Boo!*' came Lola's voice from over her shoulder, and Aphrodite's *Spiritual Guide* fell to the floor. Before she could retrieve it, Lola had picked it up and was sitting down opposite her. 'Tantric sex?' she exclaimed in an embarrassingly loud voice, scanning the pages. 'What are you reading this crap for, Delaney?'

'Ssh. Give it back, Lo,' hissed Aphrodite, reaching across the table for the book.

'No.' Lola whipped it away. 'Hey. Great menu.'

Resigned to the fact that she wouldn't get her book

back until Lola was good and ready to relinquish it, Aphrodite leaned back in her chair. 'Menu?'

'Mm. Some *very* interesting serving suggestions for bedtime treats. Bananas . . . mangoes . . . strawberries . . . Oysters. Ee-yoo. You can forget that one. The only time I tried an oyster I nearly threw up. I had to publicly confess to being oyster phobic in one of the grooviest seafood bars in Ireland.'

'God! How deeply unsensuous, unadventurous and untrendy of you, Lo.'

'I know. The thing is, everyone says they're supposed to taste of–'

'OK. As we are about to have lunch, I think we should nip this conversation in the bud.'

Lola leafed through more pages. 'Holy shomoly, Aphrodite! This reads like it's been written by a member of some Seventies hippie sex cult. I have just one question for you. *Why?*'

'I found it in a second-hand bookshop.'

'Well. I'm relieved to hear you didn't pay the full price for it. But that still doesn't explain why you're reading it.'

Aphrodite explained.

'Oh dear,' said Lola when she'd finished. 'It all sounds very – um . . .'

'It *is* very "um". I really can't see myself getting into it, Lo. All that counting does my head in. And you'd have to be acrobatically trained to maintain the Yin and Yang connection while alternating positions.'

Lola looked back at the book and flicked through another few pages. 'Pretty humourless stuff, isn't it?

I confess that Patrick and I spend half our time in bed just laughing.'

'Yeah. Troy and I used to do a fair bit of that too. Oh, hell! Am I really saying "used to"?' She fixed anxious eyes on Lola, who didn't seem to be able to tear hers away from *The Ultimate Spiritual Guide*. 'You see, my only hope is that maybe this is just a passing phase, that maybe he'll get over it and things will get back to . . .' Her voice trailed off as she watched Lola's hands turning pages. 'Lola?' she said. 'What have you got on your finger?'

Lola stopped leafing and looked back at Aphrodite. Then: 'Oh, this?' she said, holding up her left hand and admiring it. 'It's my wedding ring. D'you like it?'

'Very nice,' said the waiter, who had just rolled up. Aphrodite recognized him as an actor who'd been on a commercial she'd styled some months ago. 'Congratulations, madam. May I offer you a couple of glasses on the house to celebrate?'

'Hell,' said Aphrodite slowly, as realization dawned. 'Hell! This calls for a bottle, and lunch is on me.' She laughed and clapped her hands. 'Oh, Lola! I'm speechless!'

'Well, that *is* a rare event, Delaney.'

'May I take your order?' The waiter was looking at Lola with wolfish eyes.

'Oh. I'll have the special.' Lola bestowed a big flirtatious smile on him.

'Madam?' The waiter turned to Aphrodite, who hadn't even bothered to look at the menu.

'Oh, um – soup,' she said, 'and that couscous thing.'

The actor/waiter turned away with a last interested look at Lola, which the minxy thing returned.

'Lo!' scolded Aphrodite. 'You're not allowed to do that, now.'

'Do what?'

'Flirt. Now that you're a – God! I can hardly believe it! – a Smug Married.'

'Pah,' said Lola. 'If women stopped flirting with Patrick I'd get seriously worried, so I'm acting on the assumption that the same thing applies to me. As long as people flirt back then I know I'm not morphing into some kind of sad unattractive matronly type.'

Aphrodite scoffed at the notion of Lola ever being either unattractive or matronly. Then she narrowed her eyes at her. 'So, sly bitch Lo. Spill the beans,' she said.

'There are only about three to spill,' said Lola. 'We applied for a licence a month ago, we got married in the registry office in Grand Canal Street last Friday – oh, sorry. They say "wed" in *Individual*, don't they? We *wed* in the registry office on Friday, and then we honeymooned for three sublimely romantic days in Ballynahinch Castle. And then Patrick went back to work. End of story.'

'Well. You total sneaks! Why didn't you tell me?'

'We didn't tell anyone. I only just got around to telling my parents last night. Of course my mother's not speaking to me now. I'm the only one of her daughters ever likely to get married–'

'Rosita's definitely decided to come out, then?'

'Yeah. The day she made the announcement,

Mother actually fell on the floor in a dead faint before excommunicating her from the family for ever. So she's mightily pissed off that I got married on the QT and robbed her of her opportunity to act out the "mother of the bride" fantasy she's cherished all her married life.'

'*Why* did you do it on the QT?'

Lola gave her her best 'get real, Delaney' look. 'Hey. Can you imagine the circus *that* would have been? Family flying in from all over the world, and marquees and caterers and dressmakers and limos and speeches and bridesmaids and poor cousin Tommy as a pageboy in velveteen knickerbockers and a frilly shirt – and fucking *hats*! No thanks, darling. I'd have fled screaming faster than Julia Roberts in *Runaway Bride*, and I suspect Patrick would have done the same.'

'Wow.' Aphrodite reached across the table and took Lola's left hand in hers. 'A Smug Married! I don't think I know *anyone* married. You're the first.'

'And, before you ask – I didn't marry him because I'm pregnant, because I'm not.'

'Why did you, then?' Aphrodite was genuinely curious.

'Because we totally love each other,' said Lola.

Aphrodite's jaw dropped, and it was at least five seconds before she could speak again. Then: 'Oh! Oh! How beautiful!' she said.

And there in the middle of Fitzers' restaurant, Aphrodite and Lola looked at each other with tears welling up in their eyes and fell into each other's arms.

The pair of cool dudes sitting at the table next to them exchanged glances and one of them uttered a single word that dripped with amused disparagement. '*Girls*,' said the dude.

'Damn right,' said Lola, smiling at him through her tears. 'And the beauty of it is – you *know* we rule.'

Chapter Sixteen

Later that afternoon she kissed Lola goodbye on the street and ran up to her office for her meeting with Troy and James Gillespie, the pattern cutter. She was squirting mint-flavoured spray into her mouth as she took the stairs two at a time. She didn't want to have giveaway traces of alcohol on her breath now that Troy was in ascetic mode.

The two men were there already, Troy's portfolio lying open on her desk. Aphrodite moved across the room, feeling apprehensive suddenly. Would these designs wow her as much as the autumn stuff had?

She needn't have worried. 'Oh! Oh, Troy!' she said, turning over page after page of drawings so breathtaking she could barely speak. This stuff was fabulous. There were gowns that looked as if they'd been crocheted from soft corals, there were gowns that gleamed with the iridescence of pale rainbows, there were gowns that suggested weed underwater. There was more. There were thistledown wraps, and shrugs that looked as if they'd been painstakingly constructed from thousands upon thousands of filigreed leaves, there were fishtail trains with spangles for scales, there were capes like faded butterflies' wings, there were fichus of feathers and stoles studded with tiny sea shells. There was a gown that burned as brightly as a Roman candle.

'Jesus, Troy,' she said finally, setting aside the portfolio. 'You've excelled yourself. They are so, *so* beautiful.'

But Troy just shrugged. 'I don't care for them much myself,' he said. 'They're a bit floriferous for my taste. But what the ladies want, the ladies get.' He yawned, and ran his hands over his velveteen head. Then he took up a marker and started doodling spirals on the corner of one of his sketches.

Aphrodite turned to James and smiled. 'You'll have your work cut out for you, won't you?' He made a face at the appalling pun, and she said: 'Ow! Sorry about that.' She liked James Gillespie. He was, quite simply, the best in the business. He was diligent, reliable, unflappable, and he had years of experience.

Aphrodite returned her attention to the drawings. 'D'you know what they're like? They're like frocks from a fairy's dressing-up box,' she said. 'Look at this. That harebell blue will look fantastic on the twins. Oh – and the dotey little velvet cap! It's just edible, Troy! Hey – there'll be serious ructions about who gets to wear what! Troy? Don't you think? Troy?'

Troy looked up briefly before resuming his doodling. 'Yeah,' he said. 'I guess.'

*   *   *

The sex wasn't working. They both knew it. They'd tried to get it right over the course of the past couple of nights, but they each knew that they'd reached some barren place in their relationship: that horrible place where there was absolutely nothing left to lose. As she lay beside him now on a Saturday night, she heard the ormolu clock in his drawing room strike twelve, and she knew that the fairy tale was over. And Aphrodite felt a rush of real regret for what they'd had, for what was now slipping away beyond reach or recovery.

Troy turned his head towards her so that they lay facing each other on the pillow. 'I'm sorry.' He lifted a hand and lightly caressed the line of her cheekbone and the contour of her jaw, and Aphrodite longed to tell him how *good* it felt when she knew he wasn't counting, but she didn't. She knew there was no point. 'We don't seem to be communicating as well as we did, do we?'

Aphrodite shook her head.

'I know you blame me for that, and yes, I *am* the one who's at fault, because I've changed, Aphrodite. I've changed and I'm moving on.' He took a deep breath, and then he said: 'I'm going on a retreat to a monastery near Mount Kailash.'

'Mount Kailash?'

'It's in western Tibet. I leave on Tuesday. I don't know how long I'll stay there, but it's a six-week journey to and from Kathmandu, so I'll be away for some time. After that, I'm not sure where I'll go, but I think it's unlikely I'll return to Dublin. I've asked the agent to let this apartment, and I'm meeting with my solicitor on Monday. I'm going to sign over all my shares in Troy MacNally Enterprises to you, Aphrodite.'

'What?'

'Sell them if you like. I don't care what happens to the business.'

She clutched at his arm. 'Oh, Troy – you can't do this!'

'I can. I can, and I will. It's the only way forward for me, Aphrodite. You know it too, I think. Going to Mount Kailash will be the ultimate spiritual journey for me. I've been living in fucking torment for far too long.'

'Are you sure? Are you *sure* you're doing the right thing, Troy?'

'Unquestionably and absolutely. I've been thinking about it for ages.' He furrowed his brow. 'Do you know what I think? I think I was in danger of becoming a complete voluptuary, and I couldn't have lived with myself if that had happened.'

'But I liked it when you were a voluptuary!'

He smiled at her. 'You wouldn't have liked it if I'd carried on too far down that road. I know what the next stage would have been.'

Aphrodite gave him a questioning look. 'You're talking about drugs?'

'Yeah. I went there with Miriam. It wasn't a good place to be. It's a dark place, and I crave the light. I crave the kind of light that shone down on me that day in the monastery on Skellig Michael. That's when I hit on the idea of a quest for enlightenment. And the first step to enlightenment, unsurprisingly, is to dump some material ballast. The shares are yours–'

'But–'

'Ssh. Don't argue. Just listen. I've asked Polly Riordan to send all the stuff in this flat to auction and donate the proceeds to charity. I know you don't trust her, but she's always had my best interests at heart. She's promised not to breathe a word of this to anyone until after I've gone, incidentally, because I don't want the news dragging down company morale – especially when you've a bitch of a photo-shoot to get through on Monday. But I had to tell you face to face. I am sorry, Aphrodite. Can you understand?'

'Yes. I think I can.' She remembered the way he'd looked that time on the boat trip back from Ilnacullin, how his eyes had been those of a tortured soul. She thought of all the avenues he'd gone down, the confused maze he'd woven around himself in his thankless efforts to establish meaning in his life: the drugs, the sex, the sensual delights. A poor little rich boy. And she thought now that probably Troy had been a sick boy, too, for a long, long time, mind-fucked by a series of harpies. A manipulated boy who'd ended up in one of the most manipulative businesses of all, the business they called fashion. 'I hope you find what you're looking for, Troy.' She took his face between her hands and smiled at him. He was looking very tired, and she thought of the long, hard journey that he had in front of him, and her heart went out to him. 'I did love you.'

He managed a dozy smile back. 'And I did love you. You were very good for me, you know. You got me through some pretty scary patches. That's why you're getting my shares as a reward. You'll have a controlling interest now; you can do what you like with the company. Oh – and I want you to have my car.'

'Jesus, Troy! I can't accept that as well! I'm–'

'Please, Aphrodite. I've been hard work. You deserve some kind of perk for putting up with a contrary bastard like me.'

'Oh, Troy!' She invested his name with yearning, and she thought of the time they'd yearned for each other over the phone when he was miles away in Coolnamaragh and she was stuck in Dublin. 'You weren't hard work *all* the time, you know. We had a lot of fun along the way. Remember? I'll never forget the time we spent in Kerry together, before–' She'd been about to say 'before Jolie came along and spoiled everything', but she didn't. Instead she said: 'Before I had to go back to Dublin when my flat got trashed.'

'Yeah,' agreed Troy. 'Kerry *was* good. Drive the car down there tomorrow instead of hiring one. I won't be needing it any more.' He closed his eyes, and then he said: 'Can you forgive me, Aphrodite?'

'There's nothing to forgive, Troy. There really isn't. You're absolutely right. The thing we had going has run its course, and it's much, much better that it should end amicably rather than acrimoniously.'

Something made her think of her predecessor Miriam de Courcy, and she thanked heaven that she, Aphrodite, had survived – that she'd somehow managed to avoid all the 'pitfalls of being a muse: the open battles and the guerrilla warfare and the assassination attempts that had done for poor Miriam.

Now she stroked his velvet head, and said: 'Will I say goodbye now? Or will I stay one last night?'

'Stay,' he said.

So Troy MacNally's final muse kissed him on his cheeks and his nose and his chin and his closed eyelids, and finally, chastely, on his spoilt boy's mouth, and then she took one last look at his drowsy face before moulding herself into his shape for the last time ever, and settling down to sleep.

And the next morning she let herself out of his fabulous *fin-de-siècle* apartment without waking him and without saying goodbye, and took the road that they'd once taken together, to Kerry.

* * *

On the morning of the shoot the crew had an early breakfast in the hotel where Aphrodite had booked everyone in, with the exception of Jack Costello, who was staying in his own house on the island of Valencia. Because the shoot was going to be so short, sharp and – hopefully – sweet, gofers and assistants were redundant, so the crew was a small one comprising only make-up, model and Aphrodite.

They had been blessed with the weather. It was a balmy autumn day with few clouds in the sky and enough sporadic sunshine to keep spirits raised and puffa jackets in the boots of cars.

'But the water will be freezing,' Maggie the make-up artist pointed out over her cornflakes. Everybody had come out with the same observation when they'd heard about the shoot. 'How on earth will you manage, Anna?' was the question on the lips of everyone the model met.

'I just will,' was Anna's matter-of-fact response. 'I'm being paid a lot of money for this gig. It's high-profile, I've an upmarket hotel room and a wonderful dinner waiting for me at the end of the day, so what have I got to complain about? Models who moan in situations like this are the pits. Of course it's going to be tough, but what's the point in reminding everyone? Just keep that hip flask handy.'

'Shit!' said Aphrodite with feeling. 'I'm sorry, Anna. I completely forgot about a hip flask.' She looked at her watch. 'And the hotel won't sell us alcohol this early in the day.'

'Don't worry,' said Anna blithely. 'Jack will have one.'

The drive to Valencia took the three women just over an hour in Troy's Merc, and when they got there, there was Jack Costello waiting for them by the pier in a jeep piled high with scuba gear and camera cases. There was another man with him, a tall dark dude with biceps bulging under the cotton of his T-shirt.

'Hi,' said Aphrodite, standing on tiptoe to give Jack a casual peck on the cheek, then stepping back and sending another 'hi' to the dude.

'This is Ronan,' said Jack. 'The skipper. He's kindly volunteered to lend a macho hand.'

'The skipper?'

'I can't see you or Maggie hauling poor Anna out of the water every time she needs to change her frock. Ronan's here to manhandle her.' Aphrodite nearly said: 'Lucky Anna.' The idea of being man-handled by Ronan was rather appealing. Instead she said: 'You're the skipper of a *boat*?'

'I am. And once on board, you do exactly as I say.'

Ronan sent her a sexy smile, then started to unload the jeep, swinging down a weighty scuba tank as easily as if it was a carrier bag from Marks & Spencer's lingerie department.

Aphrodite wandered over to the edge of the pier. 'We're going on a boat? Which one?'

'The sexy little cabin cruiser over there. Isn't she a beaut? She's Ronan's pride and joy.' Jack indicated a jauntily painted boat to his right. It bore the legend *Clarabelle* on its hull. Or was that its bulwark? 'We'll drop anchor below the bridge, and Anna can dive from the leeward side. You can set up all your para-phernalia below deck.'

Aphrodite knew she'd turned ashen. The last time she'd been below deck on a boat she'd suffered serious nausea and vomiting. For some reason she'd pictured Anna diving from the bridge connecting the island to the mainland, but she saw now that it wasn't a viable proposition. The dive itself was possible, but getting back onto dry land would be fraught with difficulty. 'Won't it be very cramped down there?' she asked in a voice that bleated with uncertainty.

Jack gave her his long-eyed look. 'You're prone to seasickness?'

'Yes.'

'Take a couple of these.' He reached into his pocket and handed her a packet of tablets.

'You get seasick too?' she asked.

'No. But I always keep tablets on me for those who do. I'd rather take a leak in the jakes of the most insalubrious gin-joint in the world than venture into the head of a boat where someone's just barfed up their breakfast.'

'The head?'

'Maritime-speak for loo. If you feel nauseous, come up on deck for fresh air and focus on the horizon.'

Aphrodite looked at the cabin cruiser with distaste. 'Couldn't Anna change on deck rather than downstairs? There's lots of space.'

'No. If she was stuck on deck in open water she'd be blue with cold before you could say Jack Robinson.'

She attempted a smile. 'Before you could say Jack Robinson?' she repeated. 'I haven't come across that expression since I read Enid Blyton as a child!'

'It's nearly as archaic as "churlish ruffian and blackguard",' observed Jack. 'But not quite as sexy. Don't worry too much about the seasickness thing, incidentally. It'll take no time at all to get the boat to the site, and there's no swell. You'll be fine as long as you take the tablets.'

'What about you?' asked Aphrodite, wanting to change the subject. 'Won't you be freezing under-water?'

'I'll be in a dry-suit. The cold won't be a problem. But we'll still need to work as fast as we can. How's Anna fixed?'

'Maggie did her make-up at the hotel—'

'It's waterproof?'

'Damn right it's waterproof. We'll just need to touch up a tiny bit between shots.'

'OK. Show me the frocks.'

Troy's creations had been packed with the utmost care, layered with tissue and folded once only – horizontally to minimize creases – in cardboard cartons. It had seemed absurd to treat with such reverence garments that were going to end up submerged in sea water, but such was the beauty of Troy's dresses that they *commanded* this kind of respect. Aphrodite took them out one at a time, and after holding up the third one Jack said: 'OK. I get the picture. They're fucking works of art. It seems a shame to ruin them. Isn't there any way you can rehabilitate them afterwards?'

'Not a chance,' said Aphrodite. 'They're ephemeral as the mayfly – hatched to live one day only.'

'Or as ephemeral as a *chose de neige*?' They smiled at the memory they shared of the ghastly arthouse film. 'I suppose it's worth it, to pull off a stunt like this. I'd better get it right.'

'You better had. Imagine if we trashed Troy's frocks only to discover that you'd forgotten to load the camera!' She gave him a look of humorous challenge, which he rudely ignored.

'OK. Let's get this show on the road.' Jack clicked his fingers rapidly – once, twice, three times, and then he started to move across the pier to where Anna was having her lips retouched. He greeted her by sweeping her hand into his and kissing the palm. 'Good morning, beautiful,' he said. 'What a privilege to have you working with me on what I conjecture will be one hell of an ambitious shoot. I could have had a diva; they've sent me down a goddess.'

'Cut the crap, Jack,' said Anna, smiling back at him. 'You know it doesn't work with me.' But from the look in Anna's eyes, Aphrodite suspected that it did.

'May I borrow her for a moment, Mags?' Jack said to his colleague, who had stepped back and was inspecting her work of art with critical eyes. 'We need to do team bonding.'

'Sure,' said Mags. 'She's all yours.'

Swinging Anna's hand in his, Jack led her across to his jeep, where they stood talking for a good five minutes. Aphrodite glanced at them from time to time as she slung bags onto the deck of the boat, and she registered at once the rapport between them. She saw it in the curve of Anna's beautiful white neck as she threw her head back to laugh at something he said, she saw it in the smile he gave her as he described something in the air with his big hands, she saw it in the way he leaned in to her and touched her face, and she saw it in the way Anna touched his face back. Theirs was the easy intimacy of two people who worked well together – or, she found herself wondering with a stab of irrational jealousy, was it the easy intimacy of two people who had been – maybe still were – lovers?

Then suddenly Anna was walking towards her, saying: 'Let's do it', and Jack was getting into his gear on the deck (she tried not to watch as he pulled the horizontal zip on the crotch of his dry-suit), and

Maggie was lugging her make-up case downstairs to the cramped galley, and the engines were chugging into life, and then Anna was raising her arms as the first of Troy's beautiful gowns was dropped over her head, and the *Clarabelle* slid away from the pier.

As soon as they dropped anchor Aphrodite clambered back on deck, grateful for the fresh air (Maggie had been spraying fixative below). She stood clutching the rail of the boat, fixing her eyes bleakly on the horizon as Jack disappeared underneath the water in a fizz of bubbles. By this time they'd attracted quite an audience. Anna waved and laughed at the crowd who'd gathered on the bridge to watch, and then, as Aphrodite started the countdown to a hundred that Jack needed before he was ready to start shooting, the model stood motionless, centring herself, readying herself for the dive.

'Ninety-eight, ninety-nine, one hundred!' Aphrodite called out, and suddenly Anna was in the air. Troy's iridescent chiffon rainbow shimmered in the October sun, fluttering around her nakedness like the feathers of a kingfisher for an infinitesimal moment before she hit the water and the gown was gone for ever.

Aphrodite held her breath. Half a minute later Anna was at the surface again, droplets of water spinning from her hair as she shook her head and laughed like Disney's Little Mermaid. 'This is fucking *insane*!' she shouted. 'Aphrodite Delaney, you are one seriously mad bitch to have dreamed this one up!' And then she took a deep breath and dived down again to where Jack was waiting to catch her beautiful, exhilarated sea nymph's smile for posterity.

* * *

Not much more than an hour later it was all over. Anna had performed like a trouper, climbing in and out of the water, having yards of soaking wet fabric peeled off her body, being dried off before slipping into yet another fabulous dress, allowing Ronan to wrap her in Jack's sheepskin jacket – and knocking back quick nips of Jack's medicinal bourbon.

Back on dry land, Jack joined her for one after he'd divested himself of his dive gear. She was sitting on the pullback of the jeep, wrapped in his jacket, with her damp hair spilling all over the turned-up collar, eating a sandwich and signing autographs for her gape-mouthed audience. She still looked stunningly beautiful, and Aphrodite thanked her lucky stars that she had been able to find such a rarity – a feisty model with a real sense of fun.

Jack sat down beside her and waited until her fan club had dispersed before planting a big kiss on her cheek. Aphrodite couldn't help but eavesdrop as she rolled Troy's dresses into damp balls and consigned them to rubbish sacks, feeling like the ultimate philistine.

'Are you staying in Parknasilla tonight?' he asked.

'Mm-hm,' said Anna, taking a big bite of her sandwich. 'Are you?'

'No. I'll eat there, but I've to drive back to Dublin. Can I use your shower before dinner?'

'Be my guest. Why have you to get back to Dublin in such a hurry?'

'I've an appointment in the morning, and there's no way out of it.'

'Shame. There's a king-sized bed in my room.'

Aphrodite froze, and pretended to be consulting her checklist.

'Anna,' said Jack. 'I happen to know there's a significant other in your life right now, and I have a rule about sleeping with other men's women.' Then he gave a low laugh. 'Let me know if he ever becomes an *in*significant other, though, won't you?'

'You, my darling, will be the first to know,' she said. Now Aphrodite heard Anna's laugh – husky, infectious – and she sneaked a sideways look at the pair. Anna had leaned towards Jack, snaked her beautiful, slender arms around his neck and was dropping a kiss full on his mouth. The kiss was just fractionally longer than a kiss between friends should be, observed Aphrodite.

'Ow. Jesus. You brat. You could do with a good spanking, naughty Anna,' said Jack, taking hold of her arms and disengaging himself from her embrace. 'And I'm going to have to make that a cold shower.'

'Spoilsport. Give me another go of your hip flask, Costello,' she demanded. He handed it to her, and she swigged and then rummaged in the picnic hamper for more food. 'Shit. That's the end of the chicken sandwiches. I don't like tuna. And I am seriously starving.'

'In that case,' said Jack, 'let me run you back to your hotel and we'll get some food into you. I owe you dinner for the wonderfully intrepid panache you brought to bear on that shoot today.'

'Will you buy me champagne?'

'Of course. Will you let me watch the porn channel?'

Anna laughed. 'You are incorrigible, Jack. And anyway, I don't think there *is* a porn channel in the hotel.'

'No porn channel? You poor deprived girl. I'll let you watch me in the shower if you need to indulge your voyeuristic tendencies.'

'I don't have any. Watching does nothing for me.' She rested her chin on his shoulder and looked up at him with a foxy smile. 'Morgana likes watching herself, though. Her bedroom's full of strategically placed mirrors.'

Jack got to his feet and held out a hand to pull her up. 'I know,' he said.

And then he and a laughing Anna climbed into his jeep and drove away, leaving Aphrodite clearing away the detritus of the shoot and slinging bin bags into the boot of Troy's car.

'Nice car,' remarked Ronan.

'Thanks. Can I give you a lift anywhere?'

'Thanks, but no thanks. My girlfriend's picking me up.' Of course she was. 'Are you going to bin those dresses?'

'Yes. They're of no use to anyone in the state they're in.'

405

'They'd be of use to my girlfriend. She makes rag rugs for a craft shop. If you don't need them, she'd be glad to take them off your hands.'

'Be my guest,' said Aphrodite.

*   *   *

On the drive back to Parknasilla she tried hard not to think of Jack and Anna and the easy camaraderie they had going between them. She pictured them in Anna's room, flicking through the television channels, lobbing jokes between bedroom and bathroom, ordering champagne from room service. Why did it make her cross? They'd worked as hard as she had today. Harder. They deserved time out. She was turning into a resentful, boot-faced bat.

When she finally got back to the hotel she went straight to her room, had a shower, helped herself to a large gin and tonic from the minibar (mentally thumbing her nose at the instructions she'd read on the seasickness tablets earlier, that had cautioned against consuming alcohol). Then she dried her hair, did her face and watched MTV as she dressed for dinner, because Parknasilla was quite posh. Before she left her room she checked out her reflection in the full-length mirror, and after some consideration, she changed the rather demure high-necked silk thing she was wearing for a floaty little MacNally number that drew attention to her Wonderbra-enhanced cleavage.

Downstairs in the bar Anna was drinking champagne, Jack was drinking Guinness, and Maggie the make-up artist was drinking mineral water. Another champagne flute was magicked for Aphrodite, and they sat there for some time admiring the view, studying the menu, yawning and not making much conversation because everyone was knackered.

In the dining room, however, second-wind syndrome kicked in once they'd refuelled with extremely good food and ordered a second bottle of Bordeaux. Before coffee came, Maggie made her excuses for being a party pooper and retired. Anna and Aphrodite reassured her that she wasn't a party pooper at all, and even if she was she was allowed because she'd just told them she was pregnant, and wasn't it so beautiful?

Finally the waiter came with *petits fours*, and Jack reached into his jacket pocket for his card and asked for the bill. It was the same battered sheep-skin jacket that he'd been wearing the first time she had ever met him, over a year ago, and even though it was even more battered, it didn't look out of place in the gracious dining room. *Clothes do not the man make* or something like that, thought Aphrodite vaguely. What does then make the man? Manners? But Jack Costello *had* no manners. He was one of the rudest men she'd met; she'd always said so. Or had until quite recently, anyway, she mused, as he got to his feet and inclined his head at Anna, who had disappeared off to the loo some minutes earlier, and was now drifting back towards their table.

'Jack Costello,' said Anna, resuming her seat and leaning forward with a slit-eyed smile, 'you have the best manners of any person I know. You are the only man I have ever met who still insists on standing up when a chick enters the room. It is an endearingly old-fashioned habit of yours, and it's very, very sexy. In fact, it's so sexy, I'm going to make you do it again.' She stood up, and Jack did likewise. 'Hah! Good night, you gorgeous, talented man,' she said, presenting her beautiful face to him so that he could kiss her. 'I am now officially off to bed.' She plonked a kiss on Aphrodite's cheek. 'Good night, Musey. See you in the morning.'

'Won't you stay and help us finish off the wine?' asked Aphrodite, pouring herself another glass. 'There's buckets left.'

'No no no. I am *soooooo* knackered. Look at me. I am practically swaying with exhaustion.'

'I'm not surprised,' said Jack, 'after what you went through today.' He deposited an avuncular kiss on her forehead. 'Sweet dreams, little mermaid,' he said, and watched admiringly as Anna turned and proceeded through the dining room, her super-model's thoroughbred grace only slightly off kilter.

Aphrodite went to pour for Jack, and then realized to her embarrassment that there *wasn't* buckets left. The level of the wine in Jack's glass was a bare half-centimetre higher. 'Oo-er,' she said, squinting at the bottle to make sure it really was empty. 'I've poured myself all the wine. Sorry about that. Will we order another?'

'We will not,' he said, looking at his watch. 'Unless you want to sit here drinking it all by yourself. It's late, and I have to make tracks. I've a long drive home, and I've no intention of doing it over the limit.'

'Well,' said Aphrodite. 'You could always stay here for a few hours' – um – kip. That would really be the most sensible thing to do, and I'm sure that they have a room to spare because it's my theory that all really good hotels always–'

But she never got the chance to expound her theory, because just then the waiter arrived with the bill. Aphrodite immediately lunged for it, saying: 'No, no. Troy MacNally Enterprises is footing the bill. I insist, and so would Troy. If he were here. Which he isn't.'

But the bill and Jack's card were magicked out of sight, and Aphrodite realized that she was quite glad of this, because she wasn't sure she could handle the maths. She also realized that they were the last people in the dining room apart from a couple of honeymooners who were spooning and crooning at each other, their faces radiant with happiness and candlelight.

'What are they doing still here?' said Aphrodite in a loud whisper to Jack as he escorted her out of the room. 'They should be in bed, shagging each other senseless.' The idea of two madly-in-love people having glorious sex made tears of nostalgia spring to her eyes as she tripped over the threshold between dining room and lobby. Jack caught hold of her before she hit the deck, and then he took her elbow and guided her towards the lift. 'Oh!' she said, feeling a little *frisson* of delight when she realized that he had obviously taken her words of wisdom on board and decided to stay the night in the hotel. 'But don't you have to book in first?'

'I'm not booking in, Aphrodite. What's your room number?'

Oh God! she thought as *chi* sloshed through her, and 'Um,' she said, as she recalled with some difficulty that her room number was 232. But as they were halfway down the second floor corridor she remembered that it was actually 323, and they had to press for the lift again and wait, and for some reason he didn't kiss her as they were waiting even though there was no-one else around, and then suddenly they were manoeuvring the third floor corridor which had more twists in it than Aphrodite remembered from earlier in the evening. And then finally they were at her door, and Jack was inserting the key card in the lock for her, and the sexual tension which had been stretching like an elastic band inside her since he'd asked her for her room number was on the verge of snapping.

The chambermaid had been in, she was glad to see. MTV had been switched off, the towels that she'd scattered around earlier had been tidied away, and the bed had been turned down. Jack took her by the hand and led her across to the bed that was beckoning to them from the far side of the room. 'Oh, God,' she whispered, as he put her sitting on the mattress and knelt down to unwind the straps of her shoes from around her ankles. He slid off first her shoes, then her stockings, and then he pulled the sheets back and swivelled her legs between the sheets and gently pushed her back against the pillows. And then he pulled the blankets right up to her chin.

'What are you doing?' she asked, confused.

'I'm tucking you in,' he said.

What? 'What? You mean you're not coming to bed with me?'

'No, Aphrodite. Much as I would like to, I am not coming to bed with you. I don't bed other men's women. And I certainly don't mess with other men's muses. Goodnight.'

And then the room was in darkness apart from the golden rhombus of light that shone in from the hotel corridor. For a moment Jack's bulk was blackly silhouetted against the gold, and then the door closed and his shadow was gone, and thankfully, thankfully, sleep descended upon Aphrodite before she'd had time to register exactly what had happened and exactly how appallingly she'd behaved.

Chapter Seventeen

She registered it the next morning, though. She was woken by the thumping rhythm of a Shakira number belting out in the room next door. Someone was playing MTV way too loud. The rhythm banged on relentlessly, matching itself perfectly to the rhythm of the thought pounding in her head. *You stupid bitch*, it went. *You stupid, stupid bitch*. Pulling the blankets over her head did nothing to muffle it. Even when Shakira shut up, the thought banged on. Shut up! Shut up! Go away! *No*, said the thought. *You can't hide from your own thoughts, stupid girl. You can't hide from yourself, and I'm going to say it again. You. Stupid. Bitch. And again. Stupid. And again, and again. Stupid, stupid*.

She berated herself as she shambled into the shower, she berated herself as she pulled on her jeans, she berated herself as she flung her belongings into her bag, trying to summon the courage to look in the mirror. And when she did, when she saw the whey-faced, tousle-haired, tragic-eyed reflection looking back at her, the girl in the mirror's mouth opened and she heard her say: 'You stupid bitch.'

*   *   *

The thought pursued her all the way back to Dublin. It pursued her all round the office when she got into work. There was a minor distraction in the form of a brusque e-mail from Polly Riordan that said: 'Troy asked me to contact you. We need to talk a.s.a.p.' But Aphrodite knew that talking to Polly would simply be inviting more stress into her life and more stress was something she just did not need right now. So she deleted the e-mail and sent one back saying 'As the major shareholder in Troy MacNally Enterprises, I think I call the shots. Please do not use the a.s.a.p. word to me again. I'll be in touch at my convenience.' And then the horrible thought came back and pursued her some more, and she knew that there was only one way to exorcize it.

At around seven o'clock she pulled up outside Jack's house in Portobello. She was just getting out of the car when the front door opened, and her mother stepped out, looking impossibly glamorous.

'What are you doing here?' said Aphrodite and Thea simultaneously. Aphrodite couldn't very well say that she was calling on Jack to deliver a heartfelt apology for being a stupid bitch, so she said: 'I'm returning a lens cap Jack left behind on location.'

Thea raised a cynical eyebrow. 'Oh yes? How very convenient.'

'What do you mean?'

'I'd love to have the excuse of returning items of photographic equipment to the sexiest man in the business. I bet you filched it on purpose.'

'What *are* you on about, Mother?'

'*You* know. He is drop dead gorgeous *and* eligible.

413

And he has a thing about older women. Or so he tells me. Even though I'm not *that* much older than him.'

Thea shook back her hair, and Aphrodite noticed that her décolletage was flushed. Something Jack had once said came back to her. What exactly? And when? Oh! It had been during the photo-shoot at the Gaiety. When he'd wanted Maggie to make up the twins so that it looked as if they'd been having sex with each other . . . *And maybe a dusting of blush on the décolletage – and the ear lobes as well. That's always a post-coital giveaway . . .* A little purr escaped her mother and Aphrodite quickly checked out her ear lobes, but Thea was wearing enormous clip-on earrings, and she couldn't see what colour her ears were.

She was awash with outrage, suddenly. 'Mother! What have you been . . . Have you been . . .'

But Aphrodite shut her mouth like a trap as the door opened again and Perdita emerged onto the step. She looked surprised to see Aphrodite. 'Oh – hi!' she said. 'Jack won't have those contacts ready for you until tomorrow, you know. Didn't he tell you?'

'Oh, yes, I know,' said Aphrodite. 'I just wanted to um – to return something to him.'

Thea sniggered, and Aphrodite shot her a look that said: *Shut up, Mother.* 'You're running very late, Mum,' she pointed out. 'You're going to miss your half-hour call if you're not careful.'

Thea looked at her watch. 'You are absolutely right, darling.' She gave a languid sigh, and eased her shoulders in a sensuous, luxurious way. 'Oh, well. You know what they say?'

'What do they say?' asked Perdita obligingly.

'Time flies when you're having fun. I'd better grab a cab.'

'Don't bother,' said Perdita, extracting car keys from her bag. 'I can give you a lift. My route home takes me straight past the theatre.'

'You are a stunning, adorable treasure. Thank you,' said Thea. She leaned forward to kiss Aphrodite on the cheek. 'Goodbye, you little minx of a daughter. You've inherited more of me than I realized.'

Aphrodite wished Thea would just shut up and go away before she came out with any more incriminating innuendo in front of Perdita.

'My car's over there,' said Perdita, indicating a beat-up old Volkswagen across the road. 'Sorry it's not more glamorous, Thea. You should have asked Jack to give you a lift in his roadster. Then you could have pulled up outside the theatre in style. Here, Aphrodite.' She fished another key out of her bag and inserted it in the Yale. 'I'll let you in. You'll find him in the studio. You know the way, don't you?'

'Yes,' said Aphrodite. 'Thanks.' As she stepped through the door into Jack Costello's hall she heard her mother say to Perdita: 'What *does* Jack drive, incidentally?'

'A classic Jensen,' said Perdita.

Aphrodite walked down the hallway and out through the door that led to his garden. Her feet made a loud scrunching noise on the gravel path, and she recognized the rhythm instantly. *You stupid bitch*, it went. *You stupid, stupid bitch*. Oh, God. This exorcism was *not* going to be easy.

At the door she hesitated, screwed her courage to the sticking place and knocked. There was no reply. She knocked again, then pushed open the door a fraction and called his name. She heard his voice say: 'I'm in the darkroom. Come on in.' On the other side of the studio was a door that was partially obscured by a heavy black drape. She slid behind it, opened the door, and found herself in a smallish, crepuscular room. A dull red glimmer was the only illumination. Jack was standing at the other end of the room with his back to her.

'What do you want now, you sexy bitch?' he said. 'Don't you realize you're going to be stonkingly late for your half-hour call?' He turned round. 'Well,' he said, after a beat. 'It's not the mother. It's the daughter. You sound very alike.'

Aphrodite wanted to run screaming out of there. Why had she come? This was the worst possible scenario she could have ever imagined in a million years. *You stupid, stupid bitch* . . . 'I just – I just – I just –' What did she just want to do? She didn't know any more. She didn't know anything. And then the events of the past few days – the responsibility, the hard work, the split with Troy, the six-hour drive up from Kerry, the hangover, the hissy e-mail exchange with Polly, the humiliation, the confusion – all these things took their toll suddenly, and she felt as if she just wanted to crawl away on her own and die. And then she became aware of the tears that were streaming down her face.

'Oh, darling,' said Jack. 'Oh, darling.' He moved across the short distance that separated them and took her in his arms, and she sobbed and sobbed and sobbed. Oh God! It felt so *good* to sob. She couldn't remember the last time she'd done it. She couldn't remember the last time someone had taken her in their arms like this and held her and cradled her head on a broad shoulder and kind of *rocked* her and stroked her hair and made little soothing sounds in her ear, little sounds that made no sense – no sense at all – but which were somehow infinitely reassuring. And then she realized why she couldn't remember. It was because no-one had ever done it before.

When she was all sobbed out, she just kept standing there with her head on Jack's shoulder, loving the sensation of his body against hers, loving the sensation of his hand on her hair, and all at once the sensation wasn't soothing any more. It was intensely, shockingly erotic, and she knew he knew it too because his body had tensed, and she could tell that he was making an effort to control his breathing. Her own breath was shallow now, and behind her closed eyelids her pupils were dilated, and she could feel her lips begin to part and she wanted – God! how she wanted him to kiss her. As she went to shift her weight from her right foot to her left she felt his erection straining against the denim of his jeans. She shifted again, and felt him brush against her belly, and the most difficult thing she ever did in her life was to resist the impulse to grind herself into him. And then she heard her mother's voice in her head, the arch tone as she'd smiled her post-coital smile at Aphrodite and said: *He has a thing about older women. Or so he tells me* . . . And his remark as she'd blundered into his darkroom: *What do you want now, you sexy bitch? Well. It's not the mother. It's the daughter* . . .

Aphrodite wrenched herself out of Jack's embrace, turned on her heel and ran out of the darkroom back into the light.

*　　*　　*

That night she poured wine into the biggest wineglass she could find, took a long bath and went to bed early, craving sleep like an addict might a fix. She knew it would be the only way of silencing the voice that echoed in her head, the voice she still hadn't been able to exorcize. Stupid bitch.

*　　*　　*

She woke late the next morning and didn't care. She'd worked her ass off recently, she deserved time out. She made coffee and checked the messages on her machine. There was one from her mother – obviously left after the show last night – in which she slurred on and on about how awful the ageing process was and how unfair it was that women should get menopauses and men didn't, and there was one from James Gillespie that had been left earlier that morning, asking her to ring him urgently. How she hated that word! Everybody always needed her *urgently*. Well, now she was chief shareholder in

Troy MacNally Enterprises she was bloody well going to stop dancing this grim gavotte of attendance on everyone. Even on lovely, punctilious, obliging James. Whatever was urgent would just have to wait till she got to the studio.

She showered, did her face, put on her Troy MacNally suit, and got into his car to drive to the studio.

When she walked through the door Saskia the receptionist looked even more frightened of her than usual. On her way past the machine room she noticed that the women's machines were deathly silent, and, what was even more unnatural, so was 98FM. In the outer office, her PA was white-faced.

'What the hell is going on?' asked Aphrodite.

James Gillespie materialized wearing a grave expression; his calloused hands abstractedly working a pair of imaginary scissors. 'Come with me,' he said.

Aphrodite handed her PA her mobile. 'I'm not taking *any* calls,' she said, and then she followed James into Troy's office, where last season's stuff still hung on costume rails. It looked overly structured to her eye now – now that she'd handled the fragile, dripping wisps of gowns she'd consigned to bin bags the day before yesterday.

Troy's portfolio lay on his desk beside an A4 envelope with her name printed on it. 'Take a look,' said James, indicating the portfolio with a nod of his head. The look in his eye as she undid the ties told her what she was going to find.

The fairy tale had turned into a horror story.

Troy's wood nymphs and naiads had been obliterated by thick, black marker that spiralled down from the tip of a tiny cap to the toe of a dainty shoe. Every single one of his evening wear designs had been defaced.

There was a beat. Then: 'All is not lost,' she said, amazed at how calm she sounded. 'We still have the patterns for the evening dresses from the ones you made up for the shoot.'

'No we don't,' said James flatly.

'Why not?'

'He destroyed the patterns.' James indicated the galvanized steel wastepaper bin. It contained the charred remains of paper and what had once been calico toiles.

Aphrodite bit her lip. For someone with such little grasp on reality, Troy had been remarkably thorough. A thought struck her. 'How do you know it was Troy?' she asked James.

He shrugged. 'I've worked with him for a long time. I knew something was up. Have you spoken to him?'

'No. I can't speak to him. No-one can.' Aphrodite found herself laughing in a wildly hysterical way that didn't sound like her at all. 'He's on his way to a mountain in Tibet.'

'That figures,' said James, and his pragmatic northern accent made her laugh even more. She laughed and she laughed until the tears ran down her cheeks, and then she remembered how Troy had said: 'We're talking about a bunch of frocks, not a life or death situation', and the sanity and the self-evident truth in that observation combined with the mug of tea James had brought her made her calm down and reassess. She wiped away the signs of her hysteria and thought of the damp bundles she'd shoved into bin bags and left behind in Kerry for Ronan's girlfriend to turn into rag rugs, and that made her want to start sniggering again. 'Could you have reconstructed them if I still had the original prototypes?' she asked, not sure that she wanted to hear the answer, and hoping she wasn't going to laugh out loud again.

'What kind of nick were they in?'

'Well, let's just say I wasn't tempted to hang on to any of them.'

'I might have managed to cobble something together,' said James. 'But I wouldn't beat yourself up over it, Aphrodite. Nobody could have predicted that anything like this could happen. He left an envelope for you, by the way.'

James handed her the A4 envelope and a paper-knife. The noise of the paper being slit by the blade sounded unnaturally loud in the silent studio. Aphrodite reached in and extracted a square of folded A4 paper. 'A note,' she said unnecessarily, and she read out loud the following words: '"Aphrodite. Enclosed are my new designs. I have decided it's time for another radical change. I am no longer inspired by nature. I am inspired by the notion of cerebral purity."' She reached into the envelope again, drew out half a dozen sheets of paper, and spread them on Troy's desktop. There was nothing on them. No sketches, no spirals:

nothing. They were all as blank as the expression on James Gillespie's face.

Aphrodite looked at the pages, and then she looked back at the A4 sheet. The words were printed in standard double-spaced Times New Roman font. There was no signature. And now Aphrodite knew sure as eggs was eggs who was responsible for the destruction of the drawings. It hadn't been Troy. It had been Polly Riordan. Polly had let herself into the studio last night after receiving Aphrodite's e-mail, and she had systematically sabotaged Troy's entire spring/summer collection. She would have known that it would be of no account to Troy now that his mind was on more lofty spiritual matters. Anyway, he was winging his way to Kathmandu. But she also knew that it would be a crushing blow to the new chief shareholder in Troy MacNally Enterprises, Musey Delaney. The reason that Aphrodite knew beyond the shadow of a doubt that Polly had per-petrated this act of wholesale sartorial destruction was staring her in the face in the printed words on that A4 sheet. Because Troy MacNally had never operated a printer in his life.

She felt the bubble of hysteria rise within her again as she crumpled the page and dropped it in the wastepaper bin. Then she looked at James Gillespie and said: 'I'm going home.'

*   *   *

She rang Lola to see if she wanted to go out and get drunk, but Lola wasn't there, so she left a message on her voice mail, switched her own answering machine on, and got mildly smashed by herself at home instead. Every time the phone rang she'd sneak up on it to see if it was Lo, but it was always only her PA, fretting that she still had Aphrodite's phone and bleating piteously that she couldn't handle all the calls. Hah! thought Aphrodite bitterly. Now someone else knows what it's like to be *chargée de* bloody *affaires sartorieuses*. Then somebody rang from *Individual* magazine to ask where her 'Elegant-stupid-arium' column was and didn't she realize she'd missed her deadline? And once Jolie rang, sounding a bit peeved, saying: 'It would be a good idea for us to get together and talk, Aphrodite.' And darling model Anna rang to say: 'Aphrodite – I've just heard about Troy. I'm so sorry. If there's anything I can do, please let me know. I'm sure you need a shoulder to cry on.' Did she need one? she wondered. And then she thought, no, she didn't. She'd spilled too many tears in too short a period yesterday, and had discovered to her horror the luxury and the liberation of a long, long weep. Tears were too precious an indulgence to waste.

Every hour on the hour she put in a call to Lo, but without the satisfaction of a pick-up. In the end she knew with blinding clarity that the only thing to do was to walk the Pigeon House pier.

She located Troy's car keys, and was just getting into the driver's seat when a Jensen Interceptor pulled up on the other side of the road. Sitting behind the wheel was Jack Costello. They sat there looking at each other rather helplessly for a minute before Jack took the initiative. He got out of his car, strolled over to where she was parked and leaned down until his face was on a level with hers.

'Where are you off to?' he asked.

'The Pigeon House pier,' she said, trusting that he wouldn't assume that she was going there to throw herself off the end. She knew she must look as if that was her intention.

'Oh. Shame. I was hoping you might like to have a look at these.' He waved a manila envelope at her. 'The contact sheets from the Valencia shoot. They're pretty special.'

'I don't *have* to go to the Pigeon House pier,' she said.

'Good,' he said. Then he indicated a bottle of wine that he was holding in his left hand. 'I brought a peace offering, by the way. I thought it was about time we started to conduct our relationship in a rather more grown-up fashion.'

And to her horror, she heard herself blurting: 'Troy and I have split up.'

'So I heard,' he said, extending a hand to help her out of the car. 'Models are the best gossips. I imagine you're feeling pretty gutted.'

She didn't know whether to say: 'No, I'm not' or 'Yes, I am', so she said nothing. She zapped the locks on the car, unlocked the door to her house and veered automatically in the direction of the kitchen to fetch glasses. When she came back into the sitting room, Jack was stripping away the foil from the neck of the bottle.

'You've heard the whole story?' she said. 'About the designs and the note?'

'Yes.'

'Then why did you bring me the contacts? What's the point?'

'You need to see them,' he said. 'They're stunningly beautiful. That photo-shoot was your baby, Aphrodite, and you need to see your vision realized.' He pulled the cork and poured.

'It was *all* our baby,' protested Aphrodite. 'Not just mine. It was a collaboration between you and Anna and Maggie and me. And Troy.'

'Yep. I'll concede that. But it was your imagination that spawned that collaboration. It was *your* original concept. Look.' He drew the contact sheets out of the envelope and laid them on the table.

'Oh!' Her hands flew to her mouth. The photographs were stunning. They were original. They were as much works of art as were Troy's dresses. And they were *her* idea. She hugged the knowledge to herself. These exquisite pictures had been *her* brainchild! She thought with sudden yearning of the days when she'd got a buzz out of her creations, the days before she'd become a muse, before she'd become *chargée d'affaires sartorieuses*, before she'd become revered authoress of 'Elegant-crap-arium', before she'd become a B-list celebrity. Looking at the contacts gave her a rush of something that felt like *chi*, and then she realized that it was a surge of unadulterated creative pride. She turned a smiling face to Jack, and something was happening between them and she couldn't work out whether this *chi* feeling had something to do with him as well as the creative thing, and then the phone went.

'Aphrodite!' said her mother's voice on the answering machine. 'Did I ring you last night? I seem to remember burbling something about the tribulations of hitting – um – a certain age.' A tinkling laugh. 'Now, don't worry about that. I'm feeling *much* better this morning, and I need a favour, if you don't mind. When you next see Jack Costello could you ask him – in a *roundabout* kind of way of course – if he'd consider doing shots of this wonderful young actor I've discovered? Tarquin Swindell is his name, and I can assure you he is going to be the next hot thing. He saw the shots of me that I picked up from Jack's studio yesterday, and thought they were glorious. I know Jack doesn't do shots of just *anyone*, but maybe you could wield a little influence for me? Could you? Thank you, darling. Byeee!'

Aphrodite and Jack were still looking at each other. Aphrodite swallowed. 'You mean – you didn't have sex with my mother?' she ventured to ask.

'What?' said Jack. 'No, I most certainly did not have sex with your mother. What a totally bizarre thing to say.'

'But – but – you called her a sexy bitch. Or, rather, you called *me* a sexy bitch, but you thought you were talking to her . . .' Oh, God. She was sounding stupid. She let her voice trail off, and then she blanched as she realized that her mother's flushed appearance yesterday hadn't been down to lashings of excellent sex with Jack Costello. It had been down to her menopause.

'Your mother *is* a sexy bitch, Aphrodite Delaney. But not half as sexy as you. I think I'd like to kiss you now, if you don't mind. And then I'm going to take you up on the very kind invitation you issued the other evening, which, due to your out-of-bounds relationship status, I was unable to take you up on.'

'What invitation?'

'I'm going to take you to bed. It's through there, is it?' He indicated the door of the bedroom with a nod of his head, and Aphrodite nodded back in dumb affirmation. 'I'm going to take you to bed, and I'm going to fuck you the way I've wanted to fuck you since I first laid eyes on you.'

'OK,' said Aphrodite in the kind of breathy voice Marilyn Monroe might have envied. She actually thought she might swoon, but she managed to remain upright by winding her arms round Jack Costello's neck. 'I think I'd like that.'

And she did.

Chapter Eighteen

In fact, she liked it so much that they stayed in bed for the rest of the day. At around eight o'clock they shambled kitchen-ward and Jack made perfect omelettes. Aphrodite sat at the kitchen table watching him, thinking how incredible it was that she should be here with this man who could cook, who had beautiful manners, and who fucked like a Greek god. The one that had the furnace.

'Who taught you how to cook?' she asked.

'Necessity. I'm self-taught. I've lived on my own all my adult life, so it was something that was pretty essential to learn.'

'You've always lived on your own?'

'An actress moved in with me once upon a time, but it didn't last.'

'Why not?'

'She went away and became famous.'

Aphrodite longed to ask who the famous actress was, but she didn't want to appear nosy. She was longing to ask him loads of things: she wanted to find out everything there was to know about this extra-ordinary, shambling man with the come-to-bed eyes and the charisma she'd tried to ignore for over a year. She wondered what would have happened if he hadn't gone away to the States that time, the very day after they'd first met at awful *Chose de Neige*. Would they have got it together then? How had he felt, she wondered, when he came back and found that she'd hooked up with Troy? Had it mattered to him? Or had he shrugged her off merely as a missed opportunity? There were so many questions! And then she wondered apprehensively: *would* she ever know more about this man? Would this liaison last long enough for her to ever become relaxed about asking him stuff like that?

'Here,' he said, setting her omelette in front of her. 'Eat up. You look peaky.'

'Thank you. Wow. Delicious. I can't remember the last time someone cooked for me.' Actually, she could, because the occasion had been etched into her memory as one of the more horrific events of her life. It had been when Jolie Fitzgerald had performed with the aplomb of a celebrity chef down in Coolnamaragh all those months ago.

'Well. We'll have to remedy that. Come to my house tomorrow and I'll do something hearty and nutritious. *Cassoulet.* I'm going to fatten you up, Aphrodite Delaney. The more of you there is to feast on the better, as far as I'm concerned.' He slid his hands down the front of her kimono and cupped her breasts before kissing the back of her neck and returning his attention to the omelette pan.

She felt a little *frisson* at the prospect of having dinner *chez* Jack Costello. It was as if another brick had been added to the structure of their relationship.

He slid his omelette onto a plate and sat down opposite her. 'What will you do now?' he asked, pouring wine. 'With your life? Will you carry on working for Troy MacNally Enterprises?'

She shrugged. It was way too major a question to shrug off, but there really didn't seem to be any other response. 'I honestly don't have a clue,' she said. 'That's why I was going to walk down the Pigeon House pier. To try and sort my head out.'

'That's how you solve problems, too, is it? Watching water?'

'Yes. I find it really therapeutic.'

'Me too. Except I fish.'

'In Kerry?'

'Yeah.'

'In waders?'

'Yeah.'

'Sexy!'

He laughed and kissed his thumb, then reached across and rubbed her mouth with it. 'Damn right they're sexy,' he said. 'On ladies. I did a "country life" shoot for *Individual* once that involved a model wearing cut-offs, a skimpy T-shirt and fishing waders. The resultant image was . . . *affecting*, to say the least.'

She felt jealous of the model, and realized rather glumly that beautiful women were a major occupational hazard for this man. She gave him a look that she hoped contrived to be both foxy and snooty at the same time, and then gave up and said: 'It must be amazing to have a place like Valencia to escape to. I'd love to see it.'

'Be my guest. You might want to know that I have a spare pair of waders in girly size for visiting friends.

430

Sadly, no-one's availed of them yet.' Another brick! Then: 'Tell me,' he said. 'What would you have done if Troy was still around? What was in the pipeline?'

'Um,' she said, swallowing omelette. 'Let's see. Well, there was the new collection to get together, of course. And there was that big gig at the Point. I feel badly about that. I mean, I know it'll be a media circus, but it *is* for charity, after all. I promised them half a dozen of Troy's evening frocks. And now they're rag rugs.'

'Rag rugs?'

'Yeah. Ronan took them away for his girlfriend to make rag rugs out of them in Valencia.'

'Well. I must buy one when I'm next down there. I rather like the idea of having designer rag rugs on my floor.'

Aphrodite finished her omelette, put knife and fork together, took a thoughtful sip of wine and said: 'I suppose the whole business will go under now, without Troy at the helm.'

'But Troy never contributed much to the day-to-day running of the outfit, did he?'

'No. I did most of that. He was the figurehead. I was just the factotum.' Aphrodite spread her hands in a gesture of helplessness. 'You see, Jack, the grim reality of the situation is that I am now, courtesy of Troy, chief shareholder in the business. It's not in my interest to let Troy MacNally Enterprises go belly up. It's currently my only source of income.'

'There's always "Elegantarium". You could become a full-time fashionista.'

'Shut up about that. I'll put you in it if you're not careful. "The latest, most desirable status symbol is to have your portrait done by society photographer Jack Costello. Mr Costello can be contacted at—"'

'OK, OK. I won't ever sneer at "Elegantarium" again.' He poured more wine. 'Couldn't you just take another designer on board? Why don't *you* have a stab at it, Aphrodite?'

She smiled. 'It's funny. Troy and I once talked about the fact that there's no real demarcation between fashion and theatre design any more. But the thing is, Jack, I don't *love* it. I don't *love* the fashion industry the same way as I loved theatre.' She circled the rim of her wineglass with her middle finger, and she thought suddenly of Jolie and Polly and the poisonous twins and the backbiting and the breathtaking bitchcraft she'd encountered since she'd become involved with Troy MacNally Enterprises. Of course, the theatre world had its own share of nastiness, its Damien Whelans and its divas, but at least there was something endearingly *ingenuous* about the theatre world, with its struggling fringe groups and their minuscule budgets and their staff getting by on nothing more than poverty-line incomes and enthusiasm and *vision*. And then she remembered what Troy had said about the Southeast Asian sweatshops and the indolent, moneyed individuals who took front row seats at the *couture* shows in Paris and she said: 'In fact, I hate it.'

Jack was looking at her speculatively, with those eyes that made her solar plexus contract, those eyes that still contrived to look sexy even when he was being deadly serious. 'Well, then,' he said. 'If that is the case, you must get out.'

She gave him a hopeless look. 'But what'll I *do*?'

'It doesn't matter. When you feel that way about something, it doesn't matter what you do. Work as a waitress. Iron clothes in a laundry. Get a job in a shop. But if you don't put distance between yourself and the thing you hate, it'll get you in the end. I know.'

'Have you been there?'

'Oh, yes. I spent a year as a staff photographer with a tabloid. I was well paid, but I hated it. I hated the paper's ethos, I hated its cynicism, and most of all I hated the grubby, careless way it handled other people's lives, the way the editors looked on people as *commodities*. And when I found myself viewing human tragedy in terms of its newsworthiness, I knew it was time to get out. I was becoming a horrible person.'

'That's just what I said to my friend Lola! I told her I was scared that I was becoming a horrible person.'

'You're not a horrible person, Aphrodite. You're funny and talented and clever, and you will survive. Anyone who can make women walk around sporting puffball skirts is a survivor.'

She would have launched herself into his arms for a kiss if the cat flap hadn't just at that moment swung open with a peremptory 'thwack'. Bobcat stalked in. He'd been out in the rain, and he looked like he'd been double-knitted in damp bouclé. He gave Jack one suspicious, contemptuous sideways glance before moving directly to his bowl and saying: 'I want food and I want it now.'

'OK, Bob,' said Aphrodite with requisite meek-
ness. She got to her feet and dutifully poured
chicken, tuna and salmon Krunchies into his food
bowl and fresh water into his water bowl before
resuming her seat. Bob hoovered up the Krunchies,
then leapt onto Aphrodite's lap, kneaded it with
muddy paws and outstared Jack.

'It's all right, buster,' said Jack. 'I can tell who's
boss around here. I'm not going to mess with you.'

Bob switched his attention to Aphrodite, rubbing
his muzzle against her proffered cheek and purring
to let her know she was a good girl. Then he sniffed
at her, and that profoundly suspicious expression
came into his eyes again.

'Oops,' said Aphrodite, raising an armpit and
taking a whiff. 'I must reek of "Eau de Sex". Sorry,
Bob.' Bobcat slid to the floor in an indignant huff as
she stood up. 'I think I'd better take a quick shower
and rub myself all over with cod liver oil in an
attempt to win back the affection of my despotic cat.'

As she moved past Jack, he caught hold of her
hand and pulled her down to him so that he could
inhale her. 'Jesus,' he said. 'I wouldn't describe that
as "reeking", Aphrodite.'

'How would you describe it, then?'

'It's the sweetest smell in the world,' he said.

*   *   *

Of course she didn't rub herself with cod liver oil,
she rubbed herself with her sandalwood body lotion,
and the smell conjured up memories of Troy, who

434

had loved it so much. And she wondered what place now he had reached in his pilgrimage, and she prayed that he would find the nirvana he was searching for, and she knew in her heart that he – and she – had done the right thing.

When she came out of the bathroom there was no sign of Jack. She felt a momentary flutter of panic before she located him in her studio. He was sitting at her desk with his back to her, and she nearly fell on the floor when she saw Bobcat curled up on his lap, smiling and purring louder than the sewing machines in the machine room in Troy MacNally Enterprises.

'What are you doing?' she cried.

'Sorry,' said Jack. 'I hope you don't mind. I'm looking through your portfolio. You're a talented girl.'

'Oh, thanks,' she said vaguely. 'But actually I wasn't talking to you. I was talking to Bob. He *never* sits on other people's laps, so I got quite a fright when I saw him on yours. I thought you might have drugged him or something.'

'It's OK. We've come to an agreement.'

'Oh?'

'Yeah. I blackmailed him. I told him if he continued acting snooty around me that I would take you away to live in my house, and he wouldn't be welcome.'

'Oh!' The structure of their relationship had suddenly acquired about a million more bricks, and maybe even a roof.

'So he went all smarmy and decided he liked me

435

after all. C'mere, you.' He shooshed Bob off his lap, and reached for Aphrodite's hand, and suddenly she'd usurped Bob's place. She thought with pleasure that she could sense an erection starting to build again, so she wiggled her bum a bit. 'Stop it, you bold creature. I've something to suggest to you before I fuck you again.' Oh, God! Why was it so sexy when he said that? *So* much sexier than 'exchanging *chi*'!

'What do you want to suggest to me?' she said in a suggestive voice.

'Look.' He had spread out along the desktop the drawings she'd done at college for her degree show, the designs for *A Midsummer Night's Dream* that her tutor had described as 'refreshingly fairylike'. 'What do these remind you of?'

'I dunno,' she said, sucking his ear lobe.

'Stop it, and look again.'

She looked at the drawings, at the flower-like frocks and cobwebby cloaks and suddenly she heard Troy's voice saying *A bit floriferous, for my tastes* . . . And she looked at Jack, and said in a very small voice: 'Oh. They're like . . . they're a bit like Troy's frocks. Aren't they?'

'Damn right.'

She furrowed her brow and looked at the drawings again. They were similar in a number of aspects to Troy's designs. In cut and texture, definitely: the detail was not quite as gorgeous (Aphrodite's fairies were obviously not quite as well off as Troy's; although, she thought, a tad guiltily, they made up for it by having a better sense of humour), but the basic concept was undeniably the same. These were the beautiful raggle taggle bohemians that had inspired Troy's springwear collection.

The word 'plagiarism' sprang to mind, and the unpleasant associations that that word held for her made her flush. When could Troy have seen these drawings? And then she recalled that she'd left her portfolio behind that time she'd stayed in Coolnamaragh. Oh! Had he *stolen* her designs? She looked back at her *Midsummer Night's Dream* fairies, at Titania and Oberon and Puck and Cobweb and Moth and Peaseblossom and her favourite – little First Fairy who had no name – and she knew he hadn't. Troy MacNally had too much artistic integrity to do that – she remembered his outraged reaction when she'd told him about Damien Gobshite Whelan and the *Seagull* fiasco: he'd refused to *work* with Whelan on account of that! No. These drawings had simply infiltrated his subconscious and lodged there, waiting to spring forth in some other guise. Now she thought about it, she felt quite flattered that Troy had thought highly enough of her stuff to use it as the basis for his most stunning collection of all. Didn't they say that imitation was the highest form of flattery?

She looked at Jack, and he looked back at her, and there was a wicked glint in his eye as he said: 'Are you thinking what I'm thinking?'

'I think so,' she said. 'You're thinking that I should pass my drawings off as Troy's?'

'Absolutely. It's the answer to all your problems, sweetheart.'

'Is it? How?'

'If you do there's not a *Chose de Neige*'s chance in hell that Troy MacNally Enterprises will bite the dust. In fact, the publicity generated when the truth finally leaks out – as it undoubtedly will – means that the shares will probably rocket and you can sell them off once you've found yourself a replacement designer and start thinking about what *you* want to do with the rest of your life.'

He sounded terribly plausible. But . . . 'Oh, God, Jack. I don't think I'd have the nerve–'

'What? Is this the voice of the same woman who had fashion victims raiding Oxfam shops for puffball skirts, and who urged her readers to visit a non-existent installation in an obscure Barcelona art gallery that went by the glorious moniker of "Barbie Bush"? Where's your mettle gone, you wimp?'

Her erstwhile honest streak – the streak that had gone AWOL since she'd taken up with Troy and his cronies – made itself felt. 'Well, actually,' she admitted. 'I can't take the credit for the Barbie Bush. I didn't dream it up. My friend Lola did.'

'The girl I met with you in the IFC all that time ago?'

'Yeah.'

'She's a sexy minx, that same Lola. Persuasive, too. She managed to talk me into taking photographs of her latest set design for a fee so paltry I tore up the cheque.'

'Yeah, well, hands off, Costello. She's also a married minx now.'

He put his hands between her shoulder blades and did something so incredible to her spinal column that it made her gasp. 'Jesus, Costello! Where did you learn how to do that?'

'Hilary the brick shithouse masseur is full of useful tips.'

'Do it again!'

'No. We've business to sort out. To resume. You say you can't take credit for dreaming up the triumphant Barbie Bush, but you still had the nerve to print a big fat whopping lie in an influential style bible. Messrs Orton and Halliwell would have envied the chutzpah that was responsible for that little prank.'

'You mean Geri has a subversive streak?'

'I'm not talking about that Halliwell. I'm talking about Joe Orton, the playwright and his partner Kenneth. They penned some very funny letters of mock outrage to newspapers, as well as perpetrating pranks in their local library. They ended up in prison for their pains.'

'Thanks for that reassurance.'

'Come on, Aphrodite – go for it! Just think of the buzz you'll get out of pulling the wool over all those sheepish eyes. The Point Depot will go down in history for hosting the ultimate parade of the Emperor's New Threads.'

'No,' she said, shaking her head. And then, with more decision: 'No. Absolutely not. I can't do it. It would look as if I was being a horrifically smug bitch.'

'Why? You're not thinking of doing something juvenile like appearing on national television and saying "fooled you", are you?'

'No.'

'Come on, then. You've got a chance to save the day and your own skin.'

Oh no. This was horrific. She was going to start vacillating – she hated it when she did that. 'But *how* could we do it?' she asked. 'I mean, even if I was thinking of doing it – which I'm *not* – *how* could it be done? It would be an impossible stunt to pull off.'

'Well, the first thing you do is swear people to secrecy. If you're going to single-handedly transform Troy MacNally Enterprises from a dying duck into a phoenix soaring forth from the ashes, you will have to be sure that you only confide in those in whom you have absolute trust.'

'I'm not sure I'd have absolute trust in anyone in this business,' she said. 'Apart from James Gillespie. And Anna,' she added for good measure. 'You said it yourself, Jack – it's impossible to keep a secret in the fashion industry.'

'It won't be impossible if people's jobs are riding on whether or not they keep their mouths shut,' he pointed out. There was no denying the truth behind the remark. There *were* jobs at stake here. 'Who will you need to take into your confidence?'

'Well . . . Jolie and Gareth, obviously, as the other shareholders.'

'They're smart enough not to go fuelling gossip. Who else?'

'Um. James Gillespie, the pattern cutter. And the machinists, and – oh, God, Jack! It's impossible. The story about Troy's defection will be all round Dublin already.'

'OK. We spread a counter-rumour.' He was obviously going to be dogged. 'Let's say that the blank pages were Troy's idea of a practical joke, and that *you* had drawings of his squirrelled away that nobody knew about. That's surely not unfeasible.'

She tried to force another spanner into the works. 'James will know immediately that my drawings aren't Troy's. They're a completely different style.'

'You say you trust this James person?'

'Yes.' She could feel her argument being gradually frayed away at the edges, like one of Troy's beautiful Ilnacullin gowns.

'In that case, only he and the machinists are allowed to be in the know. They're not going to risk losing their jobs through spilling the beans. But everyone else concerned is spun the fairy tale.'

She bit her lip. It was outrageous. It was unethical. It was very possibly illegal. But, hell – it would be *fun*! The look in his eye told her he was winning. He gave her his wicked, sexy, bedroom-eyed smile.

'Do you know what you are for dreaming up such a stunt?' she said.

'Tell me.'

'You, Jack Costello, are a "ruffian and black-guard".'

He pulled aside the lapels of her kimono and slid his hands underneath. 'And you, Aphrodite Delaney, are a wanton hussy and an audacious adventuress. Do it. It's worth a try. Even if word does get out before the event, it's not that important. If you were doing this as a means to achieving fame and fortune for yourself, then yes, people would take

441

a dim view of it. But you're not. You're doing it to keep a small industry buoyant, and you're doing it for charity – and you're doing it to fuck the begrudgers.'

'The begrudgers! I'd forgotten about them. Ee-yoo! There are millions.'

'Like I said, fuck them.'

'Jack, I'm not averse to performing sexual acts that some people might consider a little pervy, but fucking *begrudgers* is emphatically not one of them.'

He laughed, then swung her off his knee and started dragging her towards the bedroom. She'd been aware for some time now as she sat on his lap that his libido had been growing increasingly – well – libidinous. So libidinous, in fact, that they never made it as far as the bedroom door. A scandalized Bobcat leapt off the sofa in the sitting room as Jack bent her over it and pulled up the silk of her kimono, and a moment later she heard the recriminative 'thwack' of the cat flap in the kitchen.

And now that she thought about it for the last time before Jack embarked on his urgent exploration of her erogenous zones, she experienced a tiny, illicit thrill at the idea of those begrudgers, and she thought that actually, yes, fucking them might prove to be something of a blast.

* * *

Lola called later to ask Aphrodite what the panicky phone messages had been about. She hadn't accessed her voice mail until nearly midnight because Patrick had whisked her off to a love nest so secluded that her phone had been out of range the entire time they'd spent there. 'What's going on?' she asked. 'What do you mean your life is in a mess?'

'It's not. It's brilliant.'

'OK. Within the space of twelve hours your life has gone from being a mess to being brilliant. How, pray, was this transformation effected?'

'Yeah.'

'What?'

'I said "yeah".'

'Ah. I take it that means you can't talk.'

'That's right.'

'Someone's with you?'

'Yeah.'

'Troy?'

'No.'

'A man?'

'Yes.'

'Are you in bed with him?'

'Could be.'

'I know who he is.'

'He? How? Who?'

'You sound like a cowboy singing campfire songs.'

'Shut up, Lo.'

'It's Jack Costello, isn't it?'

'How do you know that?'

'Easy peasy. When I heard you were going off on location with him I knew there'd be trouble at t'mill and fish to fry. You didn't have to be as wise as the Sibyl in Delphi to guess that you were going to end up in bed with that man one of these days, Aphrodite Delaney.'

'You're insufferable, Lo. Can I call you in the morning? I've loads of news. And there's something I want to run by you.'

*　　*　　*

She spent the entire morning running Jack's idea by the chosen few. She waited and waited for someone to pooh-pooh it and say: 'Don't do it. It's a preposterous idea.' But not one single person did. Not even Jolie Fitzgerald. And the very next week Aphrodite's designs were in production.

Chapter Nineteen

She'd been right about one thing. It had been impossible to keep the plot under wraps. She got back late from the studio two days before her frocks were due to strut their stuff down the catwalk at the Point Depot to find a message on her answering machine from Andrea Mooney.

'Aphrodite?' crooned the journalist's voice down her phone. 'A little bird tells me that the evening wear being shown under the Troy MacNally label on Friday night has actually been designed by you. Is there any truth to this rumour? If so, I'd love to do a piece on it. Perhaps you'd give me a call?' And she reeled off a litany of contact numbers.

The next day there were calls from members of the press representing newspapers from Donegal in the northernmost corner of Ireland to Cork on the southernmost tip. They left messages with her PA, on her mobile, and on her land line. How had they got hold of her number? she wondered. She wasn't listed in the book. She wondered if Jolie had tipped them the wink, knowing how invaluable the attendant publicity would be, so she called her cold war ally and they arranged to meet up. 'Do you want to come here, to my house, Aphrodite? Or do you want to meet for lunch? There's a new restaurant in

Ballsbridge that got the most incredible reviews—'

'Jolie,' said Aphrodite. 'I don't have time for lunch. I'm up to my eyes in stuff. You're going to have to come here, to the studio.'

'OK,' said Jolie, sounding uncharacteristically meek.

She arrived an hour later looking her usual sensational self. She air-kissed Aphrodite, told her she was looking *great*, perched on the desk that had once been Troy's, and said: 'What's the problem?'

'The problem is,' said Aphrodite, 'that the press have been on to me.'

'Me too.'

'What did you tell them?'

'I told them "No comment". I didn't think it was my place to speak on your behalf. But you're going to have to face them at some time, Aphrodite. We knew all along that it would be virtually impossible to keep this thing under wraps.'

'I don't *want* to talk to them, Jolie. I did this to try and keep Troy MacNally Enterprises afloat, not as some egotistical exercise in self-promotion. If the press is interested, fair enough – and you're right, at this stage the publicity could be helpful. But *I* don't want any part of it.'

Jolie raised an eyebrow, picked a piece of lint off her cuff, and started rolling it between her beautifully manicured thumb and forefinger. 'I don't mean to be smart, but you weren't particularly backward about coming forward until now.'

'*Touché*. But I did it for Troy, you know that. I did it to reflect the spotlight back onto him. I was never a celebrity in my own right, Jolie. I was "Aphrodite Delaney, muse to Troy MacNally". Troy had the real claim to fame. Mine was spurious B-list stuff.'

'But now you're fully-blown famous. You've *earned* your A-list status.'

'I don't want it, Jolie. I really don't. I felt uncomfortable enough being a minor media darling. I don't *want* the full glitzy treatment. I don't want people intruding in my private life. I don't want to be seen as a fashionista. I don't want to make a living bullying women about what to wear.'

Jolie's expression stiffened, and she stopped fiddling with the lint. 'You mean you're not going to take over from Troy? Gareth and I kind of hoped that you would, Aphrodite. It just seems such a natural progression that you should step into his shoes. I'm sure that's what he would have wanted.'

'What Troy wants is immaterial now. It seems to me that I've spent my entire life doing what other people want, and now it's time for me to do what *I* want for a change. It's *my* turn to be selfish.'

Jolie gave her a cynical look. 'And you honestly expect me to believe that you don't want fame and fortune?' she said.

'I don't want fame and fortune. And I don't want to work in the fashion industry any more.'

She said it with such heartfelt fervour that she could tell Jolie was finally convinced. The other woman looked at Aphrodite thoughtfully, and then laughed, conceding defeat. 'I had an inkling when I first met you that you would be an interesting adversary,' she said, with unexpected candour. 'Not like

Miriam. She was a piece of piss.' The lint was flicked into the wastepaper bin. 'She's in rehab, incidentally. I saw a piece about her in the paper last weekend. Anyway, I'm glad we didn't end up in a fight-to-the-death situation, you and I.' Her phone rang, and she fished it out of her little Vuitton purse and depressed the 'talk' button. 'No comment,' she said, smiling at Aphrodite. Then she pressed 'end call' and put the phone back in her bag. 'Are you going to sell your shares?' she asked.

'Yes.'

'Sell them to me, will you? I've a feeling Troy MacNally Enterprises is going to be huge. We'll have to think of a new name for the label, though.' She sighed. 'And scouting for a new designer's going to be tough. Can you recommend anyone?'

'Try Damien Whelan,' said Aphrodite. 'He's got the right temperament for the job. And call the new label Fag Hag.'

Jolie laughed. 'Musey shows her claws. Maybe I should be glad that you're not staying around.'

The PA put her head round the door. 'James wants a word, Aphrodite.'

'I'll be with him in a minute.' Aphrodite got to her feet. It was Jolie's cue to leave.

'I'll see you at the gig?' she said, moving to the door.

'Yes.'

Then Jolie paused and said: 'Aphrodite? As a matter of interest, what are you going to do next?'

Aphrodite smiled a secret kind of smile. 'I'm going to be very, very, happy,' she said.

The gig was nowhere near as chaotic as that disastrous autumn show of Troy's when Aphrodite had allowed herself to be so thoroughly humiliated by Polly Riordan. This gig ran on well-oiled cogs, with PAs and gofers and lackeys and liggers and security guards and champagne for the supermodels.

Aphrodite had opted not to wear one of her own designs to the show. It felt too – well, too pompously *self-referential.* She had hummed and hawed over Troy's autumn stuff, and then she'd decided against that too. Word had got out that the designs on show tonight had been executed years ago as part of Aphrodite's degree course, and she knew that anyone with a bit of cop-on might jump to the conclusion that Troy had plagiarized his erstwhile muse's ideas for his last autumn collection. She didn't want anyone levelling accusations of piracy at him. So instead she had decided on the beautiful sage-green calico number he'd kitted her out in all those months ago.

Her designs were scheduled to be second last before the interval, and because she didn't have the nerve to sit out front and watch her babies sashay down the catwalk (it had been bad enough watching the dress rehearsal), she spent the first half of the show backstage, finalizing details and gossiping with Anna, whom she'd begged to model for her. Anna had announced that she had had no intention of doing the Point gig because she'd once had a serious run-in with one of the supermodels who was appearing, but she'd relented when Aphrodite had said 'pleasepleaseplease'. The girl had vamped a blinder for her during the rehearsal, and pronounced herself 'blown away' by Aphrodite's designs. 'You're such a clever-clogs, Musey. What an ingenious ploy! You'll be able to take single-handed credit for keeping the flag flying at Troy MacNally Enterprises.'

'Actually, it was Jack's idea,' confessed Aphrodite.

'Jack Costello?'

'Yes.'

Anna looked sly. 'Hey. D'you mind if I ask you something, Aphrodite? Did you two get it together that night in Parknasilla?'

'What? No,' said Aphrodite. 'But we did a couple of nights later,' she added, unable to resist the temptation to tell.

'So! The rumour's right. You two are an item?'

'I suppose so.' She didn't waste her breath saying: What rumour? The industry was rampant with rumour.

'Ha!' crowed Anna. 'I knew that was going to happen!'

'How come everybody seems to say that when they find out about us?' Aphrodite was genuinely puzzled. 'My friend Lola said the same thing.'

'Well,' said Anna. 'You don't have eyes in the back of your head.'

'What do you mean?'

'You can't see the way Jack looks at you when your back's turned. That's why I made myself scarce that night. I wanted to give him a chance to seduce you.'

'He was too much of a gentleman to seduce me that night. He thought I was still involved with Troy. And it wouldn't have been much fun for him anyway. I was pissed.' A man with an earpiece was gesticulating wildly at Anna. 'Um. I think you're needed, Anna.'

Anna looked towards the gesticulating man. 'I hate that geezer. He's an insufferable sexist git. I'm going to make him sweat a bit. Yeah, yeah, yeah,' she mouthed at him, waving her hand dismissively. 'Send my congratulations to Jack for the Valencia shots, by the way,' she said, turning back to Aphrodite. 'They now have pride of place in my go-see book.'

'I'll do that. I'm meeting him at the interval.'

'Well. I *am* impressed.' Anna's eyes opened wide. 'He must think very highly of you, girl.'

'What makes you say that?'

'Jack *hates* gigs like this. He avoids them like the plague. Oh dear.' The stage manager's waving was becoming more frantic. 'I suppose it would be unprofessional to ignore him any longer. Catch you later, Aphrodite.' And Anna adopted her haughty model's stance and stalked towards the spotlight.

Aphrodite thought about what Anna had just said, about Jack thinking highly of her, and the thought warmed her and made her smile that secret smile she was smiling so much these days, and she skipped – she actually *skipped* – away from the backstage area to the bar in the foyer where she'd arranged to meet him. She must look completely ludicrous, she realized, stopping at once. A grown woman decked out in last season's exquisite full-length Troy MacNally, sporting a top hat and evening purse skipping across the carpet! Strike the pose, darling, she told herself. Be elegant. But, she supposed, there wasn't really anything intrinsically *elegant* about being happy . . .

She was pleased to see that the bar area was comparatively deserted. The audience would be thronging out for the interval soon, and then it would be virtually impossible to get a drink. She ordered white wine for herself and bourbon for him, and carried the drinks over to a corner just as the doors to the auditorium opened.

'Aphrodite!' She put the drinks down and turned with a smile in the direction of the voice, and then a flashbulb went off in her face. The flash attracted looks from the crowd which soon became stares, and she could make out muttered remarks along the lines of 'Aphrodite Delaney? Isn't she the one who–' '*I* know her! She's the one who–' 'Hey! I dare you to ask for her autograph!' And then Andrea Mooney was bearing down on her with her notebook and pen in hand, and saying, 'A little bird tells me that Anna Boland is your muse and new house model,' and someone was shoving a mic under her chin and asking: 'Is it true that–', and someone else was saying, 'How does it feel to–', and she heard an urgent voice say: 'Is there any truth in the rumour that–' and someone else saying: 'I'd love you to contribute a feature on your fashion predictions for next season. You know – something similar to your "Elegantarium" column, but with a zany spin? How would you like to–'

'Aphrodite!' she heard again, and it was Lola, with her singing detective bringing up the rear. A little corridor was magicked through the crowd by dab-handed Patrick, and suddenly Lola was at her side. She held up an authoritative hand. 'Ladies and gentlemen,' she said, in an equally authoritative voice. 'Thank you for your interest, but I'm afraid Ms Delaney is suffering from laryngitis and will be unable to speak to you this evening. However, as her personal publicist, I will be delighted to answer any questions on her behalf. Patrick – will you accompany Ms Delaney downstairs? Thank you.'

Patrick placed a guiding hand on the small of Aphrodite's back, and gently manoeuvred her through the crowd in the direction of the stairs. 'Stop laughing,' she heard him say in an amused undertone. 'You're supposed to be suffering from laryngitis.'

She could hear Lola's voice from behind, plangent with assurance. 'Well,' she was saying, 'there has been interest from Paris. I don't want to give too much away, but if I say that a representative of the daughter of a former Beatle has been in touch, I'm sure you'll know who I mean. Also, a sunglasses-wearing, pony-tailed, newly slim Teutonic person – sorry, sir – *you* said the L word, not me . . .'

'Your wife is outrageous,' said Aphrodite, as they ran down the stairs.

'I know,' said Patrick. 'That's why I married her.'

In the foyer, the area around the big plate glass doors had been requisitioned by more photographers. Celebrities – millions of them, including her mother – were smiling and posing and laughing for the cameras, and coming out with what – to judge by the uproarious response from their interviewers – were hilarious *bons mots* for tomorrow's gossip columns.

'This way,' said Patrick, indicating an obscure corner of the foyer where the less stellar members of the public were milling around. 'Your date elected to hide among the plebs, away from all those celebrity scalp hunters. He reckoned they'd never dream of looking for you there.' He gave her a peck on the cheek and said: 'I'll leave you to it. I'd better get back to Lola before she lets the ladies and gentlemen of the press in on the fact that Madonna's commissioned an entire wardrobe from you and that you're designing a brand new set of costumes for *Riverdance*.' And Patrick legged it back through the crowd.

'Wow. I love the riding topper,' said Jack when she reached him. 'All you need now's a crop. You could make that next month's must-have "Elegantarium" accessory.'

She made a face at him. 'When in Rome . . .' she said, accepting the glass of wine he was holding out to her and taking a very welcome gulp.

'Did you manage to shake off the posse of press? I saw them descending on you and I'm afraid I turned tail and scarpered like the yellow-belly I am.'

'Lola and Patrick came to the rescue.'

Jack narrowed his eyes, and then he shook his head at her and gave her a wicked smile. 'Tch, tch,' he said, in a tone of mock reproval. 'Look where "Elegantarium" has got you now, Aphrodite

Delaney. That'll teach you to make women covet the emperor's new clothes.'

She ignored him. 'How was the show? What did the frocks look like when they came out?' she asked. 'Would they pass muster as Troy's?'

'They looked fucking fantastic. But the Troy connection is kinda superfluous now, don't you think? You're a supernova in your own right, Delaney, not just a heavenly body reflecting someone else's glory.' He dropped a careless kiss on her mouth, and before she could demand another one she heard him say: 'Hi, David.' A man somewhere in his forties had sidled towards their corner, trying to look nondescript and not succeeding very well due to the fact that he was tall, dark and nearly as charismatic as Jack. Aphrodite gulped like a cartoon character. David Lawless, the shit-hot theatre director! 'Are you in hiding from the press, too?' asked Jack.

'Yeah. Eva's out there somewhere, though. She never manages to escape. She's too sweet – she gives them all "exclusive" stories, and they love her to bits. The only journalist who ever said an unkind thing about Eva Lavery ended up in Obits.'

Jack laughed, then turned to Aphrodite. 'Do you know Aphrodite Delaney? Aphrodite, David Lawless.'

Aphrodite managed a smile and a starstruck 'hi', and just then Eva Lavery rolled up, and she just managed another one. This was theatre *royalty*!

'Aphrodite Delaney?' said Eva. 'Are you the one all the rumours are flying around about? The one responsible for all those glorious bohemian threads that were second last on the catwalk?' Before Aphrodite could answer in the affirmative, Eva rushed on. 'Of *course* you're responsible. There couldn't be another Aphrodite Delaney floating around. You're Thea's daughter, aren't you?'

'Um. Well, yes, actually.'

'Oh, David!' said Eva. 'You must see more of her stuff. She'd be the perfect choice to design the costumes for the revival of the *Midsummer Night's Dream* you're planning. You're theatrically trained, Aphrodite, aren't you?'

'Yes.'

'Well, in that case,' said David, looking at her with new interest, 'why don't you contact my PA and ask her to set up a meeting? Here's my card. Give her a ring any time after the end of next week. She's away on holiday till then.'

'I'd be glad to,' said Aphrodite, which roughly translated as *Oh, dear God in heaven thank you, thank you! I cannot believe this is happening to me!*

'We'd better go, darling,' said Eva, laying a hand on his arm. 'I arranged to meet Deirdre upstairs. Bye, you foxy man.' She raised her face to Jack so that he could kiss it. 'Bye, Aphrodite. Glad to have met you.' And the monarchs made their exit, leaving Aphrodite gazing at David's card in open-mouthed awe.

'Why didn't you give him one of yours in exchange? You know, the ones that say "Aphrodite Delaney, design consultant"?'

She wished he hadn't reminded her of that. 'Shut up,' she said.

'That's one of the things I admire most about you, Delaney.'

'What?'

'Your mean line in repartee.' He yawned and looked at his watch. 'Do you want to go back to that wretched display of next season's must-haves now that your babies have been safely delivered?'

'Christ, no,' she said. 'Anyway, I'm supposed to be suffering from laryngitis.'

'In that case,' said Jack, 'we'd better get you home to bed.'

She pretended to consider. After all, it wouldn't do to look *too* eager. After a beat of about one millionth of a millisecond she said: 'You're on,' then turned away with a cat-who-got-the-cream smile, only just resisting the impulse to skip across the foyer.

The place was clearing. People were filing back into the auditorium. Most were young, Aphrodite noticed, and on a modest income, to judge by the plethora of Miss Selfridge type clothes they were wearing. But they were having fun, laughing and leafing through programmes they had to share because they could only afford one between them, programmes that peddled the dreams they had come here tonight to see on the catwalk, the aspirational dresses they fantasized about wearing one day, the kind of dresses they would never be able to afford. But dreams were fun, she supposed, as long as you didn't expect reality to match them, and she suspected that these girls with their Miss Selfridge budgets were probably an awful lot happier than the half-dozen social X-rays in the world who could afford the real thing.

In the loo she had her pee, then went to wash her hands. There was a woman washing hers at the next basin.

'Is the show any good?' asked the woman.

'I don't know, to tell you the truth. I haven't seen any of it.'

'What? Why not?'

Aphrodite didn't want to tell this woman that she had been backstage for the first half. If she did she'd just be inviting questions like: 'What's Kate really like?' and 'Is Jerry really well preserved and is her daughter any good?' So she just said: 'I – um – lost my ticket, and decided to stay on for a drink in the bar.'

'Shame,' said the woman. 'You should have come to me, I might have been able to sort things out for you. I work in the box office.' She adopted a confidential tone. 'D'you know? I'm raging I had to work tonight. I'd have *loved* to have seen the show. I'm a fashion fanatic. See what I mean?' She indicated the logo-covered bags stacked at her feet. Jigsaw, Kickers, River Island. 'I went out shopping in my lunch hour and just couldn't help myself. My husband'll kill me when I get home. "What're you doing buying the same old crap all the time?" he'll say. And he'll be right.' She picked up the River Island bag and held it open. 'See these jeans? I've got three pairs at home nearly identical. And I've lost count of the number of plain white T-shirts I have. And I bought this jacket today.' She rummaged in the Jigsaw bag and held up a little canvas number. 'I'm going to have to bloody return it, aren't I?'

'Why?'

'Because I don't really like it.' She stuffed the jacket back in the bag. 'It's stupid, isn't it? If I stopped spending money on stuff like this, I could save up for something like what you're wearing.' She looked enviously at Aphrodite's beautiful gown – the one Troy had hand-picked for her – and there was a note of real reverence in her voice when she said: 'It's fabulous. It's a Troy MacNally, isn't it?'

'Yes,' said Aphrodite, moving to the hand dryer. Across the room someone was doing the same thing, and she stopped short when she realized that it was her, reflected in the mirror opposite. It took her a long moment to recognize herself. Was that really *her*, that bizarre-looking creature in the fairytale frock? And suddenly she felt choked by the embrace of the high-necked bodice with its myriad little mother-of-pearl buttons that had taken her ages to do up before she left the house that evening (she'd spotted a neighbour sniggering at her get-up as she'd climbed into the taxi), and she felt constricted by the tight, tight sleeves that she'd practically had to wrench her arms into, and the weight of the stupid top hat cocked so 'wittily' atop her stupid 'signature' crop was giving her a headache, and she heard herself saying: 'Do you want it?'

'What?' said the woman. She gave Aphrodite an openly suspicious look, and Aphrodite knew she meant it when she added: 'Are you mad?'

She laughed. 'No. I may look it, but I'm not mad. I mean it. I'll do a deal with you. You're about my size, aren't you?'

'Yes,' said the woman with a touch of pride. 'I'm a standard size ten.'

'Well,' said Aphrodite. 'If you let me have your new purchases, I'll let you have my Troy MacNally.' The woman looked at her as if she'd just sprouted ears like Mr Spock's. 'It's not as insane as you might think, honestly.' She looked at herself in the mirror again, and again she had the odd sensation that she was looking at a stranger. 'You see,' she said with sudden irrefutable certainty, 'this was never really my dress. It was made for someone else – a sad girl called Miriam – and I feel like an impostor wearing it. It's difficult to explain, but I reckon that if I give the dress away to someone who really loves it, I'll kind of be making amends for . . . for . . .' For what? She thought of poor Miriam, beautiful, tragic-eyed and manacled, and of how badly she'd been injured by the monstrous, despotic behemoth that was the fashion industry. She wanted to know that there was hope, and she was glad that somewhere in the world her predecessor was healing. 'For *her*,' she said. 'For Miriam.' She turned back to the woman and gave her a level look. 'I'm absolutely serious.'

The woman was now looking at her as if she were only slightly barking instead of a full-blown loon.

'Shoes!' said Aphrodite. The woman adopted her guarded expression again, and clutched her Jigsaw bag to her chest as if afraid that Aphrodite might grab it and run. 'If you agree, we're going to have to swap shoes, too. What size are yours?'

The woman looked down at Aphrodite's soft leather lace-up boots with their dainty heel, and her expression changed again. It now verged on the voracious. 'Five?' she said hopefully.

Aphrodite reached out and shook the woman by the hand. 'Then we're in business,' she said. 'What do you think? Have we a deal?'

'Are you being really deadly serious?'

Aphrodite thought of that behemoth again, the marauding one that had so successfully camouflaged itself – for many more years than a social X-ray would care to admit to – as a glittering, delicate, ephemeral *chose de neige*, and said: 'I've never been more serious about anything in my life.'

* * *

She was just finishing tying the laces on her brand new Kickers five minutes later when she heard Jack's voice bounce off the wall of the ladies' loo. 'Aphrodite,' he called. 'What is going on in there? I know women like to spend time titivating, but you've been at it for ages. You'll come out looking like Michael Jackson at this rate.'

'It's OK,' she called out from the cubicle where she'd been changing. 'I'll be out in a sec, I promise.'

'Yeah? Good. I was worried there for a minute. I thought you might have been mugged. A woman ran out cramming something into a carrier bag and laughing like a lunatic.'

As she stepped out of her cubicle she smiled at the thought of the box-office woman running off with her booty before the mad bitch in the loo could change her mind.

The reflection looking back at her from the full-length mirror on the wall was smiling broadly back, and she remembered what she'd said to Jolie in the studio yesterday. *I'm going to be happy* . . . The only thing wrong with the way she looked now, she noticed, was that her ornate dangly earrings and the little beaded evening purse she was carrying looked a bit bonkers with River Island casuals. Oh, well. Maybe it would be interpreted as a new fashion statement, and women in biker boots would start sporting fragile *chose de neige* type accessories.

Jack was lounging by the plate glass doors talking to a couple of security men when she walked out into the empty foyer. He looked at her without recognition, and then he looked again. Aphrodite wanted to laugh when she noticed that he actually allowed his sang-froid to slip sideways momentarily. Then he recollected himself and came striding across the foyer. He met her halfway, swung her hand into his, raised the palm to his lips, and kissed it. 'Not very Versace,' he said. 'Not very Valentino. Not even very *Vogue*. But *very* Aphrodite Delaney. OK. Let's go home to bed.'

'My place or yours?'

'Mine. We're going to Valencia.'

'What? Now?' Oh, God! Could this evening get any better? 'This minute?'

'Yeah. I've a sudden graw to see you in fishing waders, Delaney, and I don't have any up in Dublin. There is, unsurprisingly, no real call for fishing waders in the city, but I'm sure you could change all that if you put your mind to it. "Elegantarium says

462

that fishing waders are *de rigueur* for all you sad broads out there who don't have anything better to do in your lives than read this perfectly specious column of mine".'

'Shut up,' she said again, and then she stood on tiptoe and started kissing him. 'Are you serious,' she said between kisses, 'about going to Valencia right now?'

He echoed the words she'd uttered five minutes earlier, to the box-office woman in the loo. 'I have never been more serious about anything in my life.' Then: 'Bye, boys,' he said to the doormen, who were looking at Aphrodite with hungry speculation. 'Give Liberty Ross one from me when you meet her.' He swung open the door and held it open for her, and then they were walking through the car park that was bumper to bumper with parked cars. Balloons had been released earlier, and Aphrodite thought how entirely appropriate they were to celebrate the event, symbolic as they were of fashion in all its frivolity, capriciousness, flirtatiousness and silliness. The kind of fashion that didn't take itself seriously. The kind of fashion that was fun.

'Do you really fancy Liberty Ross?' she asked, abstractedly noticing that there were – unusually – a few smudgy stars to be seen beyond the balloons floating up there in the city skyscape. She remembered how the sky in Kerry had been littered with stars most nights, and she wondered what constellations Troy would be gazing upon now, far away on Mount Kailash, beyond the Himalayas.

'God yes,' he said, slinging an arm around her

shoulders. 'I fancied the arse of every single woman who swung her booty down that catwalk this evening. I was thinking such bad thoughts about them that I merited a beating with a riding crop.' He slanted a gorgeous sideways smile at her. 'But I didn't get a hard-on until I saw you coming out of the Ladies with that silly, silly smile on your face. That's when I pictured you performing the ultimate sex act.'

'Oh? And what is the ultimate sex act?'

The police siren that suddenly wailed into life drowned out most of his words. She caught only two with any clarity. They were, unsurprisingly, 'Fishing waders' and her laugh rose up, up into the frosty Dublin night to join the helium balloons, and the Christmas lights that were festooned along the steel silhouettes of cranes, and the crazy lasers, and the subtle smattering of stars. Those stars reminded her of something else, now. 'Jack?' she asked, slanting him a provocative look. 'Do you remember the T-shirt I was wearing the first time I met you?'

'Can't say I do. I was more interested in what it was concealing.'

'Well, it had "Beam Me Up Scotty" on it. I've come up with a better slogan.'

'And how intellectually challenging might this one be?'

' "Scotty? Don't bother," ' she said.

THE END

Kate Thompson would like to invite you to visit her website at www.kate-thompson.com